FACES OF THE SNOW

ROBERT L. WILLIAMS

Also by Robert L. Williams

FACES OF THE SNOW

ROBERT L. WILLIAMS

Raincrow Books

SOUTHEASTERN PUBLISHING CORPORATION
DALLAS, NORTH CAROLINA 28034

FACES OF THE SNOW
A Raincrow Mystery/Suspense novel, Published by
Southeastern Publishing Corporation
3613 Dallas-Cherryville Highway
Dallas, North Carolina 28034

Copyright©1999 by Robert L. Williams

Library of Congress Cataloging-in-Publication Data

Williams, Robert L.
Faces of the Snow: a novel.
ISBN 1-893330-01-X

Cover Design by Wendell Cisco II

Printed in the United States of America

10 9 8 7 6 5 4 3 2 1

Look on every one that is proud, and bring him low; and tread down the wicked in their place.

Hide them in the dust together, and find their faces in secret. Then will I also confess unto thee that thine own right hand can save thee.

Behold now behemoth, which I made with thee; he eateth grass as an ox.

Lo now, his strength is in his loins, and his force is in the navel of his belly.

He moveth his tail like a cedar; the sinews of his stones are wrapped together.

His bones are as strong pieces of brass; his bones are like bars of iron.

Job 40: 12-18.

Hast thou entered into the treasures of the snow? Or hast thou seen the treasures of the hail...?

Job 38: 22-23

But when the children of Israel cried unto the Lord, the Lord raised them up a deliverer, Ehud ... a man left-handed.

Judges 3: 15

He alone who has looked upon the lovely and desolate faces of the snow knows the meaning of fear, and hate, and dead or dying love.

Leonard Trebor

Dedication

This book is for the people who never wavered in their faith in me and my efforts. Heading the list are Elizabeth, my wonderful wife (who is also the most patient and marvelous copy editor I have ever known); Robert, our superb son; and my incredible publisher and his family: Dean Carpenter, his loving wife Jackie, and their very special daughter and son, Anna and Adrian, all of whom worked tirelessly to make earlier works successes in every way. This book is also for Joyce Paulin and Barbara Wright, who aided in so many countless ways, from proofreading to making wonderfully helpful suggestions. To all of these people I am indeed grateful and shall remain indebted to them.

ONE

The fiery eyes winked softly from the dying embers in the fireplace. Sleet pecked like starving ice chickens against the panes of the bedroom window, and the woman on the blanket beside me stirred restlessly. Her eyes opened to the wet gray dawn and then closed again briefly before they snapped open in soft alarm.

A blistering knot of asphalt nausea rose into my throat as I watched her pasty-creature face transform from a stolid mass of lethargy into that of a nearly stunning woman.

I turned away from her before she could see the look of disgust on my own face, which I felt softening even as the detestation swelled. It wasn't her fault that I abhorred her. She was an attractive woman, nearly perfect in each physical feature. A woman who would have been welcome in any man's bed.

Except mine.

I preferred the sleet and the raging wind that lashed the cabin and flung ice pellets against the window in a clattering din that drowned out the woman's raspy voice. She had caught the look on my face, and her voice betrayed her pain.

"Do you hate me so much?" she asked. "Why did you let me come here if I revolt you?"

"You don't disgust me." It was nearly the truth. I had for too long endured what Ezra Pound called lesser brightness. But who on earth cared what Ezra Pound said about anything?

"I turned you into a eunuch," she said with only a trace of bitterness.

I attempted a failed smile. It slunk into a swamp the moment it was misborn. "You didn't," I said.

"King Midas, then." Her voice had lost its hoarseness and now absorbed the smokiness from the fireplace.

I nodded in agreement. King Midas with a new spin. All he touched instantly became cold, unfeeling, lifeless gold. What I touched turned into death. And the more I touched and killed, the richer I became.

I was in the hell of granted wishes, and it was killing me. Everyone died but me, for I had the deadly Golden Touch.

So I made certain nothing touched me, and that was Laura's great failing: she wanted to *touch* me.

Not just my flesh, which I might have endured; she wanted to touch my feelings, my *soul,* or what she believed my soul would be if I had one to touch.

She rose from the bed and in the soft darkness found her clothes that she had hung neatly on the nail on the back of the door.

"I shouldn't have tried," she said as she dressed quickly. "I won't make that mistake again. Until you ask."

I nodded. It seemed ages since I asked anyone for anything. King Midas, even one with a heart as empty and cold as an alpine cave, didn't have to ask. He could buy whatever he wanted.

Everything but the one treasure he'd have given his soul to have again. Laura read my thoughts. "She was never yours," she said with a strange calmness. "Even if she had been, she could never be yours again. She always belonged to something you could never understand. Or accept."

"Don't," I warned. "We're not having this conversation."

The tension in my voice turned my vocal cords into steel cables stiff from the icy cold and to frozen spiderwebs. I moved closer to the window, away from her and toward the icy chickens that would warm me as much as any fire or woman could.

"We've *never had* a conversation of any kind," she said. "I don't know if you could ever talk to anybody. You sulk and mope and resent anyone who tries to come near you. I give up! I don't know what else to say, what else to try. Nothing I've done is enough, or it's too much. Tell me what you want me to do and I'll do it."

I shook my head in an effort to stop her. "It's not your fault," I told her.

"No. It was my fault all the way. I was the one who came to the goat's house for wool."

I almost smiled. I had not heard the expression in thirty years. She stood in the center of the room and began to fasten her pants and button her blouse.

Goat's house! The irony of her remark struck me like a maul. In the darkness that surrounded the cabin I could see the bobbing motion of headlights as a vehicle moved along the rutted road I called my drive. A secondary wave of irritation swept over me and I fought the impulse to drive my fist through the closet walls. I didn't want to see anyone, to talk to anyone, to endure the presence of another human being. I wanted to be alone with the warmth of the icy chickens.

"Someone's coming!" she said, her eyes widening in sudden fright. She clutched at her coat, and her fingers trembled and her eyes darted in sudden fright at the gun and at me. She fumbled helplessly as she tried to button the garment.

I watched her, pathetic in her wild and sudden and senseless fear and wondered why it mattered whether she was properly dressed when she was discovered in the bedroom of another man's house in the predawn hours while her husband was away. Her only consolation was that there was no smoking gun.

Of either kind.

"Chess!" Her voice seemed to crash through the room as it rose above the noise of the icy chickens now threatening to force their way into the cabin. I mentally urged them on. "What's happening?"

I didn't answer her. How could I? How could I find words to explain to her how nauseating her whining voice was even when I felt good? And I felt like hell now.

Or had, until I reached into the dark corner beside us and pulled the Stevens to me and let its icy coldness touch me. *It* could touch me without arousing the loathing demons. I could welcome its unfeeling and remote frigidity because it asked nothing and gave everything I had wanted now for six months. I wanted to caress cold metal, to know the blinding flash and unbearable heat that could explode a world into fragments.

"Chess!" The whining had disappeared and alarm had replaced it. "Chess! What are you doing? What are you—"

She lunged at me, her body writhing like a loathsome pale reptile as she flung herself across my lap and clutched at the Stevens.

"Stop it!" she screeched. "Damn you, stop it!"

She began to scream, the shrillness of her voice begging me to put down the gun. There was the sound of footsteps pulverizing the ice that had accumulated on the deck. Strong strides were accented by the heavy clump of boots on hardwood floors. I heard the voice of Zane Andrews as she called out to us, her voice rising above the shriek of the wind as it rattled windows in their frames. Then there was a sudden shattering of glass and the noise of the door swinging open as the cold air filled the room.

Laura stepped away from me suddenly. Her face held the look of a body long dead in the icy woods. Her momentum caused her to trip on her forgotten shoes, and she fell backward into the bed where she writhed like a wounded serpent on the rumpled covers.

Her eyes were those of a person whose brain had become a stranger to her body. The flesh of her face sagged as her mouth, gaped wide and as dead as her eyes, hung open as if the hinges had been shattered.

For a sudden horrifying moment I thought that somehow the gun had gone off and had killed her in some cold, bloodless, and silent manner. Then I realized that she was bordering on mild shock. I had seen the glazed-eye look too many times before.

I slowly released my grip on the Stevens and Zane snapped open the breech and ejected the two shells that clattered across the hardwood floor before she opened the door and slung the gun into the darkness of the gray winter morning.

She turned to Laura Dennis, a look of disgust that rivaled my own on her face.

"Get up," she ordered. "Finish dressing and get out. Move!"

The strident insistence of her voice startled Laura into sudden animation. She scrambled to her feet and lurched toward the chair where she started fumbling erratically in an effort to straighten her clothes.

Zane watched as if fascinated by the woman's body as Laura fumbled helplessly with her scarf, then gave up in frustration and shoved it into the pocket of her coat. When she had jerked on her pants, her black panties fell to the floor. She left them where they fell.

Her face was flushed with humiliation, fear, and anger. Her hair hung over her face and she flung it aside with a sudden gesture of pathetic violence.

If I had not loathed the woman so desperately I might have found something to pity in her bewilderment and shame.

"Get out of here," Zane ordered when Laura was dressed. "And don't you ever come back. Do you understand?" When Laura did not respond instantly Zane advanced menacingly toward her. Laura nodded vigorously in her new terror.

"Don't you contact that man in any way." she continued. "Not now, not ever. Do you understand?"

Laura started to nod, checked herself, her lips bunched into a childish pout. Zane took a quick step toward her and the woman fled in terror, her defiance scattered like the sleet pellets. Zane stood, hands on hips, feet spread like a storm trooper, until Laura, purse falling open and the contents scattering like windblown seeds, disappeared with the dignity of a hawk-scared hen.

Zane did not move until we heard Laura's car engine roar and the tires clawing for traction on the ice. Only when the sound of the Mercedes moved away from the cabin did she turn to face me. Her face was a vortex of fury, shock, and helplessness. Her mouth opened three or four times and no sounds came forth. She tried again, unsuccessfully, three more times before she hit me. Her fist caught me just under my left eye. Before I could recover from my shock she hit me again, three times in rapid succession. A blinding flash of pain shot through my head. The pain from the first blows had completed only half the journey to my brain before her other fist landed solidly against my nose. I tasted blood, and still the blows fell like the pellets of the eternal and scalding sleet, only faster and harder.

And her tears fell faster than did her blows.

I clutched at her, our breath coming in painful and fast gasps. My head throbbed and my gut threatened to erupt. The entire scene was

11

wild, unreal, terrifying. The room spun wildly as we danced in wordless fury. Her body sagged slightly and for a split second I thought she was starting to collapse before she shifted her weight and her boot came down hard on my bare toes.

I screamed and released my grip on her just as her knee rose and crashed into my crotch.

Falling heavily to the rough pine boards I doubled up in agony as the pain turned with amazing speed into excruciating torment, a mixture of malignancy and purgative crossing my abdomen and paralyzing me. I was barely aware that I was retching helplessly, the undigested food and beer erupting like fermented lava and spreading like a decaying albatross across my chest and dripping down my neck and onto the floor. The odor was overwhelmingly vile. Blood—my blood—mixed with the filth.

The boards scraped my face and hip. I don't know how long I lay there, lips forming silent and vile curses. Zane stood over me and glared like an angry beast. She had resumed the spread-legged stance that she used on Laura, and I hurt too badly to move for fear she would again use her boots on my helpless body.

"Get up and go wash yourself," she said when it became evident that I had no intention of moving on my own. "You smell like a bus station toilet. And be glad I controlled myself."

I groaned and retched simultaneously. The room tilted back and forth, and everything within my sight seemed surrounded by violence. She stood, her fists still clenched, ready to attack. She waited, poised in silence, and I could hear the sleet pecking furiously again. My legs were weak. My body felt as if I had been gutted with a dull hoe.

The fierce throbbing and nausea abated bit by bit, and I managed to get to my feet and stagger toward the bathroom. Zane took one arm and steadied me as I wobbled slowly beside her. Neither of us paid the slightest attention to my nakedness.

When I had showered and returned to the den, she had cleaned up the mess I had made on the floor. She had folded the blanket, as if by removing the scene of the crime she had somehow by magic eliminated it. I had pulled a robe around me, and when I stopped in front of her I started to speak.

She held up one hand firmly, and the expression on her face told me it would be unwise to say anything.

"Spare me," she said, her voice as taut as catgut on a tennis racket. "Don't tell me it wasn't what it looked like." She rolled her eyes upward as if she could not bear to look into my face. I couldn't find much way to blame her.

"How could you do this, Chess?" she asked when I clamped my mouth shut. "Do you not have a brain in your head? What is it? You decide you can't get anyone else to kill you, so you decide to do the job yourself?"

I shook my head helplessly. My groin still ached badly, but the pain had diminished enough for the pain in my eye and nose to register fully.

"Look at this!" she hissed. "You face the gas chamber for killing your wife and best friend, and when you luck out of that, you inherit millions and millions of your wife's dollars." She could have etched metal with the acid in her voice. "You let a woman kick your ass." She didn't have to remind me.

"I don't know—" I began feebly.

"Damn right you don't know. You don't know your worthless ass from third base. *Some* people could be happy with just this."

"Not you," she continued. "Oh, hell no. Chess Ivy can't be content with a great house and five hundred acres of great land. He can't live with only more money than he could ever spend in a dozen lifetimes. He can't be content with any woman he wants. He has to screw the wife of the county manager. But even that's not enough. She is stupid enough to drive a new Mercedes into the woods, and you are dense enough to unplug your phone so you can't get emergency calls. Then you try to blow your brains out."

She paused for breath before she launched one final attack. At least I hoped it was the final one. "Well, let me tell you, brother, you've failed at everything you've ever done, and you'd have failed at blowing your brains out, too. You'd never hit anything as small as a pinhead. Now get your clothes on. On the way to town I'll tell you why I risked my ass to get out here to give you the message. We have a missing person. A woman."

I stared at her in shock. We never had missing persons in Sherman. Not in my memory, which was awfully vague at the moment. Our town was not a violent one in any respect. Oh, we had the Saturday night pool hall fight or the college kids raising hell after a game. And we had our share of family fights, with husbands going to jail overnight because they decided to make a punching bag out of a wife. But never a serious crime, not as long as I could remember. Not like this.

"Gone since six-thirty this morning," she said.

I dropped the robe and reached for my clothes. She dropped her eyes toward my crotch.

"She risked her marriage for *that*?" she asked.

I decided silence was my best response.

TWO

B ecause my ego was as bruised as my body, I hobbled to
the parking space at the edge of the woods and groaned
my way into the deputy's car. She hit the gas even before I had
closed my door, and the tire treads grabbed as the car lurched through
the accumulation of sleet and toward the highway and from there to my
office. It was now snowing heavily. The ruts made by Laura's car were
already covered.

I laid my head back against the rest and closed my eyes. I was still
nauseated and I hurt all over. I didn't care that the car slid wildly on the
narrow pavement, now white with ice. I doubted that a wreck would hurt
me worse than the pain I already felt.

I had started to speak a dozen times as we make our precarious way
down the two miles of my cabin road to the state road and from there to
the main highway. The sleet fell hard and was now piled like rice along
the strip of asphalt. It was going to be a hell of a morning.

The white hell I already knew about. Before Laura arrived I had heard
the sleet start, and a forty-mile wind whipped the ice like shotgun pellets. I was sitting on the deck when I saw the lights of her car. My hands
and feet were numb from the cold as I sat on the front deck of the cabin
and let the icy wind chill me to the bone. Coldness was my only pleasure when she led me into the cabin, built a roaring fire, and knelt beside

15

me and placed my hands between her legs and held me in her arms. She pulled my face against her breasts and we huddled in silence for what must have been hours.

"I tried to call," she said. "There was no answer. I figured you had unplugged the phone, so I drove out here."

I didn't answer. I had nothing to say that she didn't already know. There wasn't anything the town didn't know: that I was a lush and a full-time loser.

She somehow undressed me before she removed her own clothes. She located three more blankets and wrapped us in them and then tried for an hour to arouse me before she finally gave up and nestled against me and fell asleep.

I waited until she breathed regularly before I inched away from her so that our bodies did not touch. I lay there listening to the pecking of the cold and starving chickens on the window panes. There was an eerie light in the room, a creation of the sleet's reflection. I stared at the dying fire and waited, dreading another day. Dreading to face Laura Dennis.

I knew there would have been no point in telling her not to come. She'd done it every time her county-manager husband left town for a day or two, and for a brief time I had actually looked forward to her arrival. Now it was like looking forward to the gallows.

Laura Dennis was in her late thirties and looked, except for two important distinctions, for the world like the late movie star Hedy Lamarr. The differences were that Laura was taller and her breasts were much larger. Both women possessed creamy white skin in shocking contrast with their hair as black and glossy as anthracite.

Both had a small mouth, diminutive nose, and eyes large as full-ripe apricots and as smoky as a November brush fire.

There was another distinction. Miss Lamarr, on the silver screen, at least, was taciturn, letting her body language and facial expression speak volumes. Laura Dennis was a parrot, albeit an attractive one, and at times I found myself wanting to stuff a sock into her face to shut her up. Any form of silence would have been preferable to her voice. She seemed to be unable to endure silence for more than a few seconds at a time.

She was also sexually insatiable. Wonderfully exciting at first, Laura soon became a chore, a burden to be dreaded and avoided if possible.

16

Within weeks the uncontrollable excitement became labor without cessation. I felt as if I were trying to fill the Grand Canyon with a teaspoon. I soon tired of her, which was not an adequate emotion: I first developed an active dislike, then I found myself detesting her, and at this precise time in our relationship she began to talk of leaving her husband and moving in with me, preparatory to our forthcoming marriage.

I almost screamed the first time she mentioned marriage. The word barely left her lips before a starkly real vision of Derry filled my mind and clouded my brain. *Derry:* all joy and light and eternally witty and equipped with intelligent conversation, full of energy and ready for a twelve-mile hike, a swim in the cold waters of Lake Carrie, a cookout, a good-natured argument over politics or art, or even a foot race. I never found a topic that did not cause her to rise instantly to the bait.

One exception: she never liked to talk about living people. If she did not like a man or woman, she never spoke the name or alluded to the person. Dead people were different. She read biographies of the poets and novelists of England and soon she was teaching me about my own lecture courses. We devoted exhilaratingly happy hours debating elements of some poem that fascinated her.

With Derry marriage was a never-ending celebration, a life filled with the endless ecstasy of simply being together, two as one.

Marriage! The thought of marriage to Laura was abhorrent, odious. She had been at best an effort to find physical release, to exorcise, I had hoped, the ghost of Derry. I argued futilely, telling Laura that marriage was an impossibility, that she had her own husband who happened to be one of the most powerful and influential men in the county. She simply plowed straight ahead. I did not have to ask why. I was new and, until recently, more energetic and attentive than her husband. I am not a matinee idol, but I have one attraction that drives many women crazy with desire: I am, through no fault of my own, obscenely rich.

I also have the distinction, thanks to the quaint laws of the state of North Carolina, of being the first and only sheriff in the history of Sherman County who was elected to the office after serving a prison term.

Most people have good news and bad news days. Mine were bad news and disaster-news days. The bad news was that I knew nothing about law enforcement, except being arrested and convicted, and that I had to face people like Laura and the world almost daily.

The disaster news was that now each day I faced the world that no longer included Derry, the only woman I had ever loved.

I was also a pariah and possibly the most hated man in the county. It was a rare day that I did not get threatening or at least abusive anonymous letters or phone calls. When I visited a store or shop I might as well have been a leper or an alien life form.

I was the Cassandra and the Midas of economics. She could see into the future but no one would believe her prophecies, and he destroyed everything he loved in order to turn it into gold. I simply turned it into death.

It brought me a parade of women I never wanted even on my worst days in prison, Laura being the latest. It was mildly shocking and immensely satisfying that I learned to hate her in record time. Almost as much as I hated my own miserable self.

The onset of depression was so insidiously slow that I did not recognize it for months. I thought my emotionally honest grief would someday, somehow leave me. I was not Prince Hamlet nor was meant to be: I was not even an attendant lord. Eliot had it nearly right.

What I was became simple. I dreaded the coming of the next day without Derry, and I cringed physically at the thought of the coming night without Derry beside me in the bed. I could not look at the lake without seeing her. She was in every nook and cranny of the cabin. Her voice was in every bird's song, her joy in the exultant energy of the fawns playing at the edge of the water and in the ripple of the streams, her emotions in the crashing ecstasy of the waterfall, her soul in the sighing of the wind in the towering pine trees she had loved so much.

The depression grew deeper and deeper. I spent money like water and detested the junk I received in return. Daily I tried to drink myself into oblivion and succeeded only in inducing the most horrible sickness I ever endured. I tried rock climbing and realized that I did not give a damn if the rope broke and I crashed into the rock-littered valley below.

Impotence soon followed. I became the Jake Barnes of Sherman County. When it first hit, I became alarmed, and with each succeeding failure I fell deeper and deeper into the abyss, the bottomless pit of self-pity.

"You were really going to do it?" Zane asked, her voice shocking me back to the present. I opened my eyes with a start. I had not been asleep, but instead I had been in some type of waking trance. I turned my head and felt the sharp reminders of the blows she had landed on my face. My groin still ached dully, and I was sufficiently hung-over to feel each and every lurch and skid of the car, all of which triggered one more wave of nausea. My eye and jaw ached intensely, and I could feel my eye beginning to swell. Within hours it would be closed, I thought, and at the same time I wondered how I could explain it to others.

We had entered Sherman while I was holding my throbbing head. The streets had a surprising number of people wandering toward their jobs. An old woman, astonishingly tall and obese, waddled along, pulling a sled filled with huge sacks of what appeared to be groceries. Everyone was stocking up on the staples, in case the snow became the predicted blizzard.

Zane had mentioned something about predictions for one of the biggest snowstorms in recent history. The system had swept down from Canada, circled in the Gulf area, and was headed north again and dropping more than two feet of snow in its path.

What happened too often for comfort was that the storms bank up against the mountains and stall there, leaving us with two or three feet of snow and ice. I dreaded the thought of being out in the weather while we searched for a missing wife who would in all probability show up a week from now and confess to her husband that she had spent the week in a beachfront motel three hundred miles away.

While we froze ourselves half to death in a pointless search for her.

"Or just scare the dog dung out of Laura?"

"I don't know," I said weakly. "It isn't important."

"No," she said. "To you it isn't important. You still can, if that's what you want," she said. "I can't be with you every minute of every day. You can afford a new shotgun if you can't find the one I threw away."

"I know."

"Are you going to do it?"

I started to shake my head and realized my mistake as the fiery pains erupted in a dozen places. I hadn't realized she had hit me so many times.

"I can't say."

"And you won't let anyone help you?"

"No one can."

"No," she said, guiding the car gently into the parking lot behind the courthouse where two dozen cars were parked. Half of them, I knew, belonged to night people. Their cars were covered with sleet. The ones with clean windshields belonged to people who had come in early for the day shift. I did not recognize three of the cars at all.

"Probably not," she added. "Do you hate being sheriff so badly?"

It was a nauseating effort, but I attempted to answer her. My response came out too much like the man who refused to quit his job cleaning backstage toilets because he didn't want to leave show business.

"The deputies despise me," I said. "They ridicule me and have nothing but contempt. The people of Sherman County laugh at my stupidity. Criminals love for me to arrest them because they know I'll screw up and they'll be free in half an hour. Secretaries giggle when I pass them, and janitors feel sorry for me."

"Then why not resign? Why put yourself through this."

"I can't leave," I croaked. "Coming here is the high point of my day."

We left the car in the snow-filled lot and entered the crumbling old courthouse building by the back door. In the office we found Deputy Rick Blanton, the editor of the local paper, the high school principal, and a man I assumed to be the husband of the missing woman. His face was pale, and his hands shook so badly that he squeezed them tightly together in his lap. The clock on the wall showed nearly eight o'clock.

I dreaded the encounter. I was sick, looked and felt like hell, and, worst of all, was totally useless in my present state. Worse, I knew tomorrow wouldn't be any better.

The principal stood quickly and shook hands with me. He was a tall man, broad-shouldered and fit-looking. The ex-jock who left coaching but had not yet gone to seed.

"Marlin Rockwell," he said. "I came as soon as Bert called the school." He kept his grip on my hand firm, constricting.

"Why did he call you?" I asked, not really knowing why. I thought I ought to ask something. "How long has Mrs. Webley been missing?"

Rockwell glanced quickly at the distraught man who now sat with his head in his hands. He instantly struck me as too grief-stricken for no longer than his wife had been gone.

"Bert called at fifteen before seven. It was still dark. He told me Alicia had driven to her mother's house and would go from there to school. She had not arrived when he called me."

I extricated my hand from his and moved away from his frank and disarming countenance. The jock still showed through. The man had once been a charmer. Perhaps still was. I sat down beside Bert Webley.

"Why did you call the school?" I asked. I hung my head in the desperate hope that the booze fumes would stay in my area only. "Did you have reason to think your wife was in some danger?"

He looked helplessly at me, ready to burst into tears at any moment. He appeared to be no more than nineteen years old, the boy who never grew up, who had never worked a day in his life. I had seen him a few times around town, back in the days when I had a semblance of life.

"The phone call," he managed to get out before the tears and wracking sobs convulsed him. I turned to Rockwell, questioning. Rockwell glanced at Ed Gallager, the newspaper editor, a sallow and small man: a mole out of his burrow.

"The call came to me," Gallager said. He seemed weak, unable to control his apprehensions. "I came straight over, hoping to find you in." I didn't miss the contempt in his voice. "The caller said he *had* the wife of Mr. Webley."

"That's his exact word? He *had* her?" The words struck me like huge boulders. Nausea welled inside me; my head threatened to explode, and I felt the second wave of impotence. No man ever loathed himself more than I did at that moment. I could not bear to look into the wretched face of the man whose wife was missing and who expected me to find her, to save her. He didn't know I could not find the floor if I fell on my face.

"'I have Bert Webley's wife,' the voice said."

"What else? Tell me every word."

He sidled closer, like a wounded weasel, until his mouth was near my ear. I felt a greasy cold shiver course through my guts and I knew the coming message, if not the exact words.

"He said he would keep her till he tired of her. Then he hung up."

"What time was this?"

"Seven-thirty. I looked at the clock the moment he hung up."

"*He?* You're confident it was a man? Describe his voice as closely as you can."

"Soft, weak. As if a large and strong man was trying to make his voice unrecognizable. Like a man whose vocal cords had been damaged."

Webley found his voice again. "Mr. Gallager called me, and I called Mr. Rockwell," he said. "To see if he had heard anything from Alicia. Mr. Rockwell said he hadn't seen her. Then I came here. They said they'd call you. I've been calling the house every ten minutes since."

He blinked rapidly several times, trying to hold back the tears. His voice wavered when he spoke. "Sheriff Ivy, what are we going to do?"

What could I tell him? That I was far more helpless than he? That I had no idea where to start or what to do?

"May I make a suggestion?"

It was Zane, who had been silent since we arrived. She moved to the side of Deputy Rick Blanton, the monster man we called Lurch, after the character on the TV comedy-horror show.

"Why don't we check roads first? Rick, you and Webley ride together. I'll drive the sheriff. Mr. Gallager, you and Rockwell go back to your offices and stay there. That's sort of what you suggested on the way in, Sheriff. Is that still all right?"

Gratefully, I managed to nod somewhat authoritatively. The effort nearly nauseated me. She gave them her car phone number and we left. The sleet had formed a perfect base for the snow that was now falling. It was going to be a hell of a day, I repeated.

THREE

Everyone in the room waited for me to respond. I didn't speak until we had crossed the parking lot, brushed snow from the windshield of the car, and started across the parking lot.

"Thanks," I said "That meant a lot. I'm grateful."

"Then show your gratitude," she said as she pulled into the empty street.

"How?" I groaned, hoping with all my heart she didn't mean what I feared she did.

"By being professional," she said. Her face held all the expression of a rattler awaiting his prey. "By making at least an effort to be a lawman."

"I don't know how," I said miserably. I did not exaggerate. I know nothing about law enforcement. Nor did I pretend to know.

"Then start learning. Until then, play it by ear." The heat continued to seep through her demeanor. "I make you a promise, Chester Ivy, and I don't promise frivolously. You show up at the office hung over again and you'll find a couple of things that were once important to you hanging on a rusty nail in some falling-down barn. If you think I'm kidding, you try me."

There was no hint of humor in her voice or demeanor. She was furious with me, and rightly so. Everyone I knew had the same right. I tried for a moment to think of one person I had not let down and couldn't. I gave up the effort when my head began to throb worse. The motion of the car nauseated me, and I ground my teeth in an effort to control the gag reflex.

"Roll down the window," Zane said. "Your booze breath is making *me* sick. Stick your head out. Freezing your brain won't do any more damage than your life style is doing."

I obeyed, and the frigid air, whipping marshmallow-sized snowflakes like brass gnats, pelted my face and stung my ears.

Desperately I turned on the map light and tried to force my eyes to focus on the notes Zane had somehow made and slipped to me. I knew nothing about Bert Webley and his wife, but possibly I could learn. Bert and his wife lived in a rock house at the edge of town. They had been married two years, and she taught music in the public schools and he ran the hardware store downtown.

I vaguely knew both of them: intelligent, reasonably articulate, and attractive. Alisha Webley played the organ at the Baptist church on Main Street and Bert sang in the choir. There was no mention of any discordant note in their marital life.

The narrative was simple. Bert and his wife had spent the night together, as always, and they both rose at five o'clock in the morning. He had baked biscuits while she prepared the sausage and eggs for breakfast. While she prepared for school, he watched the television weather report for news of school closings.

The Sherman public schools were among the schools closed because of the weather, and Alisha decided to make a dash to the supermarket near my office and to stop by her mother's house on the way back. Bert was in the bathroom when he heard the phone ring, and Alisha answered. It was one of their neighbors wanting to know about the schools. Then she left. Bert drove down to open the hardware store before dawn. He did not see Alisha's car as he passed the grocery store. When he called home at nine, she wasn't there. Nor was she at her mother's house. It was barely light when he went looking, in case she was stuck in a snow bank.

An hour later he passed his house and saw Alisha's car in the drive, but when he entered the house she was not there.

He called several of his wife's friends and found that none of them

24

had seen her at all that morning. Then he checked the trunk of his wife's car and found that the groceries were still there. In one bag there were two cartons of ice cream.

At that point he called the sheriff's office.

When I saw him there he had aged a decade since our last meeting a few days earlier. I knew too well the feeling that ages a man in minutes.

Slender, with the slight build of a country club tennis pro, and with a face as youthful and energetic, Bert at that moment appeared to be an ancient man, decrepit and forlorn. When he looked at me I could see that his eyes had filled with tears.

When we talked with him, he kept his hands perfectly still in his lap and he looked into my eyes with the directness of an electrical surge. At no point did he avoid eye contact or pause even slightly before speaking, and he did not occupy his hands with pencil or other common distraction items.

We drove around for two hours before I asked Zane to take me first to my cabin so I could pick up my shotgun and then we'd drive to the school. What I didn't tell her was that I was stalling while I tried to come up with a plan of some sort. From there we went to the schoolhouse on the hill.

Marlin Rockwell met us at the huge double doors facing the street. He ushered us into his office, closed the door, and poured three cups of steaming coffee.

"Sheriff Ivy," he said warmly. "Tell me the news. Good news, I should add," he amended instantly.

"Nothing," I told him in answer to his unasked question. "We found no trace of anything helpful." I tried to keep my face averted in order to direct the booze fumes downward.

"We looked in every reasonable place," Zane offered. "We are now ready to start on the unreasonable ones."

"I called one of the cooks," Rockwell said in a voice that reeked of granite boiled in acid. It was as casual as a ramrod. "She agreed to come in and fix sandwiches and soup for your people. I'll drop them off at the department throughout the day." He added, "And night, if necessary."

He held the door wide and motioned us into the hallway. It was a short corridor twenty feet wide that opened into the long hallway that

25

stretched the length of the schoolhouse. The double offices were to the right of the short corridor and as he ushered us inside we saw that both rooms were empty except for us. No secretary, no assistants, not even brown-nosing in-trouble kids. It was a mausoleum.

I started to thank him for the soup-and-sandwich offer but the look on his face stopped me.

"I want this kid back safely," he said. His tone was soft, even, and cold. There was no mistaking his message. But even if I had, he repeated it in a manner that left no questions. "I want her found and returned to her husband and to this school. I do not want to hear excuses and rationalizing. I want results."

I felt nothing that could be mistaken for confidence.

Only chills.

He stared at me, hard. The affable nature that had met me at the door of the empty building had evaporated.

"I know your story, Ivy," he said. "The whole story." The final thrust was an ominous observation, like the dried buzz of the timber rattler.

"If you know the whole story," I said lamely, "then you know there is nothing for which I need to apologize. Not until last night," I quickly added.

He stood, feet spread in an athletic stance and studied the hangdog look on my face.

"Last night was only the most recent incident," he said. "One out of months. Let me review the facts: A college professor goes to prison; after he breaks into a university records room and steals files, he then with a deadly weapon attacks the school president and two of his deans. He serves part of his term and then persuades his flunky lawyer friend to campaign for him and then rig the election, by buying the votes of all his black so-called friends, so the convict can come out of a cell to act as sheriff."

I started to protest his careless manipulation of facts, but he held up his hand and the anthracite in his voice increased in decibel count and degree of hardness, coldness.

"Some act," he went on. "You come out of prison and immediately your wife and your black lawyer were killed while they coupled like reptiles in the dirty basement of the filthy man's house. You wriggle out of the murder charges by coercing a dying man to confess that he killed the couple, and then happen to learn that your wife had been named beneficiary of your shyster's whore-and-drugs fortune and the entire bundle of money and stocks and options dropped from the sky and directly into your lap. Then two of your deputies, a fat and stupid man and a sexually repressed woman, surprise you at your cabin and you kill both of them, after which you hand out the cock-and-bull story that it was they and not the dying old man who had done the killings. Clever, Ivy. Clever as hell. And then you go on a three-month drunk and let your staff run the sheriff's department while you sleep it off in your own private little whorehouse you call a cabin. And all you can think of is how to keep from going back into a cell. I don't blame you. I understand they have quite a welcome-back party for law officers who return to prison."

"It didn't happen that way and you know it," Zane nearly snarled at him. "Sheriff Ivy was set up by the deputies, just the way it came out in the reports. You people amaze me. You can't let it go, can you? I think you'd like nothing better than to see him returned to his cell."

I touched her on the shoulder and she became instantly silent. She knew she was on the verge of too-far. My head hurt too badly for me to engage in bickering that was pointless.

Except that it *wasn't* pointless. Rockwell was exactly right on all but a couple of minor counts. I *was* in constant danger of returning to prison, and the thought kept me in a continuous shudder of terror. Ex-law officers did not fare well in prison, particularly alongside the people he helped to put behind bars. But it didn't matter who put them there. They saw all cops as one and the same: loathsome rodents to be exterminated.

"Sorry," she said. "*If* I was out of line, I apologize."

Affability returned in full regalia. Rockwell smiled at her, then at me. "Please," he said. "I was terribly wrong. This is no time for personal viewpoints." He turned to Zane and beamed his warm and ultra-personal smile.

"As an educator, of all people, I am obliged to keep an eye on my students and on my faculty," he said.

I didn't know if the comment was apology or justification. It didn't matter now. Earlier, it might have. Or perhaps later. We sat, Zane and I, like guilt-ridden juveniles in straight-backed chairs while Rockwell seated himself in a swivel chair behind a desk that must have looked formidable to miscreants. The broad surface of the desk gleamed darkly under the florescent lights. The wood appeared to be oak or maple. Only a legal pad, a small desk calendar, and a pen set interrupted the sheen. I wondered how much the desk had set the school board back.

"What can I do?" he asked, in a manner now concerned and benevolent. "How can I help?"

"We need to get a better look at Alisha Webley," I said. There was nothing to be gained by prolonging the cold war. "How long have you known Alisha?"

He didn't stop to count. "I've known Alisha Webley two years. Before that, I knew Alisha Brady for three years. She was in the tenth grade at Sherman High when I met her. Pretty girl, smart, personable, but a bit shy. I was delighted when she and Bert decided to get married."

"You knew Bert, then?"

"He was a student here, too. It was a strange match, I thought at first. She seemed by far the stronger of the two. I sometimes wonder if women do that on purpose: marry weaker men so they can dominate them."

"You consider Bert weak?"

"Weaker than Alisha. She was a quiet girl but as strong-willed as they come when the occasion demanded. She did not mind standing up for what she thought was right. Or good."

He smiled as he spoke. A tall, athletic-looking man, his voice and personality seemed too subdued for his physical looks. He reminded me of a weight-lifter who looks perfectly normal in his build until he takes off his coat and you see what's really under it. I still nursed the feeling that he had been a college jock turned coach and then principal.

Those who can, do; those who cannot, teach. Those who cannot teach become administrators, I thought, with apologies to Shaw.

"Did she have any boy friends?" I asked.

He smiled again. "Tons of aspiring ones, but she kept them all at arm's length. She apparently wanted Bert and no one else."

"To dominate?" I asked. "What I meant was, did she ever have any boy friends after she and Bert were married? That you know of, I mean?"

He smiled patiently at me. "She'd have wanted man-friends, not boyfriends," he said. "She seemed to strengthen as the months went by. I always hoped she'd go back and complete her college work. She was a marvelous student. Always had her work done on time, never permitting mistakes to creep in, and never guilty of anything even remotely incorrect. A perfectionist."

I received a load of information. What I did not receive was an answer to my question.

"Did she graduate at the top of her class?"

His face darkened and he frowned. "Funny about that," he said. "She never graduated from Sherman High School. She dropped out in March of her senior year. Wanted to sing with some sort of rock band, or some such thing. Left home to go on the road with them. Her parents were pretty upset. In fact, it tore her mother up to see her, as she put it, throwing her entire life away."

As he spoke, I watched his eyes. They darted everywhere, like the eyes of a ferret. They were dark and hinted at a somber or brooding attitude. He had the dark good looks of a suave Latin-American movie star to accent his athlete's body that housed an educator's brain.

"This rock-singing career, then. It was sudden?"

"As far as anyone knows. She sang in the Girls Chorus and in the Glee Club. She had a rich solo voice. Not enough for her to make a career professionally, but a good amateur voice."

"Did she have any problems here at school? Anything that you can think of? Fights or feuds with other students? Trouble with teachers? Problems at home?"

He spoke crisply without losing the warmth of his tone. "No problems with students, teachers, or even custodial staff. While she was on this campus, she was a happy young woman."

"What about at home?" By now we all spoke of her in the past tense.

He shook his head, and the light caught the hint of gray at his temples.

"At school she was a totally happy person," he said. "She, if she had a fault, tended to be too book-oriented. Most of our teachers would kill to have such a student. But she let her studies, as I said, dominate her life. As for problems, there is not a student in this school—or any other school in the universe as we know it—who does not have problems."

Another non-answer.

"What about problems at home?" I repeated. He was going to answer at least one question that I wanted answered.

He smiled in a benign manner. "Like most young women, she was often at odds with her parents. Like all too many, she and her father did not enjoy a wholesome, happy relationship."

He stared at his desk for several moments, and when he looked back up at me there were tears in his eyes. His voice cracked slightly when he spoke. Genuinely concerned? Or merely a good actor?

"She perhaps wanted to move faster than her world would allow. To know everything."

"A little knowledge," I said, "is a dangerous thing."

He smiled apologetically. "A little *learning*," he said, correcting me mildly. I made a judgment at that point.

"Sure," I said. "'Drink deep or taste not the Pierian Spring.'" People who misquote the first line and don't know the next three lines demonstrate just what Pope meant by a *little* learning.

"'There shallow draughts intoxicate the brain,'" he continued with the quote, "'And drinking largely sobers us again.' A wonderful passage from a superlative poet."

"Yes," I agreed. "*The Essay on Man* is a classic."

He smiled wryly. "*The Essay on Criticism*," he said, "as you well know. Can I help with anything else, or do you want to go on playing mind games? My suggestion is a concentrated search."

He turned to Zane, who had been silent since her solitary outburst earlier. "Was that a fair appraisal of Alisha, Deputy Raines?" he asked.

Deputy Raines? I glanced at her to see how she reacted to the wrong name and to my surprise she nodded casually, as if she had not caught the mistake.

"I remember her as a student, not as a faculty member," she said. "I'm not certain I would have characterized her that way."

We left quickly and in the parking lot Zane turned to me as we stopped in front of our cars. "I was married right after school," she said. "My maiden name was Raines." A bitter laugh erupted from her. "Maiden," she said. "What a quaint term for these times. Maidenhood—maidenhead. You know what the kids say a virgin is, Chess? The ugliest girl in the third grade. Is that sick, or what?"

30

"I didn't know about your marriage. It ended, I assume."

"Like everything," she said. "It ended. My husband died, and that's the end of that short biography. Where to?"

"Let's go talk to neighbors," I said. "You take the north side of the street and I'll do the south."

We did, and after a dozen brief visits we met again at the school parking lot. When we compared notes a slightly different picture of Alisha Webley emerged. Everybody loved Alisha, who was a model wife, teacher, musician, and member of the community.

Except that she had become pregnant during her senior year and had dropped out of school. The only singing she did was in the form of lullabies.

She was the kind of woman no one could possibly hate or harm.

So they said. We had reason to think otherwise. Everybody loved her, despite the fact that as one neighbor told me, she couldn't keep her pants up. At least before her marriage. Because she had a thing for older men. Because she—

Alisha, we learned, was perfect only in an imperfect manner. And her imperfections were understated because it was bad form to talk ill of the soon-to-be-dead. Everyone else talked of her in the past tense, too, demonstrating clearly how much faith they had in me or in any other law officers. Her only trips out of town were to the tiny community of Monbo, one of the neighbors told us.

We stood in the swirling snow and I glanced back at the school and it seemed that I could still detect a faint odor of oil-soaked wood floors. In the hollow between the school and the football field I caught a glimpse of Panther Creek, a stream that three miles north flowed across Sherman University. At the northwest end of the college campus the creek fell two hundred feet over a sheer rock face of a granite cliff. A man-made dam caught the water as it left the plunge pool and formed a five-acre lake.

Two schools connected by Panther Creek. Too closely?

The snow had fallen steadily for hours now, and we again left the school and drove the rural roads for hours in increasing difficulty. It was nearly dark when the call came from my office.

"Ed Gallager is here once more," Deputy Rick Blanton said, and my heart plummeted like a stone dropped into the Grand Canyon. I was alone on a road that wound around Lake Carrie. My sawed-off shot-gun—as a paroled felon, I was not permitted to carry a hand gun, the only law officer in the nation denied that simple symbol of office—lay on the seat beside me.

"The kidnapper called again. He says that Alisha Webley is now in the trunk of a car. He said he's tired of her now and needs a new toy. He'll call back in half an hour. It might be best if you were here when the call comes."

"Be right there," I told him.

Blanton and Bum Phillips were there when I arrived, along with Ed Gallager and Marlin Rockwell, who brought along a bucket of fried chicken and all the trimmings. Zane arrived five minutes after I did, her hair and shoulders dotted with huge snowflakes. We all sat around a table and stared at the food.

Nobody was hungry, but we ate automatically. The phone rang at seven o'clock. It was a secretary from Ed Gallager's office. I didn't have to ask about her news. Her voice was taut as catgut leaders on a fishing line. She tried three or four times before she ever managed to get a whole sentence out.

"He called again," she said, her voice perilously close to breaking. "He said that the gray car with Alisha Webley in the trunk would be in the county parking lot before midnight."

I didn't try to pull anything else out of her. The others could see the tension on my face and they had stood in unison, ready to move in any direction I suggested. I told them quickly about the message. Like stock characters in an old-time movie, they stared at one another for what must have been five seconds before anyone made a move. Then we all moved at once.

Quickly we rushed outside and positioned four cars in the parking lot, one at each corner. Two of the cars were near each of the entry lanes, so that there was no way for anyone to drive into the lot without being seen. And no way for anyone to leave the lot without being apprehended, un-less he was driving a tank.

Bert Webley and I occupied my car that was positioned nearest the exit lane. I explained to him that there could be danger, but he insisted on being there. I pretended not to notice the bulge at the waistband of his pants where the jacket barely concealed the hand gun.

I have never been politically correct and didn't plan to start now. If we apprehended the bastard and Alisha Webley was dead or suffering, I felt that Bert deserved a chance to make his statement.

It turned out that he did not get the chance. Midnight came and went, and no vehicles of any sort entered the parking lot. We waited until one o'clock in the subfreezing climate and watched the snow fill up the parking lot.

I made two or three futile and embarrassing efforts to talk to him, but he had sunk so low in the car seat that I thought he had actually gone to sleep. He was as unresponsive as a department store dummy.

Then my car phone rang. The noise couldn't have sounded much louder if it had been a cannon. Webley jerked upright, his hand snaking toward the gun. My heart pounded as if I'd sprinted up Mount Everest.

I fumbled with the phone, dropped in into my lap, and finally managed to recover it and position it properly.

"The woman from Ed's office just called again," the voice from my office said. "The message is that the woman is in the trunk of a gray Honda Accord with a dented trunk lid."

I had lowered the window as soon as the phone rang, and now a sudden gust of wind picked up snow and blasted us with it. The soft flakes struck me in the face and filtered their way down my collar. A shiver of death caused my entire body to tremble with unanticipated fervor. Zane in the nearby car must have seen the look on my face, for she opened the car door and rushed toward me and Webley. She started to lean forward and place her hands on the car roof, then realization struck and she backed away in horror. She clapped a gloved hand over her mouth to prevent the rising scream.

I clambered out of my car, scrambled to the trunk, and brushed away the four inches of snow that had covered the deep dent in the trunk lid. By this time Rick Blanton, aka Lurch, and Bum Harley had noted the flurry of activity and joined me, Zane, and Webley. My slowly freezing fingers found the trunk key and inserted it into the lock.

The lid swung open slowly, and in the yellow light filtered through the snow I saw a black plastic sheet that had once covered a stack of wood behind my cabin and which now covered something I did not want to see. A once-pale hand now almost black extended from under the plastic. Before I could move, Webley clutched the plastic and yanked fiercely at it. Under it was the nude body of Alisha Webley.

Webley made a choking sound and staggered backward. I must have done the same thing, for we collided and nearly lost our balance in the deepening snow. He turned away from the car and began to sob uncontrollably.

Zane had approached the trunk of the car and stared in helpless horror at the body. Even Lurch seemed unable to move.

There was no need for anyone to ask how Alisha Webley had died and whether she suffered horribly before death mercifully intervened. She had been butchered by degrees.

FOUR

I stepped backward as the raging wind howled across the expanse of the snow-covered pavement. When I looked around me quickly and saw that no one but me heard it, I knew the sound had come from within me.

My heart pounded furiously, and the entire scene became a surreal and horrifying nightmare. Except that it was real, and I stood in a maelstrom of wind, sleet, and snow that swirled into the trunk of my car and gently kissed the Thing that felt none of the cold or wind or snow.

The shock was beyond belief. All day I had moved in a sort of trance in which my mind was incapable of compelling my body into action. I was an automaton, a robot without intelligence and motivation. In my own way I was nearly as dead as the woman whose skin was rapidly turning from blue-black to white.

Nothing about the day had been real. Nothing had prepared me for the obscenely ugly and grotesque thing in my car. Even when the phone message came in and I rushed toward the parking lot I could not make myself understand that the body of Alisha Webley would—or could!—be in my car. I closed my eyes tightly, shutting out the light from the tall metal posts that hovered like war clubs above me and the car. An instant prayer that what I had seen had been an illusion flashed through my mind, that when I opened my eyes again the body would be gone.

35

It was still there. I stood paralyzed for what seemed like light years but, I realized, had been only a few seconds. Light years without light, warmth, or reality. I felt my last meal, whenever it had been, rising inside me, and I turned my face upward and let the sleet sting my flesh and the snowflakes insulate me against my own nausea. I could not add another indignity to my life by losing my meal on the snow that covered everything but Alisha Webley.

After the wave of nausea passed, I forced myself, sheepishly because of my frightened reaction, to approach the trunk and the body. This time it was a little easier to stare at the plastic, unreal, body under the sheet, a body that seemed to have been encased for a long time in solid ice.

"Call the hospital," Rick Blanton said tersely to someone behind me. The hospital was almost directly across the street from us and in only seconds we heard the siren drawing closer and closer and saw the frantic lights dying the color of the snow to that of blood. I glanced quickly at Webley, who stood rigidly, as if he had been turned into a statue. He appeared to be on the edge of shock; his face betrayed no hint of emotion. Marlin Rockwell had stared at the body for several moments before his eyes darted around the interior of the trunk. Gallager scribbled rapidly, cold fingers holding a ball-point pen and grubby pad.

Without warning, the nausea returned like rolling and silent thunder inside me as I glanced rapidly at each of the faces in the snow. I was certain I could read their thoughts: Webley wondering how much the loss of his wife's income would affect the family finances, the high school principal calculating how to handle the reporters and board members that would invade his office and school, Gallager mentally counting the new subscribers and advertisers to come his way because of the story headlines screaming within hours across the newspaper.

And I was wondering how I would survive yet another series of embarrassments and degradation.

I wondered if anyone in the snow sensed any of the pain that Alisha Webley had endured. And whether any of us felt even the faintest twinge of the loss of the woman before us. I did not like what I concluded.

Whoever made the call, Zane Andrews, likely, had apparently explained the situation well, because the young doctor leaped from the vehicle and approached the car efficiently. He might as well have been the meter man or a mechanic.

He searched for nonexistent signs of life, fingers and eyes expertly probing into the final moments of the life of Alisha Webley. I retreated backward as far as possible into the snow and the night and still saw too much. I could only hope that the woman had died in the early part of the ordeal.

The doctor completed his tasks quickly and stepped back. We again approached the body. In a small mountain county like ours, a forensic team was only a daydream, and Rick, Zane Andrews, and Bum Phillips surrounded the body. Flashlight beams darted like lasers about the interior of the trunk.

My frigid face flushed hot with embarrassment and shame that I was totally left out of the scene. At the same time I was intensely grateful not to have to look at the body again. Rick Blanton would miss nothing. He was our one-man force: expert in the fields of explosives, martial arts, all types of weapons from knives to guns of all sorts. A decade earlier he had been a student in classes I taught at Sherman University, a school that was as much a disgrace to education as the man the school was named for had been to humanity: the man who waged war on women, children, animals, and even churches as if they were enemy soldiers.

Rick had sat in class and seemed never to hear anything I said in lectures. Then he turned in perfect test papers; he wrote with the same ease with which he jogged for miles along the shores of the lake or through the streets of town. His eyes were movie cameras, his ears tape recorders, his mind computer files. He could read a book and years later dredge up facts and details with astonishing rapidity and accuracy. He remembered faces and comments the way other people remembered where they parked their car.

Bum Phillips was the opposite: he liked to tell people that he was half-Cherokee Indian but seemed to be as Caucasian as a snowman. He had to write down everything he wanted to remember. We used to joke, when there was something to laugh about, that if he went to the store to get ten Cokes, he'd have to list them one at a time. But he was a bulldog, a bloodhound, a man who moved with the slowness of a glacier, but nothing sidetracked him from the trail. He would plod through the pages of a county or city directory in search of a name or address; he could knock on every door in town until he found the details he sought.

It used to be said that Daniel Boone could track a bear back to the place where it was born, but Bum Phillips could retrace the trail to where the parents had mated. He attended Sherman University also, but I never taught him; I just stood in front of him. He labored over each and every assignment and he barely managed to score a passing grade on any test. But in his own way he was as thorough and systematic as any law officer ever needed to be.

Rick could have worked for any police force in the nation and distinguished himself; Harley would be lucky to find another place in the South where he could work, but those who turned him down would be the losers.

Zane Andrews was the newest member of the department, and I knew next to nothing about her. Short, attractive in a round-faced and sexless fashion, she moved with the quickness of a ferret and the grace of a cow on crutches. She was the weak link in the chain. But she was miles ahead of me: I wasn't a part of the chain at all. I was the rust and corrosion that was as useful as the proverbial boobs on a boar hog.

This was real modesty. And I had a great deal to be modest about. I had been a mediocre teacher at a school devoid of academic standards. When a student once asked me why the school didn't attempt to improve its academic reputation, I told him that it was so he could be admitted and I could keep a job there.

And now I stood in the snow and let the three of them work, knowing that they would do the best job possible under the conditions. Once, while I still had illusions that I could make a place for myself in the department, I had begged for money for a real forensic team, complete with proper training and equipment, but the county fathers insisted that with our crime rate one of the lowest in the entire nation, we'd be better advised to spend money on a new press box for the football field and new mats for the wrestling team.

Mentally, I admitted that my resentment had been partly, if not mostly, the reason the county manager's wife had first come to my cabin.

The truth is that most big-city churches have higher crime rates than we normally have in Sherman County. Kindergartens see more raw violence on the playground than we have in our pool rooms and back alleys.

The only carnage we ever see occurs when the Sherman University football team plays any team not confined to wheelchairs.

"I'll go talk to Bert Webley," Zane said, finally turning away from the car trunk and the body. "Unless you want to."

I looked to the spot where Webley had been and was shocked to see only the imprint of his Italian shoes remained in the snow. He had somehow disappeared.

"He's in your office," Zane said. "I took him in there and told him one of us would join him in a couple of minutes. Would you prefer to talk to him? Or do you want me to do it?" I had not seen either of them leave.

Thank God for people with presence of mind, I thought. While I had been feeling sorry for myself, she had been acting like a law enforcement officer. I knew when I campaigned for sheriff that I knew absolutely nothing about law enforcement, and in the cold night with the frigid wind lashing our faces and the dead eyes staring back at me from the dead face that had been already lightly covered by the snow, I realized anew just how hopeless, hapless, and helpless I was.

"I don't prefer," I said, "but I have to. It's my job."

I had needed to deliver death messages before, and it was never an easy job to tell a parent or wife or child that their loved one would not ever return, that the fiery wreck, the overturned boat, the heart attack, the bolt of lightning....

But this was different. Webley knew his wife was dead. For all I knew, he had killed her. It was not the kind of thought I relished, but it had to be considered. Even I knew that much.

He was sitting across from my desk when I entered the tiny room adjacent to the waiting room where I had first seen him. He did not respond for several minutes when I told him what he already knew: how his wife had died. I did not add that she had suffered considerably. Maybe he already knew that, too.

He did not look like a killer, however a killer is expected to look. He reminded me of a child who keeps expecting an adult to tell him that it was all a mistake, that the puppy had not been killed on the busy highway. I told him that we would have updated information for him as soon as possible. I asked if there was anyone he wanted me to call, and he shook his head. He sat with his face buried in his hands and did not sob, speak, or groan. He could have been a distorted statue.

Finally he raised his head and I could see that his eyes were swollen. He seemed slight now, much smaller than he had been even an hour ago. But his eyes now burned with fierce light.

"How did the body get into your car?" he asked evenly. His wife had already become "the body." I shook my head in disbelief.

"I have no idea," I said. "I have been in the car, give or take a few minutes, virtually all day. Nearly all that time the car was moving. Whoever did this had to take an awful chance that someone would see him. It was broad daylight when she disappeared and the only time my car was parked was while I was in the office or inside a building while we talked to people. Bert, I'm terribly sorry. I have an idea how you must feel and...."

His face suddenly became hard and angry.

"Do you?" he asked viciously. "Do you know what it's like to see your wife's butchered body? Can you imagine what it's like to see—" He began to weep then, racking, body-shaking sobs that let the anguish and the pain, for the moment, escape. I walked away before he could ask the question a second time about how the body could have been put in my car without my knowing about it.

I wanted, perhaps more than Webley, to know how the body was placed in my car. Laura Dennis and her county manager-on-the-loose husband lived just at the outskirts of town, where the fairly new man-made lake inched up to their back yard boundary. There was one road, a loop leading off the main road to their house. The nearest neighbor was a quarter of a mile away and no one in the house could have seen Laura's drive. It would have been difficult for someone to know that she would leave her home in the middle of the night and drive to my place and that my Honda would be parked at the cabin.

Lurch was still outside when I left Webley, but by now he had pulled my car under the covered pickup area by the back door. He had located a powerful flashlight and was examining the interior of the trunk carefully. When I stopped beside him, Lurch straightened to his full height and towered over me by a good six inches. I thought again that he missed becoming a millionaire by not playing pro football or basketball. He shook his head as he looked down at me. "It's already been vacuumed," he said. "You ever hear of too many clues?"

"Red herrings?" I wouldn't know a clue if one bit me.

"No. Just that we are dealing with the most careless killer since Cain, the way it looks to me. We found junk of all sorts, as if it had been dumped in there with her. Almost everything else except a social security number, driver's license, and signed confession."

"I'm waiting for the other shoe to drop," I said. "Drop it." He shook his head again. The snow was falling harder now than it had all day and his hair looked like that of Bobby Cremins, the basketball coach at Georgia Tech.

"The other shoe is simple: without all the litter in there, we still have nothing. As it now stands, everyone in town is a possibility, but no one is a suspect."

"Except me," I said. "Yogi Berra was right: this is deja vu all over again. I didn't like this movie the first time I saw it. Tell me what you took from the trunk."

He grinned, barely. "A spare tire, flat, by the way. Don't you ever check on these things? A lug wrench, a pair of old and ragged coveralls, a fly rod with line so rotted that you couldn't have landed a housefly if you hooked it. A small boxful of old *National Geographic*s that you fully intended to read one day. Four bills with postmarks dated August. Of 1991. They all had twenty-nine cent stamps on them, by the way. We found your Sears catalog, still in the wrapper, and three or four envelopes with credit cards inside them. You cleaned out this space right after the Late Unpleasantness Between the States, right?"

"I've been busy," I said.

He winced. "Sorry, chief. I majored in tact when I was in Sherman U. We've contacted the state police. They say they are ready to come when we call them. Sorry about the remark."

"It's all right." He was referring to the incident only days after I took office. My best friend—I thought— and my wife were both slaughtered in his house one night just after I had left there with a bagful of my friend's money. I was stupid enough to defend myself when they charged me with double murders and lucky enough to have some good friends to help me stay out of prison. I had been there, done that. Since that time the thought of a dead body paralyzes me mentally and emotionally.

"What else?" I asked.

"A small cut stone on a necklace. Leaves, twigs, scraps of cloth, an old shoe, a section of newspaper. Nothing that will help in any way. Is Webley holding out as well as possible?"

I nodded. "He's crushed, of course. Just as I was. But I was luckier. At least I could get as mad as I wished at my wife and no one would blame me. He can only get furious at the killer. What are your suggestions?"

Lurch, as everyone in town knew, really ran the sheriff's office. I wore the badge only because Edney Parkins, the man I thought was a real friend, conned me into a web that included filling the vacancy left when Maurice Chambers died in the arms and in the private parts of June Flowers. Edney had other plans for the office once I was in it, some of which had to do with his illicit operations that I was not supposed to see.

Rick looked at me as if I were an ingenuous child. I knew what he was going to say even before he opened his mouth, and I felt like a damn fool.

"You didn't ask him anything, did you? You saw him starting to weep and wail and gnash his teeth and you couldn't stand to see a grown man cry, and you walked away. Am I right? If he had anything to hide, you gave him time to think up a cover story?"

I nodded.

"Don't worry. I'll talk to him."

"What should I do?"

He grinned quickly and gave me the old line used in a million Hollywood films about frontier life. "Boil water," he said. "Lots of it." Then he added, "We need to talk to everyone who knew the victim: her parents, siblings, in-laws, professional colleagues, choir members, friends, church members, even students. We have already started covering the neighborhood. Don't get any hopes up. No one is going to have seen anything. But first, let's get Webley home. I'd like to see the inside of his house."

The drive was short in distance but interminable in time as Webley slouched against the door and moaned softly. It reached the keening point, almost, before Lurch spoke to him in a tone that was gentle and yet insistent.

"We have a choice," he said. "We can start to work and do our best to catch the killer, or we can use our time in other ways. Do you feel like helping?" Tactfully put, Lurch had just told him to save the mourning for a better time. Webley sat up, as though he had been slapped.

"Did you and your wife have any problems?" Lurch asked. "And before you pop off, remember that in any mate's death, the first person to be questioned is the other mate. Now did you two fight, disagree on serious matters, or have other problems?"

"No problems," Webley said softly. He was retreating into his mourning mode. "We had no problems at all."

"Everybody has problems," Lurch insisted. "They had problems in Eden. Did you have or do you have a girl friend?"

"No."

"Did your wife have a boy friend?"

Webley sat up as straight as if had just had a harpoon used as a suppository. His face flared a brilliant crimson and he turned toward Lurch as if he wanted to slug him.

"Bad judgment," Lurch said. "Better judgment would be to answer my question."

"My wife was a virgin when we were married," a subdued Webley said. "I am the only man she ever knew."

In the rear view mirror I saw the expression on Lurch's face that said far more than Webley wanted to hear. We were turning into the drive of the house where Alisha Webley had spent her married life.

The Webley house was too large, too gaudy, and too showy to be a home. It had obviously been built to show the world that the Man of the House was successful in marriage and finance. The living room had been used sparingly if at all. The kitchen was all formica and polished wood, with nothing errant showing anywhere that mattered.

Quickly we searched the house for anything that would help us and found little of significance. In the bedroom Lurch turned back the covers of the bed, then remade it. He rifled through Alisha's underwear drawer and held up panties with the initials RC on them. I wondered whose initials they were and whether Webley had ever seen the underwear, on or off his wife. Saying nothing, Lurch replaced the garment and lifted another pair with the same monogram. He moved to the bathroom and dumped the contents of the laundry hamper and examined every item in it before he rose and headed toward the kitchen.

Webley had sat down at the kitchen table when we entered and was still there when we rejoined him.

"Do the initials RC mean anything to you?" he asked Webley.

Webley shook his head.

"Did you and your wife make love this morning?" he asked. A startled look crossed Webley's face.

"Damn you," he tried to snarl, "what business is it—"

Lurch's voice was as menacing as the crackle of a lightning bolt or the high-pitched whir of the rattler.

"Your wife's death is my business," he said sharply enough to make me cringe. The effect on Webley was worse. "It does not matter to me whether you approve of my questions or not; I am going to ask them and you will answer them. Did you and your wife have sex this morning? I can ask it plainer, if you prefer."

"No," Webley stammered. I expected him to say four words at once, so eager was he to please Blanton. Then, "Wait. Yes. Yes, we did. I remember now. Two times!"

"Did you wife often go to Monbo?" I asked. "If so, why?"

He colored slightly. "No," he said. "What reason would she have to go there? It's a nothing town." I looked at Rick.

He nodded. He asked nothing else, and minutes later we were in his vehicle and driving away. Webley's parents arrived as we were leaving. We did not pause to talk to them.

"Melville once remarked that the more whales, the less fish," he said as we headed directly into the face of the storm. "We have a surfeit of whales."

"Thanks," I said ironically. "What we need most is a crime that can't be solved. And whales that can't be caught."

He shook his head and snowflakes dropped to his shoulders, which could have served as parade grounds for Boy Scouts. "I didn't say it couldn't be solved. It just won't be solved by asking people if they saw anything."

"Everyone in town knew her," I protested. "Her car was also known to a few hundred people. I doubt that she could walk down the street at midnight and not be recognized by a dozen people."

"It was snowing hard," he said. "People who didn't have to go out, didn't. Those who did were concentrating so hard on their own progress that nothing else registered. The snow, by the way, has covered any tracks we might have hoped to find, in case the killer traveled on foot."

"You've had someone go to the grocer's, I suppose?" It was one of the all-night markets that somehow justified its hours by the volume of beer sold to college kids.

"Bum is at the store. He's going to find that no one saw her leave the parking lot."

"We know she did. Her car made it home."

Lurch shook his head again. "We know that somebody drove the car to her house. The problem here is that we are starting at the wrong end of town. We need to start by determining when and where your car was parked so that the killer could have put the body in it. Starting with how he unlocked it." He lowered the window briefly.

"That part is easy," I said. A sudden gust of wind filled our faces with snow, and more than a few errant flakes made their way down my collar. "I didn't lock the car. I never do. All he had to do was reach inside and flip the lever to unlock the trunk."

He pulled a small envelope from inside his jacket and passed it to me. I opened it and saw the small cut stone that was dull rather than glistening. "Then we need to decide where the body could have been put into the trunk. She disappeared shortly after eight this morning, Webley says. We know she was at the market until after seven o'clock. Where was your car at the time?"

I hesitated only a fraction of a second too long. Lurch knew I was lying when I told him that I thought it was in the parking lot only a few feet from us.

"No," he said gently, "for as long as it's possible to keep it there, your car was not in the parking lot between eight and ten. It was at your house. Right?"

I nodded.

"Whoever killed her could have put the body in your car while it was parked at your cabin?"

Again, I nodded.

"It would take some balls for someone to do it so close to your place. But that's the only possibility."

"I can't believe it," I said miserably. "It's impossible! I was awake all night, listening to the sleet."

He, like Atlas, shrugged. "Jeff Dennis will learn that his wife was at your cabin," he said. "He might come after you with a shotgun. Or get one of his flunkies to do the job. Does that bother you?"

"It's not a happy thought," I admitted. "But I really don't give a damn if it happens. There's a connection?"

"Keep an open mind," he said. "It's always possible that Jeff Dennis has been carrying on with Alisha Webley and that he knows about you and his wife. His affair turned sour and he found a way to settle two scores."

"You believe that?"

"No. It's a possibility. One of a thousand, but yours is the only car that we know of that held the body of Alisha Webley, and Laura's house is the only place we know of where the body might have been dumped. Why did you ask about Monbo?"

I told him what I had been told.

"We need to get a photo by there," he said. "Ask around town. Maybe somebody saw her at one of the businesses or at the house of a friend. Or lover."

He drove expertly along the treacherous roads. He handled the car as well as if he had been driving indoors.

"Webley lied," he said a few moments later. "He doesn't know who or what RC is, but he lied when he said that his wife did not have a boy friend or lover. There were fresh sperm spots on the sheets."

"He said they had made love that morning."

"He lied about that, too. He didn't remember it at first, or so he said. Then he remembered it twice. A man who can't remember whether he had made love is lying. Or he's such a wimp lover that it's a certainty that his wife was fooling around. A pair of Alisha's panties in the clothes hamper also had fresh sperm spots in them. He doesn't know that we know about his wife's pregnancy before marriage."

"You think she had an abortion or a miscarriage?"

"I'd bet on neither," he said.

46

I knew better than to bet Lurch on anything.

It was well after daylight when we returned to the office. When we arrived there were styrofoam takeout breakfasts from McDonald's waiting for us. Rockwell signed a note saying that his cook was preparing lunch for us, something that would keep in case we didn't find time to eat right away. I wondered what the cook thought about being the only staff member called out on a day like this.

During the final hours of the morning we called upon neighbors, friends, teachers, and others who knew the Webleys well enough to provide us with any information that, we hoped, would prove helpful as we searched for directions, no matter how slender the thread. No one we called upon seemed to mind having their home routines interrupted. At first we wasted our time, and then a neighbor or two began to talk.

What we learned was what we already knew: that Alisha Webley was a young, attractive, outgoing, intelligent, polite, energetic, and well-liked member of the community. No one could offer reason for us to think she had been selected specifically for the role as victim of a twisted and perverted mind.

Bert Webley was similarly respected and liked. He was hard-working, honest in business dealings, and involved only slightly in social and civic matters.

The Webleys were, in short, the model couple.

But we knew better.

I had seen enough of human nature to convince me that there is no one without at least one shadow in his past.

Back at the office Zane was on the phone when we entered. She nodded to me and I took the phone. It was the hospital.

"I've worked too fast," he said, "and may have to modify my report later. I wanted you to know the basic facts."

The doctor, Andrew Miller, was tall, thin, and astonishingly broad-shouldered for a man with such an otherwise slight frame. His eyes earlier had suggested that he was amused constantly, if only by the cruelties of humanity. Except for the slight salt and pepper in his hair, I'd have thought him to be in his twenties.

"The victim died slowly," he said. "She suffered greatly. Several of her teeth were cracked. Bicuspids and molars. She apparently clenched her teeth in such agony that she actually broke them. There are no external bruises to suggest the damage resulted from a blow or blows. Her death resulted from loss of blood, which in turn was caused by a series of deep slashes made with a smooth-bladed knife. Not stabbing. Slicing. She had experienced sexual intercourse recently, and lack of bruising indicates she did so willingly. Skin under her fingernails indicated that she attempted to fight her assailant or another person, but the fight may have come after the sex. I can't possibly say for certain. I can tell you that three of her nails were broken. The slashing wound was apparently made after the less serious ones—when he was tired of hearing her scream. And there are small lumps on the back of her head."

"Will the sperm samples help us?"

"If he's a secretor," he said.

He paused, and I heard a crunching sound. "Yellow delicious apple," he explained. "Recovering smoker," he said. "This is my pacifier. I must have eaten a bushel of apples during the past two weeks. You have any questions I can answer at this point?"

"Yes," I said. "Any wounds on the back of her head? Anything to suggest that she was slugged from behind, for example?"

He crunched the apple vigorously and grunted as he spoke. "I understand," he said. "You are wondering whether she was surprised by stranger or strangers. No obvious wounds, but I have more checking to do."

"She was not surprised by her killer?"

"Nothing to suggest that. We can conclude that it is likely that she saw whoever attacked her and did not regard him as a threat until too late."

He mumbled, crunching another bite of apple. "There was a huge bruise that covered the entire front of her face," he said. "As if a very strong person with a huge fist punched her in the mouth. The blow broke her nose, loosened three of her front teeth, and probably rendered her unconscious. She experienced a slight concussion. She, I think, would have been too dazed for several minutes to make an effort to fight off her attacker. Any fighting would have occurred after she regained consciousness."

"Then he didn't tie her up, at least right away?"

"No signs of rope burns on her wrists. There is one physical characteristic that may be interesting to you."

He waited for me to ask, and I did.

"Mrs. Webley had given birth at some time in her life. She and her husband have no children. The child was born, I assume, prior to her marriage. This may or may not be significant."

It was, to me. Lurch and I drove to the home of Henry and Betty Brady, parents of Alisha. Traffic in the streets of Sherman had been cut in half. A few vehicles inched their way through the streets. On a street corner I caught a glimpse of the same woman I had seen earlier: the ugly Amazon. She still had her sled with her and was waiting for the traffic, I was confident, but I had nothing to support my guess.

We arrived at the Brady house within five more minutes. Both parents looked as if their souls had been removed with meat hooks when they admitted me into their den. He was a short, nearly bald man in his early fifties. She was taller, rail-thin, and looked older. Lurch did not spar around: he asked instantly about their daughter's pregnancy. I didn't expect much. She had been crying and he had been drinking.

Surprisingly, they both agreed to discuss the topic. I had expected them to deny everything.

"Alisha became pregnant around Halloween during her senior year," Betty Brady said. "She wanted to give birth to the child, but not to keep it. She left Sherman at the end of the school term and spent the summer with my sister in Aiken, South Carolina. She gave birth to a child that died two days later. She returned here and resumed her life."

"What caused the death?"

"Something about the blood," she said. "I didn't understand it all."

"Was the baby's blood RH negative?" Rick asked.

Her eyes brightened slightly. "That may have been it," she said. "I just don't know what went wrong."

I asked, "Did Alisha go to Monbo often?"

Both parents shook their heads.

Brady was totally unlike his wife. He missed his calling by not getting a job as an anvil in a blacksmith shop.

"Was she deeply disturbed by the experience with the baby?" I asked. "Or was she able to readjust well?"

"It was as if it never happened," Brady said. "When she came back home, she greeted us as if she had just spent the weekend with friends at the beach. We never talked of that part of her life again."

"Any notion who the father was?"

"She refused to tell us," Betty said. "When she first told us that she was pregnant, Henry and I suggested that we persuade the father to marry her. Alisha simply laughed and said there was no chance that either of them would consider such a thing. That was her position each time the topic was mentioned."

We didn't learn anything else of value. They delivered their lines so well that I knew they had rehearsed them and used them many times before their daughter was murdered. I looked around the den, which reeked of hard work and saved pennies. It was the den of a couple who had escaped the mill hill or the tenant farm and had, in their eyes, moved up in the world. The ubiquitous picture of Jesus and the sheep hung on one wall. On the mantle over the unused fireplace cheap frames held photos of the parents and Alisha during happier times.

In the photos she appeared to be her mother's sister. They had identical facial structure and body frame. Even their smiles were identical.

"When did she start dating Bert?" I asked.

"Not until graduation from college," Henry said. "Bert was in her high school class, but they were just speaking friends. It was strange," he added. "She was a pretty girl, very popular, and yet she dated very rarely. She liked boys well enough, and in the middle-school grades she was always in love with someone. A new boy each week. But in high school she seemed to lose interest. She became interested in books and such." His voice trailed off to empty air.

"What about the rock band she was interested in?" I asked.

The two looked at each other quickly.

"No," Henry said. "She never sang with a rock band. That story started when she left to go to Aiken."

"She worked at the school," I said. "Anywhere else? Did she do any moonlighting?" Both shook their heads again. Their stories did not mesh well with others we had heard.

We thanked them and left. When we returned to the office Bum was typing ponderously, his stubby fingers threatening to smash the keyboard.

"Bert Webley has not been a saint," he said. "Not Son of Sam, either. DUI charges, possession of marijuana, breaking and entering. More than a dozen minor criminal charges. He never served any time, but he paid out his ride-around money in fines. His crime wave began when he was thirteen and ended two years before he married Alisha. And for a couple with two incomes, they aren't exactly rolling in money. Webley's up to his ears for the store." He went back to hammering the keys.

Lurch pulled me into my office. "I dated Alisha a couple of times," he said. "Nothing. I turned her off completely. So did all the other boys. It was as if she had no interest in men."

The phone rang and I picked it up. Answering the phone seemed to be one of the few things I could do well. It was Dr. Andrew Miller. He sounded as tired as I felt.

"I neglected to mention a couple of things," he said. "They appear insignificant, but you're the better judge of that. First, there are small lumps on the back of her head. Nothing that could be considered life-threatening or bone-crushing. Bumps, more than blows. As if she had been pulled feet-first down a flight of stairs. The injuries, while slight, are noticeable. The bruises are aligned almost perfectly, and all run in a more or less straight line from a point roughly even with the top of her ears. I also found several tiny flecks of white paint in her scalp."

"At the points of impact?" I asked.

"No, on the left side of her head. In front of and also just above her ear."

"Suggesting what?"

"That she had been knocked against or perhaps fell against the wall of an old building." I could hear a cracking sound in the background and I knew that he was eating another apple.

"How do we know it's an old building? Couldn't the flecks be from a poor paint job?"

"It's a lead-base paint," he said. "The kind that hasn't been used for decades. Not only that, there is a faint trace of decaying wood on the back of the paint. So it's either old paint in an old building or someone found a bucket of ancient paint and used it on a rotting wall."

He hung up and I relayed the information to Lurch. He was far ahead of the doctor. He took the small envelope from a desk drawer and dumped the contents onto the desk blotter. I looked over his shoulder at the flecks of paint. Turning one over, I saw what Dr. Miller had meant. The dark brown fibers looked like heart pine that had not been painted until too late to help it.

"What about the stone?" I asked Lurch.

"Rose beryl," he said. "No value as a precious stone. At best a semi-precious stone cut rather clumsily and not worth ten bucks. There's an interesting story behind this type of stone. I'll need to freshen my memory on the details and I'll let you know as soon as I can."

The phone rang then and Lurch answered.

"Sherman County Sheriff's Department," he said. "Deputy Rick Blanton speaking. How may I help you?"

Instantly his face darkened and he stood as still as a statue. Only his eyes seemed alive.

"We'll be right there," he said. "We're on our way."

I had taken off my coat, but I pulled it on quickly as Lurch grabbed his own jacket.

"That was Ben Tyler," he said. "His wife spent the day with her sick mother and left her house two hours ago. She didn't make it back home. He thinks she may have had car trouble."

We were leaving the office when Ed Gallager met us at the covered walk. The editor's face was ashen, and his voice trembled when he spoke. He seemed on the verge of tears.

"He did it again," he said shakily. "He called me a few minutes ago. He says he has Phyllis Tyler." The editor seemed ready to collapse. He stammered, shivered, and shuffled his feet uncontrollably. "He says he's already getting tired of her."

The exhaustion we had felt only seconds ago evaporated with the blast of icy wind that struck us in the faces as we raced from the covered entrance to the closest car to the building. Seconds later we were rushing slowly through the storm toward the house of Ben and Phyllis Tyler.

FIVE

Lurch and I rode together, with him driving. On snow or ice I was tentative, afraid, but he was in total control of the vehicle as we slid and slued down the deserted streets of Sherman and past the city limits where the sheriff's department's authority began. I couldn't force myself to get behind the wheel of my old Honda Accord. I doubted that I would ever be able to enjoy it again.

The Tyler house, barely outside city limits, like the Webley house, was huge and unattractive as only a cracker-box style of architecture could be. It was square and consisted of three floors. There was nothing ornate about the house, and its only attraction seemed to be its size coupled with the huge hilltop where it sat and commanded a perfect view of the shallow valley below and the Blue Ridge Mountains in the foreground and the Great Smokies range in the distance. It took us less than ten minutes to drive from the office to the Tyler house.

The snow fell so thick that we could see only two hundred feet in any direction, and the icy pellets had given way to large, fluffy flakes that appeared to be miniature falling clouds.

I had to force myself to align my days. Alisha Webley had been kidnapped on Friday, the same day, only eons ago, that I had spent the early morning in bed with Laura Dennis. Alisha's body had been discovered shortly after midnight on Saturday morning.

An unnatural chill invaded my body as I thought that the killer might have stood outside the cabin when Laura Dennis had arrived. He might have watched her drive away.

He could have placed the body in my car while I was still in bed, or while I was shaving and dressing. He perhaps watched Zane as she arrived and later as the two of us left.

Zane had taken me back to the cabin so that I could get the old Honda and shotgun, and the gap of more than an hour would have been plenty of time for him to leave the body.

But there were no tire tracks in the snow. Or, if there had been, the snow had covered them.

As we pulled into the Tyler drive we could see only the light above the front door and its restricted reflection. As we drew closer to the end of the thousand-foot drive, we could see another tiny light, this one in the center of the ceiling of the carport. There was room for two cars. One bay was empty.

Ben Tyler met us when we arrived. As Rick parked the car, Tyler opened the front door of the house and hurried out to us. He appeared tired and ill despite his immense bulk. Years ago he had played tackle for the Sherman University football team, but the post-athletic years had not been kind to him, and now he had the appearance of a man who had been in the gym only to pick up his wife or daughter. Or another man's. He was in his early thirties and looked fifty.

"Get in," Lurch told him. "We'll talk while we drive. Is there anyone in the house to take a message?"

He paused, then remembered. "Yes. My mother and father came over earlier and stayed. They were there when the call came, so they know."

His father was Jacob Tyler, founder of the oldest and most successful law offices in the county. He had in fact opened ancillary offices in a dozen nearby towns: a supermarket chain of legal representatives.

Lurch glanced quickly at me.

"When who called?" he asked.

"The man. That's all I know. A soft-spoken man."

He climbed into the back seat and Lurch turned the car around in the small backing space adjacent to the carport. "Where we going?" he asked.

I looked at Tyler. "Tell us what you know," I said.

He hesitated, his face ghostly in the pale light from the single bulb in

54

the ceiling of the carport.

"I don't know," he said. "I have no idea. I don't know what's happening." He had caught the look that passed between Lurch and me, and he suddenly realized that this was far more serious than he had thought. He seemed ready to burst into tears. His face paled in the dim light from the reflected snow. Maybe it was our urgency that tipped him off, but he became deathly ill, as if he did not realize where he was or why we were there.

He had the terrible awareness that somehow we had to search frantically but had no idea where to start. A snatching was not a crime that could be solved by a careful analysis of the microscopic clues that would eventually lead us to our target. We had to rush, which was the worst way to tackle a crime, but we had no choice. The man had killed once already, and I had a sick feeling that he did not plan to show mercy this time.

"Turn right at the highway," he said in a choked voice. He seemed to be having trouble breathing. "Two miles north. Maybe we can spot her car on the road."

Rick drove steadily but safely while I prodded Tyler to give us all the details. It was an exercise in futility. There were no details. He was almost incoherent.

"The man called only a few minutes ago," he said, his voice a mask of constricting fear. "Why? What's happening? What are we talking about?" His voice rose almost to a falsetto.

"Think," I urged him. "Tell me exactly, as closely as you can remember, what he said. Word for word. Don't leave out any grunts or sneezes. Use his words, not yours."

Tyler was silent for a long time. "Tell us," Lurch barked at him. "We have to know what he said."

Lurch was at the highway now and turning right and into the full force of the storm. I thought about the snow and what it would do to any tracks or signs of a struggle. I looked at Tyler to prompt him.

"All he said was that Phyllis wouldn't be coming home anytime soon. I didn't know what he was talking about. I yelled at him and he hung up. That's all I know. Why didn't Phyllis call me? What's going on, Sheriff? What's happening to my wife?" The alarm pushed his voice an octave

55

higher, until he was almost screaming.

His voice, taut already, threatened to break twice during the brief comment. He turned his face away from me so I could not see the tears that I knew were there.

A gurgling sound came from the back seat, and I knew that he was trying to find his voice. I turned to face him.

"I couldn't catch it all, and he hung up when I asked him to repeat it," he said. "I didn't understand him."

"What?" I asked. "Don't make us pull it out of you."

"Something—" he began, then he paused, trying to control the sudden sobbing that erupted deep within his chest. "Something about pissing against a wall. And how Phyl will soon understand it."

I turned and looked at Lurch. "Anything there?" I asked. "Did you hear anything I didn't? What does pissing against a wall have to do with anything?"

"It's in the Bible," Lurch said. "Something about the Lord saying that He would bring evil upon the house of Jeroboam. He said He would cut off from Jeroboam him that pisseth against the wall. It seems to single out only the males of the nation. If I recall correctly, pissing against a wall appears seven or more times in the Old Testament. Does that mean anything to you, Mr. Tyler?"

He shook his head helplessly.

"A jeroboam is a large wine bottle," Lurch said helpfully. "A champagne bottle that holds almost a gallon. Anything?"

"No." The word was almost a sob. Lurch tried again.

"Jeroboam was among the first kings of Israel. Does king suggest anything to you? What about Israel?"

He shook his head.

"Did he call your wife Phyl? Or is that your nickname for her?" I asked.

"His word," Tyler said. "I never called her that. She liked her full name. She said that shortening it made her sound like a boy."

"Her name is from a Greek word," Lurch said. "Phyllis was a country maiden. I don't suppose—"

"Nothing."

"Did any of her friends call her Phyl?"

"Most of them," he said. "They all liked to shorten names. You know: Liz for Elizabeth, Lin for Linda, Kat for Katherine."

I would have been amazed by the data that poured from Lurch, except that I had known him long enough that his vast stores of knowledge had become apparent to me ages ago.

We drove in total darkness except for the headlights which barely penetrated the snow enough for us to keep moving. On three sides of us the world was turning blacker by the moment. On the fourth side it was yellow and white. We had just rounded a curve when a huge buck stepped out of the forest and into our lights. Lurch fanned the brakes and slowed the car down so that the bewildered creature could command its legs to move. A few feet further and we crossed the bridge over Hunting Creek. Only when we had cleared the bridge did I let my body relax. I had not even realized how tense I had suddenly become.

Hunting Creek was once among the favorite hunting grounds of the Cherokees who did in fact use the creek for hunting and fishing. It was twenty feet wide in places and often six to ten feet deep. There were king-sized trout in the creek years ago when a grist mill stood on its banks and the fish lay in the shadows to grab the corn that fell into the stream. When the sportsmen located the spot, they pulled out hundreds of trout that weighed eighteen to twenty-two pounds and were as long as a normal man's arm. Now the stream was depleted except in the upper reaches where the sportsmen are disinclined to go. To me the term sportsman suggests a sadistic killer, and as such I had no respect whatever for them. Not when they disregard rules and laws and common decency in order to kill at random.

The thought was too close to the man who had captured Phyllis Tyler, the man who had killed Alisha Webley.

"Describe the voice," I said. "Cultured? Educated? Deep? High-pitched? Nervous? Confident? Angry?"

He hesitated. "What can I say? It was the voice of a stranger. Not the voice of a football player or weight lifter. The voice of a quiet man, maybe weak."

"The voice of a small man?" I repeated. "Could it have been a woman?"

"No. I mean, I don't think so. I never thought about it till now. I can't say. I don't know what to think." His voice rose anew to the falsetto range.

"Think hard," Rick prodded. "Was it the voice of a woman or a man? Maybe a man pretending to be a woman?"

"I don't know," the tiny voice from the back seat said. Despite his bulk, he had shrunk into a tiny blob of a man.

"Who were your wife's closest friends?" I asked.

He shrugged. "She had lots of friends at the hospital where she worked. And at church. She stayed in contact with some of her old school friends."

The drive took much longer than we had feared. The snow was so deep now that we were barely moving, and I knew that if the storm did not abate soon we'd have to call off the search until the plows could clear some roads. Except that there was no way we could call off the search. Not while a helpless woman was being tortured by a madman.

"Who were her close friends?" I repeated. He seemed anxious for us to believe that his wife was loved by all.

"Elizabeth Clanton, Linda Burton, Katherine Thennis, Helena St. Clair, Alexandria Mulholland. People like that. They tried to get together once a week for coffee."

"At a public place? At the home of one of them? Did they take turns visiting in each other's homes?"

"They had about six or seven houses where they met. Ours was among them. They met at our house a month ago, I guess. I wasn't there. I was at work, as usual."

"Were you at work today, Mr. Tyler?"

"Till the snow got so bad nobody was out."

I remembered Tyler well but had to ask. As a lawyer, he had months ago represented an acquaintance of mine, a man I'd had to arrest, who had been accused by a thirteen-year old of rape. Tyler had told the client that his only hope was to plead guilty and ask for the mercy of the court. The man insisted that he was not guilty, but eventually he accepted the lawyer's word that if he did not plead guilty and save the state the cost of a jury trial he'd spend the rest of his life in prison. A guilty plea would get him out in five to seven years.

The man went to prison, after first paying Tyler all the money he had. He had once owned the house that Tyler now lived in. The deed to the house was part of the attorney's fee.

A faint light gleamed through the wall of snow, and Lurch pulled into the drive. The three of us climbed out and made our way to the front porch where the light burned. The door opened as we reached the steps and a woman and man emerged from the house.

"I'm Flicka Collins, the mother of Phyllis," the woman said. "This is her father. Won't you come in?"

"No," I told her. "We can't stop. You haven't heard from Phyllis?"

She shook her head and a tear squeezed its way past her closed lids. Her husband gripped his wife's shoulders and said nothing. He was a huge man, burly and rough around the edges. He looked more angry than worried. His wife, like the wife of Henry Brady, was thin and athletic-looking. She, like Betty Brady, could have passed as the sister of her daughter.

They opened the door automatically, as if I hadn't spoken, and ushered us into a small living room. Benjamin Tyler looked around the room as if he had never been there before. I doubted that he had been there except when necessary. The house was one step above the mill-hill economy. Like Alisha, Phyllis had married upward.

"We wanted to have a chance to search the road in case she had car trouble," I said. "We need to keep moving. Soon it'll be too hard to travel."

The husband cleared his throat timidly. "You won't call off the search for the night, will you?" He seemed to be begging or threatening. It was not clear which.

"No, sir," I said. "We'll find a way to travel. Deputy Blanton has a four-wheel drive truck. We'll load the back with cement blocks or cordwood." I'd have promised him to take the QEII out of dry-dock if necessary. I understood. I would not have wanted to think of anyone's daughter in the clutches of a sadistic killer, particularly on a night like this. On the walls of the room where we stood were inexpensively framed photographs of the family. Phyllis Tyler starred in the display. I looked at the photo and found myself amazed by the similarity to the photo I had earlier seen of Alisha Webley.

We left the two on the porch and retreated to the car, which Lurch had left running. Before we left I asked for a recent photo of Phyllis. They quickly took one from a frame and gave it to me.

"Let's drive on to the lake," I said. "She may have somehow gone off the road. We can hope, at least."

I didn't believe what I said, but the road behind us was clear and I saw no reason to retrace our steps. It had now been close to twenty-four hours since I had slept, and I was feeling the effects of the day and night, but adrenalin kept pumping and Lurch seemed as alert as if he had just risen from a full night's sleep. I had looked for signs that a car or truck had traveled the road before us. There were none.

Lakeview Road was in slightly better condition than the secondary roads were, and we drove for miles and checked out several roads on each side of the highway before returning to the office. Each of the roads led eventually to Lake Carrie, the huge inland sea that now covered about a third of what had once been dried-up farms of Sherman County.

The lake's name was a corruption of Tucumcari, the name of a Cherokee princess who had reportedly leaped with her lover from a cliff and into the waters of the Catawba River, long before the idea of a lake was even a glint in the eyes of a realtor who would have sold the Washington Monument to the Japanese if the terms were right. Princess Tucumcari became Cari and then Carrie long before the lake was filled.

I asked Tyler if he wanted us to take him home, but he said he could not bear to go into that house. I understood. I couldn't have spent a night in the house. For two reasons, one of which was the memory of the earlier owner who hanged himself in his prison cell shortly before the young girl who accused him had recanted her story.

At the office we found Zane still there. She looked as tired as I felt.

"Get some sleep," I told her. "It might be a long night."

"I dozed a little," she said. "No calls. It's been quiet."

"Do we have a high school yearbook here?" I asked. "One that goes back eight or nine years."

"Ten," Tyler corrected me.

"Got them all," Zane said. I remembered that Zane had brought her high school yearbooks so in case of problems involving local graduates we'd have a photo on hand at a moment's notice. She opened a closet and returned seconds later with the yearbook for Sherman High School.

Tyler opened it to the seniors pages and flipped rapidly until he found the right one and pointed to a tiny face that looked at us as if she had found the world funny.

The caption said: Phyllis Collins, who cares and will always care for everybody. The smiling face only vaguely resembled the photo we had borrowed from her parents. She had gone from happy to anxious within months.

"She wanted to become a doctor," Tyler said. "It was her dream from the time she started to school." He paused to let the brick in his throat move. "She couldn't afford medical school; her grades were good enough, but her father's checkbook wasn't. So she became a nurse. She worked while I was in law school. As soon as my practice built up, I was to send her to med school, if she could still get in."

His voice had trailed off to a whimper, and he backed weakly to a rickety couch and sat down and, like Webley, buried his head in his hands. His law practice, it seemed, had been good enough for him to have whatever he wanted but was never good enough to send his wife to med school. Hell, he could have bought the med school. I had the feeling his income would have never been good enough until she was too old to be a candidate.

Lurch, Zane, and I stared at the thumbnail photo, which told us nothing. Phyllis Collins had been pretty in a faint way, with huge eyes that dominated a small face with a slightly pointed chin. She looked tiny.

We scanned her high school activities: Boosters Club, to which, apparently, everyone in school belonged, school paper, dramatics club, yearbook staff, and band.

Lurch turned a few pages until he found the photo of Alisha Brady. She, too, was pretty but not beautiful. She had taken part in girls basketball, Boosters Club, camera club, and home economics club. She sang in the Glee Club and Girls Chorus.

"You know about Mrs. Webley, don't you?" I asked him. He did not respond except to jerk his head in a quick nod.

The photos seemed to be those of persons caught helplessly between childhood and death. They had scrawled their neat and mushy notes to each other in the margins of the yearbook. They were careful not to let the pen trail across their faces. I stared, fascinated by the vows of eternal friendship for each other and everlasting love for Sherman High School. The curling letters seemed drawn rather than written. All the letters seemed to lean the wrong way.

Lurch closed the book and turned to Tyler, who sat like a huge, soggy mushroom that threatened to overflow the chair in which he had collapsed as soon as we entered the room.

"Tell us about your wife," Lurch said. "First. We're going to ask you a series of questions that may seem meaningless to you. We're not sure what we're looking for, other than a thread that runs through both of the victims, past and future. Start with her age."

"She was twenty-eight." he said, almost defiantly.

"Religion?"

"Baptist. Sherman Baptist Church."

"Political party?"

"Democrat."

"How long have you been married?"

"Seven years."

"Any illnesses that required medication. For her, I mean."

"No."

"Hobbies?"

"Other than her music? Hiking, photography, camping now and then, some rockhounding. Gardening. She liked ball games. At the park, not on television."

"Is your wife left-handed or right-handed?" Lurch asked. I looked at him sharply. His eyes seemed to penetrate Bert's mind. He, too, was startled.

"Left-handed," he said. "What on earth could—"

"Did she have a favorite stone she liked to hunt for?"

He shrugged. "All the girls wanted to find valuable stones, like emeralds, but they never did. Nothing except stones they could have cut and mounted just for looks. Look, what does this have to do with what's happening?" He had noticed that we had slipped into the past tense.

"Did she like rosy beryl?" He disregarded Tyler's query.

I had stopped asking questions. It was obvious that Lurch had a destination in mind, and I knew enough about police work to know that I knew nothing. He was a hound on a scent, and I let him run free.

Tyler seemed startled, then he regained his composure. "Yes," he said. "How did you know? I mean, she didn't seem to like it, but she had one.

I never understood why she insisted on wearing a stone she didn't like."

"Did the other women in the group also like rose beryl?"

Tyler seemed dazed now, unable to comprehend. He started to speak and stopped. He tried again.

"Yes," he stammered. "What does this—how did you—?

"Your father is still living," Lurch said. He already knew that.

"Yes. Why?"

"I'm not being nosy," he said. "Your father is a wealthy man."

Tyler started to protest, looked at Rick's face, and then changed his mind quickly.

"Yes."

"How rich?"

"What difference does it make how much money he has?"

"Damn it, how rich?" Rick thundered.

"He's a millionaire," Tyler shouted. "He owns law offices across three states."

"Did you and Phyllis have a contractual marriage?"

Tyler slumped noticeably. His shoulders sagged and the life seemed to have left him momentarily.

"Yes," he said finally. "We did."

It took several minutes, but we finally learned that the marriage contract stipulated that if there was a divorce, the children, if left in the custody of the wife, could not inherit any part of the family fortune. If the father had custody, the children could inherit. If the marriage ended in the death of Tyler, Phyllis would inherit only a small amount of money. She could not retain the property or the business.

"This group of women who remained such close friends after high school," Lurch said gently, allowing Tyler time to regain part of the self-respect he had just lost, "did their group have a name?"

"Yes. They called themselves the DOLLS. All capitals."

"Was Alisha Webley in the group?"

"Yes."

"Who else?"

"Elizabeth Clanton, Linda Burton, Katherine Thennis, Helena St. Clair, and Alexandria Mulholland."

The same set of friends he mentioned earlier.

63

"How many of these women are left-handed?"

Tyler sagged forward, his face buried in his arms, which were extended across the table. He mumbled something inaudible. Lurch clutched the man's hair and lifted his head roughly.

"How many?" he demanded. The room was deathly quiet. Only the spasmodic jerking of the hands of a wall clock could be heard. It seemed to me that even the snowflakes fell softer.

"All of them," he said.

We started out of the office, but before we reached the car we heard Ed Gallager calling. My breath seemed to stop, and the hum of the tires over snow became hypnotic.

"That car you are hunting," he said tentatively. "The man who calls himself Zimri called again. The car is parked near something that sounded like the Blue Gloomp." He peered at me. "Does that make any sense?"

"Yes," I whispered. "That helps. And hurts."

Lurch started the car and was pulling out into the main drag when he turned to look at me.

"How bad is it?" he asked.

"Bad," I said. "Worse than bad."

I thought of Gallager's voice. It was soft, educated, and almost apologetic; yet there was a strength in it that seemed to exude power over an audience. He would have made a good preacher, I thought. Or a teacher.

The car fishtailed before gaining traction and moved erratically toward the outskirts of town. Tyler had now become instantly alert. "What car?" he demanded. "What is this blue thing you're talking about? Tell me, damn it."

"The Blue Gloomp is my old pickup," I told him miserably.

SIX

The drive took half an hour to get to the driveway that leads into my place. The cabin I call home is located a few feet from where Buffalo Creek feeds into Hunting Creek and then the two empty into the new lake started years ago and still filling. My drive leaves the state road and wanders aimlessly for two miles or so through the forest. I kept my old pickup, which I used to haul firewood I cut from the storm-downed trees, near my cabin.

As the three of us, Lurch, Tyler, and I, made our painfully slow way through the snow, dozens of eyes peered at us from the darkness. It was a rare night when I arrived home late that I did not see deer, bobcat, raccoon, opossum, or other night creatures wandering in search of food. I once saw a mountain lion, long thought to be extinct in this part of the country, and a black bear, within two weeks of each other.

Tonight I wondered if any of the eyes watching us belonged to a killer.

As Lurch rounded the final bend, I could see the headlights reflecting off metal and glass. Tyler lurched forward and began to point and shout.

"That's Phyllis's car," he yelled. "Son of a bitch! What's her car doing here?"

Even before the car stopped he opened the back door and leaped out. I yelled at him to stop, but he didn't slow down as he plodded through the snow toward the car.

In a blur of movement Lurch was behind him, tackling him while he was still twenty feet from the vehicle. As I climbed from the car I could see the two forms wrestling in the snow. By the time I reached them Lurch was sitting on the helpless lawyer and was holding the man's shoulders pinned to the snow.

"Listen to me," he was saying. "You can run up there and risk contaminating the entire scene. Now are you going to follow along behind us, or am I going to have to drag you?"

The man mumbled something and Lurch rose to his feet and pulled the lawyer to a standing position. He brushed snow off both of them.

"Sorry," he said, "but we can't allow you to touch anything. You stand behind the car and we'll let you know what we find, if anything."

The lawyer nodded numbly and remained, shaking from either the cold or the memory of those awesome hands on him seconds earlier. I had brought flashlights from the car, and the two of us approached the abandoned car slowly. There were no tracks to be obliterated in the snow; the snow had covered them long ago, but there might be fingerprints or trace evidence that could be preserved. My faith in such luck did not amount to the weight of a snowflake.

Our search did not last ten seconds. We could smell the blood almost as soon as we opened the door. The interior of the vehicle was almost unrecognizable. Dark stains appeared nearly everywhere. There did not seem to be any place that had been spared.

While Lurch returned to the car to call in for a team to screen the car interior, I used a gloved finger to trip the latch to the glove compartment. There was a pistol inside. I used a finger inside the trigger guard to lift it out. It was a .38 special with a two-inch barrel. It was fully loaded, and none of the bullets had been fired.

The compartment also contained the inevitable road map, folded incorrectly, facial tissues, a small notebook that seemed to be filled only with mileage notations, and an assortment of pens and pencils. Three quarters lay against the fire wall. They were atop a folded sheet of paper.

I removed the paper and unfolded it. It contained two words written in what appeared to be blood: the victim's, I knew.

Chestnut log.

There was no more. Lurch was back by this time and looked over my shoulder. He said nothing, but I knew that he, like me, knew what the brief message meant.

In the early years of the twentieth century the chestnut blight had destroyed the American chestnut tree, except for a rare specimen occasionally found in the deep woods. One of my treasures when I first bought my tract of land was that it had a huge chestnut tree growing on the side of a deep hollow. Somehow the blight had missed it, and it appeared healthy and strong. And then the tornado that leveled part of my woods uprooted the tree, and I had intended but had never gotten around to cutting long log sections from the tree and chain-sawing some rough boards to use in building a table and benches for my kitchen. From the roots of the tree another chestnut had sprung, and it was now large enough to look as if it, too, has escaped the blight.

Lurch motioned to Tyler, who had not moved from his tracks after Lurch had rescued him from the snow.

"Come with us," he said. "But stay behind. It's a long walk but it's better than sitting in the car and freezing."

Tyler followed obediently, like a beaten dog. Clearly, he had already accepted the fact of his wife's death and all that now remained was to recover the body. He seemed amazingly calm now, almost serene. As if he was happy that she no longer had to suffer.

We reached the chestnut log in fifteen minutes, and it took us less than ten seconds to locate the body of Phyllis Tyler. The scent of blood in the snow had already attracted the scavengers, and there were fresh animal tracks in the snow. The body had been mutilated as the first one had been.

It had grown dark somehow, and I realized dully that it was now Saturday night. The night an earlier generation looked forward to as if it were a holiday. And, for many of them, it was, in an age when the work week consisted of six full days and Saturday night was the only time for fun because Sunday was the one day that many of them did not have to rise early.

No more.

I directed the beam of the flashlight into the snow-covered underbrush. Every limb, every twig was coated with snow, and every cluster of honeysuckle now became a heap of pure and uncluttered snow. In the cluster I could see the faces of the snow: the incredibly varied designs that became eyes, mouths, ears, fingers.

And flesh and blood eyes stared back at my light.

"The team should be here within a few minutes," Rick said. I knew what he meant. He had called in the state emergency team that remained on call for emergencies such as this.

We were still there at dawn. Sunday morning, when mountain housewives by the hundreds rose, as they had done for countless years, to bake the innumerable biscuits and fry the slices of ham or bacon or patties of sausage. The mountain wife baked thirteen thousand biscuits per year, prepared a thousand meals, washed fifteen thousand dishes. Sunday morning was no exception.

On this Sunday morning there would be no interruption of the cycle, the ritual, and the celebration of life. In spite of floods, fires, famines, or murders, men woke hungry and expected and received food. Not the cup of dirty water city folks call coffee or the buns that are half preservatives and half sugar and no taste, the fare of many city dwellers, and not the bowl of cardboard cereal with watery milk splashed over it.

But a real breakfast of eggs, meat, hot bread, gravy, real coffee brewed over a fireplace or woodstove burner, butter, honey or molasses, and stewed fruits. A ton of cholesterol, the world said, but somehow these people managed to live out their eighty or ninety years of life without being sick a day in their lives.

Some of them did.

Others, like Alisha Webley and Phyllis Tyler, would have no breakfast and would never again rise when the alarm clock screamed at them. Phyllis was now one of the faces of the snow.

By the time the crew arrived and completed its preliminary work, the area had been trampled so that it appeared that an army had marched through the forest.

The army included some familiar faces and one new one. The old ones included Montgomery Wooley of State Tactical Operations Police, a man I had met on less-than-friendly terms once before. On that occasion he placed me under arrest and charged me with murdering my wife and, until then, my best friend. And for a few weeks it looked fairly certain that I'd be victim of the good-news-bad-news revelations. The good news would be that my prison term would be very short; the bad news was that I'd spend it in the electric chair or gas chamber.

Another familiar face was that of Dallas Wadsworth. Jhon Rance stood shoulder-to-shoulder with him. The three men worked in tandem with STOP which, in this state, can choose to take part in the investigation of any crime, with or without formal or even unspoken invitation or permission from local authorities. The SBI liked them less than I did.

Personally, at this point, I was happy to see them. A tall, red-haired woman with a rather severe face detached herself from the group and crunched her way through the snow to me.

"I'm Rowena Cullen," she said. "With the STOP. I am, for better or worse, the replacement for Agent Broughton who worked here earlier. I think you recall her." She removed the glove from her right hand and extended it to me. Her fingers were long and cool, and her grip was comfortably masculine.

I recalled Agent Broughton with vivid detail. She was a ball-busting gung-ho butch whose idea of heaven was the testicles of the men she knew in a vise and she was at the crank. She testified as an expert witness in my recent murder trial and did not fare well. Even now I could not escape the feeling that she had been set up as the classic straw man for me to knock down and burn. Somebody wanted rid of her and put her head on the block and handed me the sharp hatchet.

I nodded. Cullen had reclaimed her hand and was pulling the glove back on. Snowflakes, now light and airy, remained in her hair and on her shoulders.

"I remember her well," I said. "And how is Miss Broughton faring these days?"

"Well and not well," she said. "She is pushing a pencil until her retirement application is approved. She plans to enter private practice as a consulting psychologist. I sincerely wish her the greatest of success, though I doubt you share my wishes."

"I bear her no malice," I lied. "No more than I would hold against anyone who tried to have me fried." The truth was that I would have cheerfully driven the Blue Gloomp across her.

"It was her job," she said.

"Goering and Himmler had their jobs, too," I said. "So did the men who fired the furnaces at Buchenwald and Dachau."

She smiled faintly to suggest that the conversation had come to an end and that a new topic needed attention.

"What can you tell us?" she asked. Wadsworth, Rance, and Wooley had detached themselves from the cluster at the chestnut log and stood nearby.

"Overkill," I said without a trace of a smile. "I don't mean it as a pun. The killer took one woman yesterday morning and left her body for us less than twelve hours later. He took his second victim, apparently, within two or three hours after we found his first one. In all probability he has already selected his third one by now and may have already taken her."

"That's insane," Rowena Cullen said. "I mean, really, truly insane." She stopped short, then began again. "You don't need me to tell you that," she added softly.

"Tell us everything," Wadsworth said. "From the beginning until now." He was five and a half feet tall, with unruly hair that seemed to have recently escaped from captivity. He wore thick glasses in heavy rims. When he moved he had the grace of a heron with hemorrhoids.

I stood there in the snow while I recounted the killings to this point. They listened in silence. When I had finished Jhon Rance spoke softly, as if the snowflakes might hear. He was a huge black man I had known for years. A darker version of Lurch, he was, I knew, deeply intelligent and tried hard not to show his brainpower, and he was also a thorough investigator that little ever slipped past. Unlike Lurch, he had never learned not to take his work personally.

He'd like nothing better than to skewer me.

"We're standing here in the snow," he said, "while a killer may be picking up another woman, hauling her into the darkness of the storm, and disemboweling her. Damn it, we need a direction. We need a lead of any kind. Something to get us on a trail."

I told him about Lurch's noticing that Alisha Webley was left-handed. I also mentioned the fact of the wealth of the in-laws of the two slain women.

Rowena looked at me curiously. "You really think that being left-handed has something to do with all this?"

She waved one gloved hand in the direction of the huge chestnut tree. "What earthly connection could there be?"

"I have no idea," I said truthfully. "Possibly none. But I know that if I

70

sneeze and a tree falls in this forest, it is in all probability nothing but coincidence. If I sneeze twice and two trees fall, we have established a relationship at least. What if I sneeze three times, six times, and three or six trees fall?"

"You have correlation, not causation," she said.

"If I sneeze a million times and a million trees fall, we still have no causal relationship," I admitted. "But if finally only one tree in the forest is left standing and I feel a huge sneeze coming on, are you going to stand near that tree?"

She nodded. "If we have more murders, and if the victims all are left-handed, I'll start to see your point more readily. For now, though, what can we do? We can't guard all the women in the entire town."

"We may not need to," I said. "Both women were members of the same high school class. They were the same age, give or take a month or two. They belonged to the same small private club. The first victim had given birth before her marriage."

Wadsworth looked at me sharply. "Is this a connection, or another sneeze?"

"I haven't asked him, but I don't think the husband knew about the birth. Alisha Webley delivered a child that died at a very early age. I'm making it a point to ask the doctor who performs the post-mortem if Phyllis Tyler had a child. I might be completely off base, but right now it's one of the few possible leads we have."

"You say both of these dead women are left-handed?"

I nodded. "There is a photo in the yearbook of her holding a pen in her left hand. Her handwriting slants backward. We'll get more complete verification, but I'm positive."

The crime scene analysis was over quickly, and the body of Phyllis Tyler was carried out of the woods and to the rutted drive where the cars were parked. There was very little that could be done at the scene itself. The snow had covered everything, and trace evidence on the body would still be there when the final examination was made. We followed the body, and a half-hour later the four of us sat inside the den at my house.

"Let me add some wood to the stove and I'll get us a cup of coffee," I said, raking through the coals in the bottom of the cast iron stove. I had not fed it in more than twenty-four hours but a thick bed of coals remained. The house was toasty warm. Luckily, before I left the house I turned the damper knobs to the closed position, then turned them backward one-fourth of a turn. There was enough ventilation and draft to keep the fire burning but not enough to let it consume the firewood quickly. I opened the damper all the way and added three chunks of well-dried poplar and an equal number of seasoned oak. Within minutes the warmth began to fill the room.

When I set the tray holding the cups of instant coffee on the crude table I had made months ago, Montgomery Wooley sipped his coffee, replaced the cup in the saucer, and looked directly at me.

"Somebody is trying awfully hard to make you look as bad as possible," he said. "The first body in the trunk of your car. The second in the woods near your house. What's the message someone is trying to send?"

I shrugged helplessly. "Don't think I haven't spent hours in wondering," I said. "The only explanation I can come up with is that only a few weeks ago I was charged with killing my wife and my best friend. You know all about that. I'm the chicken-killing dog, and every time there is a dead hen, someone will check my mouth for feathers."

"A decoy," Rowena said. "Someone wants everyone to look in your direction. It's more than probable that a couple hundred or so people in this county still think you killed your wife and her lover. And hundreds more who didn't think so will change their minds when the news of this body gets out."

"So who's trying to get you?" Rance asked. "Somebody has a reason for picking your property or your car. Who? What reason, real or imagined, can they have? Chess, I've know you for years, known you well enough that you must have some idea. What is it?"

"I can think of several," I said. "Most obvious is that some person I arrested wants to get back at me. God knows that's a small number: I haven't arrested more than half a dozen people, and most of them were drunks. Another possibility is that some former student is carrying a grudge. Maybe I refused to fix a speeding ticket and angered somebody. It sounds trivial, but we all know that a demented, perverted, and twisted person doesn't always need logical thought progression."

"Any business deals gone sour?" Wadsworth asked.

"None. I don't have any business deals. I buy groceries, pay my bills, and that's ninety per cent of what I deal with."

"Someone you knew in prison who is now out and wants to get his kicks by killing these women and adding to your misery by dumping the bodies in your lap? You inherited a wad of money that some people might have thought they had claims to."

"Nobody and nothing," I said. "Ollie One-Eye is the only person from the prison that I know of in the county. I'd trust Ollie with my life. The fact is, he saved my life and damn nearly lost his own. I can't see him as a suspect." Ollie was a huge man whose work release came shortly after mine, and I immediately hired him to clean and cook around the jailhouse. People were practically committing crimes just so they could eat Ollie's food.

Wadsworth shrugged his shoulders slightly and turned to Rowena. She looked at me and said, very softly, "What do you know about serial killers?"

It was my turn to shrug. "Little or nothing," I said. "I've read a few magazine articles written by psychologists who take us into the minds of the killers. I used the articles to wrap my garbage in."

"You have a low opinion of psychologists? Like me."

"I have a friend who is a fortune teller. I like him in spite of his work."

"You think psychologists are fortune tellers?"

"I'm glad my friend is one, rather than a psychologist."

She learned forward, her face intense, drawn. Wadsworth, Rance, and Wooley waited for the attack.

"You can lump hundreds of years of intensive study into one ball and toss it into the garbage?" she asked. "Did someone not tell me that you were once a professor of literature? You can teach fiction, products of the imagination without foundation here or hereafter, and you can devote your life to this bubble-chasing. Yet you can disregard the work of brilliant men and women who have made the most amazing breakthroughs in history?"

"Not to get bogged down in fancy footwork," I said, "because there is a killer out there and we need to be making our presence felt in as many places as possible, you speak of hundreds of years of study. The word 'psychology' means a study of the human soul. Half the practitioners are atheists. How can an atheist make a scientific study of something which, to him, does not exist? The Greeks saw the soul as a butterfly emerging from a cocoon from which an ugly, dying worm was reborn into a beautiful and delightful new life. So you are a student of butterflies."

She only smiled. It was a tense smile; her lips were a thin dry line, but it was a smile.

"You are making a point," she said. "I'm curious. Go ahead."

"I have worked with psychologists in one manner or another for years. One at the college spends nearly all of his free time watching porno movies and collecting girlie magazines. I don't recall ever seeing him with a scholarly book or magazine in his hand. I taught a silly young thing who could not and did not pass one single test I gave on any topic, yet she managed to make her way through college and is now a psychologist. Her IQ was somewhere in the eighty-five range. How can I possibly consider her an expert in a scientific field of study?"

"Do any poor students ever become teachers of math, English, or biology?"

"Yes," I said. "Too often. But you know what happens? They are all weeded out of the field almost immediately. You see, in a real course, a person can be demonstrably wrong. In your field, the more wrong a person becomes, the more likely he is to find a great following. Was there ever a more misguided thinker than Freud? A man who saw sexual perversion in everything we do: a man who thought that cocaine was the greatest wonder drug in the history of modern medicine. Today virtually every idea the man had has been junked, discarded, or ridiculed into obscurity. Those who refuted him will one day become as obsolete as he is. Name me one literary figure who has ever been recognized as great and then discovered to be only a mediocre writer or thinker. The writers of fiction are dealing with the greatest reality possible: the truth of human nature. Now can we get back to the killer? I don't think that this is a man who will fit into a neat psychological profile, but if you can help, go to it. I'm not doing so well on my own."

"The serial killer," she corrected.

"The killer," I said in turn correcting her. "A man goes into battle and kills forty men in a single encounter. He is not a serial killer. He is a one-time killer who got into multiple situations resulting in deaths. A man sees five men raping his wife and he kills all five of them. He is not a serial killer. The person killing these women has an agenda, and when he has completed it, he will stop. But not until."

I meant only a portion of what I had been saying, but I fervently meant that portion of it. Some of the most brilliant men and women I had ever known had been psychologists, as well as some of the densest asses who ever drew breath. Still, baiting her had been my primary objective.

Her tone was mocking, a reflection of her facial expression.

"You are speaking as an authority, are you?"

"I am speaking as one who knows that the word of authorities is often worthless. You measure one multiple killer by all others you have known, when a dolt would know to measure each one only by what else he and he alone has done."

Wadsworth cleared his throat as a preamble to one of his sermons on police science. "I'm interested," he said, disappointing and relieving me. "Why isn't this person a serial killer?"

"He's working too fast," I said. "Every multiple killer I have ever heard of kills his first victim and then waits until the urge overpowers him again, perhaps months later. Then, his attacks come closer and closer together. Six months apart, then four, then two, then every two weeks, then every three days, and finally daily, hourly if he can find the victims. He is a drug addict whose opiate is blood and suffering. That is, if your colleagues' theories hold water. The man we are after killed one woman early in the morning and by evening he had already picked up another victim and killed her. He is probably at this moment stalking his next victim."

She frowned and sighed in exasperation, as if she were dealing with a teenager who would not listen to reason. I didn't blame her. I'd have been impatient with me too. I was being stubborn on purpose, keeping in mind that Polonius advised us that by indirection we can find direction out. What I was doing had a point, if only to me.

I was not disregarding the obvious facts facing us, but I also wanted to know what type of person I was working with. Not just that: I had spent many years as a colleague of psychologists, the vast majority of whom were respectable, intelligent, thorough, and reasonable. But there were some of them who, as in all professions, were total kooks. We had our share of them in the English Department when I was on the college campus, and I dreaded the thought of trying to have a cogent conversation with most of them. To listen to them, you'd have thought their work *mattered.*

"Do you really have such a low opinion of our profession?" she asked. "Can you be that far removed from reality?"

"Reality has nothing to do with any of our professions," I said in my most stubborn tones. "Reality is the maniac or the cold-blooded killer out there who is slaughtering people. And we happen to have one of them in our midst, and I doubt very seriously that he will be finished with his work anytime soon."

As if on cue, the telephone rang. It was Lurch.

"Another woman has disappeared," he said. "She was in the same class as all the others. Hang on."

Seconds ticked by slowly. In the background I could hear the rustling sound of pages being turned. Then his voice came back over the phone.

"Her name is Katherine Thennis. Also left-handed."

SEVEN

The call, like the first one, had come to Ed Gallager's office and he relayed it to me. I hung up the phone and turned to the STOP agents who sat staring at me.

"Who took the call?" Jhon Rance asked. Leaning forward in his chair, he stared at me as if I were something repulsive, and I had to agree that he was not far wrong. Since Zane Andrews had come to my cabin, I had moved mechanically. My mind refused to work, and it required all of my will power to force my body to respond.

"Ed Gallager," I said. "The newspaper editor."

"I know who he is." His eyes were cold, hard, cruel. A brawny man of immense strength and incredible quickness, he liked to give public demonstrations of his martial arts skills. He said it was like the police dog epics he often staged: letting the criminals know what they would face when they broke the law kept most of them honest.

It might work with petty thieves and muggers, but it had done nothing to bring us closer to whoever was killing the left-handed women from one high school graduating class.

"He took all the calls?" Rance asked.

"Yes," I said.

"So far." Dallas Wadsworth had put his cup on the coffee table and was standing at the window and watching the snowfall accumulate.

"What does that mean?" Cullen asked. "That there will be more calls? More killings?"

"Is there any doubt? When did a serial killer ever stop, except when he was arrested? They're like a shark. They get a scent of blood and go into a frenzy. That's your term, not mine."

"And while we sit here in this cozy cabin, Katherine Thennis is being tortured to death." It was the first time Montgomery Wooley had spoken since their arrival. "We ought to be out there looking for her. We can't do any good here."

Now Rance stood, his huge bulk rising like a tower until he hovered over all of us. "I'm not so sure," he said. "We might be able to do as much good as we could out there risking our lives in the snow. He isn't out there riding her around. The risk would be far too great. In all probability, she is already dead and he has left her body for us to find."

"What can we do?" I asked helplessly, feeling like a child caught in an embarrassing moment. My ineptitude was no secret. They all knew I was incompetent, and I had no way to prove them wrong. Especially since I didn't disagree with them.

I wasn't angry at what they felt; I was humiliated, furious with myself for being unable to function, horrified that there might not be an end to the killings as long as I was in office, which could not last for very long.

What could I do? The killer knew where he was at all times, and he knew where his next victim would be found. I had no idea where to look, what to expect next, or how his mind worked.

I did not accept the others' belief that we were dealing with a serial killer; a multiple killer, yes, but serial, no. The serial killer murders out of compulsion; he often selects his victims randomly. This monster was not acting out of need but out of fear or ambition. He knew that the women represented either a reward or a danger to him. He knew from the start that he would kill the women. And he knew who his next victim would be, and the one after that, and the ones after that.

There would be no end to it until he had accomplished what he set out to do, or until we somehow caught him. I knew well that the typical criminal is caught, not through superior police techniques but through the loudmouthed goon who can't resist the temptation to boast about how he or one of his friends pulled off the perfect crime.

The man who had called himself Zimri would not be one who blabbed. Nor would he, like the infamous serial killers, keep souvenirs and mementos around to convict him in case someone with a search warrant gets lucky.

This man, or woman, although I remained convinced that the killer was a man, had his own agenda. He was not killing for thrills or through obsession. He was killing through nature's strongest motivations: self-preservation.

During the few minutes of private time we had, I listened to the arguments of the professionals and their pontifications on the psyches of serial killers, sermons that explained every urge these perverted people had experienced from the time they were improperly potty trained until they were caught with the blood of a dozen victims on their hands. But not on their consciences: they were not provided with these, or they misplaced them when it got in the way of their savagery.

I listened but said nothing after my outburst in the cabin. I had my own ideas about serial criminals, from punks who cheat their way through school and college and medical school and every other kind of school to the shoplifter who is too worthless to work.

So sue me because I don't buy the explanations. Some people are sick; that is a given. But others are as mean as a snake or a mad dog, and they kill for a handful of reasons: to get something they can't get any other way, to protect something that others want, self-preservation, blind animal fury, and resentment that twists their minds beyond repair.

Zimri was not sick; I was convinced of that. He was cruel, but not sadistic; he was in a rage but not in the throes of some bizarre compulsion; he was not killing because of sickness but because he knew that it was far more dangerous for him not to kill. Someone represented a threat to him, and that someone was a woman, especially a left-handed woman.

I had never been guilty of being politically correct, and I didn't plan to start in that direction. Sometimes I was convinced that the sickness of the killer is equalled only by the stupidity of the educated people who salivated at the thought of making a national hero out of some sadist who raped and killed a ninety-year old woman because she didn't tip him when he delivered the groceries.

I returned to my thoughts of the killer whose victims were left-handed women. Make that more specific: left-handed women who gave birth before marriage and who married wealthy men who insisted on having a prenuptial agreement. Women from the same high school class who were all members of a tiny and very private club and who for some reason kept rose beryl stones around for no apparent reason.

All the time they talked we were pulling on coats, checking in corners of my cabin and, later, behind the trees in the forest. The onset of paranoia that hit me almost as soon as I found myself in jail and awaiting charges had struck again with a vengeance, and each time I saw one of the self-styled experts glancing at me, I knew what the person was thinking.

I felt the heat rushing to my face, and I knew I should be in the face of Rance when I read his lips as he whispered to Wadsworth. "I don't think Mrs. Thennis is in any great danger as long as all of us are here," he said.

It was clear what he meant: Katherine Thennis was safe as long as I was in the room. Rance saw that I caught the message and started toward his four-wheel drive vehicle. Seconds later we were on our way to town.

To try to avoid the worst roads, we took a circuitous route back, and it took us half an hour to get to my office. Ed Gallager was in my office when we arrived. His face told me all I needed to know.

"The caller was the same one, my aide said," he told us. "She said she'd recognize that voice anywhere and under any conditions. I had been working on the next issue when the call came. We had just answered dozens of calls from the usual people wanting to get their names in the paper, and we simply weren't prepared for the call."

"You didn't tape it?" Rance asked. "You didn't use callback to see where the call came from?" He towered over the tiny and terrified Gallager, a miserable man cringing before the wrath of the enormous black man whose face was like a thunderstorm.

"We didn't think...." Gallager didn't have the courage to complete the sentence. Rowena played the good-cop routine and went to him, speaking softly, understandingly. She turned Gallager away from Rance, who stalked his way across the room like a storm-trooper.

I stood beside Gallager, who told us briefly what the caller said: he had "taken" his next toy and would play with her until she bored him. He had also added that he hoped none of us became ill because of the time we spent in the cold and snow. He had given Gallager a personal message for me.

"Tell Ivy that Zimri said he ought to be arrested for impersonating an officer of the law," Gallager said timidly. He turned away from me, his tiny shoulders bunched under his weak chin as if he expected me to hit him. Me, the spineless sheriff who wouldn't arrest a bird for jaywalking.

"What else?" I demanded, my face burning with humiliation. "He told you something else. What is it?"

Gallager stammered helplessly. Finally he mumbled the brief message. "He said to tell you that if you weren't such an idiot you'd know who he is. He said to tell you it was no wonder your wife slept with everyone in the country, with a wimp like you at home."

The flames leaped anew to my face as embarrassment coupled with anger flooded my numbed brain. I groped for something to say, to do when the phone rang. It was Dr. Miller from the local hospital.

"I did some instant checking," he said. "I knew you needed to know. Same story. Almost a carbon copy of the first one. It appears as if the same weapon, or one almost exactly like it, was used. The wounds were frequent and the slashes were long. No stabbing wounds. She died from loss of blood and shock. And, yes, the victim had given birth. This is only a guess, but I'd say it was when she was about seventeen at the time."

Phyllis Tyler had died, apparently, less than an hour or two before we found her body. I realized that it would have taken the killer almost an hour to carry her body, if she was dead at the time, to the chestnut log and return to his car. This meant that we were apparently within an hour of making contact with him. What I did not know is how he managed to leave her car at my place and still have a way to escape.

"She had to drive one car," Rowena said. "Either that, or he has a helper. I have trouble accepting the latter."

"Why?" Rance asked.

"Serial killers don't work in tandem. They don't trust anyone. No, he had to force her some way, or deceive her into driving her own car."

"Why wouldn't she escape when she was in the car alone?" Rance asked.

"I didn't say she was alone. Perhaps the killer was in the car with her.

81

He forced her into the woods and tied her up or even drugged her."

"The doctor said there was no indication that she had been tied. No abrasions on her wrists or ankles. And at this point we don't know if there were indications of drugs in her system."

"Then she drove on her own free will, or he was in the car with her. That brings us right back to the question of how he was able to escape on foot," Wadsworth said.

"If that's what he did," Wooley interjected.

During the brief exchange, I had been leafing through the Sherman High School yearbook. I stared at the photo of Katherine Thennis. She was a pretty girl, as the other two had been, but not a raving beauty. You could pass her on the street and notice her even, delicate features, and then you'd go on to the drugstore to get your sinus decongestant medication.

None of the girls had been real beauties, but all had been attractive, cute, or appealing in some way. Zane had entered the office and stood by my shoulder.

"Do you know her?" I asked.

She nodded, biting her lip. She reminded me in a suddenly chilling way of the three girls, now women and now dead, in her casual prettiness. I had known Zane for only two months, since she had come to me to ask for a job and she disarmed me with her confession that she had no qualifications except a genuine desire to learn the work.

I agreed that I would hire her on the condition that she take courses in police science taught at the local college. She enrolled, accumulated perfect scores on all tests, and scored at the top of her class. She had been working for the sheriff's department on a provisional basis while she was in the college program.

My discomfort was beyond words when I had to tell her that I had never taken the police science courses and that I could not have ever become a deputy. The law would not permit it.

I could be a sheriff, although I had served a prison term for a felony, but l could not be a deputy. One position was elective and the other was appointed. And, by law, the deputies were not supposed to be around me. Their code required them not to associate with known criminals.

"How well did you know her?"

"We were in several classes in high school," she said. The icy chill increased in intensity when I realized that she not only knew the girls but was in the same graduating class. "I didn't know her well. I didn't know Phyllis or Alisha except to speak to them in the halls or in class. We were from different sides of the tracks."

I nodded. I knew what she was saying. In Sherman there is no such thing as the wrong side of the tracks. There are tracks beyond estimation. Part of the county's and the town's population worked at tobacco or cotton farming as they had done almost from the time the first settlers came into the Blue Ridge Mountains and would continue to do as long as the sterile soil was watered by the two rivers and countless creeks that cut their way through the hills.

Still others were tenant farmers in the traditional sense: these tenants rented small farms and cultivated the plots and grew their crops and then shared with the owners. More than a few had apple orchards, someone having discovered decades ago that apples love the crisply cold spring mornings and sharpness of the autumns, with the abundant rain and warm days between.

A segment of the population worked at town and county offices, and still others fed the cabbages into the choppers at the county's kraut factory. Another small part of the population manned their own offices and small businesses.

Then we had the college professors and administrators, who occupied their own corners of the town. Students accounted for more than half the total population of the town and a huge chunk of the county. In the hills beyond the town countless residents somehow grubbed a living from the land. They killed their deer and bears and wild hogs, adding rabbits and squirrels to their diet when the large bodies of meat were eaten. They grew a few vegetables in backyard gardens and pulled in small trout and hornyheads and smallmouth bass from the streams that crisscrossed the county like veins through a body.

Zane didn't fall into any of the categories. Her parents had been writers and illustrators of children's books, and they split not just the blanket but the royalty checks and went their separate ways when Zane was in the fifth grade. Her father stayed in Sherman and her mother made her way first to New York and then to Los Angeles and finally to Taos, New

Mexico.

Zane remained with her father, who developed a keen interest in booze as his interest in writing declined, until he died of a heart attack two months earlier and she was left with no visible means of support. She couldn't afford to stay in college unless she found a job, and she made her way eventually to my office. She had been with me since that day and seemed delighted with her work in the sheriff's office.

"You never went out with them?" I prodded. "No double-dating, no after-prom parties, or weekends at the beach?"

She shrugged. "I saw them on occasion. Sometimes we got together for coffee or just girl talk. But that was after we had graduated from high school."

"Never at meetings of the morning club?" I didn't like having to ask the question, but I didn't think I could afford not to. She flinched as if I had struck her. I added the clincher. "Or at the DOLLS meeting?" I did not have any idea what the club included, but I didn't think the girls would have called themselves dolls without a reason. It was bad enough when a man called them such; it was unthinkable that they would apply the label to themselves except through sarcasm. The name of the club had been mentioned in one of the yearbooks, but I received the impression that it was not formally accepted by the school.

She flushed, bit her lip again, and touched me on the shoulder and walked outside into the snow. I followed. She stood in the parking lot, her face turned upward so that the snow fell onto her cheeks and closed eyes.

"Sorry," I said. "I had to ask."

She now bowed her head and compressed her lips tightly. "It's all right," she said. "You need to know. No, I never attended meetings of the morning group, but when the DOLLS group splintered off, I met with them a couple of times."

"What were the clubs all about?"

She shook her head. "I wasn't there long enough to decide. I didn't fit in. I'm not married."

"What does marriage have to do with it?"

"Everything, apparently," she said. "Most of the girls had been married shortly after high school graduation."

"To rich young men."

She nodded. "To very rich men. I suppose they were bored by their easy lives. The morning club, at least. At least that's how I interpreted it."

"What about the DOLLS?"

She flushed. "I never learned, not fully. They talked about little except local scandals, sex lives, and clothes. But it was different. It wasn't that they tried to get personal, and they didn't giggle about it. Not when I was there. They had one basic attitude: they hated men. Or most of them, it seemed."

"Are you still a member?"

She nodded. "Technically, I suppose. There are no dues, and no one is required to be there. They don't take on projects or get involved politically. They explained it to me as a support group."

"Is it an acronym? Daughters Of Loony Lovers or something of that sort?"

She flushed slightly. "The Den Of Left-handed Lovers," she concluded weakly. "Because they were all left-handed."

I started to pursue the topic when Rowena rushed into the parking lot. Her face was white with fear.

"He called again," she said. "He asked to speak to the editor. He's inside. He wants to talk to you. The editor, I mean. We're on the other lines. Get in here!"

I left Zane in the snow and hurried inside. Ed Gallager was holding onto the phone and Lurch was hovering over a large and sophisticated tape recorder. I grabbed an extension just in time to hear a soft, almost guttural voice whisper, "Good-by for now." Then the line went dead. I looked at Lurch, who shook his head, indicating that he was unable to capture any of the conversation.

"What did he say?" I asked the editor, knowing what I'd hear.

"The same message. He's already grown tired or her. He says he may not keep her much longer. What do we do? We don't have time to waste. We've got to do something!" He let his eyes jump nervously to each of us in turn.

I wished I knew. I asked if he had personally talked to the killer, and the answer was the same. The message was too brief for the tape recorder to get much of it. The voice I had heard was not one I'd heard before. I floundered helplessly. I had no notion of what we ought to do, and I looked at the others for help. They seemed as bewildered as I was.

For endless hours now I had felt guilty each time I paused to talk, to rest, or even to eat or go to the toilet. I had the urge to rush frantically around the entire county, and all that kept me from doing it was the realization that, snow or not, I'd be doing exactly what the killer wanted. If I were on the road in the southern part of the county, it was an easy matter for the killer to dispose of a body in the northern part.

Lurch punched the telephone dial and wrote a number on a pad and gave it to me. My heart leaped with excitement. We had the number from the phone where the call was made. Maybe the killer had become careless and we had him.

"Find out whose number it is," I told him. Ed Gallager leaned closer to me and stared at the number. His face became almost as white as the snow that seemed to cover the world. He sat down heavily, his arm knocking papers off the desk.

"Don't bother," he said in a weak and terrified voice. "I know whose number it is." I glared impatiently at him.

"It's mine," he said.

"He called from your office?"

He shook his head. "From my house." I told Blanton to come with me, but Gallager held up his hand.

"It's no use," he said. "That's what he wants you to do. You'll find an empty house, and by that time Mrs. Thennis will be dead. You have to find him!" His voice trembled, and he buried his face in his hands. His shoulders shook violently.

I quickly told Rowena, Wooly, Wadsworth, and Rance what Ed Gallager had just told me. Zane, snow still lingering on her shoulders and in her hair, joined us.

"Describe the voice," Rance said. "Tell me what the caller looks like. Is he tall, thin, fat, weak, strong, whatever."

I had heard only a phrase. Gallager lowered his hands from his face and looked at us through watery eyes. He spoke with surprising strength. "Same as before," he said. "Medium size. Educated. No grammatical errors. No mispronunciations. He did not falter, stammer, hesitate, or flounder, and yet it was not a well-rehearsed speech. It was off the cuff. Believe me, interview enough people and you can tell."

An amazing recovery after appearing to be nearing a nervous collapse seconds earlier.

"You people are the experts," I said to the state people. "I'm the raw rookie. Tell me what I can do. I never felt so helpless and so furious in my life. Dallas, what can I do? What can any of us do? We can't stand and wait for him to kill again, but where do we begin to try to stop him?"

Wadsworth stared at his feet. Apparently he had felt the same helplessness I experienced.

"This is not an easy situation to get a handle on," he said pointlessly. "In my years in law enforcement, I never encountered anyone who seemed to kill at a frantic pace. Sooner or later, of course, we're bound to get him, but how many will he kill before he makes a mistake? I frankly admit to being paralyzed. We don't know one thing about the killer except that he is clever and he has a four-wheel drive. I don't suppose the department of motor vehicles could help us."

I shook my head. "Not a chance," I guessed. Lurch agreed.

"In the first place," he said, "the killer may not even live in the area, and in the second place half the people in the outlying areas own four-wheel drive vehicles. In the third place, the guy may be as good in the woods as any of us. Better. If he's in good shape, he could carry a body a considerable distance in the snow, particularly if the body is that of a woman. He could then hike cross-country to where he left his car."

Wadsworth was wagging his gray head like a worried bull. "How far could he travel on foot?" he asked. "Five miles? Eight or ten at the most?"

"Try twenty, even thirty, if he's desperate or driven," Rick said. "I'm not in good shape, but I could do close to three miles an hour, even in this snow. In five or six hours I could cover close to twenty miles."

"But the cold—" Rowena said.

"He could take the cold. We have a couple dozen guys around here who winter-camp. Some of them go out West and camp in the Rockies to elk hunt. They spend hour after hour exposed to the cold and the wind and snow. This would not be a problem for them. And it's possibly not a problem for the killer. Besides, the north of the county is crisscrossed with roads and he could walk only three or four miles and be on safe ground."

I was impatient to be moving. I had not slept in God-knows-when and I was ready to collapse. The only thing that had kept us going was the food that Rockwell brought, as promised. During one moment of respite I called to thank him, and he said that it was the least he could do. Then, strangely, his voice broke.

He paused for several seconds, then resumed as if nothing had happened. "You must understand," he said, "that I'm an incurable romantic. These girls, and the boys they married, are not adults in an adult world. They are still teenagers, dreaming their dreams and planning their futures. Whoever is killing them is killing my people."

I tried to tune out the din in the office. The talking was to me merely an exercise in semantics. We could theorize all night and not be one inch closer to the killer. And while we talked another woman might be, and in all probability was, being tortured to death.

Gallager shared my restlessness. "Look," he said, "I can't sit here and wonder whether the man had an unhappy childhood. Let's get on the road. The chances are microscopic that we'll see him or be able to help her, but if we stay here the chances are even lower. I suggest that we take three or four vehicles."

"Just what I was going to say," Rance said. "Why don't we split up. Take three cars. Two to a car. Ed can be the third person in one car. How shall we do it?"

"I'm going," Zane said, "and I'm riding with Chess. Anybody else who likes can come with us." She spoke with surprising and sudden feeling. She, too, had been smoldering inwardly for as long as I had, and she wanted to do something, right or wrong.

"I'll ride with Rance," Rowena said. "I don't mind admitting this guy scares me. A lot."

"That leaves you and me," Wadsworth said to Wooley. "What about the editor?"

Gallager nodded toward me. "I'll ride with them," he said. "And before you ask, I'll not get in the way, and I'll not even consider printing anything without getting it cleared with you, Chess."

I nodded. I was surprised that he made the offer. In the past he had shown little restraint in printing what he felt like writing. He attacked with equal opportunity attitude: he could blast the preacher one day, me the next, the college the third, and the Statue of Liberty on the fourth. He claimed that the secret to a newsman's success was to have half the people love you and the other half hate you, and every six months you change them around. He had a lot of spunk, but I never considered him to be a paragon in the area of discretion toward the news. He seemed to read my mind.

"I think I understand what you folks need," he said, "and a wild and frightened public is at the bottom of the list. If we print too much, they'll be shooting each other across the back fence daily. When it's over, I'll have my day. I'm ready when you are."

"Besides," he added, "if this snow doesn't stop, we'll not be able to get the papers we've printed to our readers."

"You're going to do a book about this," Rance said. It was not a question. The editor shrugged.

"There's a demand for them," he said. "If not from me, then from someone else."

We left the office manned by Bum Phillips, the sheriff's department's curmudgeon-in-residence. He was one of the few who did not turn against me when I went into office. He was a good man, but he had put on a few pounds in recent weeks and I did not want him running through the woods. Besides, I could trust him to keep the office under control and to alert us in the event of a breakthrough of any type.

As we entered the vehicles, I realized that I didn't know what day it was. As we left the office I didn't even know if it was daylight or dark until we reached the outside door. To my shock it was growing dark. I wanted to ask but did not dare if it was still Sunday.

Some Sabbath. Keeping it holy.

"I'm driving," Zane said as we reached my car. "I don't want you crashing on me on some mountain road." I didn't argue. I was not certain I could make it around the block. "You rest," she added. "If you can sleep a few minutes, do so. I'll wake you the moment I see or hear anything that seems unusual."

We had agreed before we left that Rance and Rowena would take the south part of the county. Wooley, Wadsworth, and Ed Gallager would take the middle of the county, and Zane and I would patrol the north part.

You have to understand that Sherman county is like a Dali watch and the Unaka Mountains are the table edge. Except that in this case the table is the crest of the range, and the county is draped over the ridge like a tablecloth. Two-thirds of the county lies to the south of the ridge, and the northern part that Zane and I would patrol was lapped over onto the north side.

The mountains of North Carolina are not typical of many ranges that I know of. There are six major ranges in a state that is thought by many to be small and flat. And while we do not have peaks like those in the Rockies, Mount Mitchell is the highest peak east of the Mississippi. We have forty other peaks higher than six thousand feet and more than a hundred that reach five thousand feet.

It is a shorter drive from Murphy to Columbia, South Carolina, Atlanta, Georgia, Nashville, Tennessee, Charleston, West Virginia, Richmond, Virginia, and Frankfort, Kentucky, than it is to Raleigh.

In North Carolina the climb is so steep and the curves so acute that it takes not only a skillful driver but a car in good condition to handle many of the roads. The most dreaded sight on the roads in summer is the white Cadillac with the Florida license plates and the short, fat man at the wheel.

We also have snow. Most people think of the sunny South as flat and hot, but sometimes it snows for three and four days in a row, then we get a day of sunshine, followed by another three-day snow.

In fact, it had been snowing for three days in a row now, and I was hoping, praying for clear weather. The snow plows had no chance to keep the roads cleared. As fast as the plows moved the snow off the roads, the snow behind the plow covered the road again even before the plow was around the next curve.

We also have forests. I mean miles and miles of deep, green, and impenetrable forests where a large army could hide for months and never be seen. Occasionally a child wanders away from parents, and hundreds of volunteers scout the area for signs of the toddler, and often no one ever finds even a scrap of cloth.

The mountains are filled with wild boars, black bears, and far more mountain lions than the naturalists would have you to believe. There are rocky cliffs, gorges, whitewater rivers, and laurel slicks that no human can move through at any speed faster than a slow crawl. Along the mountain roads the houses are spaced miles apart, and the people hit by blizzards tough it out and have nothing more to eat than roast beef, steak, country ham, fried chicken, hot biscuits, apple pie, and assorted vegetables.

During a terrible blizzard some years ago an emergency Red Cross vehicle finally plowed through the snow to the house of a farmer and his wife who had snow piled up past their windows. When the volunteers shoveled their way to the door and knocked, the man of the house opened the door, saw the Red Cross insignia, and without cracking a smile said, "I already gave where I work." Independence at its best.

While I was ruminating about where I live and why I live here, Zane was weaving the four-wheel around sharp curves; half a dozen times we saw headlights reflecting from the eyes of deer, and twice a fox darted across the road in front of us, his tail dragging in the snow as he glided across the soft surface.

Then the headlights caught the metallic glistening of chrome and steel and glass, and she stopped, backed the vehicle to the tiny side road we had just passed, and pulled in so that the headlights illuminated the vehicle parked in snow that was now close to two feet deep.

It was Katherine Thennis's car.

We sat and stared at the vehicle, barely visible beneath the covering of snow. Instead of an automobile, it looked more like a soft pyramid of cotton. Except for the headlights it could have been the fresh earth from a grave covered tactfully not with artificial grass but with snow. Slowly we emerged from the car. Zane held her Glock .45 at the ready position and I carried the legally sawed-off shotgun which had become my constant companion. Since my release from jail I had lived with the strict regulation enforced by the state: that no convicted felons, whether cat burglars or county sheriffs, can carry hand guns.

The law in North Carolina states that no one can hold the position of sheriff unless he is a citizen of the United States, but when a felon loses his citizenship, he can regain it when he has, in the opinion of the justice department, paid his debt to society. At this time he is permitted to hold any elective office in the state.

In my case, I considered that I never owed society a debt of any sort, but the courts ruled otherwise. And when I was still in jail my friend Edney (at least, I was his friend) pulled strings all over the place and I was paroled in time to apply for citizenship reinstatement so that he could buy me the election.

And he bought it in admirable fashion, by purchasing newspaper ads intended to inflame the public and to split the support for the two leading candidates, those who had some notion of what law enforcement work was about, and then he bought the votes of all the fringe population by a series of gifts and promises of what was to come once I was in office.

And I owed a great debt to my friend and to my wife.

Some friend. Some wife.

EIGHT

A t first I was naive enough to think the votes came my way because of the political clout of Edney; it was not until my wife and Edney were murdered that I learned that Edney's string of cathouses all over a three-state area, coupled with his drug merchandising, included nearly everyone with some clout in the entire county, and all Edney had to do was make a few calls and hint of sensitive materials that might "accidentally" find its way into the hands of the newspaper editor.

Overnight I became the front-runner and won the election. I did not know at the time why Edney was so interested in having me wear the badge. It took less than a week to learn that what he really wanted was for someone to look the other way while he ran his illicit operations.

The gun I held was cold, icy cold, despite its being in the car with us. I had pulled on thin leather gloves which kept out some of the cold and at the same time allowed me the free use of my fingers. Just in case.

We both carried flashlights. I held mine far out to my right as I walked, remembering the lessons from the prisoners with whom I spent seven months and twenty-nine days. They told me that when they were pinned down, they always shot at the light.

"You hit the light and the man can't see you, which is good," they explained to me. "You miss the light and you hit the man holding it, which is even better. Stupid to carry the light in front of his body and you hit both of them. Smart, he carry it to the side, and the man with the gun don't know which side to shoot at, if he don't make no contact the first shot."

I passed the message on to the staff, but I didn't try to enforce it. I mean, out of all the people on the sheriff's entire department, I was the one with the least experience and with the poorest background. Even as I crunched through the snow, I had no real idea what I'd do if someone opened fire on us. I liked to think that I could drop the flashlight and fire at the muzzle light of the gun. What I'd do might be completely different.

The concern was purely academic. The car was empty. To my relief there was no sign of blood or indication of a struggle. The interior of the car was as neat as if it had just come from the auto-wash.

It was not locked. Using my gloved finger, I gently lifted the door handle at the outside edge. If there were prints, they would likely be in the center of the handle. I did the same with the glove box, which was empty except for a box of facial tissues and a note pad with a ball-point pen clipped to it. I flipped through the pages quickly and found only a list of telephone numbers, all with local prefixes. I slipped the pad into the pocket of my coat.

Zane flipped the trunk lock lever and the two of us made our way to the back of the car and opened it wide. I've probably seen too many made-for-TV movies, but I fully expected to find a body inside. Instead, we found just what anyone would expect to find: a spare tire, lug wrench, jack, and floor mat that covered the well where the spare was kept.

I pushed on the spare. Like those in probably half the cars in the nation, it was flat, as mine had been when Lurch checked it. If she'd needed to change the tire, I doubt that she'd have known where to begin. Even if she had known, her knowledge would have been worthless. I wondered how a practically new car could already have a flat spare. Maybe it was flat when her husband bought her the car. The car had snow tires, but the flat was regular all-weather tread.

"We'd better call the others," Zane said. "After we check the engine for warmth."

She had the tact and the kindness to look after me without letting me know she was doing it. So, of course, I had to know. But there was no need for either of us to communicate the help.

I reached inside the automobile and pulled the hood release handle. Zane raised the hood and placed an ungloved hand on the engine.

"Still hot," she said. "It wasn't parked here more than an hour ago. Let's check our own."

We raised the hood and felt the engine cylinder cover, then rechecked the Thennis car engine. They were almost identical in their heat, which meant that the Thennis car had not been parked in its present location for more than a few minutes when we arrived.

I don't know why it was necessary or even important to call the others, but we did. I already knew what they would find when they arrived: they would see exactly what we saw, learn what we had learned, and arrive at the exact same conclusions we had already reached.

The reasoning was not simple. There would be no prints, no clues of any sort that were meaningful, and nothing to be learned from the interior of the car.

For several reasons: first, as cold as the weather was, the killer would undoubtedly wear gloves when he drove, just as all the honest people in the county pulled on their gloves before they turned the door knob as they left their houses.

Secondly, anyone but a blithering idiot could prevent trace evidence from being found and used. The killer could easily drive to a nearby town and buy coveralls. Wal-Mart sells them by the thousands, as do other discount stores and general stores, and there was no way anyone could ever trace them. Gloves, cap, and coveralls would prevent nearly all possible trace evidence. The only other items would be boots.

Oh, in time, perhaps, the coveralls could be traced. If we had time to search the coveralls, find the inspection marker, contact the manufacturer to learn where the batch inspected by that one person at that one time had been sent, and so on ad infinitum. And we'd narrow the list to about forty thousand people and twice that many if you consider that a woman might have bought them for her man. And we'd already narrowed the list of suspects to people within the county. In this weather it was not likely that anyone from outside was killing our women.

We didn't even have the coveralls. We didn't know for a fact that the killer wore them. For all we knew, he could wear an expensive Italian suit, or work buck naked. He could wear woolen long johns or any of a thousand other possibilities. For all we knew he wore the apparel of the women he killed.

Consider it: a man, a killer, wearing gloves on his hands, new clothing on his body, a cap on his head, and disposable rubber boots on his feet is not going to have much of his body showing. No hair can fall, no fingerprints can be left, and any tracks made by the boots would be useless because the boots were either discarded, burned, buried, or dumped into the lake before the killer called us. The lake was only a short stone's throw from where we stood, and even though it was frozen the killer could knock a hole in the ice and dump in the boots, and within minutes the new ice and snow would cover his tracks in a very literal sense.

The more I reflected on it, the more I was certain that the killer had planned the murders for weeks, even months. He was just waiting for the first five-day snow. If he was intelligent, and there was no doubt that he was, he knew that the snow would in essence make him invisible. It would also account for his absence from whatever job he held. Too many of Sherman's businesses and offices were either closed or were operating on a reduced staff basis.

There were no notes; there were no samples of handwriting or typing for us to consider. We know that certain typewriters have certain quirks or identifiable characteristics: part of a key is damaged and the impression shows that defect. Perhaps the typist makes certain errors or mistakes repeatedly. There were myriads of possible answers or conclusions.

But we had no notes.

We had telephone calls. And we had no points of comparison of the voice types. We had only a couple of second's worth of noises, but even that was difficult at best. Besides, it's easy to disguise one's voice. Not to the point that one could fool voice print experts. Ask Clifford Irving about that. But anyone can disguise his own voice enough to fool even those who know him best. Hold your nose and your voice is totally different. Hold a handkerchief over the mouthpiece and the voice is muffled and indistinct. Pitch your voice higher into a falsetto or lower into a bass tone and even your own mother wouldn't recognize it. Make the call from a pay phone and the phone company records can't help much, other than to tell you where the pay phone is located.

Then all you have to do is find someone who just happened to be passing a certain pay phone at a certain time and just happened to see a certain man dressed strangely and acting highly suspiciously.

Or you can go to Las Vegas and bet the farm on one roll of the dice and become instantly wealthy.

I mentioned the telephone trace to Zane.

"I've done it already," she said. "I called the telephone company for a record of calls. I figured you'd want me to do it but hadn't had a chance to ask."

We both knew that the lie was told out of kindness. The idea that had occurred to me only minutes ago had hit her from the start. But then that's the difference between us: she's a super law officer and I'm a fish out of water. Or rather a swimmer in a pack of sharks.

"And what happened?"

"No records," she said. "Which means that either the local company does not record all calls made from all phones, or the numbskull I had helping me did not know where to look. I suspect the former. Pay phone calls may not be recorded. There's only one other possibility, other than the call from Gallager's."

"Which is?"

"The call was never made through normal channels."

"What other possibilities are there?"

She shrugged. "I have no idea. I'm waiting for something from the local company supervisor. We know that one call was not made from a car or cellular phone, and it was not long distance. One possibility is that it was an interoffice call."

We had turned off our flashlights, and now we stood in total darkness and let the soft snowflakes swirl around us. Neither of us had suggested turning off the lights. We just did it. But in the backs of our minds I suspect that both of us considered the odds that the killer could be as far away as Florida by now, or dangerously near us.

"He could be in the thicket," Zane said. "Watching us."

The thought had occurred to me. "Listening to our absurd theories."

"Laughing like a maniac."

"He is a maniac."

97

She moved closer to me and lowered her voice. "You don't really think that. Neither do I. He could have been aiming a rifle at our heads."

"I know. Being shot is the least favorite part of this job."

"I thought you didn't care if you died. Or if someone killed you."

"Only dying," I said. "Not being killed. That means somebody sucker-punched me."

"Somebody else."

She knew about Edney and Derry. She had to. Everyone else in the county did.

We stood close to shield each other slightly from the snow and wind. We had elected to stand outside in the event we heard any sudden and alarming noises that we should investigate. We heard nothing but the sound of the wind in the trees surrounding us and the occasional swishing noise made when an overloaded limb suddenly bends and drops the snow onto the forest floor.

"There might be deer in the woods," she said.

"Or bears."

"Bears are hibernating."

"Maybe this one is having trouble sleeping. Maybe he woke up hungry."

"There are foxes and bobcats out there."

"Maybe a mountain lion. They're supposed to be extinct. I heard one a couple of weeks ago. And saw the tracks."

"There's one left, then."

"Two, I hope. It wouldn't be much fun to be the last of anything. Nobody to see you gloat."

"Better than being the next to last."

"Good point."

We ran out of anything to say. We stood and listened to the silence and thought.

About the insanity of murder, particularly the murder of two and probably three vaguely beautiful and apparently happy young women who had, to our knowledge, never harmed anyone, never existed as a threat to anyone, or in any way motivated such savage cruelty.

About the apparently senselessness of the related factors: all left-handed; the two first victims having given birth out of wedlock and while still in their teens; all members of the same seemingly silly and informal social club; all girls from the less affluent circles and perhaps having married wealthy men and under the guidelines of prenuptial contracts.

This latter factor was something I would have to check as soon as we stopped chasing our tails. I'd been over it a hundred times in my mind already: the plan was apparent, if the motives were not. The killer had an agenda, and he planned to carry it out to the letter.

Whatever his reasons, he had the urgency to kill at least three women: not in a rabid frenzy but with what must have been a cold, calculating, unspeakably cruel, and totally amoral manner. He was not a shark driven mad by the smell of blood. He was a killing machine. And I hoped, but doubted, that he'd stop at three.

"Tell me again what you think," Zane said softly. After the moments of silence, her small voice startled me.

"First, I'm scared."

"Me, too. I didn't think men were ever scared."

"We're always scared," I said. "We just don't admit it."

"So what do you think, scared or not?"

"When I was a kid we kept chickens. One night a weasel got into the coop and methodically and coldly killed every chicken we owned. No reason. Just animal lust."

"But that's not what we have here?"

"No. If five of us robbed a bank, I'd want the other four to die before they could finger me."

"The killer is eliminating people who could incriminate him?"

"Something like that."

"What's the secret crime?"

"If we knew that, we'd stop him." I called the office and Bum answered. As usual, he seemed to have been awakened from a deep slumber, but, again as always, his mind was alert and his body was ready.

"Anything else on the wire?" I asked him.

"No calls of importance," he said, "except that everyone is scared to death and every noise is a killer trying to break in and slaughter them. Can't say I blame them. If I was a young and pretty woman, I'd not go to the toilet except in a crowd."

"Do me a favor," I said. "It'll get you a cussing, but call the county manager and ask him if we can meet for a few minutes tomorrow morning. Tell him it's urgent. Besides, it'll save him a call. He's probably been trying to call me all day and night."

"Only eight times," Bum said. "I assured him that you are hot on the trail of the killer but that you are hip-deep in snow and can't get to a phone."

"Thanks," I said. "A lot."

"A pleasure," he said. "I don't much care for important people."

Another one of my subordinates looking out for me.

"I'll call him," he said. "I been cussed before. Once more won't hurt. Just another mosquito's wing. Be careful in the dark."

I wanted to be careful; I just didn't know how.

His comment about the mosquito's wing was something I had borrowed from Thoreau who advised us to spend one day as deliberately as nature and not be thrown off the track by every nutshell and mosquito's wing that falls along the rails. I used the quote one day and Bum latched onto it. He was like that. You can say something and you'd think he never heard a word. Then six months later he'd repeat the comment word for word.

He was quite easily the most dangerous man I had ever known, and that includes the ones I shared a prison cell with. He never blustered, threatened, or boasted, but I had seen him sit totally unruffled while a huge redneck threatened to cut his throat, and then with a blur of motion lay the attacker unconscious with one quick movement. He never talked about his experiences in Vietnam, but inside his desk drawer he keeps a small box holding the medals he received: enough of them to make me want to salute him when he passed me. Sometimes he'd open the desk drawer and simply sit with his hand atop the box: he never smiled, frowned, or moved for minutes at a time. It was as if he was in a different world, if only for a few moments. Rick informed me of the one citation that described how he slipped through the jungles and slit one throat after another as he led a patrol through enemy lines.

He was the weasel with a motive.

I, too, had a motive. I had to keep the job I hated. Without the job I had only apprehension and trepidation.

"May I harass you for a few moments?" I asked Zane.

"Anytime," she said. "Fire when ready, Smedley." When she was a newcomer to the office, I had savaged the old "Fire when ready, Gridley" quote to the Jimmy Hatlo bastardization, and Zane had picked up on it.

"You ever been married?" I hated to ask questions I already knew the answers to.

"Yes."

I could sense her stiffening in the dark.

"I'm not being nosy," I said. "You were in the same high school class with the murdered women. Are you left-handed?"

"You never noticed?" she asked. I couldn't tell if she was hurt or merely pouting. "Yes, I am."

"Did you ever do any rockhounding?"

She moved closer to me and seemed to shiver with sudden chill.

"Yes, and before you ask, I have a necklace with a single rose beryl stone on it. I never wear it. I don't even know where it is."

"Was your husband wealthy?"

"Incredibly. His father operated a fleet of trucks that covered the entire South."

"Are you divorced?"

"No. I'm a widow."

"Oh. Sorry. The war?"

I could see her nodding her head in the darkness. "Without a doubt the war killed him," she said. "He was so scared that he'd be drafted that he left me and headed for Canada. He was killed in a car wreck near Jackman, Maine."

"Prenuptial agreement?"

"Yes," she said. "When Jack was killed, I signed over all my claims back to the family. I didn't want any of their money. Now may I harass you?"

"Fire when ready, Smedley."

"Are you going to keep on seeing Laura Dennis?"

I didn't answer for several moments.

"I take that as an affirmative," she said in a voice much colder than the wind or the snow or the frozen lake only yards from where we stood. We could hear the groaning of the ice that had formed on the lake days before the snows began. It sounded like a mourning whale. I thought of the days not many years earlier when loggers actually drove teams of horses that dragged monster logs across the small river that now fed the lake.

"One more time," I said.

"You're insane," Zane said. "You know you can't go on seeing her. My God, Chess, she's the county manager's wife."

"I didn't know she was married when I first dated her," I said.

"You damn well know it now. Break it off, Chess. When, not if, the county manager finds out, he'll have your job."

"I know."

"He has enough money and influence that he could have himself fired, if he set his mind to it. You have nearly everyone at the college hating you as it is. You have every black person in the county thinking you killed Edney Parkins and then killed Pawnee and let the world think she and Jernigan killed Edney and your wife. You have to face it sooner or later, Chess, that the people in this county who don't hate you actually loathe and abominate you."

She stopped short, then began again. "You know I don't mean that, Chess. It's just that I don't want to see you lose this job and go back. I don't want to see you leave...." She didn't have to complete the thoughts.

"You love your cabin and your woods, and you love the classroom. Maybe some day—"

"Not in this lifetime," I assured her. "I'll go back to the university when it has been reliably ascertained that hell has frozen over and the imps of the perverse are ice-skating down there. No, when I leave this office, I leave town."

She bristled. "All the more reason to keep your pants zipped," she almost snarled. "Or at least find you a woman whose husband isn't a threat to you."

Then, before she could stop herself, she blurted out, "Someone like me."

"Oh, damn," she said quickly. "I didn't mean to say that. I promised myself I'd never say it."

Her chagrin turned to anger, and she lashed out at me again, this time with more fervor.

"Forget I said it! To hell with it and with you and with me. You are a damn fool for caring about her and I'm a bigger one for caring about you. Get yourself fired! Get yourself killed! Get yourself into more trouble than you'll ever get out of. Lose your house and your woods and your life and everything you care about and everyone who cares about you! Damn this snow, these killings, and you. I don't care anymore what you do!"

I couldn't argue with anything she said. I found myself in trouble the first time when I tried to help a helpless old lady who had in one of her toes more nobility than most people will see in a lifetime, and the stupidity that led me to try to become Sir Galahad left me more as Don Quixote who drove a battered old Honda rather than riding a skinny and decrepit old nag.

I preferred to think of myself as an idealist, but I knew the term was flawed. No. I was flawed. It's not courage to leap into a shark-infested ocean to save a person who is beyond salvation; it's stupidity.

And I had leaped into far too many of the shark pools, with the results never varying: I was lucky to get out alive. Frost said that innocence often gets its own way, but he never wrote that stupid judgment wins that many battles.

I turned to Zane in the darkness and awaited her next attack. She had more to say, but the glow of headlights and the sound of tires crunching snow stopped her. Seconds later Wadsworth and the others arrived.

"One more time," I said gently. "Not for sex. That hasn't been part of it for a long time. I need to ask her about the killings and to tell her that it's all over between us."

I could see her face glowing in the dark.

"You mean it," she said simply. "God! You mean it."

"Yes," I said.

We didn't have time to say anything else. I was grateful. Already on thin ice, I was ready to plunge again, stupidly, into the same frigid waters that had nearly claimed my life on half a dozen occasions.

The cars pulled to a stop and the occupants seemed to tumble from the cars at once. Rick advanced toward me and said very simply, "He's killed Katherine Thennis. He told us where to find the body."

I didn't ask where the body was. I thought I already knew. First, my car. Then my woods. Each time it was closer to something closer to me.

103

"He said that it was where you first seduced the wife of the county manager. He said it was in your groundhog burrow."

"Did you talk to him?"

He shook his head. "A nurse from the hospital."

I tried not to remember the first night Laura Dennis came to my place; we made love on the couch in the basement. It was a hot night and the basement was cool and perfect. I had called the basement a groundhog burrow because it was dark and secluded and I was protected there. I thought.

What didn't make sense was how the killer knew. Another question was how long before everyone in town knew.

Lurch was still waiting for an answer.

"Let's go," I said. I told them where the body was.

NINE

There was no way we could hurry. All we could do was creep through the snow at a snail's pace. The seconds ticked past with agonizing slowness. Our drive could not have taken more than half an hour, but to me it seemed that we could have driven to the West Coast in the same amount of time.

I felt ill, lethargic, and incredibly sleepy. Overcome with a soporific contentment, all the way to Buffalo Creek I fought to stay awake, and my sleepiness had nothing to do with the fact that I could not recall the last time I had closed my eyes except to blink. I had not seen a newspaper since the first call came in, and I had not taken the time to watch even one second of television news.

It was the short-circuiting of my mental switches that debilitated me.

There had been no time for anything normal. And that, of course, was part of the killer's plan. He was practicing overkill in the most literal sense of the word.

He had planned it carefully. Either that, or he was in a panic.

I could not imagine panic on his part. His scheme was a good one, in a perverted, evil sense. He simply was leaving us no time to gather our forces, make plans, produce evidence and gather lab results.

We were in a hornet's nest and thousands of insects were buzzing, biting, stinging, and terrifying us, and standing still and staying calm and rational was an impossibility. Frantic running and fighting back seemed to be the only logical reactions.

And the killer knew that. His plan was obvious: he would keep us in such a frenetic pace that we could have no time in which to use reason and common sense.

Killers don't do that. They typically, if typicality is even possible to assess, commit their act, go into hiding, and stay there until the heat is off, at which time they strike again. Or they sate themselves with the blood and agony and suffering of the victim and the victim's family, and only when the satiety wears off and they need a new fix do they kill again.

This killer either did not know the rules or he deliberately planned to avoid them at every turn. To me, the latter was far more likely.

He killed with careful premeditation. The fact that the women were all in the same high school class was cause enough for us to start looking for a link. I reviewed the characteristics of the dead women: married to wealthy men, left-handed, same high school class, rose-beryl stones, members of the same club.

And I came up with nothing.

But I could not afford to overlook anything, no matter how trivial it might seem. If all had been redheaded, we'd need to try to find the linkage. If all shopped at the same market, drove the same model or even color of car, or liked pizza, we could not disregard the possible tie-ins. Not as desperate as we were.

All victims so far had no children since they had been married, and all have given birth before marriage. Presumably the husband and the father were not the same man, which caused me to think, idiotically, of the old Benny Hill line in which the mother says about her newborn child, "He has his father's eyes but my husband's mouth."

All the members belonged to the same private club, and, as far as we could tell, they all belonged to an unofficial offshoot of the club or to a group that met because of common interests or backgrounds or motivations. It was not even a real club; it was only a group of women sharing a single interest. Or passion. Or frustration. Or fear.

Or hatred.

And we needed to follow up on the high school ties, to learn what these women had in common then and now. We felt a compulsion to

106

study the fact that they were all of the same age, give or take a month or two. Killers often choose children, but they take them where they find them. Same with older women. Rapist-killers often want good-looking women, sexy-looking women, or big-breasted women. There are no fixed criteria. Sometimes they want only the available women. At times it is the power thing: they can scare, terrify, frighten the women into hysteria, and from the fears of the victim the rapists derive their gratification.

It was crucial that we explore the social club and its little corollary. We had to learn why the club was formed, why only women were members, and why the ancillary club came into being. We could not afford to allow anything to keep us from delving deeply into the deeper-seated motivations behind the clubs, if any existed.

The left-handedness could not be overlooked, nor could we wait even another hour before we searched for links. The same was true of the pre-marriage births. We had to learn what became of the babies, whether they lived or died, whether they were adopted by local parents or out-of-town or state parents.

But we could not pause in our frantic pace even to make a quick phone call or question the parents, the husband, the social circle, work place colleagues. We could not pause to do one damn thing. Except to look for hostage or kidnap victims.

Or for their bodies.

It was an ingenious tack, unquestionably. A man in a flood-swollen river or wildfire cannot pause to worry, to reflect, or to ponder. He must beat at the flames frantically or swim with all his strength and energy.

Above all, he cannot afford to lose his head and abandon his sense of perspective.

Yet that is precisely what we were doing. We were dashing ineffectually and frantically in all directions. We had to hurry to a location, ask three or four quick questions, and dart to the next danger area. We drove up and down the roads of the mountain county as fast as conditions would permit. We hesitated to try to question or investigate by telephone because we needed to keep our own lines open.

We could not sleep because the killer could be selecting his next victim while we were getting our beauty rest. Even if it were only because of negative publicity, and it was a great deal more, we could not afford to rest. We did not need to be told what the effect would be if a young wife was killed brutally while the entire sheriff's department—or only the sheriff—slept like a baby, oblivious to the carnage.

I kept coming back to the same thoughts. Because only the killer knew where he was at all times and what his next moves would be, we never knew where he was, what he was doing, or what he was planning. All we knew was where he had been. Yet he could know where we were at any time.

He could eat casually, sleep as he wished, watch television, engage in chess games, take long and relaxing hikes, or go bird-watching.

He was completely in charge. He had all the advantages. He could send us to the north of the county while he picked out his next victim in the south. Or the east, or west, or even in the north, within a mile of us, and we'd never know it, unless we got lucky. And luck had not favored us.

I detested the idea of luck because it suggested that we were so inept that we must rely upon freak chance to help us defeat one man. Worst of all, it was like the preacher I once heard who prayed that a new liver could be found for a preacher friend whose own liver failed. He did not realize that he was praying not simply for a liver but that a young, healthy, and vital young man or woman must be tragically killed in order for the liver to be available. I could not bear to hope, even in the darkest recesses of my mind, that the pervert would kill one time too many and we'd catch him.

The victim would undoubtedly have hoped that he had killed one time less even if he had never been caught.

I did not want to see another woman killed, injured, frightened, or even put in danger. But I wanted the animal destroyed.

Our killer had chosen the most secluded spot he could find. My cabin.

And if I was on the road or at the scene where the latest body was found, there was little danger that I'd surprise him at my place.

We could split up, as we had done earlier in the night, and have three cars, rather than one, patrolling, but the division of forces did nothing to help us. The killer had dumped his latest corpse, and no one, as far as we knew, had seen him or his car or his motor scooter, snowmobile, skis, roller blades, or mule.

Most people were at home in bed, with their doors locked and their loved ones around them. Most, not all. Some people worked the night shift, but they were inside the mills or the stores or the hospitals. Others returned home late from trips, but the odds were incredibly great that they would see anything suspicious. Even the deer spot-lighters were not out. They ran too great a risk of being stuck with a deer carcass in their trucks.

No. Everyone was indoors. Except for us, the killer, and the latest and possibly the newest victim. The hornets were buzzing and stinging and all we could do is run frantically or slap ineffectually. There was no time for rest, sleep, or meals. But the killer had perhaps slept soundly all day and was ready to spend his night pursuing whatever sickness fascinated him. I wondered, and feared, where it would end. Did it go on until the killer ran out of victims, died by his own hand, or of old age? Was there nothing within our powers that we could do? Except ride the snowy roads of Sherman County?

I remembered the note pad in my pocket and pulled it out, directed the beam of the flashlight on the telephone numbers, and dialed the top number. Benjamin Tyler answered in a grumpy and fatigued voice.

"Sorry to bother you," I said, "but I need to know about the DOLLS club some of the women had formed. Do you have anything that would help me?"

He was instantly alert but not happy. "Ivy?" he said. "Is that you? Do you know what time it is?"

I assured him that my Timex was running perfectly and asked again if he could help us. I noticed that he did not bother with a title before my name.

"A stupid club," he said finally. "A pointless club. Not even a club. Just an excuse for some old hens to get together and dish the dirt and waste time."

"Your wife never talked about it?"

"She never told and I never asked. What did I care about their recipe swapping? They didn't bother me and they didn't cost a lot of money. So what's to tell, and what does this have to do with my wife's death and your not doing your job?"

I didn't argue with him. It would have been an exercise in futility.

109

Instead I asked how long the club had existed.

"It started in high school, then they quit meeting after they graduated. Then a couple of years ago it started again."

I dialed another number and heard the slurred voice of Bert Webley. I went through the same questions.

"I asked Alisha about it once or twice," he said, "but she wouldn't talk about it. She never told me anything. To this day I have no idea why they met or how they got started in the first place. You think this club had anything to do with the killings?" I told him I didn't know what if anything it had to do with anything and then dialed another number as soon as we had hung up.

"Marlin Rockwell," the voice said. He didn't sound as if he had been to bed at all. Some men—and women—are like that. They can wake from a sound sleep and be alert and cheerful, just as some women look like a million dollars the moment they open their eyes, while others require an hour to get the puffiness from their faces and the bile from their voices. "May I help you?"

"It's Chess Ivy," I said, apologizing for the lateness of the call and asking him about the club. "Yes," he said after a short pause. "The ladies started the club here at the school, I understand. The left-handed club, I presume you mean. From what I knew, it had to do only with the fact that all of them were wrong-handed. It was more of a running joke that involved some kids who were peripheral at best in the social life of the school. It appeared to be wholesome enough. I never heard anything to the contrary."

I thanked him for his help and for his civility and again I apologized for the lateness. "No problem whatsoever," he said. "You feel free to call anytime you think I may be of help. If you happen to miss me, leave a message and I'll call you as soon as I can get back to you."

"Thanks for the food," I said. "And thank your people for me."

"I'll do it," he said, "and you are more than welcome."

I thanked him and hung up again, then called Ed Gallager's newspaper office. As I expected, there was no answer. I dialed the operator and asked her to put a call through to his house.

There was no answer for several rings. Then a sleepy, fat voice answered. A woman's voice.

Fat was the only word I could think of that described the way she sounded. The talkie movies proved that looks and voice often are strangers to each other, but this voice was thick and raspy; I could hear a wheezing that so often accompanies obese body styles.

"Hello?" she rasped.

"This is Sheriff Ivy," I said. "I need to talk with the newspaper editor. Tell him it's rather important."

"He's not here," she said. "I don't know when he'll be in."

I thanked her and hung up. I had no idea why I called. I had never heard Gallager mention a wife or children. I made a mental note to ask him about his family later.

I felt myself becoming instantly sleepy again. Zane and I were in the final car of the short entourage. She had pointedly waited for the others to proceed so the others could not see my bobbing head as I found myself falling asleep every few seconds. I rolled down the window, stuck my head out into the frigid air, and was shocked into instant alertness. Then, within seconds of the time that I closed the window, my head seemed to topple off my shoulders. My chin rested on my chest, and I thought I felt Zane's hand, strangely warm, cover my own.

When the car stopped, I woke suddenly and stared in sudden and renewed disbelief that I, who had for years been a staid and stolid English professor, was out in a blizzard to search for dead bodies and the killer of them.

Zane's hand was gone, if it had ever been there. I opened the door and felt the blast of cold air against my face, and again all semblance of drowsiness vanished like a burst bubble.

The others had parked in the wide parking space and had started toward the house. Flashlight beams darted into the woods, along the edge of the road, and even into the uppermost tree branches. We had spread out and moved up slowly to the porch. Rance made his way around to the back of the house to where Buffalo Creek flowed within a hundred feet of the cabin. Zane and I followed him. The creek is, except for a few places, shallow, swift, and narrow. It heads atop a gentle mountain on the northern tip of my property, is fed by two dozen or more springs as it begins its descent, and then pours over the rock face of a cliff that stops a hundred feet from my cabin. The creek runs behind my house, making a graceful rainbow around the cabin site, then flows into the lake three hundred yards downstream. The creek starts as a rill three feet wide and enters the lake after reaching a width of more than twenty feet and a depth of six to eight feet.

We started at the roadside and moved from the cars in the direction of the creek, and we had gone less than the length of a tall poplar before Rance paused. I saw it at the same time.

The basement door of my cabin was standing open. My first reaction was outrage that the interior of the cabin would be freezing. Then, before the thought had taken form, I recoiled at the awareness of what the open door meant.

From where I stood I could see that the basement door had been forced, as if the killer wanted to be certain we saw it. I held my breath as we covered the final space and paused outside the doorway.

"He could still be inside," Wooley said. Rowena Cullen had appeared to the left of a huge white pine, as if the pine would somehow protect her from the wind or worse. Her .45 was in her right hand with her left hand curved over her other hand. I hoped no one made a sudden move. STOP training or not, she appeared terrified, ready to fire at the first sound or movement.

"He may have called from the cabin," Wadsworth suggested as we neared the cabin. The thought chilled me more than the wind had done. I had heard people talk of how they felt defiled, contaminated, when someone had illegally entered their residences. I now knew the feeling. I didn't know if I would ever be able to use the telephone in my house again. Or the basement. My only consolation, and it was a slight one, was that we did not know whether there was a body inside the house.

Not yet.

It did not take us long to find out. Jhon Rance, weapon held high and at the ready, held his flashlight in his other hand and approached the door. He shoved it open with his foot and quickly directed the beam of light around the huge room.

He hesitated for several long seconds, like a hound warily sniffing the still but tense body of the copperhead. I imagined that I could pick up the faint but certain scent of fear in him as he waited, expectantly, at the doorway of the room.

We waited, too. The first and perhaps the last thing we wanted to do was walk in on the killer. There was no doubt in my mind that he had departed earlier, possibly even hours ago.

But if he happened to be in the room, there would be blood, and not all of it was likely to be his. Rance leaned forward, as if cantilevered, his dread at the thought of entering that room measurable, tangible as mire in a swamp.

I could hear the faint whisper from somewhere behind me. Wind sighed mournfully in the tall snow-laden pines behind my cabin.

My cabin!

Not any more. It had been contaminated, polluted beyond all purification. I did not think it would ever be clean again.

Then Rance stepped inside and flipped the light switch and the basement room was flooded with light. The body of the woman, Katherine Thennis, lay on the couch near the south wall. One glance told us that she had died in the same manner as the others had.

She was fully clothed, but the garments she wore had been slashed to ribbons and crimson seeped from the vents.

For a long moment there was a chilled silence in the room. From upstairs I could hear a creaking sound that in my wild and vivid imagination could have been the soft footsteps of a killer crossing the board floors of the cabin.

Then I realized that I was hearing the ticking of the old clock that stood on the bookshelves in the den. The clock had long been one of my treasured possessions, but now it, like nearly everything else I owned, had been contaminated by the evil presence of the man who wanted to spill the blood of the young women in Sherman County. I couldn't call anything my own any more. It was like trying to salvage the treasure you had accidentally dropped into a cesspool.

Shakespeare had Ophelia warn us that rich gifts wax poor when givers prove unkind. The Bard could have added that treasures lose their value when they are smeared with blood and filth and when the most hateful and despicable forces in life demean and debase them.

Another sound registered in my brain. It was the heavy, almost sensual breathing of Jhon Rance, who stood, legs spread wide apart, like a pagan god of some sort. He was almost panting, partly from fear but largely from excitement. I could not tell if it was the scene of the crime or the exposed body of what had earlier been an attractive young woman.

Then everybody was talking at once, but I was not hearing them. I turned away from the body and stumbled outdoors. I did not want to think about the progression.

The first body had been found in the trunk of my car.

The second was in the woods near my cabin.

The third was on the couch in my basement.

I did not want to think where the next one would be.

TEN

The snow had started again, lightly this time, as I stepped into the morning darkness outside my own house and leaned heavily against a huge white pine tree and trembled violently. A body in my car, in my woods, in my basement, and there was no way to guess when it would all stop.

Ed Gallager had been kind in the Sherman *Guardian*. I knew this when I picked up one of the papers that someone had brought in from my mailbox. I was halfway through the story when I saw the words written in ballpoint pen beside a quote I had made to the effect that we were turning up leads and were getting closer to the killer. "Dream on, you incompetent hayseed!" At the end of the challenge was the double signature: Zimri and Ehud.

I nearly dropped the paper. Instead, with trembling hands I laid the paper down on a table and walked away from it. He had sat inside my house and read my paper and doubtless eaten my food and drunk my beer. In a mixture of rage and horror I walked away from the table and saw that my fears were confirmed: a dirty plate and cup were in the sink. I opened the garbage can and saw three empty beer cans.

I picked up the paper again and stared at the words and the signature. I pored over the neat loops and swirls that tilted backward with grace

115

and flourish.

A left-handed person had written the words! I dropped the paper and hurried to my library, picked up a dictionary and looked up the phrase "left-handed." One definition that caught my eye was "morganatic." Other definitions were "inferior" and "weak."

I flipped to the *M* section of the book and found the word. The definition included a reference to the marriage agreements made between royalty and commoners, or persons of inferior rank.

In the set of encyclopedias I kept in the office I found that rose beryl was the stone commonly associated with morganatic marriages. There was no entry for Zimri.

I replaced the book on the shelf and turned to leave. Then I pulled out the index to the encyclopedias and turned to the *Z* section. I found Zimri between Zimocca sponge and zinc. The page reference was for Volume 16, page 788A.

Turning quickly to the entry, I scanned the brief article rapidly. The reference was to I Kings, Chapter 16, verse 16. I was intrigued. Volume 16, chapter 16, verse 16.

Then I began my search for Ehud. I found him in the Book of Judges, Chapter 3, verse 15. The phrase leaped out at me: "a man left-handed."

I read frantically, flipping through pages, scanning as fast as I could and still derive some semblance of meaning. It was taking too long. I'd be there the rest of the day.

I called to Rick Blanton, who told me to give him a minute. It took five. I could hear him rustling pages of books twenty feet away from me.

"Best information I can find," he said, "is that there are only two left-handed people mentioned in the Bible. One is Ehud. A questionable one is Zimri, not left-handed but a man known for his cruelty. He was not only a murderer but a rather sadistic person. For recreation he apparently killed the king. His reign of terror lasted seven days. He was the son of Zerah, but there must have been two of them. One passage says that Jehoadah begat Zimri, whose daughter was Moza. Any of this help?"

"I think so," I told him.

I put down the paper and hurried to the bathroom and found the damp towel and spots of blood in the shower. The son of a bitch had used my bathroom and shower and towels. I made a passionate mental note to go through the house and discard anything that I even suspected that he might have defiled.

As I paced, not knowing anything else more profitable to do, I let Ed Gallager's account run through my mind. He had assuredly been generous. He could have used the opportunities to flay me alive, but he had been very reserved. He reported the crimes matter-of-factly and with every effort to subdue the elements of sensationalism inherent in such tales. At no time did he attempt to direct public invective toward me.

That surprised me. Ed surely realized that my position was not a good one: not with every body having been dumped close to where I live—in every sense. Ed had come to Sherman shortly after the former editor of the paper, up to his ears in a white slavery racket, seemed to have committed suicide in his parked car late one night.

I say "seemed" to commit suicide because in such cases it is often impossible to know precisely what happened. Most people guessed that the late editor knew that his involvement would be impossible to cover and chose the cowardly way out. I never saw it in exactly those terms. To me, deliberately sending a bullet crashing up through your brain is not the sort of thing a fragile person would do. I always thought that if I ever chose that option of dealing with a problem, I'd try my best to be killed by a jealous husband. Failing in that, I suspect an overdose would be the most pleasant way, if such exists.

Wrist-slitting, hanging, shooting, drowning, and leaping off a tall building or flinging oneself in front of a speeding bus always seemed to me to be too much in the category of performing your own frontal lobotomy with a mattock. Cold showers are preferable.

What really happened to our late, unlamented editor? While no one knows for certain, with one possible exception, my guess is that he did not fire the bullet into his own brain, and it wasn't simply the absence of a note that pointed me in that direction. Lots of suicides do not leave notes. They just leave, and they don't come back, so don't leave the latchstring out for them.

One person may know for certain, but I've never found the opportune time to ask him about it. I don't ever intend to ask him. That particular hound is snoring loudly, and I'm not about to whistle. I was tired of waking anything with fangs.

My chief deputy, who by every right ought to be sheriff and would be if he were not such a friend, Rick Blanton, aka Lurch, was the one who found the body.

He says.

He just might have caused the man to become a body rather than a person. Rick was with me when Pawnee Traynor, an old girl friend who also happened to be a deputy when I was released from prison to be-

117

come sheriff, and Candy Jernigan, an egg-with-legs blob who had as much business in law enforcement as a eunuch had with a credit card at the whorehouse, met their Maker in highly unpleasant manners.

They had planned to kill me and claim the insurance money to add to the money they had stolen from me earlier. Rick helped me to keep money that had come to me when Derry was killed. He also helped them change their minds about killing me. Nothing is more persuasive in mind-changing than being killed brutally and legally.

But Rick knew that the editor had been as guilty as Candy or Pawnee or any of the others had been, and nothing seems to rankle Rick as much as seeing criminals go unpunished. It is his one real weakness, if that is what it is. He is unperturbed by all sorts of unpleasantness; I doubt that an atomic bomb blast would unnerve him severely. But when he hears of child abuse, he goes into a rage. He also has a thing about being loyal to friends.

He somehow in spite of the evil surrounding him every time he sees a newspaper or answers a call has managed to hang onto a large chunk of chivalry, a word that has all but lost its meaning in the modern world. He cares about children, dogs, stray cats, and ladies.

Not women: ladies. He respects them, opens doors for them, and speaks in his best English to them. He would never dream of using an obscenity in the presence of a real lady. But if you or anyone else hurts one, he goes into a rage.

He and Derry were good friends. They respected and admired each other greatly. And when Edney Parkins and the editor found a way to ruin me and corrupt her, Rick let the animal inside him out of its cage. And when the editor ate his gun inside that lonely car one dark night, I had reason to think that Rick may have tied the napkin around his neck.

Do I think that Rick somehow lured the editor out to the lake and somehow forced the man to blow his brains out? I don't want to know; therefore, I shall never mention the topic to Rick or to anyone else. And Rick will never say. Like Walter Mitty, he will be inscrutable to the last.

But, as Byron said about the Prisoner's brother, why deny the truth: he died. And the *Guardian* was left editor-less, until Ed Gallager, who told me he had spent his life working as a reporter for a series of small papers and editor of a string of tiny ones, took all of his savings and bought the

Guardian from the editor's estate and has been in Sherman ever since.

I not only appreciate but admire his restraint in the way he handled the murders, but I didn't know how long he could keep it up. Three women killed in three days, and all three bodies found on my property. How could he keep from commenting on the series of horrible crimes? How long could he keep from wondering out loud about my involvement with the women?

How could he avoid speculating about the progressions? One in my car: I drove it around town much of the day; one in my woods where I spent part of nearly every day and where I could find pleasure in all types of weather; one in my basement. I wondered how Ed could explain his own role? In the first case, the killer had called his office. Ditto the second. Why? He couldn't simply be wanting ink. He'd get the coverage, regardless of whether he called the editor, me, or the tooth fairy, unless the latter was dating his dentist at the time. It would be only a matter of time before Ed was forced to take a stand, one way or another, and it would be a nanosecond later that those who don't already want my scalp would be howling for it. There would be hundreds, or more, demanding that if I don't put a stop to the killings and find me a murderer, I should be removed from office.

And they'd want Rick Blanton to take my place. Even I could not argue the point. The only reason Lurch was not sheriff now is that he doesn't want to be. No, that's not totally true. He may want to be, but he doesn't want me not to be.

Confusing? Not really. As I've said, when I was in prison, the only way I could be released was to have a job, and the people at Sherman University did not like me greatly. They, in point of fact, hated me. The president would have enjoyed seeing my eyes eaten out by fire ants, but since he could not arrange that, he did the next best. He pulled more strings than a puppet master and kept me from getting a job anywhere in the county.

It was elementary: I had to have a job. Either that, or stay in prison, the world's equivalent to fire ants and unprotected eyes. So when I had an opportunity to run for sheriff, Rick Blanton could have beaten me without making a single speech or kissing a single baby's mother. He refused to run, telling the press that, like an infamous predecessor in the area, if nominated he would not run and if elected he would not serve.

Actually he told the reporters to engage in aeronautical intercourse with a revolving pastry. He stayed in the background and let me win the election.

But that same ugly specter reared its ugly rear every time I pause to think about the murders as they relate personally to me. If there is enough public clamor, I could be booted from my job. If that happens, I find other employment or I go back to prison.

I had gone over this earlier, while I stood in the middle of a country road in a snowstorm. I didn't like my conclusions then and I liked them less now.

If he could do it legally, Rick could accept the job, if I were booted, and then appoint me deputy. But the law will not permit me to work as a sheriff's deputy. I am a former felon, and as such I cannot be deputy.

But I can be sheriff! I don't make the rules, and I don't pretend to understand them. But if the public should decide I must go, then I'll go, if unwillingly. The public, once it realizes its power, can have anything it wants. And it can get rid of anything it doesn't want.

I don't know how long I stayed there, leaning against the tree and feeling the soft flakes of snow filter down the back of my neck. I didn't want to go into my own house, and I wondered how I would manage to sleep there again, assuming that I found the time to sleep in the foreseeable future.

But I had to go in, and did. Rick was standing in the middle of the basement floor and making copious notes in the little book he carried with him everywhere he went. He once confessed to me that the notebook contains more poetry than crime notes. I never asked to read his poetry and he never offered. But I'd bet my last job, this one, that he's as good at poetry as he is at everything else.

When he saw me he came over and spoke softly. He was not being secretive; he is simply a very quiet person.

"A carbon copy of the others," he said. "It's as if the guy processed them all through a fax machine. He's not very original, but that's as much as we can determine. Nothing in the pockets, no marks that weren't on the others. The wounds are very similar and may have been made with the same weapon, or one like it. As before, not one hint of where

120

she has been or who took her there. The medical examiner will be along soon, but I can tell you that he's not going to find anything that he didn't find earlier."

It was incredible to me. "How?" I asked Lurch. "How can any man, woman, or beast kidnap three women, haul them around, and then kill them, and not leave a clue, trace evidence, or some hint of what happened and where? How can it be possible that no one saw the women as they were captured? The guy can't be invisible, and even if he is, his victims aren't."

He shrugged, his massive shoulders moving like tectonic plates on a fault line. "You remember Chesterton's 'Invisible Man'? Maybe it's the same."

Lurch would be the last of the Renaissance men if it were not for the fact that there are some topics he doesn't give a hoot about and therefore refuses to learn. He hates math and will master only enough of it to balance a checkbook. And he does not care greatly about psychology and sociology. But nearly all else is one constant lesson for him.

I knew the story. G. K. Chesterton wrote of a murder committed in broad daylight and yet no one saw anyone entering or leaving the premises, and yet someone had to do so. The solution, as Father Brown explained it, was that the killer was the postman who was, for practical purposes, seen daily for years and years by so many people that they no longer see him. He is a fixture in their minds and would be noticed only if he did not appear. Like the buzz in a florescent tube that we notice only when it stops. "I think G. K. Chesterton did it," Lurch said. "Or Father Brown was the mailman."

I knew what he meant, and it wasn't an idle guess. I doubt that Lurch ever thinks lightly. He can give you an opinion off the top of his head, it seems, but he had given it the thought process it deserved. He just happened to think much faster and much better than most people.

"She has not been dead long," Lurch said. "We're getting closer. He's only a matter of hours ahead of us."

I was still disconsolate. "If it were only seconds, it would still be too much."

"Don't forget," he urged. "He's had days, weeks, months, even years to get ready for this. He's had time to make all sorts of arrangements, to plan every step, to have everything in total readiness. He had too much of a head start on us for us to catch him instantly, except for a fluke."

He started to add a thought when the phone rang. I held up a hand for Lurch to hold his thought and answered the jangling phone. My heart was pounding.

"Chess," the soft voice said, and instantly I was flooded with both relief and apprehension when I heard Laura's voice. "Can you talk?"

I wondered why she thought I couldn't. The news of this latest killing couldn't have spread yet.

"Somewhat," I said vaguely. I had no way of knowing when someone would enter the room or whether I could be heard from the steps to the basement.

"I needed to hear your voice," she said. "We've in trouble. Jasper suspects."

I felt the oily cold oozing down my spine. The last thing I needed was to have an angry husband gunning for me, with all the other violence the town was experiencing. Jasper was her mild code word in case anyone happened to overhear. In addition, I strongly suspected, she does not even like to mouth the name of her husband. Jeff had been mouthed enough, she once told me, and the sales of Listerine had soared.

"Has he said anything specific?" I was trying to be as vague as possible in case we had eavesdroppers. "Or is this a personal evaluation?"

There was a long silence, as if she was trying to think of a soft way of saying it. "I lied," she said simply. "I just need to talk to you."

"Not wise," I said. "Very unwise."

"It's important," she said.

"To you or me?"

"Both of us. But more important to other people. Like Katherine Thennis. And the others."

My pulse quickened incredibly. My chest thumped with anxiety and excitement.

"You know something?"

There was a long silence. Rick had moved discreetly out of the cabin. I could see him through the window. The cabin was icy cold and I shivered each time the wind gusted. The timbers creaked ominously in the high winds.

"I know everything," she said. "Can I come see you." She added quickly, "Just to talk."

"Tell me now." I had no patience with people who had to have the stage set for them to make their dramatic revelations.

"Jasper is near," she said, her voice dropping to a near-whisper. "I can't take the chance. I can't be left without anything. I've put up with too much for that to happen."

Seconds earlier all I wanted was a bath, a giant steak, a twelve-hour nap, and a killer behind bars. Or dead. And I wanted them in reverse order. Was she offering him to me? I became acutely aware of how long it had been since I had a shower.

I felt unbearably filthy. I had worn the same clothes since the horrors started. I had passed the point of needing sleep. I doubted that I could have slept under any circumstances, other than having the killer behind bars or in the morgue.

I thought in a flash of the hundreds of books and movies I had experienced in which the hero of the story says through clenched teeth that he will get the killer, that the heroine can bet the farm on that.

I felt no such confidence. I was facing stark reality, and it told me that the way things were going the killer would die of old age, or run out of victims, before any of us had any notion of where to search for him.

"He'll divorce you," I said. "Leave you without a cent? It can't happen. The courts will see that you—"

"No they won't," she said, her voice thick with anger and fear. "I signed that damned prenuptial agreement. I get clothes and that's all. He even gets to keep the jewelry."

I felt my own voice thicken. I dreaded asking the question, but I had no choice.

"All of it?" I said. "Even the rose-beryl necklace?"

"I get to keep that," she said. "As if I wanted it." Then the realization struck. Her voice rose half an octave. "How in hell did you know about that? I never told you."

"You are left-handed," I said.

"Sure," she said. "What's that got to do with anything?"

I didn't answer her. She knew the answer, and she knew that I knew. My heart thumped even more furiously and my voice had grown thicker

123

than winter molasses.

"I'm coming over there," I said. "Right now."

"No!" She nearly screamed the word. "I'll come to your place. Please, Chess. Don't do this to me. I can drive the four-wheel thing, whatever it is that Jasper bought. I'll tell him that I need some female things. He'd rather I'd freeze to death than to ask for the stuff in the pharmacy."

"Don't come near me," I warned. "This place is swarming with officers. Stay away until I call you."

"You'll call? You're not just promising me?"

"I'll call," I said. "It may take me a couple of hours. Maybe more. But I'll call as soon as I can."

I hung up and thought about not just what she had said but how she said it. She sounded hurt and humiliated and embarrassed, as if her husband had done her wrong. And maybe he had, but I'd never live long enough to understand how a woman can sleep with men other than her husband and then whine because he doesn't trust her.

I went outdoors quickly and rejoined Lurch, who was still writing notes in his tiny book.

"Find anything?" I asked. "Any tracks?"

"Snow fills tracks as fast as somebody makes them. Look where you walked a few minutes ago. Damnedest thing you can imagine. If it wasn't for this snow, we might have a chance. With it, it's as if we are blindfolded. You'd think it would be the opposite, that the snow would help us. In fact, it would help, if the stuff would stop falling and leave only the old ground covering. "I've put in some calls," he said, tapping his pocket where he kept his phone.

I looked a question mark at him.

"Concerning Gallager," he said. "You ever see Ross Perot and Alfred E. Newman of *Mad Magazine* at the same time? Or Clark Kent and Superman?"

I knew what he was saying. Calls had gone to Gallager's office, and each time one of the workers answered. Never Gallager himself. Could he have dialed his own news room from his office and then altered his voice enough to fool the women? It was a possibility. And one call had come from his house.

"How old is he?" I asked Lurch.

124

He shrugged again. "Fifty. Fifty-five. No more. Why?"

"Just wondering. Have you ever read anything by or about him from one of his other newspaper jobs?"

"They were out of the area."

"Did you ever see any copies in his office?"

"No, but I've been in his office only a couple of times."

"But newspaper people put full pages on the walls. They frame them and create a mini-shrine. Gallager has nothing like it on his walls."

"You doubt that he was in newspaper work earlier? You think he lied about it?"

"Are you familiar with *Editor and Publisher?*"

"Vaguely."

"Want to call them and ask if they will do a computer check on Gallager?"

"He was with us most of the day when Alisha Webley was taken."

"She was already in the trunk of my car. Or her body was."

He nodded. "He was with us when one call came, but I see what you mean. Sure. I'll call."

We had walked down toward Buffalo Creek and followed the deer trail alongside the stream. There was no point in staying in the basement. Rance, Cullen, Wadsworth, and Wooley surrounded the body of Katherine Thennis and we'd be doing our own version of the Keystone Kops if all of us hovered like vultures inside.

Besides, those four have roughly a thousand times more real experience in law enforcement than I am likely to ever have. My only claim to education in law work is a knowledge of my severe limitations. Not only that, there simply wasn't anything to see. We could all stand and stare at the grisly scene, at the body, at the clothing, and at the basement, and we'd know no more four days from now than we know right now. I wanted Lurch's take on this and asked.

"All this song-and-dance bit about trace evidence, transfer, and DNA testing and all that," I began. "What can it do for us in cases like these? I hate to appear totally ignorant, but I have no choice. I *am* totally ignorant."

He smiled, almost pleasantly. "To paraphrase Henry David Thoreau," he said, "to know that you know what you know, and to know that you do not know what you do not know, that's the start of an education. In police work or anything else. Trace evidence? It's wonderful in books and movies. In real life, you get some help from it if the killer is as dumb as a stump or as careless as a tornado. Same with transfer."

He paused, staring straight ahead. I looked where he did, and it took me two minutes to pick out the form of the deer that stood at the edge of the water. It had a nice rack and a body that seemed to me to be engineered to perfection.

"How would that look over my fireplace?" he asked. "I could use a zoom with high resolution film and get a twenty-by-thirty-six enlargement with little if any grain. What a trophy."

I breathed easier. I am not a hunter of animals and not a good hunter of men who are killers. I can look at a deer and have as great a thrill, I think, as can the man who shot and killed the animal. The difference is that I can have my thrill and the deer does not suffer. I do not suffer from a Bambi complex. If the deer became a problem, a real problem, I'd kill them if I felt justified in doing so, just as I could trample black widows and uproot kudzu. I have never found any pleasure in causing pain in other people or creatures. It was pleasing that Lurch only wanted a trophy-sized photo over his mantle.

I could never be a sportsman. To me, a sport is a contest in which both of the teams or individuals agree to compete, and both have an equal or nearly equal chance of winning. The best the deer can hope for is a tie. I don't like no-win situations.

"Transfer," he went on, "is wonderful in movies and useful at times in real life. But if the killer is careful enough, he can dump his clothing in the washing machine, turn the hose on his shoes or boots, or burn his outer clothing and nobody is likely to catch him."

"What about the woman? She's wearing clothes."

"With trace from everywhere she's ever worn the dress."

"What about the rose beryl?"

He nodded. "It was there. On Phyllis Tyler, too."

The snow had now stopped and the sun seemed to be trying to peek through the clouds. And as we made our way through the woods, I was thinking about clothing, melting snow, and telephone calls.

At the house we tuned in a weather forecast and learned that we could expect two or three days of clear and cold weather. More snow, the weather bureau spokesperson said, was expected by as early as Thursday.

The weight returned to my shoulders. We would not have any melting, I knew, and the best we could hope for was a respite from the death-per-day rate we had been experiencing. The killer would realize that within a few days the roads could be snow-plowed and nearly normal traffic would resume. His chances of being seen would become greater, and his chances of survival would correspond with the weather.

I was betting that he would at least cool off enough to let us have a little breathing room. I walked down toward the creek, and seconds later Blanton joined me.

"Nothing," he said. "The people at the publication were very helpful but his name did not show up anywhere."

"You want to stop by his office?" I said. "Maybe direct the conversation to his past, if possible. If he had one."

"Oh, he had one," Blanton said. "I just hope it's not the one we think it might be. You staying here?"

"No. I'll be back later, though."

"A visitor coming," he asked. "Is this wise?"

"No," I told him. "It's stupid. And also crucial."

I contacted Zane and asked her to meet me and to bring photos of all the dead women. It took her less than thirty minutes to meet me.

"We're going to Monbo," I said. I explained that one man had occasionally met Alisha Webley on the road between the two towns.

She drove expertly over the snow-covered pavement, and when we reached the tiny town we began showing the photo around. No one in any of the handful of stores knew her, and we were ready to leave when Zane pointed to the post office.

"Try there," she said.

We did, and the man at the window recognized her instantly. He was a tall, gaunt man with a tiny bow tie at his enormous Adam's apple and thick glasses on his nose. His eyes looked like those of a tall and undernourished owl.

"Sure," he said, looking at the photo of Alisha Webley. "Been coming in here once or twice a month for three or four years. Maybe longer."

"Does she buy stamps? Mail packages?" I asked.

He shook his head. "Picks up mail is all," he said.

"Only once or twice a month?"

"The box gets mail only at the end of each month and the first of the next month."

"Specific dates?" I asked. "Always the same day?"

"Usually. On the twenty-seventh and on the third."

"Always the same days?" Again, he agreed.

"What kind of mail?"

"Same as everybody gets on those days."

"Bills?"

"Retirement checks. State employee checks are mailed out on the twenty-fifth and get here the twenty-seventh. Social security checks arrive on the third."

"Never here at any other time?"

"Nope."

"Is that unusual?"

"Nope. Lots of people do it. They don't want their checks sent to their banks. They like to see the money, to hold it in their hands."

"Then why not have it delivered to their homes?" Zane asked.

"People steal checks from rural mailboxes," he said. "This is safer for them."

"Do you know the number of the box she rents?"

He shook his head. "Don't rent it. Somebody else does. She just picks up the mail."

My heart pounded wildly and I felt my breath coming in hot gasps. "Who rents the box?" I asked.

"Man named Benjamin Collins."

"What does he look like?"

"Can't help you. I don't think I ever saw him. Been here just a shade over three years. He already had the box when I came to work."

"Does he pay the box rent?"

"She does," he said, pointing to the photo of Alisha Webley.

"And in cash," I guessed.

"Right. Always cash."

"Don't you have to keep a residential address for all of the box-holders?"

"Sure do. You want his?" He pulled a ledger from under the counter and ran his long finger down a short list.

"Here it is," he said. "261 Church Road. That's off the main highway a few miles. Out close to the river."

We asked him about the other women, and he knew none of them.

We drove to Church Road and at the end of it we found a tiny and run-down trailer. No car was in front of it. It looked vacant. Weeds had grown up around it, and one window of the door had been knocked out.

"It's what I expected," I said. "What next?"

"What about some of the other tiny towns?" Zane suggested.

It was what I should have thought of instantly. We drove to Mica, which was, like Monbo, barely large enough to have a post office.

The clerk recognized Katherine Thennis. We knew what was coming: she came in to pick up mail on the twenty-seventh and the third day of each month. She did not rent the box, which belonged to a man named Ralph Brett, who lived at 740 Jed Brantly Road.

"You want to drive out there?" Zane asked.

"Sure," I said. "I want to see who doesn't live in the old trailer there."

As expected, it was a tiny, rusty trailer with no signs of life anywhere.

In Cato we learned that Mrs. Tyler had collected the mail at the same dates as the others and that the box was rented by Herman Brittain. At the physical address we found another empty and neglected trailer.

In all three instances the trailers stood on lots that were at the end of the roads. There were no mailboxes or any other forms of identification. There was no indication that a newspaper had ever been delivered there or that children ever laughed and played in the yards. There were no dog houses, occupied or otherwise, and no hint that anyone ever wanted the place to look a little better than rust and rot.

In truth, I saw no reason to think that anyone had ever lived in any of the trailers we visited. I took into consideration the deep snow and the remoteness of the trailers, but there had to be a reason for them to be in the neighborhood in the first place. But if there was one, it eluded me. The effect of the scene was that someone had simply bought the lots and parked the dilapidated trailers there.

"Don't they have to pay taxes?" Zane asked, and I reached over and hugged her tightly and kissed her quickly. I pulled away as if I had been burned, and she looked at me, a soft smile on her lips.

"I have lots of other questions if they bring the same results," she said. "Ready?"

"Not now," I told her. "Call the court house and see who owns the land."

She made the call, repeated the names given to her, and I wrote them down.

"Charles Lutwidge, Thomas Sterns, and Ernest Miller," she said. "I don't know any of them."

"I do," I told her. "Let's get back to town. I have a damn good idea of who killed three women. Hurry!"

ELEVEN

Turning over the Thennis investigation to the STOP people, Lurch returned to the office, and Zane and I went to the office of the *Guardian*. As the car plowed its uncertain way down the snow-laden streets, I wondered how much longer we could navigate the lanes and roads of Sherman County.

To my surprise Gallager was in his office. He looked up in surprise and, I thought, fear, when I opened the door.

"I thought you'd be at the scene of the crime," he said, recovering and rising to shake my hand. He seemed tired, sapped of strength and energy. But the newspaper, even an oldspaper like the *Guardian*, had to go on. Like the show.

"I thought you'd be there, too," I said.

"I've got to get the next edition out," he said. "It's a matter of great principal."

"Subscribers are demanding?" I said.

He managed a soft laugh. "Who cares about subscribers?" he said with only a trace of mockery. "It's the advertisers I worry about. You think a tiger is fierce? Try facing a car dealer or supermarket manager who had a big sale going on, and he took out a whole section of advertising space. And then we don't get to the streets until a day late, and the produce has spoiled or the buyers have gone elsewhere. Anyway, what's new out there?"

"Does your wife work outside the home?" I asked out of the blue. He looked startled, his pale, weak eyes darting like those of a cornered rodent.

"No," he said quickly. "Why?"

"I called your house earlier," I said, "and talked with a woman who didn't seem to know when you'd be in."

His eyes filled with instant fear. His face, already ashen, turned two shades lighter, and he looked as if he had suddenly heard his death sentence.

"Cleaning lady," he said, recovering quickly. "She comes in once or twice a week. Just to indulge my wife a bit."

"In weather like this?" Zane asked.

I too wondered how and why the cleaning lady was out in such a blizzard. But Gallager had pulled off the lie so easily I decided to let him run with the bait.

"You know about Mrs. Thennis," I said, changing the subject.

He nodded. "In the issue on the presses right now." He stood up and walked to a window and stared at nothing. Then he said, "Chess, I have no choice in this. I have to hit you hard in the new issue. The mayor has been all over me. So has the county manager. So have the commissioners. These people, as you well know, run the town and the county. They left here to go over to your place. Your office, I mean. These people could put me out of business, and God knows I can't take another beating."

"I know," I said. "It's all right. You're doing your job."

His job wasn't as hard as mine, I reasoned. All he had to do was tell what did or did not happen. I had to learn who caused it to happen or who kept it from happening and to make certain that he would not do it again.

In fairness, I told myself, he could do his job and I could not do mine. Period. End of story.

"Be right back."

He stepped into what I thought was a closet and closed the door behind him. I could hear his footsteps descending into the basement that I did not know existed. During the brief time the door was open I could hear the gentle clatter of the presses: a strong humming noise that seemed to cause the building to vibrate as the power coursed through the motors. There was a mild odor of a chemical nature that I assumed was printer's ink or its modern-day equivalent.

I wondered what was in that basement, other than printing presses. Old wood? Rotted wood with polish or oil on it?

As soon as I no longer heard his steps I walked quickly to his desk and glanced at the day's mail, which consisted mostly of bills, a couple of magazines, and yesterday's edition of several of the regional papers. In the center of the stack I could see an envelope with a familiar return address. It was from Raleigh, the state capital. I had seen dozens of checks like it when friends received such checks. But schools do not mail out them monthly. His was a retirement check.

I wondered how a man could spend decades in the newspaper business, all over the country, as he had said, and still be able to retire from the state.

I could hear him climbing the steps, and I moved quickly to my chair and waited for him to appear. He carried a still-warm copy of the *Guardian*. The entire front page, except for one boxcd-in two-column section, was devoted to the latest killing and to sidebars and follow-ups on the earlier killings.

The two-column box was headed: HOW LONG MUST WE WAIT?

I didn't have to read it to know what the article said. How long, the editor was asking, was the community expected to wait for law and order, security, and peace of mind.

I folded the paper, thanked Gallager, and made my way down the totally deserted streets to the small cubicle where I had once hidden from prison. I had nowhere to hide now.

The room I called my office was packed.

Jeff Dennis, the county manager, sat at my desk. He smiled menacingly as I entered and stared at him.

"You don't mind, do you?" he asked with a badly faked effort at politeness. "I mean, if you're welcome in my bed, I feel that I have a right to sit at your desk."

I glanced at the others: William Herrin, a well-dressed man in his sixties, was shorter than I but much broader. He looked as if he and Charles Atlas were brothers. He was also chairman of the Sherman County

Board of Commissioners. Herrin sat in the corner near the window, and in the other corner I saw Elvin Stackhouse, the mayor. Five other people were wedged into the remaining space.

"We'll come directly to the point," Stackhouse said. He was tall, slender, and self-assured. His too-black hair and too-tailored clothing spoke volumes. "There has been a murder every day of this week, and something has to be done. The people are clamoring for my scalp."

"And you want mine," I said. "Let me assure you that I can and do understand your concerns. We're working around the clock, all of us, and we frankly have made no progress at all. The STOP people are still as helpless as I am."

"We're not asking for excuses," Stackhouse said. "We're asking for action. If we don't get it from you, you get it from us. We're asking you to resign, effective immediately."

"I won't," I said. "You'll have to fire me, and you don't have the power to do that."

"The governor has assured us that he will see to it that the proper machinery is put into action," he said. "We want you to do the right thing and vacate this office by evening."

"That's insane," I said. "What can anyone do that I haven't done?"

"Catch the killer," Stackhouse said.

"How? The man hasn't given us a chance to stop to gather our forces. It's like a flood pouring in everywhere. There's no time to investigate one murder before another is committed. What else can anyone else do?"

"Stay out of other people's beds, for starters," Jeff Dennis said venomously. "The killer is not in my wife's bed."

"Your wife told me she was divorced when we met," I said. "I was not married, and we went out."

"You mean, you stayed in. Inside your cabin the whole night. As for you, we all know why you aren't married."

I disregarded the insinuation. The people of Sherman County, at least a portion of them, would go to their graves convinced that I had murdered Derry.

"I have not slept in three days," I said. "I don't know when I last ate. I can't remember going to the bathroom. I am giving every second of every minute to these deaths. Where can you find someone on such short notice who will agree to take over?"

As soon as the words died, I knew the answer.

"Jhon Rance has agreed to accept the position as interim sheriff," Herrin said. "We have told him that the job is his."

I slammed my desk with the palm of my hand. It sounded like an explosion in the tiny room. Heads jerked in alarm. "It's out of the question," I thundered. "I demand a formal hearing. I insist on having time to talk to an attorney. You can't railroad me like this."

Jeff Dennis grinned. "You'll see, young feller," he said. He made the label sound like a curse.

I walked over to my desk, snatched him up by the shirt, and held him so that his nose was within an inch of mine.

"The name is not Young Feller," I said. "My title is Sheriff Ivy. I occupy a position of respect, and you will treat it with respect, or I will give you a real reason to fire me: I'll kick your scrawny backside all over this office."

I shoved him back into the chair. He was pale now, suddenly emptied of all his bluster. The slob was scared witless. I had started twice to tell them that I was almost certain who the killer is, but some perverse reason kept me from it. The one I gave myself was that if I blow the whistle before we have any proof, there won't be any proof left when we try to find it. A man clever enough to carry out the murders was also too clever to keep incriminating evidence around him.

"Do what you think best," I said. "I was looking for a job when I came here."

"Yes," Stackhouse said, "from between bars."

I glared at him, then at the others, and then I reached into the gun rack and pulled out another sawed-off scattergun.

"Gentlemen," I said, "I have not used a gun in years, and I may be a little careless. If both barrels of this thing should go off, someone would have to scrape you off the walls. And while they were scraping, I'd explain to the media how I solved the killings and cleaned up the government at the same time. If I were you, I'd be looking for a safer place. Now get the hell out of my office before I put you all behind bars for obstructing justice and interfering with an officer of the law investigating a capital crime."

They looked at each other in bewilderment. I had no earthly idea whether such laws or charges existed, but they sounded good for the spur of the moment.

"Do I need to remind you who the highest law officeholder in any county in the state happens to be?" I demanded. "The sheriff, who has the power to arrest the county manager, the mayor, or the governor if he happens to be in town. I'll give you ten seconds to clear out. After that, you'll find yourselves in a cell. The choice is yours."

They knew to a man that no sheriff in his right mind would pull the triggers, but, also to a man, they were not at all sure that I was in my right mind. Neither was I: for a moment I gave serious thought to doing just what I had vaguely threatened to do. I was exhausted, hungry, sleepy, frustrated, and mad as hell. Almost past the point of thinking rationally.

I closed the door when they left and returned to my desk, looked up a state department number, and dialed.

"Yes," I said. "This is Sheriff Ivy of Sherman County. I am investigating three homicides and need help. I'd like for you to fax me immediately the employment record of Edward Gallager who for a period of time was employed by the State of North Carolina."

Somebody pecked at a computer keyboard. It took them less than ten minutes to get the information to me. And it took me half that time to see what I had dreaded to see: that William Edward Gallager had briefly taught journalism in the public schools of North Carolina. His first employment was in the Wilmington schools; the next was in Greensboro; the third was in Charlotte. The fourth was in Fayetteville. I kept reading until I came to the end of the road for him.

Then I called the Wilmington school system and spoke with a slow-talking woman who informed me that employee information was not available to the public. I explained to her that I was not the public but a law officer who could and would get a court order that would open their files and her underwear drawer as well to the public. She experienced an apotheosis and informed me that Ed Gallager had been terminated at the school after an incident involving a financial matter.

I didn't ask the particulars; she gave them to me. It was hard to get her started and impossible to stop her. It was not an unfamiliar story; nor was it a pretty one. Gallager had students in his class, primarily girls,

136

selling ads for the school paper. The students turned in the ad money to Gallager, and somehow it never made its way to the school office. Gallager went to trial and actually spent time in a work-release program. I called the Raleigh prisons and learned that he would have spent much more time behind bars if it had not been that some of Gallager's students refused to testify against him. Some, in fact, did testify on his behalf and praised him to the heavens, saying that he was by far the best teacher they had ever known.

In his trial Gallager had insisted that he had turned over the money to the principal, Lawton Calvin, who denied having seen any of the money. Students wrote letter after letter in his defense; they urged their parents to apply pressure on officials. They helped get him back on the streets in a hurry. That, plus the fact that Lawton Calvin, while denying that the money had been turned in, had testified persuasively that Gallager had been singled out for persecution because of the high standard of work and the elevated failure rate in his classes. A number of faculty members and former students testified that Gallager was a superb teacher who saw to it that they learned the material and developed self-discipline.

Calls to three other offices revealed that Gallager's students went on to earn the highest marks in college work and that a number of them were now prize-winning journalists not only in the South but throughout the nation.

"You want the truth?" the man in the last office told me.

"Yes," I said. "I want the truth."

"So do we," he said. "But I tell you this: if your daughter wanted to take his class, I'd recommend him highly."

"What if your daughter wanted in the class?" I asked.

He did not answer. Instead, he hung up.

The response puzzled me. Gallager was a tiny man, utterly devoid of sex appeal. There was no way he could have been in any way involved with students. Yet at Sherman University I had seen professors of all persuasions sexually involved with students by the dozens. And a college freshman is only a year older than a high school senior. Maybe less.

I called Bert Webley, who was not at home. The funeral had been held the previous day, I knew, although dates had become generally a blur for me. Blanton and Zane came into the office and waited until I was off the phone.

"I'm going to the school," I told them. "I need to talk with Rockwell again. I need you to call the state school board office and find out where Lawton Calvin is now working, if he is still in education. Keep an eye on Ed's office. If he leaves, let me know. I'm on my way."

I left the office and brushed snow off the windshield of the state vehicle with four-wheel drive. Zane suddenly appeared on the other side of the car and climbed in.

"I'm going with you," she said. "Don't argue. Drive."

I drove. As I passed Gallager's office I noticed that another four-wheel drive vehicle was parked in front. So he could handle the snow, too, I thought.

We drove past the Webley Hardware store and another four-wheel vehicle sat in front of the door.

Zane read my thoughts. "Everybody drives one up here," she said.

"But not everybody is killing people," I said.

"You suspect Webley? And Gallager?"

I told her about the fax and phone calls and about how Gallager had lied about spending his life as an editor.

"Webley's wife was sleeping around," I said. "Men have killed for less than that."

"There was a prenuptial agreement," she said. "He could have divorced her and kept everything."

"Maybe this wasn't about money. Maybe it was about jealousy and revenge."

"Why would he kill the others?"

I had no answer.

Minutes later we were at the schoolhouse and in the office of Marlin Rockwell. His own snow-vehicle was in the parking lot. Apparently he was a dedicated professional who devoted every waking moment to school business. He greeted us with friendly reserve and led us into the inner office where he gestured for us to sit.

"Any developments you can share?" he asked softly.

I shook my head. "I'd like to lie and tell you we're getting close. I can't. We'd like to talk with you for a few minutes. Without interruption."

"My secretary is off," he said. "I told her not to try to travel during the bad weather. I have to leave the office for a while. In fact, I need to check on the pipes in some of the buildings. Why not go with me. Is this all right?"

I told him that it was fine.

He smiled, showing a lot of teeth, and rose. He was wearing Timberland boots and khaki pants. A plaid shirt was shoved into his pants. He could easily have passed for the Marlboro Man.

He spoke, as before, in a rich but clipped manner that reminded me of Ronald Coleman or Anthony Hopkins.

We made our way down the hallway that smelled faintly of oil and a mixture of other indistinguishable odors. At the end of the hall we turned to the right, left the building, and headed toward a low, flat building two hundred yards away.

"The Board of Education," he said, smiling comfortably, "is of the opinion that kids do not get enough exercise. So they build the classroom complexes as far apart as possible." He smiled again to let us know that he was joking, then added, "I am told that it's all in the interest of fire protection. In case one building catches on fire, it will not spread easily."

He walked in huge, graceful strides. He seemed oblivious to the bitterly cold wind that whipped across the campus. As we walked, I mentioned the rose beryl to him.

"Rose beryl," he said, as if he had not heard the term in a decade. He mused for several moments. "I'm familiar with it," he said finally.

"Tell me about it," I said. I didn't bother to tell him that I already knew. What interested me, though, was why he knew.

"The morganatic marriage was an older version of the prenuptial agreements we have today," he said. "The term means 'a morning gift.' From the German *morgengeba.* It was a gift made by a husband to his wife on the morning after their marriage. The gift, once accepted by the wife, meant that she was surrendering all rights to any share of the husband's title or property or his money. The woman was always of a lower social class than was the husband."

"He was buying her off, then," I suggested.

He shook his head. "Not really," he said. "He was also guaranteeing

139

her that any children from the marriage would be considered legitimate. They, like the wife, could not inherit any property or receive any money from the estate, but the children were at least citizens with all the legal rights of free men."

I glanced at Rockwell while he talked. The principal strode effortlessly, leaning into the wind the way veteran hikers do.

We looked into the science lab before heading back to the main building. Along the way he paused outside a doorway, then unlocked it.

"The catacombs," he said. "Actually the boiler room. I am a one-man crew while the staff is off. We have to keep the rooms warm enough that pipes will not freeze. Look at this beautiful old wood. I'd love to have this in my house."

He led me down a dark stairway into a huge open space that held a massive furnace and little else except for ancient wood stacked almost to the floor joists. I looked. The wood had never been painted. There were no paint flecks here. The wood he had wished to have in his home was also unpainted.

We left shortly afterwards, walked through the cutting wind back to the main building, and from there to Rockwell's office. He shook hands with us at the doorway and wished us well.

I had asked him a series of pointless questions and then he had invited me to do what I had been prepared to demand: to see the insides of the building, the storage areas, and the furnace room. Zane and I drove back to my house to view the carnage.

When we arrived, it appeared that a small army had set up camp there. Cars and trucks were wedged against each other and the snow in the yard had been trampled as if a herd of the bison that once roamed the area had wintered there. At least a dozen men and four women wandered through my house, poking into drawers and closets and even shining lights up the chimney flue and into the crawl space at the front of the house where the even ground had precluded my digging a full basement.

The body of Katherine Thennis, shockingly, still lay on the small couch where it had been when it was discovered. I wanted not to look, but I could not avoid doing so.

Her face had once been if not exceedingly beautiful then at worst attractive. Her long reddish-brown hair reached past her shoulders. Her lips, I saw, had been full, and her cheekbones high, very much like the face and hair of Maureen O'Hara, one of the most gorgeous women ever to grace the stage or film. She was wearing what appeared to be an ill-fitting gray sweater and sweat pants. It was tempting to say that such a woman would never be caught dead in such attire, but she had been.

The doctor from the hospital was bending over her body. On the end table near her head there was a lamp and beside the lamp was a small plastic bag. Wielding tweezers, he had deposited strands of hair, a portion of a dead leaf, what appeared to be a leg of an insect, a tiny scrap of withered vegetation that once had been yellow, or so it appeared, and a tiny piece of matter that could have been the hull from a seed.

"In her hair," the man said. I assumed he meant that the matter had been found in her long and luxuriant hair. "She had been dragged," he said.

I looked puzzled, and he gently, almost lovingly turned her body and lifted the sweatshirt so that I could see the scrapes and abrasions on her back. The shirt seemed large enough to fit a whale.

"Her buttocks are the same," he said. "Note the direction of the scrapes. Like the flow of a river. You can tell that she was pulled by her legs, rather than by her hands and arms. Look." He lifted her head and parted the hair. Smaller but identical marks were visible in her scalp.

"We found this," he added, gently lowering the head after first smoothing her hair. I was impressed by his devotion to the dead woman. He pointed to an almost invisible black or dark brown elongated object in the bottom of the bag. It appeared to be the tip of a thorn or a splinter. It was no more than a sixteenth of an inch long and less than half that amount in diameter.

"Will this help?" I asked, thinking of what Lurch had told me earlier. He shook his head slowly.

"Can't say," he said. "Been in this line of work a while. I've seen hundreds of hours wasted, because the trace stuff was worthless. I've seen it solve less than a dozen real cases in all my time, but for the people connected with the dozen, I'd say it was worth it. Will it help? Can't say till we have all we can find."

Without attribution, I paraphrased what Lurch had said. He, without hesitation, agreed.

"Movies would have you believe that we are magicians," he said. "Truth is that we are not looking for the needle in the hay stack but for all the other stuff in the hay that might tell us whose needle it is and why it was lost or put there."

I assured him that I welcomed all the help we could get, and as he continued looking for his own private needle, I filled him in on the latest we had investigated, leaving out the interview with Marlin Rockwell. "Same man, same location," I said. "All of the women were killed within the same enclosed area. That's the premise upon which we are working."

He made a humming sound and didn't look up. "Interesting," he said. "I reached the same conclusion as soon as I started examining this young lady. She must have been a fine person. A damn shame. We both agree that her clothes don't seem right for her. Not unless she was cleaning the attic. She'd not be the type to go out in public dressed like this. Woman like this would want her clothes to look good on her."

"The third thing?" I prompted.

"Marks on her shoulder. Look." He lifted the sweat shirt past her breasts and pointed to a small rectangular mark on the inside slope of her shoulder, just under the collar bone. The mark was the size of a small paper clip.

"Bra adjustment," he said. "She wore a bra not long ago and for a long time. Wasn't wearing one when she was left here."

From his speech it was clear that there was Irish in him. His hair was the color of sand, and his unshaven face was like sandpaper that had been used on barbed wire.

"Anything else?" I asked. He nodded and pointed to the bag. His short, stubby finger, sans anything more than a suggestion of a nail, poked at what appeared to be a dirty snowflake. He tilted the bag and the snowflake flipped. On its back side there were dark smudges.

"That was in her hair, too," he said. "Sharp edge of it had kind of caught in one of the abrasions. We'll do a lab analysis on it, but I'm willing to bet my last pair of tweezers that it is a fleck of paint, old paint, from the days when leaded paint was all you could buy."

Again.

"Which tells us?" I again prompted, although even I knew the answer

142

to that question.

"That she was kept in and probably killed in a building that is very, very old. The same flecks were found in the hair and on the clothing of the others."

"How old a building?"

"I'd say at least fifty to a hundred years. Can't tell yet. See the dark smudge on the back. It's sort of hairy-looking."

I looked again, and he was right. Strands of something that looked like the hair from a dark cat clung to the snowflake.

"That's wood fibers, unless I miss my guess," he said. "That tells us that the building is old, the wood was unpainted for years, and then when the paint was first put on, the wood had not been cleaned and primed. When humidity and temperature changes acted on the paint and the wood, the paint chipped and pulled part of the decaying wood with it. Look for a building with the paint chipping on the east side."

It was the second time the detail had been presented to me.

"Why so?" I asked. "Why can't wood decay on all sides of a building?"

"Morning dew," he said. "In summertime the dew drops stand on the wood surface, and the morning sun is magnified by the water as if it were a magnifying glass. The heat inside the water bubble is horrendous, and the paint under pressure starts to crack. At the first crack, molecules of water are forced into the slight fissure and then the next day the heat inside the fissure causes expansion, and the paint begins to chip. You can sometimes simply rub your fingers along a painted surface and the paint will flake."

I considered what he had told me and then tried to put it into perspective.

"All right," I said. "It makes sense. Now how do I find the building that the paint chips or flakes came from?"

He smiled at me, like Barry Fitzgerald in "Going My Way," a slightly mischievous yet grim grimace.

"I don't know," he said. "I've done my job. Now it's your turn."

Later I conferred with Lurch and Zane, sharing what the doctor had told me. Like me, they seemed helpless to make sense of the information.

143

"Old buildings," Lurch said. "The older churches in town. All of the outbuildings are old. We could start there."

"The courthouse building," Zane added. "It's the oldest building in town. Is this animal using a storage room there?"

"It's something to check," I agreed. "Why don't you and Rick check it out. And then try the churches."

"Add the older houses in town," I added. "Sherman was built more than a century ago. We're talking about nearly every house on nearly every street. It'll take eons to check out all of them."

We spent most of the day checking old churches, warehouses, and other antiquated buildings. When we returned to the office the phone rang almost as soon as we closed the door.

When I took over the duties of sheriff, I welcomed the phone calls when people asked me to send a deputy over to investigate a break-in or a prowler who had been spotted nearby. The calls let people know that we were ready to help day and night.

For three nightmarish days, now, the phone's jangling was like having icy needles shoved under my fingernails. I reached for the phone. I did not expect to hear good news.

The entire experience had been worse than I could have dreamed possible: for the victims, first of all, and then their families. Down near the bottom of the list I put myself. I was in good health, and I had a ton of money. I had a job that some people might consider a good one, and under any sort of normal conditions I'd have been happy.

But happiness had migrated South for me. It hurt most that I was an incompetent in a job requiring the greatest of all professional skills. I needed to take action but didn't know which way to turn.

The one positive aspect of it all was that I was no longer moping about and feeling sorry for myself. My brain somewhere back had kicked in, and at least I was functioning.

One reason I had thrown off the melancholy was that I had to look into the faces of the families who looked to me and to my department to help them, to find the killer of their wife or daughter, and to create some semblance of law and order.

I had failed them, of course, but I wasn't back in a cell in a huge cage. Not yet.

144

TWELVE

The first four somber words were like a benediction: "Dr. Andrew Miller here."

I had, needless to say, been terrified that it would be Ed Gallager, with another message of a missing woman. Bum stepped into the office to glance at my face. I nodded to him, a signal that all was as well as we could expect.

I had left him instructions to start calling the women who were members of the social club that the other three women had joined years ago. The club had been formed roughly three years after high school graduation, and while I saw no connection, I thought it prudent to alert them to the possibility that their membership was linked, whether causally or not, to the killings.

"A little more news," Miller said in his sad voice that made me wonder if he had just left a production of "Fiddler on the Roof" before coming to Sherman. "The paint chips? I found two more of them, both in the woman's hair or scalp. One of the last two also has a substance on the front of it, in addition to the wood fibers on the back."

I waited. He would get there efficiently, effectively, I knew, and hurrying him would be counterproductive.

"The substance appears to be oil. Not motor oil but more of a polishing oil. And I'll tell you what it reminds me of, and at this point I have no earthly way of justifying this. It makes me think of furniture polish, the kind grandma used on the homemade table and chairs. I'd suggest a building that used or uses oil on the floors as a preservative. I'll leave here and take everything into the lab. I should be able to let you know more by late tonight."

He didn't need to tell me. He was going to work all day and all night, if necessary, to bring me into the loop as closely as possible.

"Thanks," I said, without thinking. His response told me that I was not the only one who wasn't thinking.

"My pleasure," he said.

I thought of the aroma of oil and old wood in the hallways of Sherman High School, and I wondered how many rooms in the huge basement of the school were painted with lead-based paint. I also wondered about Rockwell and the fact that he was always among us or in contact with any of us when the death messages or kidnap messages were phoned in.

The voice descriptions did not match the principal's, but that was not convincing. Anyone with any knowledge of speech patterns and tones could have disguised his voice effectively. And telephones, no matter how sophisticated, always manage to distort voices slightly. But there was no way around the fact that he had been with us when some of the calls came.

One suspect: Ed Gallager was a convicted thief and, unless I missed the innuendos during my phone call to Wilmington, he also had run into other problems. Thieves of a few hundred dollars, petty cash by today's standards, do not serve active time unless there is more to the incident than money.

Did he have a problem of keeping his pants zipped? Was he an exhibitionist? Was his past only shady, or was it soiled? He had started his life in Sherman on a false front, and if he had not deliberately lied, he allowed us to accept and believe a false background. Maybe my months in prison had twisted me more than I had feared: at least, in prison you know all you want to know about the people closest to you. You knew, for starters, that they were all criminals, many of them murderers.

We knew next to nothing about Gallager. I called his house on occasion, and, with one exception, there was no answer at all. If his wife was a homemaker, she was out of the home a suspicious amount of time, particularly during a blizzard. Either she did a great deal of shopping, walking, gardening, or visiting, or she simply chose not to answer the phone.

And the housekeeper had not braved the blizzard a second time.

As soon as I finished talking with Dr. Miller I closed the office door and motioned for Lurch and Zane to pull their chairs closer. I told them in quick detail what Miller had told me.

"Has he had time to determine whether she had given birth?" Rick asked.

"Bull's-eye. It had to be before she was married. She's had no children since she was married."

The phone rang, and seconds later Bum entered the room. "Call from the northern part of the county," he said. "Not another kidnapping."

"Thank God!" Zane said softly. I realized how tense I had suddenly become. My body started to relax slightly.

"People saw a scruffy-looking pair of people going into an old store. You want me to check it out."

"That's it!" Blanton said. "The old stores all had lead-based paint. They must be two hundred years old. They're ideal places for people to hide their activities."

There were a dozen stores that had catered to the needs of farmers and home owners at the turn of the century. These stores went out of business when chain stores, like the one the Webleys owned, came into the area and undercut all the old merchants. The stores featured crosscut saws, kerosene lamps, seeds of every basic type, sickles, scythes, pitchforks, double-bladed axes, wood mauls, and manually operated tongue-and-groove files, among hundreds of other items. Most of the stores also sold shoes, coats, rifles and shotguns and their ammunition, slabs of cheese, fatback, side meat, and enormous slices of country ham, all exposed at room temperature to whatever happened to come by for a taste.

The stores also carried a line of furniture, most of it very basic and often semi-crude, and the proprietors kept the tables and chairs in an upstairs room that would be called a gallery today. I could recall from my childhood visits to the stores that had clung to life as long as possible, and I, like every other child who entered the store, left my fingerprints on the greasy surfaces of the tables.

Which is why, now that I think of it, the furniture polish was so liber-

147

ally applied. Now all we had to do was find which of the old stores remained open, which had closed, and which still stood after all the years. I still wanted to see more of the guts of the high school, an old building which had been constructed about the time the area was settled and which had been updated on occasion since that time.

I could not escape the conviction that Rockwell had known that I would get a court order to get into the boiler room, and he volunteered to take me there, where I found nothing.

And I could not believe the scruffy pair entering the old store had killed the women. It had to be someone the women knew and trusted, and it had something to do with their club. It also had something to do with post office boxes in the tiny towns that dotted Sherman County.

I told Lurch and Zane to go together. I knew Lurch could take care of himself and half the county. I had confidence in Zane, but she was, and I can hear the women's champions screaming already, a woman and less likely to be able to fight off a killer than Lurch would be.

Or, if it makes the advocates feel better, I wanted Lurch to have backup, if he needed it. Two heads and four eyes are better than one and two, respectively.

I called Webley and asked him how many old stores still stood in Sherman County.

"Thirteen," he said without hesitation. I was afraid that would be the number he gave me. Still, I recalled that Lurch used to lecture me on the number thirteen. He informed me that it was the number of Jesus and the twelve disciples, the number of letters in *e pluribus unum,* the number of the Constitutional amendment that freed all slaves, the number of doughnuts in a baker's dozen, the number of original colonies, the number of stripes on Old Glory, and a host of other information. Still, I could not escape a twinge of superstition.

"How many are still standing?"

"All of them. One was fire-damaged back in the sixties, but the shell of the building is intact. What does this have to do with the murder of my wife?"

"I'm not certain," I said. "It's a lead, and we are tracking it down. How many of the stores are open today?"

"Three. One in Sherman, one in the north end of the county, and one

148

in the south. Do you need the locations of the others?"

I told him that I did, and he quickly reeled off the roads on which the stores stood. I wrote down the addresses in a small notebook I had started to carry in obvious emulation of Lurch. It worked for him, so why not.

Before he broke the connection, I asked the question every law officer dreads and which every marriage partner expects.

"I'm sorry to ask this," I began, "but did you at any time have cause to believe that your wife was having an affair?" I had broached the topic before, and now it met with the same reaction.

"No!" The answer came too fast, too loud, and too defensive. Again.

"It's an important question," I persisted. "If you ever had even the slightest—"

"No. Damn it, I told you my wife never had an affair."

"All right," I said. "I have asked and you have answered the question." I started to hang up when he appended every husband's staunchest defense.

"My wife was a virgin when we were married," he said for the second time to me. "In her entire life she never knew another man but me. Is that clear enough for you? During our marriage she was never away from home at night unless she was with her parents or at a school meeting. Did I make myself clear?"

"Totally clear," I said. "Did you know that your wife gave birth to a child before the two of you were married?"

He slammed down the phone, but not before he gave me an earful of invective. And I was left with nothing but general stores to investigate. But Bert Webley had lied to me and he knew that I knew. I thought about stores.

I didn't see a reason to tell him that it is the easiest thing on earth for two rutting people to find a time and place. If it's the time, any place will do. When I was at the college the professors seduced students in motel rooms, cars, bushes, dressing rooms, swimming pools, and ball parks. They did the big trick standing up, one of them seated on a desk, stretched on the grass, and anywhere else that would accommodate them for a few seconds. I thought of Dr. Johnson's appraisal of the sex act with its fleeting pleasure and ludicrous position.

In my life I have known male and female to make love, if that's what it is, and it isn't, during ten-minute breaks between classes, before the start of a meeting, and during telephone calls.

Before I started on my trek, I called Ben Tyler. I caught him at home, too. After several softening questions, I hit him with the one that disturbed Webley. His response was different.

"My wife and I never questioned each other's private lives before marriage," he said. "I knew the first time we made love that she was not a virgin. That wasn't hard to figure out. It was also fairly clear that she had perhaps given birth. A woman who has had a baby is not at all like one who hasn't. She gave me a cluster of clues, in addition to the looseness of her body."

"Like what?"

"She'd look at a baby and suddenly get teary-eyed. When we were first married, it was two-year olds that did it. The next year it was three-year olds. I could imagine that she was seeing the child she gave birth to. I never questioned her."

"What about later?" I asked. "Did she at any time ever give you any hints that she might be having an affair?"

"Yes," he said bluntly. "I am confident that she was, in fact, seeing another man. But so what? I was getting it on with other women."

"I don't wish to be graphic," I said, "but what clues did you find suggestive?"

He laughed bitterly. "When she came home smelling to high heaven of Cupid's gymnasium. There's no other smell on earth, just as there is nothing else that smells like a woman in heat."

"Smegma," I said.

"Exactly. It made me wonder if they dated in a parked car." He didn't seem to like the latter idea much at all, and I wondered why a parked car was worse than a seedy motel. I returned to my general store thoughts.

There were thirteen stores, three of which were open. I started to scratch the open stores because of the likelihood that witnesses would be around all hours of the day, and then I thought that an open store would be far more likely to attract young women with money to spend. So I put them back on the list.

My major concern was that of the decaying wood, which might be absent in the operating stores, and again I reflected on the inherent charm evoked by the timelessness made manifest by the disintegration of the timbers.

The deserted stores were the most likely places, simply because on a snowy day a killer could park behind the store, drag his victim inside, and with a gag in her mouth he could keep her as long as he wished, or until she froze to death.

Which brought up another point. If she froze to death, it stood to reason that the killer would also be cold, even deathly so. Temperatures in Sherman dropped regularly into the single digits and often below zero in winter months. Everyone has heard the old saw about places like ours that have eleven months of winter and one month of poor skiing. Or that summer came on a Tuesday last year. One old mountain man swore that one night the cold snap caused the mercury to drop so fast that it knocked the thermometer off the post.

I concluded that he had to be kept warm, and if he had a fire in a woodstove in the old buildings, someone would see the smoke, sooner or later. I knew that he could use kerosene heaters or bottled gas, but this is cumbersome and might alert witnesses to the point that they called on the sheriff's department.

No, I decided, the place had to be one that was easy to heat and would not attract undue attention. If the killer parked behind one of the deserted stores, he had to leave tracks in the snow, and there was the chance that his car would be seen, unless he could drive it inside or park it so that it was not visible from the road.

A place that was easy to heat. I kept coming back to that. Alisha Webley shopped at old-fashioned general stores. Probably the other women did likewise. There was a good chance that when the women shopped, they went together. There was an even better chance that some lecherous shopkeeper spotted the women and decided that he'd have them, one way or another.

But it was not likely. Store owners lived in the community and could not afford a scandal. Or a murder.

Possibly the women went as part of a club meeting. I made a mental note to ask Zane about it. She had told me that she did not attend meetings, but she may have heard the girls discussing their shopping excursions.

The old stores that I knew of all had a second floor and, most probably, a basement. A basement is easily heated, as is a second floor. A bound and gagged person on either level would have a hard time making enough noise to attract attention of the other shoppers.

All the time I was mulling over the probabilities, I had alerted Bum that I was going to check on the abandoned general stores and that I'd be out of radio or phone contact for several minutes at a time but that I'd call in before I entered any of the buildings. The last thing I wanted was for me to become the first male victim of the madman.

And it would be the last thing, for me.

My first stop was in the tiny community of Avon, which had been so-named because the man who built the first and only mill in the town was a lover of the Bard. Avon was little more than a crossroads, but in the community there was a used car lot, a convenience store, a tractor-repair shop, and a service station, in addition to two abandoned general stores.

The first I visited was the Avon General Store, and for years it had functioned as a company store for the mill. Workers who came into the area did not have to worry about moving furniture. They simply moved into town and into one of the company-owned houses. They rented it from the mill owner, and they bought their furniture on credit from the mill store, where they also bought groceries and clothing. So the mill owner built the houses for five hundred dollars, paid his workers fifteen dollars a week, and then collected all of money back in the form of rent, heat, furniture, or food.

When the mill closed, the houses were abandoned and soon fell into disrepair, after which they simply fell. The store was built of sterner stuff and as I parked in front I was impressed by the obvious sturdiness of the building. I called Bum and took my shotgun from the car. I slipped an ammo belt over my shoulder. The belt was packed with shells.

The old store was one of the three-story variety. It stood on a gently sloping hill and I could see basement windows under the main floor. More windows were visible on the second floor, which meant that if there was anyone in the store, he probably heard and saw me as I arrived, and he would be watching every step I took, every move I made.

I thought about the darkness of the basement and returned to the car for a flashlight. Any way I sliced it, I was the one at a tremendous disadvantage.

Loading the shotgun, both barrels, I shoved the light into my belt and mounted the four shallow steps that led to the wide porch where the furniture once was kept on display during winter and summer alike. To my knowledge, not one piece was ever stolen or vandalized. The balcony roof over the porch kept the goods dry, except in blowing rains, and the polish protected the wood from dampness. A solid wall three feet high enclosed the entire porch except for the area in front of the steps.

The steps, made of wide boards that now were bowed and cracked, gave perilously under my weight, and I shifted my feet to the wood above the stringers. When I reached the porch, I took care to walk over the joists. I planned to get to the basement eventually, but I wanted to go down via the steps.

The front door, half-wood and half-glass, was locked. The lock itself was one of the old-fashioned simplicities that anyone could open with a bent wire or nail. I walked around the waist-high wall until I found a small nail that warping of the wood had pulled from the railing. The nail slipped easily from the wood, and I shoved one end of it into a crack in the wood and then pulled down on the head. The nail bent like baling wire.

I stuck the pointed end into the keyhole, turned the nail gently until I could feel the nail make contact with the key groove, and wiggled until the lock slid home. The door creaked open ominously.

The interior of the store seemed as large as half a football field, but in reality it was only about a hundred feet wide and twice as long. A musty smell of freeze-dried history permeated the entire area. Windows admitted enough light for me to see without the flashlight, and it took only seconds to see that the main floor was completely empty except for some empty beer cans, a wine bottle collection, and a mildewed quilt that had once served as a trysting bed.

In line with the front door and at the back of the store were the stairs to the second floor. I tested the stairs, found them sturdy enough to support me, and climbed to the first landing where I paused to look upward. I could see the highly ornate ceiling with ornamental scroll work. The paint was a smoke yellow.

I climbed the rest of the way and found another cavernous room that, like the first floor, contained evidence that druggies and lovers had used the place in lieu of a motel room. The walls of the room were the same color as that of the ceiling.

The next stop was the basement. As I started down the steps I could hear the scurrying of tiny feet, and I knew I had struck out on my first search. At least no one was likely to be in the space at that moment. Rats do not like the company of people, and the ones that ran at my approach would have fled had any other human beings been in the room.

Still, I searched. The room, unlike those above it, was not empty. Remnants of old furniture, most of it broken, stood against the wall. A huge cardboard box, large enough, it seemed, to hold a small auto, was pushed against one corner.

I directed the beam of the light toward the box. Nothing moved. I stepped closer. When I reached the box I pushed at it with the toe of my boot. It moved easily. I reached out and grasped the open corner of the box and turned it toward me. As I did I trained the light beam on the inside.

I don't know what I expected, if anything, but what I saw made the hairs on the back of my neck stiffen and waves of coldness coursed up and down my spine.

The bottom of the box was covered, except for irregular patches of the original cardboard, with a black substance that I knew without touching or smelling to be blood.

Whirling, I directed the light around the entire room, just in case I had missed something. Or someone. Nothing moved. The room was empty.

It held just me, my shotgun, flashlight, a timid rat that was somewhere hidden and, doubtless, was staring at me with its pale red eyes, and the box of blood.

Then I looked again. In the far corner there was another small object, this one a smudged white. I used the barrel of the shotgun to pick it up. It was a bra. There was dried blood on it, too, and ground-in dirt. Whoever wore the bra, I judged from the marks in the dust at my feet, had been dragged across the floor from the base of the stairs.

Taking out my handkerchief, I unfolded it, then lapped the fold over the bra so that I could carry it without smearing whatever facts the bra had to tell a forensic scientist. Then I hurried to my car and returned to my office where Wadsworth, Rance, Cullen, and Wooley were waiting for me. The look on their faces did nothing to restore my flagging spirits.

On the way out of town I had driven by the school, and Marlin Rockwell's vehicle was not there. Neither was it at his house near the southern part of the lake. I parked in front and pounded on the door, but no one came.

Then I had gone to the stores. What else could I do?

The snow that had fallen on the Sherman County mountains, roads, and hills and valleys had created what many would call a winter wonder. I could see the racks later to be filled with postcards depicting the perfect scenes.

But to me the scene lacked beauty. I thought of the idiot who once lived near me: a truck driver who would go into a rage when any of the kids voiced a wish for snow. He'd snarl and sulk for hours at the thought of his having to leave his warm bed in the middle of the night and drive to the terminal where he'd climb into the cab of his huge truck and spend the night fighting snow and ice.

I used to remind him, before I realized that he was incapable of ever seeing another viewpoint, that wishing did not cause snow. If dreaming brought such results, everyone would be rich, handsome, loved, and studly or sexpottish.

I could look around me and see that wishing had not done much for most of the people I knew, and in my own case, having dreams come true was only the beginning of nightmares that apparently would last for the remainder of my life.

The snow crew had done their usual admirable job, but it was a losing proposition. Still, the highway efforts had piled heaps of snow on the roadsides and somehow the crews kept the main arteries passable. Even the back roads were not impossible, as long as you had snow tires and four-wheel drive.

It was clear, for starters, that the killer found a way to travel in and around the county. But he had all the advantages.

I was limited in what I could do or say. I was certain the man had somehow killed the women. I'd have bet every cent I had on it. But if I had arrested him, that's exactly what I'd have done: bet my last cent on my chances against a libel suit.

I watched the swirling flakes and tried to make sense of what had been happening. Sherlock Holmes used to say that when you eliminate all the impossibles, what is left is your answer. Like most simplistic cliches, this one had drawbacks. By the time we had eliminated all the people who couldn't have killed the women, my beard would reach my ankles.

But, as in all problems, there seems to be a common denominator of sorts. In this case, we started with murders of people, then we reduced it to women. Then to young women and from there to young left-handed women who all belonged to some sort of kooky club and who had been less than virtuous prior to and apparently after marriage. All the women were married to rich young snots whose only reason for existing was that their mothers did not keep their legs crossed.

Beyond that, it was guesswork. Facts were rare.

And I had no proof whatever. Much as I hated to admit it, Rockwell would not qualify as one of the usual suspects.

THIRTEEN

The roads remained virtually impassable except for vehicles with chains, snow tires, or four-wheel drive. The huge snowflakes had given way to tiny, almost invisible blurs of wind-driven crystals of ice that pecked against the windshield that could only make the road even more treacherous. It took me half an hour to reach town and another ten minutes to lurch and slide my way to the courthouse and into my basement office.

Zane met me at the door and nodded toward Ed Gallager, who sat in a straight-backed chair against the wall. He held his head in his hands. Blood trickled between his fingers. Bum hovered over him and gently pulled the frail man's hands away from his crimson-streaked face and daubed at the blood with a damp cloth.

"What happened?" I asked Zane. "Is he badly hurt?"

"Deer hunters," she said wryly. "They shot at a deer and hit his windshield by mistake. He has minor glass cuts."

"Deer hunters?" I repeated. "In this weather?"

"So he says. I don't believe it either. Bum filled out the report. It's on your desk."

I walked over to where the unlikely nurse tended to the editor's scratches.

"What happened, Ed?" I asked. "And don't tell me it was deer hunters. Hunters may be stupid, but they're not always total idiots. Who did

157

this?"

He looked up at me, a furtive weasel-look, then averted his eyes instantly. "I don't know," he said.

I grabbed him by the shoulders and twisted him violently toward me. I shook him as if he were a rag doll. Flecks of his blood spattered my hands and coat sleeves. The editor winced and seemed to collapse inwardly.

"Don't lie to me!" I thundered at him. "You know damn well who did this. Now tell me what happened?"

He looked like a man being crucified might look. He shrank from my grasp and slid down in his chair. Bum grasped my wrists in his huge hands and looked at me steadily.

"Turn him loose," he said, his voice rumbling around in his cavernous chest. "He'll tell us. Give him time."

"Ed," I said, releasing him, "You must tell me who did this."

He tried to shake his head without moving it. "Damn fool deer hunters," he mumbled. "One of the idiots blew the windshield out of my car. Coulda killed me."

He hesitated, then described in painstaking detail how he had been driving from his house to town when the windshield exploded in his face.

"Not deer hunters," I said. "Not in this weather."

"What do they care?" he said. "If they can get their rack they don't care if it's below zero or over a hundred. And they don't care what they destroy while they are at it."

Before I became a part of the law enforcement scene, I thought that the well-trained state-level officers could walk into a crime scene, sniff the air two or three times, and not only point out the killer but tell you what political party the parents belonged to and whether they liked lasagna and bluegrass music. I thought the officers could detect a lie eight miles away.

After working with officers for a while, I came to see them as mostly dedicated and highly professional men and women who do the most they possibly can with what they have. But they are not wizards, and they cannot work miracles. They are as stymied as laymen would be, much of the time, while criminals walk away.

Then somebody walks in and confesses to the criminal acts, and the crime is solved.

Except here nobody was confessing, and our man was a one-person operation and nobody was ratting on anybody. One person knew who the killer was. And maybe another person had a damn good idea. But Ed Gallager wasn't talking.

The words came freely, once he started, but he managed to say a great deal without getting rid of many facts.

"Great," I told him. "Keep lying and women will keep dying. It's your decision. I can't make you tell me the truth, but I can promise you this: if it turns out that your refusal to help us has anything to do with these killings, you are through in Sherman. I will personally do to you what the people of this area should have done when Sherman the Vermin rode into town. Now where is your car?"

"Outside," he croaked. "At the office."

I motioned to Zane and the two of us crossed the street to the newspaper office. Gallager's car was nosed into the curb, but we could see the gaping hole in the windshield long before we reached the vehicle. Flakes of snow filtered into the passenger area and had already covered the seat.

"Convenient," Zane said. "The man who fired the shot managed to miss Gallager completely but demolished one side of the glass. It was a pretty effective warning."

"Meaning what?" It should have been obvious to me. During the past days much of the lethargy I had lived with for months had disappeared, but I still had not learned to think like a law enforcement officer.

"That whoever would normally be riding in the passenger seat would have been blown to bits. Now who would that be?"

I shrugged. "Girl friend? Wife? I never hear him speak of any children. I never saw him with anybody but people in town."

I told her about my visit to the old store. Pulling out the folded handkerchief, I showed her the bra and described the scene inside the huge cardboard box.

"What do you make of it?"

She turned her face toward me, and for the first time I was aware of her delicate features and perfectly formed face. She was not a beauty in the classic sense of the word, but she looked good enough to turn heads

159

on the street.

"Could be any number of things," she said. "Kids making out after school. Or during. We don't know if it's human blood. Best bet is to take the bra to the hospital. And when this is all over we're going to have to make someone buy us a lab."

We stood looking at the shattered windshield for several more moments. Zane picked at the tangle of glass that looked as if it had started to melt.

"Buckshot, most likely," she said. "Fired from straight on, the way it looks. If the shooter had been on the left side of the road, there would have been damage to the passenger window. If he fired from the right side of the road, there would have been damage to Gallager."

"So he stood in the middle of the road. He didn't try to hit Gallager. Just wanted to scare him."

And did a fairly good job of doing it. "What next?"

"Ed Gallager is playing it as cool as he can. Close to his chest. In an editorial he admits that he has been on the wrong end of a cluster of crank calls. He writes calmly about it and suggests that anyone with real information should contact us. I don't know what kind of message he's sending. Whatever it is, it's starting to get to him pretty hard."

I had not mentioned to anyone what I had learned about Gallager, except to Zane and Lurch. I did not want to keep secrets from either of them. Zane, in fact, had informed me that Gallager and, she assumed, his wife lived in a small house just outside town and in a secluded part of the county. She had learned that Mrs. Ed Gallager, if such a person existed, stayed at home most of the time, because there were signs of life inside the house despite the fact that there was no vehicle there. I wondered what Mrs. Gallager would do in case of an emergency.

I also wondered what the story might be on Mrs. Rockwell. I decided that I'd find out as soon as possible.

Zane had told me earlier that she knew there was someone at home because shades went up and down and lights went on and off during the time she watched the house. I knew that lights could be set on timers, but the shades required human operation.

"When have you people slept?" I asked. She laughed without humor and didn't answer. Her fatigue was showing, and I knew it would not be long before she and Rick began to lose their poise. I wasn't much to brag about, either; I could not remember my most recent meal, and Lurch, Zane, and Bum had been on duty every hour I worked.

"What about you?" she asked. "You look as if you have been dead for about two weeks. When did you last eat?"

I told her the truth: that I could not remember. I had eaten most recently whenever it was that Rockwell's wife had made sandwiches and he had delivered them to us.

Zane admitted that she had ordered pizzas. "I had them sent to the county clerk's office," she said. "I did not want the delivery boy to go around telling people that we were in your office pigging out and partying while women all over the country were being murdered. The clerk will bring them to us when the delivery person arrives. I urged him to say nothing about it to anyone. He understands."

I nodded my gratitude to her. At the very mention of food I began to salivate more than a whole pack of Pavlovian dogs would if every bell in town rang. I felt suddenly incredibly weak and useless. I realized that I was weak from hunger and leaned against the car.

"Rick called in," Zane said. "He's been to two of the general stores. The first one is operated by two sisters, both of them in their sixties and frail. They say there is no way anything untoward took place there. The second is owned and operated by a Mister Peepers type of person. No chance of anything wrong there, either. The third is closed for the winter, and Blanton says they checked all around the building and there was no sign of forced entrance or even that anyone had been there in weeks."

"I have other closed stores to check," I said. "I can believe that the killer used the Avon store one time. I can not believe that he would risk using it twice. How long does it take to type blood?"

"Minutes," she said. "We might have early reports before we finish eating."

"Let's walk to the hospital," I suggested. "We can leave the bra for testing."

She looked again at the windshield. "Ed might have shot it out himself," she said. "And then used a piece of shattered glass to scratch himself. Just a thought."

We left the hospital and returned to the office. Ten minutes later Rick

161

joined us, and we closed the office door and asked Bum to admit no one unless there was an impending disaster. Gallager was still sitting in the outer office.

We received the call after the pizza was only a bad memory. The blood could be typed, I was told, quickly. I knew that from my old army days when you could get stuck at one end of the line and learn your blood type by the other end. That wasn't news.

The news was that the blood did not match that of Alisha Webley or any of the other women.

The blood, they told us, was that of a human being, but that was about all they could divulge at the time except that it was Type RH negative.

I thought again and again of the left-handed women and that all of the three had given birth before marriage and not since, and all were members of the same high school class. Coincidence does not extend to that degree, I concluded for the thousandth time, but where is the final line and what is the connection?

It had to do with Ed Gallager. I was convinced of that. I made up my mind to make a visit of my own to his house as soon as possible. And when he was not at home.

"What does Rh mean with reference to blood types?" I asked Rick, the walking encyclopedia. "I've heard it all my life and never took the time to understand it."

He didn't hesitate. "The Rh part of it refers to the rhesus monkey," he said. "It means that the blood type is common to the human being and to the rhesus monkey. At least, that's what it meant when it came into usage."

"It's very rare," I said.

"Among white Americans forty-five percent have type O blood," he said. "Give or take a percentage point here and there. Forty-three per cent have type A. Nine per cent have Type B, and three per cent have AB type."

"What about the Rh types?"

Rick shrugged. "The figures I mentioned add up to one hundred per cent. That means that all other types make up such a small part that they aren't even counted as part of the general population."

I stood, unable to sit any longer. The hot food and coffee had created in me an incredible urge to sleep. I could have lain down on the desk and slept as well as if I had been in a water bed. Dimly, I noticed that Rick was the only one of us without the glazed look that precedes sleep by only seconds.

"Now that we know this," I asked, "what do we know? How, if in any way, does blood type relate to the killer?"

Lurch, too, stood. "Don't know," he said. "Except that I'm interested in who had been in the wood pile."

Zane's eyes widened and she looked sharply at him.

"What I'm asking," Rick said, "is grounded in the adage that explains too many children who look like the milkman or the wood chopper."

"Can they tell us what race person the blood came from?"

He said, "Blood, as far as I know, has no connection with any racial types or characteristics or any other social or biological divisions. The blood of an Afro-American might match that of an African or a Finn, but it may not match his own brother. The same is true of Caucasians. We are concerned with the fact that a very rare blood type shows up but is not like that of any of the victims. That isn't unusual in and of itself, but we wonder whose blood type is Rh Negative."

Gallager, who had remained in the reception room, tapped on the door and opened it slowly and limped his way into the room. He looked old suddenly, decrepit and unstable. I thought he was going to fall and rushed forward to support him. As my arm went around his waist, he winced,

"Are you all right?" I asked. "You need to see a doctor."

Gray-faced, he leaned against the door. "No," he said. "No doctor. It's just that when the bullet went through my car, I ran into a ditch and banged up my ribs. I'll be all right in a couple of days. I'm going to the office. I just wanted you to know." He made his way through the door and disappeared.

I returned to my discussion with Rick.

We have four lines entering the office, and I grabbed a phone and called the Wilmington school offices and asked about the blood type of Ed Gallager. It was type O. I asked the secretary, when I dialed the Wilmington hospital, for the chief of staff, and when I managed to get through half a dozen secretaries and volunteers, I finally made contact with a Dr. Pearson. I explained the problem to him, and he readily supplied me with the name of the only Rh blood carrier he knew.

"The name of the man is Lawton Calvin," he said.

I thanked him and sat there, dazed, for several seconds before I told the others what I had learned.

"What we have," I said, deciding to clear the air, "is an editor who comes and goes as he wishes, never having to answer to anyone. He was once a high school journalism teacher, and he was convicted of theft or misappropriation of funds and was fired from his job and driven out of education. The only people who stood up for him were a principal named Lawton Calvin and a group of students who said he was the best teacher ever to come along. Folks, I don't think we can wait any longer. We are going to do a little checking on Ed Gallager, who has type O blood, and then we are going to try to find Lawton Calvin, who has type Rh Negative blood. But just in case the parents of the murdered women are not in fact the biological parents of their children, I suggest that we call them and verify some blood types."

Hands reached for directories and telephones, and less than two minutes later Zane said, "Tyler's parents both have Blood Type O."

"Thennis' father is Type O and her mother is Type A," Lurch said.

"Webley's parents are both Type A," Wadsworth reported. "So where does that leave us?"

"With two distinct possibilities," Lurch answered. "Either the parents are lying or in error, or there has indeed been an alien in the woodpile. There is no possible way that either of the dead women could be Rh negatives, not with the parents they have. It could also start to explain why there seems to be no history or record of the children of the dead women."

"So we need to get a medical verification of the blood types of the parents of all the victims," I said. "If it turns out that they are correct, then we have to start searching through the old woodpile."

"I'll make some calls," Zane said. "I know some of the local doctors. I might be able to talk them into giving out some of the information. All right if I threaten them with a court order if they don't feel talkative?"

"Threaten them with castration with the old ubiquitous dull hoe if that's what it takes," I said. "I'm going to drive around. There are some old stores I didn't get to explore."

Lurch rose as I left and followed me outside. "I thought we'd do this together," he said. "It's hard to watch your back trail and see where you're going at the same time. All right with you?"

"You betch-um, Red Ryder," I said, quoting the Fred Harman comic strip character. "Let's ride."

We checked the newspaper office and learned that Gallager was reportedly at home to catch up on his sleep, so we postponed that visit. I saw no reason to alert him until we had concrete evidence. So we drove around the countryside.

Ten miles from Sherman was the tiny town of Riverside, which did, in fact, lie on both sides of the Rocky Broad River, and managed to accomplish two feats simultaneously. It polluted the river hopelessly and created the dirtiest town in the prettiest setting that I could imagine.

The river a hundred yards upstream is quiet and flat, wending its way through mountain valleys, splashing and eddying over and around immense boulders. It provides life for trout, smallmouth bass, perch, and bream and offers mild canoeing thrills for the outdoorsmen. Deer drink from the clear waters, as do other forms of wild life, and they all survive.

A hundred yards downstream from Riverside the stream is dull brown, sluggish, and congested with the detritus from the two cotton mills that the owners euphemistically named the Bards and Ariel Mills. The names obviously sprang from the owner's love, at least his expressed love, for Shakespeare. I wondered if the same owner had founded the Avon Mill or if the second owner wished he had thought up the idea and swiped it.

The mills stood on either side of the river, and the general store for each mill was located in a grove of oak trees a stone's throw from the mill itself.

We tried the Ariel first and found nothing of interest. Like the Avon Mill store, the Ariel offered three floors of space as well as a covered porch that also served as a balcony for the upstairs floor. It looked as if the same architect designed both mill and store.

Lurch and I entered by the front door, again. This time Lurch picked the lock, which was as easy as picking your teeth.

We entered the main floor and shined our lights around the walls. We then climbed, as I had done before in the other store, to the upstairs floor. The scene was similar to the other one: empty bottles and cans, a quilt spread across the oily floor, styrofoam cups and sandwich containers, and other evidence that the store had been used by other human beings and for reasons that I did not even want to contemplate. Used condoms lay in a half-circle around the quilt, and against the wall lay a wadded section of newspaper with dark stains on it. A string protruded from one crease in the paper.

There was no need to touch it. The tampon was anything but sanitary. I wouldn't have touched it even with gloves. Spread across the quilt were short lengths of rope and nylon apparently cut with a very sharp knife. From the quilt came odors that managed to survive and even defeat the cold and the wind and time.

"Love in the nineties," Lurch said. "You've read 'The Waste Land.' You think this is what Eliot had in mind?"

I shuddered at the thought that the frequenters of the old store and the quilt could have under any circumstances thought they were engaged in making love. If I were a woman I think that I would prefer the grossest Anglo-Saxon four-letter words in a proposition from such slime to the suggestion of making love. Love was never intended to be dragged through the sewers.

We descended the steps slowly. This time I flashed my light across the surface of the treads and against the waist-high rail I could see more strands of rope, nylon, clothesline, and other evidence of bondage.

At the bottom of the steps there was a wide landing before the steps led to the basement. On the treads and even on the rail I could see dark stains that I'd have bet were human blood of indeterminate age. We sidestepped these carefully.

The steps stopped before a wide expanse of open floor. Again I saw broken furniture, cardboard boxes, and every imaginable form of litter. Some of the boxes were as high as my head and as wide as the length of my outstretched arms. From a dozen places I could hear the scritching of tiny feet and claws on wood, paper, cardboard, and garbage.

Holding my shotgun in my right hand and my flashlight in my left, I used the barrel of the gun to turn the first cardboard carton so that I could see inside it. A modest-sized rat glared at me, its eyes pale red in the flow of my flashlight. It sat up on its haunches and bared its teeth, as if ready to do battle. Then it thought better of its decision and dropped to all fours and skulked away, its belly dragging the filthy surface of the bottom of the carton.

It was in no hurry, its pace a deliberate insult to me and the danger I posed to it. I was tempted to launch a swift kick at its sagging belly but thought better of my impulse.

Two rats, both equally defiant, inhabited the second carton, and they both glared their anger at my interruption of what is loosely called mating. I thought again of the most insidiously evil and perverse description of sex I had ever heard or read: Shakespeare's depiction of the beast with two backs. Except even beasts defy the description.

Their callous efforts to fill the earth with more of their foul breed overpowered my judgment, and I kicked the two of them viciously. They sailed through the air, collided with the side of the carton, and landed, their frustrations equalling their anger, and crouched to attack me. I aimed the shotgun at the pair of them and my finger tightened on the trigger when I felt, sensed, a movement to my left. I turned to face Lurch and felt something slam into the left side of my face.

I reeled sideways, crashed into the carton wall, and felt it collapse under me. My finger instinctively tightened on the absent trigger and dimly I realized that the gun was gone. The windowless basement became totally dark except for a tumbling, reeling glow that somehow I recognized as my flashlight rolling across the floor.

Then the light stopped moving and the beam was directed into my face. I tried to adjust my body and realized that I was flat on my back on the carton that had seconds earlier been a love-nest for rats. Something moved under me and I squirmed wildly to escape the tiny but sharp teeth of the rats, both of which had somehow been imprisoned under my helpless body.

Something cold and hard butted sharply against my belly, and I recognized the double barrels of what had seconds earlier been my shotgun but which now belonged to someone else.

"Get his billfold," a thin masculine voice said. "If he moves I'll blow his guts all over this place."

I did not move as the hands found the wallet in my back pocket and unbuttoned the flap on my pocket. I felt the slim bulk of the billfold move smoothly and then the contact with my body was broken. The pocket area was suddenly cold and empty.

"What now?" the voice of the second person asked.

"We kill the son of a bitch," the first voice said. I wondered where Lurch had gone, and it occurred to me that he had been overpowered before the assailants had accosted me.

"No," the second voice said. I could not tell if the owner was a girl or an effeminate male. It didn't matter. A girl can pull a trigger as well as a man can. Not even a child could miss, not at this range.

"No," the first voice said. "We kill him and leave him for the rats."

Of all the words I have heard in my life, I could not think of any more disheartening than those. I shuddered at the thought of those pink eyes and sharp teeth and my helpless body.

"Why don't we tie him up and gag him and let the rats eat him alive?" the girl voice said. I instantly retracted my earlier estimation of disheartening words. I thought of Edgar Allan Poe's "The Pit and the Pendulum," easily one of the worst short stories ever written, and the absurd gnawing of the victim's ropes by the hordes of rats in the pit. I never understood why the rats did not eat the food in the dish while the hero of the story had been drugged. There were a dozen other stupidities in the story.

Neither did I understand why I thought of such inanities when my life was at stake.

"We kill him," the rougher voice said. "I'm not taking any chances. We take his money and his credit cards and we buy as much as we can as fast as we can, and then we get the hell out of Dodge."

It was insanity, I thought. Often in my life I have spent minutes, even hours, wondering about the circumstances that resulted in my being in a peculiar or even bizarre place at a particular time. But never did I in my wildest imaginations think I would be immersed in filth in the basement of a falling-down country store where perverts casually discussed the fact that I'd have to be killed.

I thought of the Robert Louis Stevenson character who insisted that none of the faults has been his own. "Giants have dragged me by the wrists from the moment of my birth," he whined. Or words to that effect. "The giants of circumstance."

I had no giants to blame. I was here in this filthy, smelly, dark, and loathsome basement of a decaying country store for reasons of my own making. I wanted out of prison and agreed to let Edney Parkins buy the sheriff's badge for me. I was in prison because I did a damn-fool thing in order to vent my frustrations for an earlier and even dumber damn-fool action I had taken. I had, even before that, tried to help an old and helpless woman to what was rightfully hers.

Why couldn't I have done what thousands of others do each and every day? Why couldn't I have turned my back and walked away, and left her to the rats and the roaches of the modern world?

But the old and helpless woman was not my reason for being in the basement and at the mercy of the two crazies who coldly planned to kill me. I was the problem. I clung to some of the old stupidities of honor and chivalry when every ounce of common sense screams to think of ourselves. Not of others. And we become relics of the past when we try to import the values of the earlier ages into the crass modern world that values a dollar over a drop of blood and another notch on our guns over the basic values of decency and respect.

Mentally I cursed. Myself, Edney, Derry, and all the others who had put me in this hell-hole. But even my silent cursings were silenced by the shrill voice of the creature who earlier had been a girl, before the modern world had created her in its own image.

From the dark recesses of my mind three names popped up and demanded my attention, even as I prepared to die. The names were Charles Lutwidge, Thomas Stearns, and Ernest Miller. I wished I had some way to convey the answer to that particular riddle before the two killed me.

Thomas Stearns was not unknown to me, in the larger sense. These were the first two names of the noted poet and critic T. S. Eliot. I might have passed off the trivia as accidental if it had not been for the fact that the first two names of Papa Hemingway were Ernest Miller.

To nail down the logic, there was the third name: Charles Lutwidge, the first two names had to be the start of another celebrity's name. I was unable to think logically, not with the two poised to destroy me. There is no explanation of the way the human mind works under stress, and my feeble brain was racing, largely in an effort to keep from facing what was coming my way within seconds.

As I faced what I fully expected to be my last moments on earth, my head was filled with wild and crazy thoughts and sensations. My nose was filled with the stench of the basement and the thick, pungent aroma of my two captors, both of whom smelled worse than any stable ever could. I was acutely aware of the cold, my discomfort, my fear, and my impending end. I felt myself jerk all over when I heard the next words.

"Then do it," the girl voice said, and there was a sudden explosion of noise and light and the room was filled with the odor of cordite and fear. I felt myself crashing a second time to the floor and realized with disgust that my face was jammed into the bottom of the carton where the rats had mated only seconds earlier. Everything else was black.

FOURTEEN

The flashlight beam burned into my eyes, forging an ache that reached behind the sockets and seared my brain. A voice strong yet soft rumbled in a nearby cave. It took me several seconds to recognize the voice as Blanton's.

"You're all right," he said. "Just lie there for a few more minutes."

A few more? How long had I lain there? And where was I lying and why? What did he mean: I was all right? How did he know? He hadn't been gut-shot at point-blank range with a double-barrel 12-gauge shotgun.

The shotgun! I suddenly remembered everything with ringing clarity and tried to rise, but Rick held me down as if I were a newborn infant. Once again I registered my thanks that the man was a friend rather than an enemy.

"What happened?" I asked, lifting my head again. He must have decided that it was safe for me to do so; he lifted his huge arm and helped me to a sitting position. I took the light from his hand and flashed the beam around us.

Six feet away lay my shotgun. The barrels, I noticed, lay on the crumpled shape of a used condom.

Ten feet from the shotgun lay a man wearing ragged, dark, and filthy trousers and a grimy plaid jacket. A knit cap covered his head, all but his

171

face, which was an unrecognizable mass of blood and cartilage and a substance that I could not identify.

"Who is he?" I asked.

Rick shook his head. "Just a man, at this point. A man who tried to kill you."

My head throbbed with exaggerated tempo at the new mention of the attempted murder. I directed the beam of the light around the room and saw another human being, this one lying face down in several layers of filth. A pool of blood surrounded the face of the person.

"They were going to kill you," Rick said. "Bums. Holdup punks with a gun and greed."

"My God!" I said. "What did you do to them?"

"Talked them into not killing you."

He was never talkative about anything he did along that line. I had been only dimly aware of his presence in the room until the action had ended.

He was lifting me from the floor and steadying me until my legs supported me. "If you feel up to it," he said, "We can drag these two to the jailhouse. Might be some paper out on them. At least get them behind bars. We can check them out to see if there is a link between them and the killings."

But as he spoke I knew that it was wishful thinking on his part. These two had nothing to do with the murders. The killer had to have access to a vehicle of some sort, and these two looked as if the only things they possessed were lice and fleas.

"Better get them to a hospital first," I said. "What did you hit them with?"

"Fist of death," he said, quoting Alice in "Dilbert" and grinning sheepishly. "Ready?"

I nodded, and he reached down and grasped each of the inert forms by the collars of their coats and dragged them to the stair well, then up it. Their bodies bumped like arthritic snakes as Lurch pulled them as if they were bundles of old clothes. For reasons I cannot explain the sight reminded me of the old and stale vaudeville skit in which a man asks his companion why he was dragging the rope. "You ever try to push one?" his friend answered. These two could never have been pushed.

He didn't ask or expect me to help him. He continued to drag them all the way across the open floor of the store and through the front door. He bumped them down the front steps and then dropped one and then lifted the other bodily and dumped him into the back of the vehicle, then deposited the second one on top of the first one. I hoped they would not have the clout or the knowledge to launch a lawsuit against us for brutality. The message has been made abundantly clear in this country: the criminals can batter police to their heart's content, but woe to the cop who fights back. But maybe these two had not heard the news.

We drove to the office where Bum jerked awake and then went into his routine. Within minutes he had the two standing naked against a shower wall where he waited until they were reasonably clean before he tossed them some jailhouse clothes and then took them into the interrogation area, which was only a large closet converted to that purpose.

I watched with only casual interest. Personally I did not care if their lice ate them alive, but for the first time I realized with certainty that one of the bums might be a woman. I thought she was, but only her voice suggested sex. There was certainly nothing suggestive of femininity about her.

Actually, she was a girl, and without her layers of filth and grime she might have been close to attractive. Now, though, her wet hair hung limply across her face and neck, while streams of water coursed across her body. She made no effort to cover herself. I wondered how many lawsuits we'd get out of this.

She appeared to be no more than seventeen or eighteen years old, but the miles had been rough ones. Her companion was older: thirty or so years old and equally hard-ridden during his time. Both had been so stoned out of their heads—or pretended to be—that they did not appear to know where they were or what was happening to them. Except for the girl, who for some reason became modest when she began to dress. If there is a lesson in there, I missed it.

For several minutes afterward we had to question them, but their replies were incoherent. Neither seemed seriously hurt, although to be on the safe side I had asked a nurse to come in to check them out. She said that the man had a badly broken nose but little else wrong with him that several days of healing would not cure. The woman had a badly discolored eye and a swollen face. I did not ask if that was the result of Rick's fist or her crash onto the floor. I thought it best not to know.

Zane told us that the pockets of the girl's clothing contained nothing. Not even a book of matches.

The man's clothes, Bum told me, were slightly different. He had a wad of money in his left front pocket. Bum laid the thick envelope before me and together we counted the money.

The bum had nearly three thousand dollars on him.

So why were they living in near-freezing conditions in the old store? Why didn't they stay in a motel? Why didn't they eat in a decent restaurant—after they bought some new clothes and had a bath long enough to wash away eight or ten of the outer layers of filth?

It seemed obvious to me at first that they could not survive for long in the abandoned store. Hypothermia would kill them, assuming they survived the rest of the weather-related perils. Yet, I thought again, the winter campers manage to live and even tell us that they like living in Arctic simulation. And the old store had a basement that surely remained fairly warm even in the coldest of weather. I knew that in my cabin the basement was in the summer the coolest part of the house and in the winter the warmest.

When the two were in a cell and the money had been counted and the envelope had been sealed and locked away, Lurch and I returned to the store and found nothing of help to us. There were articles of soiled clothing in the cardboard boxes but nothing that offered a hint to the identities of the pair. In a far corner we found extra thermal underwear and sleeping bags, so at least one question was answered: we knew how they managed to stay alive in the cruel weather. In a closet area that had perhaps once been a dressing room, we found the detritus of half a dozen Rainbow Arches meals.

My head throbbed despite the four aspirin I had taken. The only immediate result of the medication was the recollection that aspirin and X-Rays and the telephone and telegraph all came about within a decade after the modern version of the bathtub was invented. Which meant that in Victorian England for about ten years it was possible to take a bath without having to get out of the tub to answer the phone.

Rick had convinced me that I had not been shot, but the blast and the

174

unconsciousness had come so close together that I had for several minutes assumed the obvious, but if the way I felt was any touchstone, I'd have guessed that I was terminal.

There are thirteen tiny towns in Sherman County, and in each town there was a general store and a mill. Lurch and I devoted the rest of the day to searching all of the vacant stores. In three of them we found reason to think that there had been recent human habitation. It was possible that the pair we arrested had moved from store to store, although it seemed unlikely to me. I saw no benefit in their doing so.

In the final store, this one located in the community called Cato, we found a heap of clothing that had been piled in a grimy corner. Apparently the clothing doubled as a bed and as a wardrobe. We used a stick to pull the garments, one by one, from the pile. There were jeans, khaki trousers, shirts, underwear, for both male and female, sweatshirts, socks, and handkerchiefs. The clothing appeared to be of all sizes, which made me think that whoever used the bed had stolen the clothes from a line in the area. Some housewife had hung the clothing out to dry days before the storm and then had found it missing when she returned to take it in.

A small electrical heater, also stolen, I assumed, stood in one corner of the room. Cardboard boxes had been stacked into a fragile wall across part of the room.

The discovery was not exciting. The college attracted several thousand students of all ages, and while most of them attended classes and held part-time jobs or played ball, there would invariably be a handful who bombed out of their classes and rather than return home to face wrathful parents they found their version of a commune in one of the abandoned buildings.

"The two hippies lived here," Rick said. He flicked a light switch and the overhead bulbs came on.

"The electricity is still on the meter," he said. "They could run the heater and no light could be seen from outdoors."

"You think they've been here long?"

"A week. Two at the most."

"Just passing through?"

"Looks that way. We've had no reports of robberies or thefts of large sums of money. Where'd they get the three thousand?"

I had no answers for him.

It was nearly dark when we called off the search for the day. In each of the stores we had found the oiled floor and the presence of well-preserved bits and pieces of furniture, but in none of the buildings was there white paint to flake off. Other than the pair of scruffy bums, we had found nothing other than the expected rats and filth.

We talked little as we rode. Occasionally one of us would offer some weak theory about what was happening, but for the most part we rode, searched, and thought.

My thoughts were simple and unsatisfactory. Three women had been kidnapped and murdered. In each case the husband had called to report a missing wife, and in each instance the killer had called the office of Ed Gallager, the newspaper editor, or the Sherman Hospital. In the first two deaths there had been tiny specimens of rose beryl either on the body or nearby. In the third there had been paint flecks embedded in the hair or scalp of the victim. In addition to the rose beryl.

The beryl had a definite connection, I was convinced, as did the left-handedness and the births prior to marriage. But what was the connection? And with whom? Rick as always had theories.

"The women wore the beryl as reminders of what the men in their lives had done to them," he said. "The stone symbolized that the women had been bought and paid for, and if they proved to be unsatisfactory they could be returned to the store where they were purchased. And the women had to refund all that they had been given: money, house, car, furs, jewelry."

"And children," he added.

I wondered how long it could continue. I could not imagine that there would be an endless string of deaths, but even as I tried to comfort myself I thought of the Atlanta children who had been killed at such an alarming rate and in such numbers.

In Atlanta there had been a modest-sized army looking for the killer, and he eluded them for months. Here we had only a tiny fraction of the population of Atlanta, but we had many times the geographic area.

Plus the snow.

I kept going back to the left-handed women. All three had married a wealthy man who obviously exercised a morganatic form of marriage.

At least the women apparently thought so. All had belonged to the point-less social club that seemed by its nature restricted to a handful of people. Almost a high school clique rather than a functioning club with its own purpose and reason for being.

"Want to go back to the office?" Rick asked. I told him that I pre-ferred to keep on riding. I knew that it was pointless to do so, but it was better than sitting and waiting.

"Let's swing by the post office in Grassy Knob," I said. I told Rick about the visits to earlier post offices. "It's only a couple of miles from here."

We caught them at a busy time. There was one customer in the store: a grossly obese woman who appeared to be eighty years old and who looked like a beached whale in her bulky clothing. She was unlocking a mailbox near the door.

She was the same woman, I was certain, that I had seen as she pulled the sled down the main street in Sherman when I went with Zane to the office to see Bert Webley that first morning. I shuddered at the recollec-tion of the horrible body odor that had nearly overcome me, even on the street in the wide open space.

And she had been in the post office in Mica.

It had to be the same woman. How many women are that obese and that tall and that disagreeably smelling? I wondered how she traveled.

Years earlier I had written a handful of short stories but then I hesi-tated to submit them for publication. I asked a writer friend if she thought I had a chance of selling the stories if I submitted them. She replied that she didn't know, but she knew what my chances were if I did not submit them.

I knew how slim our chances were of seeing somebody or something that would lead us to the killer as we rode the roads and byways of Sherman County, but I also knew that if we went to the office what our chances would be.

I was totally frightened, frustrated, and defeated. I had no earthly idea how to go about investigating the crimes, but at the same time I knew we were getting close. In all the books I had read and movies I had seen there had always been the brilliant scientific investigator or sleuth who could take a tiny scrap of paper or a button or the scent of bath oil and

177

follow the trail directly to the killer.

Horse flop. The killer in Sherman had left what seemed to be an abundance of clues, but nothing led anywhere. It was as if someone left me in the middle of a jungle and told me to start looking for the lost gold mine. Where to look? What to look for, other than the obvious? In all the books there is a knife blade that makes a peculiar cut, and the blade, which was manufactured only on Maundy Thursday in an Alabama village inhabited only by old men and former Slobbovian military officers from World War II, can be traced to sloe-gin drinkers in the South.

In real life there is no such convenience. The injuries we had seen could have been inflicted by any knife bought in any store in the state. The only difference was that the slashes were long rather than deep. There were no stab wounds. The vehicle, if any, used in the kidnappings could have been any car in the state, as well.

Each time I tried to reason logically, I'd wind up asking if I had a redheaded brother would he like cheese. I came back to where I started, invariably, and more and more I realized that all the others felt essentially the way I did. The state people were as helpless as I was. The only good news is that we saw them only on rare occasions.

Like when they came by the office to mooch food.

Wadsworth with all of his list of crimes solved and criminals imprisoned did not seem to have any more sense of direction than I did. Neither did Rowena or Lurch or Rance or Wooley.

Worse, the state people did not seem intensely interested in solving the crimes, a realization that left me with chills not related to the weather that coursed up and down my spine. Why weren't they more involved? Why had they assumed a laid-back attitude?

I thought I knew the answer. Three of the four had testified against me when I had been charged with killing my wife and Edney Parkins. And, more through dumb luck than through skill, I had managed to make all of them look more idiots than experts. I don't think any of them appreciated the farce they became a part of, but neither would they look the other way while a killer went about his activities.

Years ago I adopted the theory that if a man goes out on his back deck at three o'clock in the afternoon and blindfolded fires a rifle into the woods, eventually he would kill a deer, if there is a deer in the woods.

He might kill a dozen people along the way, but given time and repetition he would ultimately succeed, if killing the deer was what he wanted to do.

And we would solve the crimes eventually, but after how many more women had been killed? I thought of the Unabomber case and how the best police with the best equipment had failed for years to capture the elusive bomber or even have a verifiable lead to help them. They were helpless, waiting for someone who could point them on the correct route.

The mountain-woman finally moved, and as we passed her she turned her face toward us. Her flesh was gray, and her odor had not improved. She had on the same clothes she had worn each time I had seen her previously.

I wasn't surprised. I couldn't imagine that many stores carried anything that would fit her. She must have been six and a half feet tall and her weight couldn't have missed three hundred by more than a couple of ounces. Maybe she weighed even more.

When she moved and her aroma faded slightly, we approached the man on duty, a short and eternally smiling man in his early fifties who greeted us with a disgusting amount of good cheer. He seemed to be elated that the snow kept falling. I did not share his enthusiasm. Instead, I opened the high school yearbook in front of him, identified myself and Rick, and asked if he had seen either Webley, Tyler, or Thennis in the post office before.

He studied the photos for several long seconds, then he shook his head slowly. "Not a chance," he said. "I have a fairly good memory for names and faces, and I never laid eyes on any of them."

He flipped back and forth from one page to another, then quickly flipped back to an earlier page.

"This one," he said, pointing at the photo, "has been in here. I've seen her a dozen or so times."

He had not pointed to the photo of either of the dead women. Instead, he pointed at Laura Anson. I knew her as Laura Dennis.

My heart quickened and I could feel the pounding in my chest. "Are you sure?" I asked. "Be totally certain. This is more important than you will believe."

He grinned happily. Small triumphs were not common in his life, apparently.

"No chance of a mistake. In here twice a month. When you have only a small number of boxes, you don't forget them."

"Who rents the box?" I asked.

"No problem. Man named William Harrison. Lives out on the Panther Creek Road. Woman just in here picked up his mail. You walked right past her. Couldn'ta missed her. Big as a battleship. You can catch her if you hurry."

Rick and I bolted from the post office and into the snow-filled parking lot. It was empty. There was no sign of a vehicle in any direction.

"What was parked here when we arrived?" I asked Rick. "Did you see a car of any sort?"

"Lot was empty," he said. "She must have parked nearby and walked to the post office. What do you want to do?"

"Ride," I said. "Try whatever direction you like. We need to catch a glimpse of her and her vehicle."

So we rode, and I thought, and I became more and more frustrated, which is undoubtedly what the killer wanted.

It dawned on me that we, not he, were the prey. He would keep us running frantically in all directions until we were totally exhausted, too tired to think effectively or correctly, too bewildered to know how to move in a logical straight line or to see the relevance of events to each other.

He couldn't have planned the post office encounter, but it had only added to our frustrations.

"Why don't you go home and rest?" Rick asked after an hour of fruitless searching. "You've been nodding off and jerking awake for the past half hour. If we run upon the guy, we'd both fall asleep while chasing him. Want me to run you by your place?"

I shook my head emphatically. The effort roused me into total wakefulness. The thought was horrifying. The first body had been left in my car. The second in the woods near the house. The third was in my basement.

I didn't want to think, couldn't bear to think where the next one would be. I was terrified to sleep. I was scared that in my dreams there would be bodies in my closet, in my bathtub, sitting at my table, in the fireplace.

180

What I needed was obvious. I needed to catch a killer, and I needed to see Laura. It seemed ages ago that she had called and told me that she wanted to see me about something important. I returned to the office, leaving Bum and the bums to work matters out among them. I knew he'd not get anything as long as they were stoned out of their heads. I went into my office, closed the door, and called Laura.

She answered the phone on the first ring. She seemed terrified at first, but when she recognized my voice her own was flooded with instant relief.

"Chess!" she nearly shouted. "I've been worried sick about you. I've called your house a thousand times." She giggled nervously. "Well, at least a couple dozen times. I know you have been unbearably busy and—preoccupied—but I wanted so much just to hear your voice."

I was starting to wish she would pause for a moment so that she could, indeed, hear a voice other than her own. She did, and I spoke quickly.

"Listen," I said, "You said you needed to talk. What did you want to see me about?"

Her voice dropped to a whisper. "Not now," she said. "My husband is here. I'll be at your place in an hour." She had already started to slur her words, and I knew that in another hour she would be incoherent. I started to tell her to lay off the tranquilizers and booze and start on coffee.

She hung up before I could argue with her. I would have cursed if it hadn't required so much energy.

I looked at my watch. It was seven-forty, dark, and incredibly cold. The skies had cleared and the wind had risen, dropping the chill factor to minus thirty, according to the local radio station.

The news was both good and bad. The bad news was that the weather was life-threatening; the good news was that the killer would perhaps need to stay inside, too.

But I took no comfort from the thought. The killings had started as the blizzard hit us on that first day, and as the storm intensified, so did the actions of the murderer.

I suspected that it was far more than coincidence. In the mountains of this state, we occasionally get the four-day and five-day storms that dump tons of snow on our area. The sophisticated weather instruments can track the storms from the time they start pushing down from the north in the forms of the Siberian Express until they sweep down to the Gulf of Mexico before turning and starting up the East Coast. So we had four or five days of warning before the first flakes fell.

Zane tapped at the door and then pushed it open. Her face was somber and frightened. But there was not a suggestion of new horrors; it saddened me beyond words to realize that for days she had worn the same fixed expression on her face.

"Got a minute?" she said. "Before we both fall asleep?"

"Sure," I said. "What can I do for you?"

The faintest of smiles broke through the tragic mask.

"Anything you wish," she said, and she closed the door.

FIFTEEN

She quickly crossed the distance between the door and the chair in front of my desk. At the chair she paused, hand on the back rail, before sitting.

"The news first," she said, her face flushed. "The Beautiful People in the cell have been identified. They are Bert Ragsdale and Nita Richie."

"So what does this tell us?"

"Neither is what you would call a spotlessly clean citizen. Ragsdale stayed in trouble in high school. Then he enrolled at Sherman University to major in—guess what?"

I felt my pulse quicken. "Journalism?" I asked.

"You win the turkey, Chief. Now guess where he attended high school."

"Wilmington," I said.

"You now have two turkeys. Now guess the background of Miss Nita Richie. Or I'll give you the shortened version."

"Give," I said. "Is she from Wilmington, too?"

"Classmate of Ragsdale. Also a journalism major, except that she was waylaid somewhere along the line."

"She became pregnant in high school?" I guessed.

"You could open a frozen turkey farm," Zane said. "I called the Wilmington police department and they had her records there. It seems she and Ragsdale led a gang that assaulted a man. They succeeded in

183

permanently injuring his wife. They raped her over and over, and not just with their own equipment. She was messed up internally something awful, the police said. And externally. They said her face was scarred hideously, and she suffered from severe damage to the thyroid and pancreas. Nothing helped. She became totally dysfunctional as a woman."

"Am I to guess the man and wife?" I asked. "If so, I'd guess Lawton Calvin and whoever his wife is."

"You now own a flock of frozen turkeys," she said. "The man himself managed to escape and leave his wife in the hands of the gang. The Wilmington police say it was a real pity. She was Miss New York Something or Other. Had a minor career as a decoration in some mildly good movies. A real beauty: a Marilyn Monroe who never got the breaks. The only break was marrying Calvin. After the attack, she started to gain weight and she never stopped. One theory is that she wanted to become so hideous that no man would ever lust after her again. Another is that the internal injuries left her metabolism completely screwed up, and I'm not punning. So instead of Miss New York she's Miss Apprehension."

"Could they tell you the location of Calvin now?"

"All they know is that a couple of years, maybe less, after Gallager went on trial, they left town. He taught at a small two-year college in the mountains. He had the weird habit of creeping about the campus at night. He was fired and no one knows what happened after that."

I studied her face, which was eager yet expressionless.

"You're holding out on me," I said. "What's the rest of the story."

"Nita Richie's blood type is RH negative."

"Lawton Calvin is her father?" I knew it was a stretch, but it was also a good possibility.

"Maybe," she said. "Which means that Lawton Calvin is perhaps living in Sherman County."

"And killing the women?" I asked. "Is that what you think?"

She shrugged. "Do we have a better guess?" she asked.

"What about Gallager? He has the criminal record."

"Theft is not a sex crime."

"He was charged with theft. Some of the people I talked with are of the opinion that they got him for what they could, not what they wanted to get him for."

"Which is?"

"He began dating a former student. A student who graduated two years earlier. She was twenty."

"Not a crime," I went on. "Almost as old as Lauren Bacall was when she married Bogart. Bad judgment? Maybe. Criminal? No."

"They were married two years when she left him."

"For another man, obviously. You want me to guess who?"

"You'd be right. She ran off with Lawton Calvin."

"And Nita Richie is their child?"

She nodded. "At least, she thinks she is."

"And Ed Gallager is not married?"

"Looks that way."

"Then who answered the phone at his house?"

"No turkeys for me. I have no idea."

She told the rest of the details of the check on the two we had taken into custody, which were sketchy at best, and when she had finished she stood, awkward and helpless, before me.

"This is awful," she said. I had no earthly idea what it was that was so awful, unless she was referring, as I suspected, to the killings. To find them awful at such a late date was in and of itself interesting.

"Yes," I said, not knowing what else to say.

She shook her head and for a moment I thought she would burst into tears. I had no idea how to handle such an incident and dreaded the prospects. A man can comfort a distraught woman, but how can one law officer comfort another law officer? The uniforms made the difference. There was something inherently wrong in hugging a uniformed person. I felt my stereotypical attitudes showing and desperately tried to reel them in.

"No," I said, reasoning that if an affirmative word did not answer the remark, perhaps a negative one would.

She shook her head again, her hair sweeping back and forth across her mouth and chin.

"Should I try a maybe?" I asked.

She almost smiled. "There are no proper words," she said, "and even if there were, this would be a hell of a time to try to say them. Sorry about the intrusion. I'll get out of your hair and let you do whatever it was you came in here to do."

"I've done it," I said. "Stay where you are and tell me what's bothering you. I'm notoriously inept at solving problems, but I listen reasonably well."

She shook her head again, and this time a smile peeked past her troubled expression. "You don't listen worth a damn," she said. "You haven't heard what I've been telling you for two months now. But you try, and I guess that's something. I know it is. I'm talking about your phone call. The one you just made."

She waved her hand impatiently as I started to speak. "Don't deny it, Chess, for God's sake. It's written all over your face. You just finished arranging a date with that woman. The only question I have is which one of you will wind up dead. My bet is that both of you will."

"We shouldn't be having this conversation," I said. "What can either of us gain from it?"

"Gain? Who's talking about gain? What I'm talking about is damage control. The loss of your life. Loss of your job. And what is left of your future."

Her face was nearly livid by this time and she had risen from her chair and walked across the room to the window that overlooked the parking lot. She turned back to face me, and now her expression had softened slightly.

"Chess," she said, almost pleading, "this county has had three murders in one week. Are you hearing me? In one week! One of the lowest crime counties in the entire nation and we have three killings in one week. Not barroom fights. Not riots at the prison camp. Not domestic fights." She took a deep breath and plowed straight ahead.

"All three have been cold-blooded killings that were premeditated and cold as the weather. And what do we have to show for our work? Nothing. We can't offer to the public even a single clue that might conceivably lead us to a killer. We can't even know whether the killer is man or woman or both. We are at ground-level zero and digging ourselves in deeper with every passing minute. Right now, while we are fighting—or at least, I am, while you sit there and look as if you can't decide whether you need to go to the toilet—the killer is planning, setting up, or even carrying out his next crime. He might be stalking his next victim. He might even have her by now. He could be slicing her clothes from her body. He might even be slicing her! And what do you do? You set up a meeting with your girl friend."

She paused for breath and contented herself for the moment simply to glare at me. She was breathing heavily and her eyes had filled with tears. She was about three minutes from a complete and total breakdown. She composed herself for her next attack.

"Have you read the paper? Gallager has been as kind as he possibly can be, but he has his limits. He has said as gently as possible that one man, presumably, operating in snow and under the worst of conditions, has somehow kidnapped three prominent women in broad daylight and has killed them and stashed the bodies in the sheriff's car and on his property and in his house. All this while the sheriff, his deputies, and four STOP detectives are chasing their tails and at this point have nothing whatever to show for their time and efforts. He held back as much as he could, but he said that he felt that it was his duty to warn, to scare, to terrify, if necessary, the people of this town so that they would be more careful, that they would look out for suspicious characters, strangers, or people we all know who seem to be doing anything even remotely suspicious. Then he turns around and commends all of us for our untiring work and efforts on behalf of the people of this county. He stresses that we are going without sleep and food and rest in our attempts to stop the killings."

She looked me straight in the eye and hissed: "If we can go without food and sleep and time off, you sure as hell can do without sex for a few days. Do you hear what I'm saying? How can you possibly set up a bedroom meeting while there are people out there being killed? How can you defend yourself if another body is found while you are in the sack with another man's wife? Chess, damn it, do you not care whether you go back to prison?"

There it was. It was out, now, and she could afford herself the luxury of tears. She sat down hard and laid her arms across the desk and dropped her face between her arms and cried like a child. Between wracking sobs, she mumbled past her tears and runny nose, "Damn it, *I care*. Even if you don't."

I heard what she was saying, loud and clear. She added nothing that I hadn't already considered too many times. I don't think there has been a waking moment since I was released from prison that I didn't shudder at the thought of returning. I did not need Zane to remind me that I was a free man only as long as I had a job that was acceptable to the prison commissioners, and if I lost the sheriff's post I had no job, and I'd be back in jail before I could change my underwear.

And I knew too well what happens to law officers who find themselves in a prison compound. They suffer from a sudden and acute attack of stretched sphincters and bruised tonsils and bruised and broken bodies and bleeding from countless points on their bodies. At all costs I had to stay out of prison, which meant that I had to keep my job as sheriff, which in turn meant that I must find a killer before too many more women lost their lives.

I tried to comfort Zane. I rounded the desk, knelt beside her, and put my arm around her shoulders. She caught her breath sharply, then exhaled with excruciating slowness, and then leaned lightly against me. Little my little, glacier-like, her fingers slipped sideways until the tips touched my arm. Then she sat up, flung her arms around my neck, and held me as if she were drowning and I was her only source of rescue.

I don't know how long we remained in that position, but when she finally released me my knees had cramped until intense pain coursed through my legs, and every joint seemed to be stiff and immobile.

She pulled away slightly, then with renewed effort pulled me closer and kissed me long and hard. Then, as if shocked, she jerked away and rose quickly to her feet.

"Damn!" she said explosively. "I can't believe I did that. After lecturing you on how stupid it is to meet a woman at your house and then I try to seduce you in your office."

She turned and fled from the room, closing the door quietly but hurriedly behind her. I stared after her in surprise if not shock. The shock stemmed from what I had felt during the brief moments of closeness: something I had not felt in months.

I had to find time to tell her what I had felt, why I was going to see Laura Dennis one more time, and that I had to find some proof of who the killer was. I wanted her to know that I knew his name, or thought I did, and why he had killed the women. But I did not have a shred of proof.

I heard the door open to the outer office and heard the soft rumble of Rick Blanton's voice. Then another voice reached me.

There was another tap on the door and Jhon Rance entered. He spoke quickly and located a chair.

He did not come to bring me good news. He wanted an all-out confrontation. Powerfully built and enormously strong, he looked as if he had been ill; his massive upper body seemed to be all bloat and bile rather than muscular force. He slumped when he walked, and his shoulders sagged as if great weights had been long fastened to them.

The greatest devastation apparent had been visited upon the person of Dallas Wadsworth. Short, he stood at no better than five feet and six inches, and he held himself rigidly erect and walked like a career military man. His suits were tailored to fit him like uniforms, and he moved, spoke, and, I suspected, thought with military precision.

Now, however, he appeared to have aged at least twenty years during the past three days. He dragged his feet when he walked, and when he sat his head began to sink immediately, as if he could no longer hold his head erect. He looked like the ancient rummy who had collapsed, drunk and exhausted, among the debris and detritus of the alley.

I wondered where he was and what he and the others had been doing. They had not increased their respect for me; they had only lost respect for themselves.

And what, I wondered, about me? How could I look any better? It dawned on me that I must have smelled like a sewer. My shirt and pants would have to be peeled from me when I finally took a shower. If I had dropped my shorts I would have broken them.

Rance sat there, asking me one pointless question after another and clutching desperately at any straw that crossed his mind. When we ended the conference we had accomplished nothing. And we all knew it. Worse, we knew when we started that nothing would or could come of the meeting, and we began with a defeatist attitude as we completed our self-fulfilling prophecy.

What could we do? We had a man, at least we assumed that the killer was a man, a single man, acting alone, at large in the county. The county consisted of over four hundred square miles and a population of twenty-eight thousand persons. If we checked out each family dwelling at the rate of one dwelling per hour, and if we worked around the clock seven days each week, it would take us months to locate the house where the killings occurred. That is, assuming first of all that the killer actually lived in the county. And assuming that he lived in one place during the entire search. And that he continued to live in the county while we conducted our house-to-house search.

If he lived in the neighboring counties, the number of dwellings increased to more than half a million. We all knew that if we started in one section of town, the killer could wait until we had searched one area and then move to that location and watch as we beat our brains out against impossible odds.

"He might be a college student," Rance said, "and they show up in thousands and leave almost as fast. The killer might have left the college last week and then left the county twelve hours ago. There is no way, no way whatever, that searching at random could do anything but help the killer. If we are all involved in a search, he can have the town to himself. He and all the other criminals, that is."

I nodded. This land had been plowed several times.

"If we knew why he's killing the women," Rance added. "He may be a thrill killer. He'll kill as long as his victims have blood to shed, and once he gets a taste of it, he cannot stop until we kill him or lock him up."

There was nothing for me to say.

"For him to commit his crimes, he must ask three basic questions: what can he gain, what can he lose, and whether the gamble is worth it. He agreed that the gamble is worth the risk when he killed the first woman. Now we need to know what he can gain and what he can lose."

I listened, not expecting to hear anything useful. I was not deceived.

"He can gain his freedom, or he can keep it. He can lose his life or his freedom if he does not kill. Or he can lose his standing in the community, his money, his power, or his reputation. Who stands to lose these things?"

He did not wait for an answer.

"Someone who already has them," he said. "Now who are the most powerful, wealthy, prestigious, and vulnerable people in the county?"

He answered his own question. "The bankers. Preachers. The artists and writers. The politicians. The educators. The doctors and lawyers. The industrialists and merchants. The wealthy. We haven't pinpointed anything at this point, but we've eliminated more than ninety per cent of the population. There aren't half a dozen writers and artists. No political activity is going on. The teachers are always in public view. There are no industrialists in this entire town. You know who the wealthiest person in this whole county is?"

I waited.

"You might be," he said. "You have the opportunity to get to know people. You stop them on a traffic charge. You can have half a hundred reasons to be at anyone's house at any time."

It was obvious where he was heading.

"You were a college professor," he said viciously. "College professors are notorious for their seduction of the coeds who need to improve a grade. You have double opportunities as a cop and as a college teacher. I'm going after cops, and I'm starting with you, Ivy."

I looked at him sharply to see if he was joking. He wasn't.

"How many cops arrest young women driving alone and find any of a dozen reasons to ticket them? And how many of the women agree to drop their undies rather than tell hubby they got another ticket? I want half an hour with you, Ivy. I want it now."

"Damn it," I said, "I was with some of you every moment during our search and when the calls came in. There's no way I could have made the calls without some of you knowing about it."

"Everybody has alibis," he said. "But it's too easy to fake a phone call or have someone make it for you. Half an hour. I want it now."

He was right, of course. I had seen it done too many times. But I was not comfortable with the role I had been given as suspect.

Still, I could understand how anyone would at least consider me as one of the prime possibilities. The mere fact that the bodies were all and in a very dramatic way connected with me was enough reason to consider me in the list of possibilities.

Add to that the fact that I had just weeks earlier been charged with the murder of Edney Parkins and my wife Derry and you have what to some people would be an ironclad case.

By the same token, there were those who had to be concerned that the early calls came to the local editor, who just happened not to have a past of any sort, it seemed at first. I heard the impatient breathing of Jhon Rance, almost a snort, as he waited for my response.

"As long as I'm out of here by nine-thirty or so, I'll do it." I did not think for a moment that he wanted to interrogate me. He was far too devious for that.

I had to see Laura, and I needed to tell Zane that I was keeping the date with Laura for one reason: information. I wanted to tell her that my desire for Laura had long ago dropped into a bottomless pit. But for now I had to talk with Rance.

I'd have preferred meeting a king cobra.

SIXTEEN

After Rance and I were alone in the office, he pulled a chair up directly in front of my desk and stared silently at me for several moments. When he finally spoke his voice was like the cold wind off frozen peaks. I pulled open a desk drawer, took out a legal pad inside a plastic folder, and pushed the record button of the tape recorder I always keep in the desk. I learned a long time ago to have a record of what is said relative to important topics.

"Doc Wallace," he said. That was all. He waited until the full impact of the statement had registered.

"Alive and well," I said. "Free and happy as a man can be when he is facing a short tomorrow and even an uncertain today. He has his classical music and his Kipling and enough money to see him through the hard times."

"He was not a killer," Rance said.

"No," I agreed. "He was not a killer. There was not an ounce of rancor or hate in his entire being. The man loved; he did not kill."

"Yet he confessed to having killed your wife and your best friend."

"No," I corrected him. "He confessed to killing the man I believed to be my best friend. A man having an affair with my wife while I was in prison. A man who ran the biggest drug and prostitution ring in the South. A man who didn't care who got hurt as long as he got what he wanted. Doc Wallace killed him, he said. My wife was already dead, according to Doc Wallace."

"He lied. On all counts. He lied to protect you."

"I was innocent. Doc had no reason to lie."

"Doc didn't know that. He assumed the worst. He was willing to lie for you simply because you talked to him about Kipling and let him quote poetry to you by the hour."

"Quoting Kipling is not a crime."

"Killing is. Lying to a police officer is. When a man admits to committing a crime he did not commit, his crime is just as great as that of the man who denies a crime he did commit."

"Hardly the same," I said.

"Exactly the same," he countered. "A man confesses, and right away if we believe him we stop looking for the man who did the killing. The investigation stops. Then when we learn that the man had lied to us, we are forced to try to pick up a cold trail and find the real killers."

"I think you are using the point I made against you when you were on the witness stand," I said. "I found the killers for you after you stopped looking because you thought you had already found the killer: me."

"The killers found you, which is not the same."

"Exactly the same," I said, echoing his earlier comment. "You get the bad guys behind bars, or in a grave, and the good guys go free."

"The point is that people will lie to protect the guilty. You might lie to protect a person you believe to be innocent."

"Does this mean that I am not a suspect?" I smiled lightly but felt no humor.

"It just means that as long as the ghost of Doc Wallace hovers over us, I have a hard time believing anything you say."

I understood. He was referring to the double homicide that took place in Sherman County two days after I took office. I had been in prison until I was elected sheriff. Edney Parkins, the man I thought was my best friend, engineered the election. To be more accurate, he bought it for me. I did not question the whole transaction very seriously. He got what he wanted: a friend in the sheriff's office. I got what I had to have: freedom and a job. When Edney was killed, I was charged with murdering both him and my wife. The plot, as they say, thickened considerably when the terms of Edney's insurance policy became known: in fact, the plot not only thickened; it curdled.

My wife was named beneficiary of the bulk of Edney's estate: a chunk of change equal to more than twelve million dollars, and that was just on the surface. But she died shortly after Edney did, according to Doc Remington, the medical examiner, which meant that I as the beneficiary of her estate inherited the twelve million, plus whatever else was in the Christmas stocking. The entire amount has not been resolved at this point, but it seems fairly clear that I have my own personal estate of more than fifteen million—and counting.

But my conditional release from prison stipulates that I must work. I cannot be retired; I cannot live on my bank accounts. I must have a legitimate job. And because no one in Sherman County would hire me, some because they never fully believed I was not guilty and some because they knew the repercussions would hurt them badly if they challenged the county powers, I had to keep my job as sheriff. I knew that there were people who would stoop to almost any depths in order to see me fired. They'd love for me to be the richest convict in the entire prison system.

"In view of the way you twisted evidence, I haven't found much reason to believe anything you say, either. You haven't asked me anything, yet," I said, smiling.

He did not smile back. "I'll ask you one now. Did you kill either or all of the three women?"

"Of course not."

"Why should I believe you? You have lied to me before. You lied to everyone."

"I told the truth. You chose not to believe it. You were so determined to prove me guilty that you never heard what I said. But I heard what you said on the witness stand."

He knew what I was alluding to: he had admitted that he, too, had been in bed with my wife. I could not in good conscience blame a man if a superlatively beautiful woman agrees to go to bed with him. Under normal social conditions, that is. But I can damn well blame him if the woman had been drugged or otherwise forced to do so against her wishes.

If she did not consent, then I surely could and did blame the man. The men, I should say. All of them.

He sloughed off the reference and bored in at me. "Were you sleeping with or having sex with—any of the women?"

"No."

"Never? At any time?"

"No means just that. It does not mean at the present time or at some past time or to occur in some future time. It means no. I'm rather like Alice in Wonderland. When I use a word, it means what I want it to mean. Nothing more or less. You know why? Because I make a concentrated effort to use the word correctly. Until a few months ago, words were my life. When I say I never had sex with any of the women, that's exactly what I mean."

"Did you know any of the women socially or any other way?"

"To my knowledge, I never met any of them. I may have seen them at the mall or at a ball game, but I don't recall such an event. I don't think I ever spoke to any of them."

"Did you at any time know any of the women—not just the murder victims but any of the women—in the so-called club they had?"

"I don't know who is or was in the club."

"The three women, for starters. Laura Dennis, for another."

"I know Laura," I said, keeping it as simple as I could.

"How well?"

"I can answer that question for the next eight hours and you will know no more than you do right now. The president of this country taught us all to do that. If you want specific answers, ask specific questions."

"Are you sleeping with her?"

"At present, no." It was true. At present I was sitting in my office and answering questions.

"You have slept with her in the past?"

"Yes."

"How many times?"

"I don't know. I don't carve notches on my wooden leg."

"More than twice?"

"Yes."

"More than a hundred times?"

"No."

"More than ten times?"

"Yes."

"Twenty?"

"Maybe."

"Does her husband know?"

"You'd have to ask him."

"Does he suspect?"

"See above."

"Do you think he knows?"

"I think he knows somebody has been having an affair with his wife. I am certain that he knows who. He's indicated as much strongly."

"Has he accused you?"

"To my knowledge, we have seldom spoken, except on matters of official county business."

"Would you know him if he walked into this office right now?"

"Yes. He's the county manager. I'm not certain if he would recognize me if we met in church. I doubt he has ever been in a church since he was twelve years old. But he'd know me anywhere else."

"How many other married women have you slept with?"

"Show me the relevance of that question to the investigation at hand and I'll answer it."

"Did you know any of the husbands of the murdered women before the women died?"

"No."

"Where were you on the morning when Alisha Webley was killed?"

"I'm not certain she was killed in the morning. Her husband reported her missing in the morning. She may not have been killed until later."

"Where were you at seven o'clock on that morning?"

"With an acquaintance."

"In bed?"

"Yes."

"Who was the friend?"

"Laura Dennis."

He was smiling broadly now. He enjoyed himself immensely. He had never forgiven me for having butchered him on the witness stand. Nobody digests his own words well.

"You've been sleeping with Laura Dennis for how long?"

"Three months."

"And she never mentioned the club she was in?"

"No. We had other interests, until recently. In the past few weeks we have no shared interests whatsoever."

"I'll bet. Do you expect to see her again soon?"

"It's a good possibility."

"How soon?"

"In half an hour or so."

"Your place or hers? Or a neutral field?"

"My place."

"What time?"

"Check your watch. Thirty minutes from now. That means Mickey is on six and Minnie is on...."

"For what purpose?" He cut me off abruptly. Maybe he doesn't have a watch.

"Use your imagination."

"For sex?"

"Yes. For pure, raw, savage, steaming, illicit sex. Is that what you want to hear? Or do you want the truth, which is that we are meeting for the express and exclusive purpose of my asking her questions relative to the murdered women?"

"No. I don't believe you."

"That's why I didn't tell you," I said.

I wondered if he seriously thought that a married woman would sneak out to see a man simply for the joy of holding hands or conversation. I wondered if he thought the man would be content with such a tame pastime, but I shouldn't have wondered: I knew the answer.

"How long were you with her on the morning Alisha Webley was kidnapped?"

"From midnight until nearly dawn the next morning."

"You were on duty at the time? Is that correct?"

"I was on duty. As sheriff, I am always on duty."

"And you spent duty time in the sack with another man's wife?"

"Would it be any different if I had spent the time eating doughnuts and drinking coffee? Or fishing or hiking or just riding around? Or sleeping? Or reading a book?"

198

"On active duty but out of uniform," he said, the faint gallows smile playing around his lips. "Did anyone know you were there?"

"I don't wear my uniform to bed. And, yes, someone knew I was there. Laura did."

He smiled grimly. "But no one at the office knew? So if there was a serious crime—like a woman being snatched—no one knew how to reach you?"

I didn't tell him that Zane knew and that she had called to leave a message on the answering machine.

"My home number is known to everyone here at the office." I saw no reason to tell him that the phone had been unplugged that morning.

"Do you think that Laura Dennis would alibi you if the need arises? Is she willing to make a statement that you were at her house and in bed with her at the time the kidnapping occurred?"

"No. She will not. She was at my house. You'd have to ask her if she will admit to being there."

He nodded. "Maybe not," he said. "For the moment. You know that if this somehow gets out, to the newspaper, for instance, your reputation will be smeared from pillar to post. And, just between us, buddy, you didn't have a hell of a lot of reputation left to lose."

"It didn't hurt you," I said acidly, "when you testified in court that you had been sleeping with my wife."

He grinned. "Still rankles, does it? Well, you know what they say. If a woman is getting what she wants at home, she won't be looking for it somewhere else. Your wife was a whore and you were the only one in town who didn't know it. She slept with every man who had the price of a fix. What bothers you most: that she slept with a black man or that she was the town whore?"

He is a huge man, a powerful one, and I would never have hit him if I'd stopped to think about it. The truth is that I didn't know I was going to hit him until I felt my fist crunch into his broad nose, and I didn't know then that I was going to hit him hard enough to knock him flat on his back, and I damn sure didn't know that I would keep on and on hitting him until he stopped flailing. Two or three times he tried to get up, and each time I hit him so hard that I felt the jolt up to my shoulder. My entire fist felt as if it was made of broken bones.

199

I stood over him, panting with exhaustion and nervousness. My heart pounded in my chest. My lungs burned. And I desperately wanted him to try to get up again. I wanted to beat him to death for what he had done to a woman who couldn't help herself, who got herself into trouble only because she wanted to help me. She had no way of knowing all my alleged friends were vermin.

I had done great, I told myself. Not only was I stupid enough to bed down with a married woman while another married woman was being kidnapped, raped, tortured, and killed, I was also stupid enough to knock hell out of a law officer who asked me about the incident.

No! I contradicted myself instantly. I didn't hit him because he asked about me and Laura Dennis. And I didn't hit him only for what he said.

The truth is that I wanted to kill him. I wanted to smash him senseless not because my wife was unfaithful with him and with no telling how many dozens of others but because of why she was unfaithful. My one-time best friend Edney Parkins had hired my wife to work for him when I was sent to prison. Then, somehow, he got her hooked on cocaine, and when she could no longer make it through the day and night without it, he not only took total advantage of her himself but he invited his friends to do likewise. And when they tired of her, he sold her to whoever had the purchase price.

And Derry, the most beautiful woman I have ever seen in my life, would have never been lacking for customers. I did not learn until much later that the tactic Edney had used was to tell her that the only way she could keep from losing the property I owned on the lake front, and the house as well, was to raise more money than she had ever heard of in less time than it took her to get high on her first hit. He kept her high for months after that, and she never knew how many men shoved themselves into any and all of her body orifices.

To make it worse, if it could possibly be worse, Edney had been my attorney, and I learned, also much after the fact, that any second-term law student could have helped me beat the rap. I did not have to go to prison. I had not really committed any crime except in the most technical sense.

What happened was this simple. A woman on the faculty of Sherman College, now University, suffered from Alzheimer's Disease, and she desperately needed to retire. The only problem was that she lacked three months having enough time to retire with full benefits, which meant that, as the college retirement policy had been written, doubtless with people like her in mind, she could receive only fifty per cent of her benefits. This in turn meant that she would have to sell her house and car and all else that she owned in order to eke out a living.

So I broke into the records office, swiped pay records for a chronic drunk who missed a full year and never missed a paycheck, to show that the college had in fact practiced a cumulative sick leave policy and that the woman had enough built-up sick leave that she could apply it to her employment record and retire at full pay.

I was dumb enough to shove the copies under the nose of the college president, who was intimidated into giving the woman the full retirement benefits, and when I broke back into the office to replace the records, the president and half his staff lay in wait for me. I pushed the son of a bitch and in the process I dropped a crowbar on his foot. His cronies later testified that I had assaulted him with a deadly weapon. I had used the crowbar to pry open the door to the old cell where the pay records were kept. And someone hid a packet of white powder inside my cabin.

So I was charged with assault with a deadly weapon and with possession of an illegal substance, and I was grateful to Edney Parkins for saving me from a lifetime in jail! Any other attorney in the country would have had me out on a suspended sentence and a small fine. But I never knew that.

I never wondered whether Edney had done right by me. I have this bad habit of thinking that all my friends are as loyal to me as I am to them. And it never occurred to me that Edney wanted me in jail and in debt so that he could latch onto the two things on this earth that I cared about: my forest property on the shore of the lake, and Derry.

I didn't know when I bought the land for an out-of-key song that the man-made lake would shortly rise to the point that my land was now lakefront property and worth millions. Nor did I know that a hurricane-spawned tornado would take down trees and block a creek, diverting it over a rock ledge, that I would have my own waterfall practically in my back yard.

I had a paradise, an incredibly good and beautiful woman for a wife,

201

and then because I helped an old lady, I suddenly found myself in danger of losing both. That was when Edney sold Derry to anyone who had a fifty-dollar bill.

Jhon Rance was among the buyers. He was also among those who tried to send me back to prison, or to the gas chamber, for the murder of Edney and Derry.

I doubt that I had enjoyed one full waking hour without having the dull pains of hate and regret course through my body, and the pains became worse when I faced Jhon Rance. They became unbearable when he leered at me and insulted my dead wife.

I stood over Rance's inert body and waited, both fists ready, for him to move, to give me any reason to hit him again. I desperately wanted to smash his face until he resembled nothing human. I felt him move slightly beneath me, just as I felt two pairs of hands, one on each side of me, close upon my arms.

Rick and Zane tugged gently at me, urging me in quiet tones to leave Rance alone, to let them handle the man on the floor. By this time Rance was fully conscious and sitting up. He snarled at me through split lips and past broken teeth.

"You son of a bitch," he said. "You'll go to prison for the rest of your life for this. You'll never see the world again." He stumbled twice as he tried to get to his feet and it took both Lurch and Zane to keep me from going after him again.

"So much for martial arts," Rick said. Rance was known far and wide as a zillion-degree black belt karate expert. I have never known any form of art that can resist a good hard blow to the beak, and he was not the exception.

"He assaulted me," Rance screamed at them. "He hit me for no reason and from behind. He didn't have the courage to face me, man to man. He hit me when I wasn't looking and...."

"I was in the outer office," Zane said. "I heard all of it. I heard you provoke him beyond belief. You're lucky he didn't kill you. He had every right. Besides, how did he flatten your nose from behind?"

"I heard it, too," Rick said.

I took a tape cassette out of the drawer, showed it to Rance and the others, and locked it in the office safe.

"Just in case," I told Rance, "that you want to make an issue of what happened. I think you recall what you just said. Now, is the interview over, or do you have more questions?"

He didn't answer. Instead, he pulled out a soiled gray handkerchief and began to wipe his face gingerly. He was still wiping as he left the office.

"Thanks," I told Lurch and Zane. "I don't know what else I might have done if you hadn't come in."

"It's snowing again," Zane said to no one in particular.

She didn't need to tell me that. I wasn't thinking of snow but of Rance. I knew I'd have been much wiser if I had actually killed him.

I left shortly afterward. The clock on my desk showed that I was more than an hour late for my meeting with Laura Dennis.

It's nothing short of astonishing how a good fight can make a man lose track of time. Especially if he won a fight that had been a long time coming.

I wanted to tell Zane why I was going, but she had already left the office.

I started to leave the office when Marlin Rockwell tapped gently and entered.

"A couple of minutes?" he asked. He was dressed in a coat of suede leather, Arctic boots, and his khaki pants that he seemed to wear each time I saw him.

"Sure," I said. "What's on your mind?"

"What's on everyone's mind." He smiled again, and reminded me of a cross between Cary Grant and Gary Cooper. His voice was soft, as always, and persuasively innocent. Understanding.

"The murders," I said. "We're doing all we know to do."

He held up a hand to stop me. "I know," he said. "You need not worry that I'm sitting in judgment. I want to know what I can do to help. There will be no classes at the school for no telling how long. I have a four-wheel drive vehicle. I can make phone calls, haul people around, bring in food, or whatever will help most. I want this person caught. None of us is safe."

"No men have yet been attacked," I said.

"I meant no family is safe," he said. "If a man attacks my family, he might as well attack me."

"Your family," I said. "I've never met your wife."

He smiled again. "She remains very busy most of the time. She writes children's books and has little time for social life."

"Children?"

"One daughter," he said. "Dell. For Adele. A marine biologist, until a month ago. She has decided that she wants to write a book. Doesn't everyone?" He smiled again. "Anyway, she's what I wanted to talk to you about. She wants to come spend some time with me when all this trouble is over. And it will be. I have great faith in you, Chess. I know that you have been published widely and have nineteen books out. I have read all of them and enjoyed them thoroughly. I want you to meet Adele."

"Does she live locally?" I asked.

"Fort Lauderdale, for the moment."

He paused, standing ill at ease. "I had another reason for coming here," he said. "I don't know if you are aware of this, but we have a man in our community who has a history of sexual misconduct. I don't suggest that there is any guilt here, but I thought you ought to know."

I nodded. "I know already," I said.

He sat down, obviously relieved.

"Thank God," he said. "A friend of mine called and told me about Ed's past. I was shocked, but of course I wanted to let you know, but at the same time I didn't want to betray Ed. Still, if there is a chance—"

"I understand," I said. "Thanks for coming by."

We shook hands and he left. So did I, my hand hurting agonizingly.

But before I did, I dialed directory assistance and asked for the number of Dell or Adele Rockwell. I was told that there was no such listing. So I figured she has no phone, an unlisted phone. Or another name.

I asked then for Dell Calvin, and the recorded voice gave me the number. When I called it, I heard another recorded voice, this one telling me that the service to that number had been disconnected.

The news did not surprise me. What would have surprised me is for her to have been at home.

Because I was fairly confident that she was in the jail cell in the basement of the Sherman County courthouse.

SEVENTEEN

Before I left my tiny office Ed Gallager limped into the room, his face beaming crimson with excitement. Marlin Rockwell was with him. The two had met outside and Gallager had dragged Rockwell into the courthouse building with him.

"Chess," he said breathlessly, "I just had another call."

My heart seemed to stop for a second, and then it began to thump as though it would burst my chest. I tried to speak and found no words.

"He's changing," Gallager said. "He's telling us in advance of his next victim." He was panting so loudly that I was worried that he'd have a heart attack.

"He called *you*?" I asked. "Not a secretary, but you?"

"He called me," Ed said rapidly. "He said he had already picked out his next toy. He said he'd catch her on his way home. He said you'd be—" He paused, embarrassed and concerned. I urged him to go on. "He said his next catch would be interesting, that you'd be amused by its impertinence. He's sick!"

"What else?" I urged him. "What else?"

"He said she was Rahab. He said if you didn't know who Rahab is, to ask your Frankenstein monster."

At that moment the phone rang. I answered it, lifting it with trembling fingers.

"Sheriff Dumbo," the soft voice said, and immediately I felt the chills coursing up and down my spine. I didn't have to be told who the caller was.

"This is Sheriff Ivy," I said, desperately trying to control the quavering in my voice. "How may I help you?"

"No," the voice said. "You are not Sheriff Ivy. You are Poison Ivy. You are Sheriff Dumbo. *The Dunciad.* I'm certain you know whom I mean. You are Ignaro. But not a dunce. Oh, no. You are not a dunce. You're not nearly smart enough to be a dunce."

"Who is this?" I asked, knowing I'd not receive an answer. I stared at Rockwell and Gallager, both of whom watched me with a terrible intentness. "Tell me where you are."

"I'm everywhere," the voice said. "I'm everybody. I am the personification of Evil, of Malevolence, of Depravity. I am the Goddess, with a capital letter." I strained to hear the voice more clearly. It was a voice I had never heard before. I was certain of that. Or if I had it was under far different circumstances: in a movie or television or radio program.

It was almost a Peter Lorre voice, the one he used in the classic motion picture *M,* the one in which he was the child killer. The voice was soft, like velvet, with an educated, cultured, rich quality couched in a silky and delicate tone.

"I know who Rahab was," I said. "And I know Pope's Dunciad. I know the Ignaro of Spenser's *Faerie Queene.* And, yes, I am well familiar with the Goddess."

"Then you'll know where I'll strike next, won't you? Within the next hour I shall catch my next toy. Look for my work at the home of Laura Dennis, your own private Rahab."

The line went dead, and I quickly told Rockwell and Gallager what I had just heard. I had not tried to record the voice or to trace the call. It would have come from a pay phone, and the voice was disguised enough to keep me from knowing it.

"Rahab is one of the whores in the Old Testament," I said. "Ignaro is the essence of stupidity. It's the Goddess that we have to fear. In *The Dunciad* the Goddess, the anti-Messiah, works toward the destruction of science, morality, truth, art, and all that every age has held precious. Order is gone. The kingdom of the Dull is established. Universal darkness buried everything at the end as *humanity* is destroyed. What the hell does it mean?"

Rockwell and Gallager looked at each other. Seconds earlier I had been certain that one of the two was the killer, that Ed was, after all, guilty of the charges that exiled him from the world of public education and that he had come here to start the cycle again, this time at a vicious and perverted depth. I was convinced that he was Lawton Calvin, even though the two existed separately in every way. I had even suspected Rockwell. I had wondered if the messages had been recorded, but the voice I had just heard responded to my comments.

Rockwell seemed ready to collapse. His face was colorless, empty, and his broad shoulders sagged. I knew it was pointless to ask them for answers. And all my theories had just been tossed into a cocked hat. I was back at Square One.

I called Laura's number and listened to two rings, then her voice on the answering machine. "Laura," I said loudly. "Don't leave the house. Lock the doors. Get a gun and keep it handy. If you don't have a gun, get a knife, a baseball bat, *anything!*"

"She's gone already," I told them. "To my house. I'm going out there. Maybe I can beat him there."

"She may be unable to answer the phone," Gallager said. "She may be tied up or...." He paled even more, unable to complete the sentence.

"I'll call Deputy Blanton," Rockwell said finally, "and I'll meet him at the Dennis house. He may need help. We'll take Ed with us. We'll call you as soon as we arrive."

Then the three of us hurriedly left the office, and in a matter of seconds I was on the way to my house.

It was growing darker by the minutes and snowing lightly when I reached my place. Darkness had settled in immediately, as if someone had slammed a lightproof door, hours earlier, and the yellow gleam of my vehicle's headlights became spears cutting through the dark.

Snow almost waist-deep bordered the unpaved state road, and in the center of the gravel stretch leading from the paved highway to my cabin area the snow had been packed enough that it was like driving through a plowed field. My vehicle lurched and bounced relentlessly, causing the yellow spears of light to dart and pierce erratically. I had not driven the

Honda since the day the body of Alisha Webley was found in it. I doubted that I would ever be able to drive it again.

I kept a watch for deer. Even though I was moving slowly, if a deer suddenly found himself caught in my headlights and froze, as they often do, even at slow speeds I had no braking power and I might crash into the bewildered animal.

There were no deer. No raccoons, possums, or even rabbits. When I left the secondary road and turned into my drive, I saw that the snow was still packed from the earlier traffic. At once I was overwhelmed with relief that Laura Dennis, or somebody with a friendly smile and warm voice, would be waiting for me. Since Derry's death, the chore of entering the empty cabin had been sheer torture.

One of my great fears was not that there would be a villain in the cabin, lying in wait for me, but that there would be no one. Sometimes even Dr. Pangloss, my huge yellow cat that remained convinced that I was *his* pet, deserted me for the thrill of the hunt in the forest and nearby shoreline of the lake.

Another terrible fear is that one day the emptiness of the cabin would become so great that I would ask someone to move in with me or, worse still, marry me. At these moments I recalled with a shiver the brief time that Paris Constantine, as she liked to call herself, shared the cabin with me.

She had loved me intensely, she said, but she loved someone or something more, and she moved out after three months and the last I heard from her was that she was working at the *Post*, which is the ultimate hell masquerading as Heaven for all journalists who think that life must be a continual search and never a total discovery; a trip without a destination or even an arrival; a tattered magician's hat with an endless supply of unsatisfying and mangy rabbits to be pulled out and immediately discarded. Or fried.

When I turned onto my driveway I saw at once that there would be no wild life. Which alerted and excited me as much as if there had been a herd of deer on the deck. I could count on the fingers of one hand the times I had arrived after dark and had not seen at least one deer or other major form of wild life, and on those rare occasions there had always been someone waiting for me at the cabin.

I thought again for the ten thousandth time what an easy target I would make for anyone seriously wishing to do me harm. The trail I laughingly called a driveway was only a swath cut through the trees. At any point I could roll down the window and grab a low-hanging tree limb. In summer I could pick wild fire cherries, blackberries, and blueberries from my seat inside the truck; in winter I could break small dead branches to use for kindling wood, or I could grasp a handful of snow to rub on my face to remind me that *this* was reality; this was my dream.

There was no snow on the branches near the road, which told me that some vehicle had passed up the road just minutes ago. I knew that Laura would be at the cabin and that it had been her car that dislodged the snow.

But I also knew that anyone wanting me dead could stand behind any of the immense trees that lined the drive and as I passed in slow motion he could put a pistol barrel to the truck window and pull the trigger. I would never see him. The only hint of his presence would be the sudden explosion of noise, the rain of glass shards, and the disintegration of my cranial cavity.

For months I had toyed with the idea of using a spotlight to illuminate the forest, but I knew I would never do it. To do so would be to admit fear, and the admission of fear is the first step in the direction of abject cowardice. At the same time I never overcame the compulsion to look over my shoulder as I left my car and headed up the walk to the deck. I told myself that the reaction was a holdover from prison days or a by-product of my new job as sheriff, but inwardly I called myself a liar on both counts.

When I reached the cabin and parked in the space beside the car I knew to be Laura's, I felt an immense relief at seeing the lights on in the den and also in the kitchen. Through the drawn curtains I could see her form as she moved about the house.

Even as I rejoiced at the sight of the hearth and fireplace that for so many years symbolized home to so many, I realized how foolish it was for her to come to my cabin. If her husband went on a jealousy kick, he'd come here, if he could maneuver in the snow, particularly if he had heard the message left by me on his answering machine. And if he came here and saw her car, there was little he could assume other than that the two of us, his wife and I, were fornicating frantically inside the house. Then, if he happened to be of the bloodletting persuasion, he could simply wait among the trees and kill hell out of both of us as she left. If he caught the two of us at a restaurant and having a cup of coffee or a plate of spaghetti, there would be a reasonable explanation offered. But to be at my house, alone with me, at this hour? No way.

Still, I wondered, what the alternative could be, if I had any intentions of seeing her again. If I met her in town and drove her back here, her car would be left at the mall, and he could simply wait for me to drop her off. If we went to a motel, he could drive by and see the cars.

The one solution that I resolved to honor was that of never seeing her again, except on business. The truth is that I don't even know why I wanted to see her in the first place. I never loved her: that was a given. She never loved me; another given. When we met, I thought she was single and on the make. When I learned that she was married, the damage had been done. Infidelity does not consist in the number of times but in the agreement to do it one time. Even the act is not necessary, if the consent and the desire and the arrangements are there.

A man looking at a woman with lust in his heart: has he already committed adultery? I wondered. Did simply thinking and wishing make it reality?

If so, I planned, as soon as all the killings ended, to spend hours each week thinking about giving huge sums of money to the church and to the poor and about doing all sorts of good works for humanity. Then I'd be known as Saint Chester. I was already a saint in my heart.

I opened the door of the truck and stepped out into the cold night air. Heaters in vehicles and air conditioners in houses have ruined us. We forget just how cold or hot it is outdoors, and it is always a shock to the system when we change climates with traumatic suddenness. A few light flakes of snow brushed like a dead lover's kiss against my cheeks as I made my way up the steps to the deck and entered.

Laura did not wait to see if I was alone. She whirled when I entered, rushed into my arms, and kissed me with such abandon that we were lucky not to collapse onto the floor. I struggled to escape her clutches.

"No," I said. "The killer is going to your house. He plans to kill you, Laura. Listen to me. You've got to explain what's going on. I have to know. He's gone completely berserk." I extricated myself from her grasp and pushed her down into a chair at the kitchen table.

Her face was utterly unafraid. "I knew he'd come after me, sooner or later. I'm not worried."

"Laura," I nearly screamed, "don't be idiotic. The man is a monster, and he'll destroy you."

"No, he won't," she said. "Because I'll be with you. I'm leaving Jeff, and I'm moving in with you. When you go to town, I'll go with you. I'll get me a job as a secretary and we'll ride home together. We'll never be apart."

I stared into her face. She stared back at me with eyes that were dull and sleepy, and only then did I realize that she had numbed her brain with tranquilizers. Or worse. She looked as if she would fall asleep even as we talked. Each word seemed to take her several seconds to pronounce it. Within seconds she had gone from frenzy to lethargy.

"Going to sleep now," she said. "Going to sleep in your bed. He can't hurt me there." Her eyes closed and I had to shake her vigorously to wake her.

"Laura, stay awake and listen to me. Did your husband hear the message on the answering machine?"

She nodded.

"He knows we've been having an affair. You know that, don't you?"

Again, the nod.

"Are you left-handed?"

"Yes. Don't you remember?" She giggled.

"Did you have a child before you married Jeff?"

She nodded again. "Two of them," she said.

"You are a member of the DOLLS club, aren't you?"

"I'm the first-class doll," she said. I wondered if she had any idea what she was saying.

"Who was the father, Laura?"

No answer.

"Laura, is your husband the killer?"

Her eyes widened for a moment, then closed like wrought iron gates. I caught her as she slumped and started to fall from the chair. Picking her up, I carried her into the bedroom, turned back the covers, and placed her in the center of the bed, then covered her.

I called Blanton then. He answered instantly.

"No one was at home at the Dennis house," he said. "We came back to town. Gallager and Rockwell left. Do you need me?"

I explained the situation to him. "I need you here when she wakes," I said. "Bring a doctor with you, if you can find one. We want witnesses when she makes her statement. Is Rockwell with you?"

"No. He met me on the street and told me he was going out to Gallager's place."

That wasn't what he had told me.

I left the bed and stepped into the bathroom. Turning the shower on full blast and as hot as I could stand it, I soaped myself three or four times and let the hot water cleanse me of all the evil and cruelty and anger that had threatened to consume me during the past week. I scrubbed relentlessly until nothing tangible remained of the unclean week. Hurriedly I toweled off and then returned to the bedroom.

"Close your eyes," I told her. "Lights are coming on."

I didn't know whether she heard me. She didn't move. I was hoping that the tranquilizer would begin to wear off in time for us to question her before the killer struck again.

I flipped the light switch and hurried to the closet to locate another coat. Laura had covered her head and seemed to have fallen asleep.

"Get dressed," I said, shaking her foot through the covers. "We need you to get up and be ready to answer questions."

I pulled on socks and then boots. Laura still had not moved.

I flipped the covers back and was startled to see that she had taken off her clothes. She had been fully dressed when I put her into the bed. I bent over to shake her awake when I realized that the angle of her head was impossible.

Then I rushed to the telephone and dialed the office.

Zane answered.

"Get Rick and the others to my cabin," I said. "Quick. We've got another body. Laura Dennis has been killed."

EIGHTEEN

Within minutes my cabin was again swarming with the teams sent out by the county and the state. Everywhere men and women were swabbing, collecting, probing, and questioning. It was Dallas Wadsworth who zeroed in on me. He had failed once before in his efforts to nail me to the cross, and now he had his second chance and tried hard not to show his elation.

"We found abundant sperm samples inside the vagina of the dead woman," he told me. "Can you help us out here?"

"Sure," I said, equally determined not to lose my cool. "The sperm is there because someone deposited it there. The woman is married. Which means that she is likely to have sex with some man, preferably her husband. Whose is it? Why not have the lab check the samples against the husband's?"

He didn't sneer but came as close to it as possible and still fall short. "You admit, then, that the woman was here alone with you?"

God! I thought. What did I just tell the man. "No," I said. "We had a whole television network filming crew. We were to be featured on America's Horniest Home Videos as well as on the eleven o'clock news. Oh, and the Guiness Book of Records people were here. They wanted to know how so few could do so much with so little."

He permitted a faint smile to flicker and then die. "Sarcasm is not the

213

recommended route," he said, as staid as an old maid. "Do you want me to repeat the question?"

"Which question?" I asked, then quickly decided that, as the man very properly said, this was not the recommended route to take. "No," I amended. "I recall the question. Let me make it as easy as possible for both of us. Laura Dennis is the name of the deceased. She arrived at my cabin, I assume, around nine o'clock this evening. All I can say for certain is that she was here when I arrived. She had, by telephone, earlier informed me that she would be here around nine o'clock. Or nine-thirty. I forget which. I arrived only a few minutes ago. You know fully well that I was in the office until half an hour ago. She was here when I arrived. No other vehicles were in evidence. I entered the cabin and realized that she was under the influence of some type of drug. I tried to talk to her, but she was incoherent. I put her into my bed, then I took a quick shower. When I came out of the shower she was dead. Her body was still warm. Probably still is."

"You never had sex with her?"

"Not in weeks. It was over between us. She didn't come here for that. She told me we needed to talk about the killings. She was afraid to talk from her home phone, so she came here. She was on some kind of medication. Probably tranquilizers or sleeping pills."

"Why did you call your office?"

"I wanted her to make a formal statement, and I wanted Rick Blanton here when she did."

"She never told you anything useful?"

"Nothing."

"She was in your bed."

"Yes," I said simply.

"She was naked."

"No," I said. "She was fully clothed when I put her there."

"She's naked now."

"Then somebody undressed the body."

"But you say you did not make love."

"No. Or yes, depending on how you mean the question. Yes, I say we did not make love. No, we did not make love."

"Will you agree to permitting the lab to have a sperm sample?"

"Hell, no. Why should I? No, wait. I will if every other male in town will. I'm as curious as you are as to whose sperm was inside the victim."

"You say she was willing to make a formal statement?"

"She agreed to answer several questions that were pertinent to our investigation. She informed me that she, like the others, was left-handed, that she had been given, as had the others, a rose beryl pendant on a gold chain, and that she, again like the others, had given birth prior to marriage. Twice."

He wrote rapidly in a shorthand form I had never seen before. When he looked up, a signal that he had written down all I had said, I waited for the next question.

"She was alive, you say, when you went to take a shower?"

"She was alive but asleep. When I came out of the shower, she was still in bed. The difference was that her head was covered. I assumed that she did it in her sleepy stupor. I warned her that I was turning on the light and that she might want to cover her eyes. Her entire head was covered when the light came on."

"Did you speak to her?"

"Yes. I shook her foot and told her we'd better get a move on. I thought she had fallen asleep."

"And what sort of response, if any, did you receive?"

"None. I didn't worry, because I thought she was fully relaxed or in a deep sleep."

"Did you check her body temperature?"

"Not then and not later. When she didn't move, I uncovered her face and saw that her neck had been broken. Whoever did it had to come into the house while I was in the bathroom. He used the noise of the shower to cover his own noise."

"Or he was already in the house," someone at my elbow said, and I looked around quickly to see Rick standing beside me. "How long were you in the shower? A guess?"

"Five to ten minutes," I said. Wadsworth glanced at Lurch with undisguised irritation, but I knew that Lurch would not back off or retreat. He felt as much urgency to get at the facts as the rest of us did. With one minor exception: me.

"Give or take a couple of minutes," I added. "I had not had a shower

215

in days, and I admit that I enjoyed it greatly. I might have been in there even longer than ten minutes."

"You heard no noises in the house, during the time that you were in the house alone with the victim?" Blanton asked.

"We made noise of our own," I said. "Talking. Walking around. Even if I had heard a minor noise, I'd have thought the cat made it. Sometimes he can be cranky if he wants in badly enough. Or out. But, no, I did not hear any suspicious noises."

"You saw no tire tracks leading into your place?" Wadsworth asked.

"I saw tire tracks. I assumed that they were made by Laura Dennis. Some might have been left from a day or so ago, but I doubt it. The snow has covered the old tracks. I saw no new tracks that aroused any suspicions, other than Laura's."

"No footprints?" Wadsworth continued.

"The place had been overrun by investigating officers only hours earlier," I said. "There were footprints everywhere."

"Did you check for signs of forcible entry?" Lurch asked.

"After I called the office, I made a quick check of the house. No locks were forced, no windows were broken, and no door facings or locks were scratched. If you're asking how the killer came in, I assume he used a key."

"Where did he get the key?" Wadsworth's eyes bored into me.

"Laura had one. He may have taken it from her purse earlier and had a copy made. I'm assuming at this point that the killer had access to her things. If not, I have no idea; the killer may have found the key somewhere around her house. I keep extras here in case I lose mine. The locks are all dead-bolt and I didn't want to wake some night with the house on fire and not be able to find a key to let myself out. Anyhow, we know he was inside the house earlier."

"Where did you keep the spare keys?"

"One in the front door, one in the back door, and one in the basement door."

"What about outside keys? In the mailbox? Over the door trim? Under the mat?"

"Under the bottom rail on the deck," I said. "I attached a small magnet on the underside, out of sight, and the key was stuck to the magnet."

"You haven't checked to see if any of the keys are missing?" Wadsworth asked.

"Not yet," I admitted. "I spent the majority of the time after I called to searching the house. I found no signs that anyone had been concealed in a closet or anyplace similar."

Lurch moved in a little closer. I could feel his immense bulk nearly touching me. "He could have hidden in a thousand places and you'd not have looked," he said. "In a closet, under a bed, behind a door or behind furniture, in a little-used room, in the basement, in the second bathroom, in any of dozens of places no one would think to look. Unless he had reason to think someone had broken into his house."

"When I saw that Laura was here," I said, "it never occurred to me that someone else might be in the house. Frankly, when the snow stopped, I thought the killer might wait a few days before he tried again."

"And succeeded," Wadsworth said. "Not only succeeded, but in the sheriff's house. Not just on his property, as before. Not in his car, as before, and not in his basement, as before. Not while the sheriff was gone, as before. But inside the sheriff's house, in his bedroom, and even in his bed, while the sheriff was a few feet away. Are you getting the picture, Ivy?"

I nodded my head. The truth was that I had few waking moments when my mind was not on the picture he painted.

"You're going to have to resign," Wadsworth said.

"The hell I will. They'll have to throw me out," I said, more for my emotional welfare than for his.

"Sherman County has the provision and the courage needed to do so," Wadsworth said.

Blanton, as always, had a handle on the topic, whatever it might be. "Get enough names on petitions," he said, "and any local election can be challenged, if the town or county charter includes the clause. Otherwise, state laws prevail. You'd need weeks, months to get Sheriff Ivy removed."

"It's underway." Wadsworth smiled with grim satisfaction.

"In a state-of-emergency situation the law can move rapidly. This is such an emergency."

"Jhon Rance," I said. "This is the sort of thing he'd love to do. Particularly after this evening."

217

"He's been a busy boy. The word is that he will take his petitions to the county commissioners tonight. They are holding a called meeting. You could be out of a job when you get back to the office. Maybe before. What do you think your chances of surviving this are? A trillion to one."

I faked a sigh of relief. "That's terrific," I said. "Not many people would give me any chance at all."

"Unless you capture a killer," Lurch added.

"I had one," I said. "If I had pushed a little harder, Laura would have given me the name."

"Without her to testify, it would have carried little weight," Wadsworth added, "but at least we'd have known to exert all of our forces into that direction. You are assuming that the father of the children is the killer."

"Why not?" I asked rhetorically. The truth was that I did not think the children had any direct bearing on the killings at all. But everything I had been sure about had evaporated.

"Let's compare theories later," Lurch said. "Right now, let's check the house from end to end for signs of a visitor."

He was right, of course, and the three of us went as a group from room to room. My cabin has a modest floor plan. Underground there is the basement, which is where we started. On the ground floor I have a kitchen, den, two bedrooms, and two baths. On the third level there are two bedrooms and a sitting room that overlooks the kitchen and den-dining room area.

In the basement we turned on all lights, peered into the coat closet, into the half bath, and behind all doors and all large items of furniture. As usual, we didn't know what we were looking for, other than evidence that someone had spent time in the area.

Someone unknown.

The basement consists in part of a huge open room that includes a pool table, wood stove, and some battered and incredibly heavy chairs and sofa made of real wood and with leather-covered cushions. In the back area of the basement there is a work room where I tinker with bird houses and whatever else I want to knock together, an office where I keep my books and my computer, and a long, narrow room at the very back where I have my darkroom. I had envisioned, one day, having the time to process film and print enlargements of my favorite photos.

"When's the last time you shot pool?" Rick asked.

I shrugged. Then I looked quickly at the pool table.

The balls were neatly racked and ready for breaking. I shook my head. Beside the pool table there were oblong moist spots.

"He walked in the snow," Wadsworth observed. "Some of it fell off here and melted."

"He's cool," Rick said. "He casually shot pool while he waited for you and Laura to arrive."

We moved to the workshop. I felt myself trembling, both with fear and anger. I nearly shook with fury at the thought that the arrogant bastard had earlier read my paper, eaten my food, drunk my beer, and now added another insult to the injury he afflicted at every turn.

I glanced at the table where I often worked, and another wave of fury and helplessness swept over me. The last time I worked, which now seemed months ago, I had used the table saw. A thin covering of sawdust remained on the floor. In the sawdust someone using his finger had written the single word: MESSY. The same spots of moisture were there as well.

In the darkroom we found the paper-safe box open. The paper in it, of course, was ruined. The last time I had printed photos had been one day when Laura wanted to learn how to process film. We had spent the day together and I had taken several shots of her along the shoreline of the lake, in the woods, on the deck, and in the house.

And the ubiquitous spots of dampness were there, and later in my office, and on the steps.

On the drying line I had hung about a dozen photos of Laura. She had tried her hand at printing the photos, and a small stack of dry prints lay on the work surface. On the line was a photo of her leaning over a tree that had been uprooted but had caught in the branches of a nearby tree. The trunk where she stood had been little more than waist high. The next photo was of Laura leaning against my battered old Honda Accord. A third was of Laura sitting on the leather-covered sofa in the basement. She was holding Dr. Pangloss and he was nuzzling her with his head shoved against her cheek.

Then there was a photo of Laura in my bed, with the sheets pulled tightly up to her chin.

Someone had written WHORE in heavy grease pencil across each photo.

"Is that the log where we found the body?" Wadsworth asked, pointing to the photo of Laura leaning over the tree trunk. I nodded. He pointed to the one of Laura and my car.

"Yes," I said. "Where Alisha Webley was found."

The third photo Wadsworth fingered was one of Laura and Dr. Pangloss on the couch. A chilling sense of fear coursed up and down my spine, leaving me shivering both inside and out.

"Were these photos you left hanging here?" Wadsworth asked.

I shook my head. "No. We printed two dozen shots. The line was filled with pictures. Someone took down all but the ones we see here."

I riffled through the stack of photos on the table.

"Any missing?" Lurch asked. "Anything special that you don't see?"

I didn't know what to look for. "We took three rolls of film," I said. "I can't recall what was on every shot. We did not print some of the photos, but we printed at least three dozen."

I counted the prints. There were thirty there.

"At least six missing," I said. "There was one of Laura in the kitchen. She was sitting at the table. She had fixed a huge turkey, and as a joke I had put the entire bird in front of her and she held a knife and fork poised, as if she would eat the whole thing. I don't see it."

"Would it help to look at negatives?"

"Right." I went to the negative folder and found the three rolls we had developed. Quickly I spotted the frames for the five missing photos. One was of Laura in my office. She was sitting in the reading chair I kept there and she had been holding the complete works of Shakespeare. Except that she had let the book fall across her breasts and my reading glasses dangled from one ear. In one photo she was holding a book of the complete works of Chaucer. In the other photo she appeared to be sound asleep.

Or dead.

"We know he was in the workshop, the basement den, the dark room, and the bedroom," Wadsworth said. "He apparently enjoyed the run of your house while you were driving all over the county trying to find him. What's in the next room?"

He indicated a door that led from the workshop.

"My office," I said numbly.

As soon as we opened the door I knew that the killer had been in the room. The computer monitor light was on, although the screen was dark. I know it's better to leave computers up rather than close them down when you need to be away for an hour or two, but I had an electrical storm demolish one while I was at the college one day, and I lost a full-length novel I had been writing. Now if I had to be away from home for a considerable period of time, I not only turn off the machine but also unplug it from the wall socket.

Rick seemed to sense what I was thinking.

"Considerate of him," he said, nodding toward the darkened screen. "He didn't want to cause a burn-in on your screen."

"He also didn't want the glow to be visible from outside," I said, turning up the brightness knob. Immediately I wished I had not. The screen was filled with the killer's message for me.

It began: To: Incompetent Boob Sheriff

From: Someone Too Smart to Catch

RE: Fun Yesterday, Today, and Tomorrow

The rest of the page consisted of taunts, insults, and some of the vilest descriptive phrases I have ever read. Among the mildest were "wife-killer" and similar recriminations, most of which cast considerable doubt as to my ancestry and to my major forms of recreation.

I felt the waves of nausea return. The sickness did not stem from the insults; teach as long as I have and you'll hear them all, mostly from students who loafed all term and then became wildly furious because you refused to give them a sympathetic acceptable grade.

What sickened me was the realization that a cold-blooded, sadistic, merciless, and thoroughly evil man had not only broken into my home but had defiled it beyond all powers of cleansing. I had loved this house from the day I began digging the basement with a shovel, and each day I worked I loved it more. Now I began to wonder if I could ever again feel good in this cabin, if I could ever again lie down to sleep, to cook a meal, to enjoy the deck and the lake, to read by the glow of the fireplace, to sit in the office and write the things I wanted to say to the world, whether or not the world ever read them.

"A photo of Laura Dennis in all the places where he left a body," Wadsworth said. "Do you think these other photos are telling us where the next bodies will be found? Chess, just how coincidental is it that you took photos of Laura just where the killer planned to leave a body? What are the odds that he chose places you had photographed—with Laura Dennis in them?"

I shook my head. "He's working backward," I said. "He broke in, apparently, a long time ago and found the photos. From that point it was a matter of leaving bodies where Laura had been in the photos. I imagine it's like filming a suspense movie. You know which scenes to highlight, to enhance by special lighting. The next question is whether he actually plans to leave a body in my office. I can't believe he'd be stupid enough to try that. He knows all we have to do is leave someone to guard the house. We could work shifts. Keep someone here every hour of every day. It would cut back on our manpower, but it would keep him from carrying out his plans. At least in this direction."

"You think it's Jeff Dennis?" Rick asked. "If not, why use photos of Laura Dennis? Was she the only woman you entertained out here?"

"Not the only," I said. "Maybe the only one whose husband learned about it. Or the only one whose husband found out but was not sadistic enough to kill innocent women in order to punish me and his wife. I didn't know Laura Dennis was married when I first went out with her, if that makes any difference. Maybe these photos were too handy not to use."

Wadsworth did not respond. He walked to the basement door and stepped outside into the cold air. Rick and I joined him.

Flashlights in hand, we walked down the shore line a quarter of a mile and found tracks of deer, raccoons, foxes, beavers, and musk rats, but none of human beings. The new-fallen snow had obliterated any signs of tracks except those made by animals during the past minutes. We turned left up into the forest, and we slowly made a huge semicircle around the house and back to the shore line on the other side of the house.

Again, we found tracks of the forest creatures, but nothing that suggested two-legged company.

"Remember," Lurch cautioned us, "the guy could have been here and the snow covered his tracks. He could have brushed tracks away. It can

222

be done easily. If he was wearing snowshoes, it would be even simpler."

We hiked back down the shoreline toward the house and when we were two hundred yards from the house we made another half-circle, then made another at a hundred yards and still another at fifty yards. We found nothing to suggest that anything human had been in the woods.

"Let's go to the Dennis house," I said. "Someone has to be the messenger, at least. And we can have a few minutes with him before anyone else gets at him.

We had been inside the house less than thirty seconds when the phone rang. Wadsworth answered it, spoke tersely, then handed the instrument to me.

"It's Jeff Dennis," he said.

My hand was shaking when I took the phone. It's one thing to see a husband whose wife you have seduced and have to talk to him, but it's another to have to talk to him when he had just learned that his naked wife has just been murdered in your bedroom while you were in the bathroom. My twisted brain reminded me of the man who was having an affair with the wife of a man who was overseas in military service. The man told me that he was in a sense doing the husband a real favor. His argument was that if it were not for him, the lonely wife might be out and rutting around with total strangers, rather than with a friend of the family.

He added that by sleeping with his friend's wife he was keeping her out of places where she might be beaten, raped, or killed. He was also making certain that she did not get diseased or pregnant.

I had to wonder how the missing friend would have shown his appreciation. Greater love hath no man than to lay down his wife for a friend.

"Sheriff Ivy speaking," I said.

"Within a week it'll just be Ivy," the surprisingly soft voice said. "I wanted to give you the news: the commissioners just held a called meeting and they have agreed to take the necessary steps to have you suspended. You are relieved of your duties as of this moment."

"You don't have the clout," I said. "Whether you like it or not, I am the highest-ranking law officer in the county here until someone with more authority relieves me."

"You'll be relieved," he said. "And when you are, I'm coming after you. I'm coming after you and I'm going to get you. You don't know how I'm looking forward to it."

"I'll make it easy," I said. "We are coming to your house right now. We have several questions we need to ask you. There will be three of us." I replaced the phone gently, with far more patience than I felt.

It was snowing slightly harder when we left my house, and the three of us rode in my truck into Sherman and then north of town to the small lakefront development where the Dennises lived. I felt close to tears as I urged the truck slowly through the streets that were piled high on each side with dirty snow that refused to melt and go away.

Laura was dead, I kept telling myself, but the disbelief would not disappear. She was gone, and her husband wanted me destroyed. I saw little to keep him from his goal.

NINETEEN

The drive to the house where Laura Dennis lived stretched the trip to nearly an hour. On the way the snow tires on my truck clutched ineffectually at the tractionless surface, like a cat frantically clawing its way up a greased pole.

The snow had let up slightly as we made the drive, but our pace did not improve. The back end of the truck veered and hawed as we slipped our way through town.

Sherman was a ghost town. The streets were vacant and bare. Nothing and nobody seemed to stir. As we made our way down Main Street and to the north of town I kept searching the streets and doorways for the sight of the giant woman, but if she was on the scene she blended with the streetscape perfectly. In the brief moments of respite from the snow we had been permitted during the frenetic days I had heard only rare and disrupted weather reports, but the phrase on all tongues seemed to be the Storm of the Century.

As I fought the snow, I forced myself to think of better times, of sunny days and peaceful nights. But I could not escape either the snow or Laura Dennis.

Snow in Sherman County is not rare, and it is commonplace for the ground to be covered throughout much of the winter, but for nearly a full week, we had seen the sun for only a few brief moments. As soon as one system passed us by, another seemed to follow only hours later, like wolves on the trail of wounded prey. To the south there had been rain during the same time, and already weather experts, whoever they are, had started warning of flooding when the snows melted.

I had to wonder if we were doomed to repeat the fearful experience of 1916 when the floods washed away entire towns. We had tons and tons of snow piled on every street, every mountain, and in every valley. If a sudden warm spell hit, the snow would begin to melt instantly, and the towns below us would have our water to add to their own rainfall.

Right now, though, I'd have given a month's salary for the sight of the sun for about a week. If we could travel, we'd have a hell of a lot better chance to catch up with the killer. At least this is what I thought as we pulled into the driveway of the house where Jeff and Laura Dennis lived.

And I'd have given a year's salary if I did not have to face Jeff Dennis. While we were on the phone he made suggestions that were, to say the very least, unkind. I shuddered at the thought that someone could actually do some of the things he threatened to another human being.

To me.

One car was parked in the drive. The lights in the house were on, and the front door stood open. There was no sign of life inside the house. I did not like anything we saw. Beyond the house there was only the stretches of snow covering what appeared to be an endless field. I knew that it was the lake, frozen solid across the surface, and the ice deepened each night as the temperatures dipped before the new front moved in and the new storms dumped more snow on us.

My first thought was that Jeff Dennis realized that he had given us too many clues and had packed his clothes and split. I mentioned this to Wadsworth and Rick. Wadsworth agreed; Rick did not.

"He's to New Mexico by now," Wadsworth said. "He hit too close to home and realized it. He might as well have signed his latest work, like some artists do."

"There are hundreds of forgeries in art," Rick said. "And in crime. My guess is that we find the dead body of Jeff Dennis in the basement or bedroom of the house. There will be a cryptic note beside him: something to the effect that he can no longer live with what he has done. And that, friends, will be that."

He was almost exactly right. But the body was not in the basement or bedroom. I knew there was no basement but saw no reason to spoil the theory of Lurch.

We found the body instead in the man's office, a small bedroom that had been converted to a small shrine to himself.

When we entered the house, Lurch stopped as if paralyzed. He did not sniff the air, the way Indians and Tarzan do in the old movies, but he did almost the equivalent. In the center of the living room floor he now stood, rigid, every muscle tensed.

"He's here," he said. "And he's dead. Chess, you try the bedrooms. You know where they are."

He did not smirk or even sneer when he said it. With Rick it was simply the most efficient method of searching the house.

I followed his orders, opened the guest bedroom and saw that it was empty and tidy. Then I went to the bedroom Laura Dennis shared on occasion with her husband. It, too, was orderly and empty. Even the bed was made, and I wondered where, if anywhere, Jeff Dennis had slept. My bet was the bedroom in the house of some girlfriend.

From the other end of the house I heard Rick call me. I closed the door on the bedroom, a carload of bad memories, and an equivalent amount of regrets. Following the sound of Rick's voice, I hurried to a tiny room that looked as if it had once been a garage that had been closed in.

The smell of death was everywhere. I sensed it even as I crossed the living room and headed toward the north end of the house. Jeff Dennis lay sprawled in a chair that had been placed against a wall. The wall behind him was spattered with blood and fragments of bone, clumps of hair, and other matter that I had no desire to have identified for me. A huge part of his head was missing.

I looked away quickly and stared at the wall behind him. It was filled with plaques, certificates, and a series of tiny trophies mounted on a small shelf. The plaques, four of them, had been arranged in a diamond shape, much like the infield of a baseball field. The top and bottom plaque, like the two side ones, were five feet apart and occupied or controlled a huge portion of the wall.

Arranged in a large circle around the plaques were the framed certificates, each of which attested to the fact that Jeff Dennis had led his district, wherever that was, in total sales for an entire quarter. They were dated months apart, and the most recent was only two weeks old.

Inside the circle was the tiny shelf filled with trophies. One was for bowling, another for softball, one for ping-pong, and a fourth for the largest fish in the company tournament. A small one attested that Dennis had also won the company golf tournament on one occasion.

It was no great wonder that Laura Dennis had been lonely. Her husband was gone on business three or four days a week, and when he was home he wasn't at home. He was fishing, playing ping-pong, bowling, hitting a softball, or chasing a golf ball around a course. I wondered what it was that drove a man to court and win an attractive woman only to neglect and essentially desert her until she sought the bedroom company of the closest stud she could find. And if she couldn't find one, she chose me.

Maybe it was because no one gives trophies for being a loyal and good husband or wife.

I could feel no sympathy for the man. He had, apparently, killed his wife, destroyed three other women and their families, and attempted— and perhaps succeeded—in destroying me. The jury was still out on that call, though perhaps not for long.

My sympathies were with the victims, with the loved ones of those victims, and with a town terrified into becoming a cluster of hermits. And, admittedly, with me.

A shotgun lay across the dead man's feet. I noticed that Lurch stood and stared at the gun, as if he could not bear to gaze at the body. I stared around the room. Other and larger trophies decorated the east wall; the south wall was covered with photos of Jeff Dennis and bigwigs of his company: Dennis in his softball uniform, in his bowling shirt, in his golf togs, with his rod and reel and a huge fish that looked better than he did.

The west wall was filled with framed letters, testimonials to his salesmanship, all signed by executives and by two or three mayors of nearby towns of two or three hundred people.

On the north wall was a huge color photograph, a studio portrait, of Jeff Dennis himself. In the photo he was wearing a tuxedo jacket with a red bow tie. The portrait appeared to be twenty-four inches wide and thirty-six inches high. Spaced two feet away on all sides were smaller photos of Dennis in a high school football uniform, in midair as he launched a basketball shot, and with a bat on his shoulder as he waited for the pitch from the hapless pitcher.

"It's a sick shrine," Rick said to me. His voice was soft but crisp, almost bitter. "No wonder the man's wife ran around on him. He was cheating on her with himself."

A small couch was located on the south wall so that whoever sat there had little choice but to stare at the portrait. I knew, or thought, how it felt to be in Dorian Gray's presence.

During the many times I had been in the house, I had never seen this room. The door was always closed and, of course, I never asked to see inside. Laura never mentioned the room; she made no references whatever to her husband's work, although she chatted with delight about other aspects of her personal life and of her house. We couldn't go outside, but she stood at the window with me and pointed to where she would put in her asparagus bed, her tulips, or her roses.

Inside the house she often made references to what color of paint she'd like to put on the door and window trim, and often she mentioned some remodeling she'd like to do in a certain room. But the Shrine was never mentioned. It was as if the room never existed.

It was almost embarrassing to be inside the room. Never before had I seen such unadulterated adoration of oneself.

"You remember Oscar Wilde's comment when someone mentioned that a certain man was very modest," Lurch said quietly. "And Wilde replied that the man had a great deal to be modest about. I get the opposite feeling here. What we have is a man who never in his life amounted to anything in anyone's eyes, other than the fact that he could sell a product and catch a fish. So in his own eyes he projects himself into a larger-than-life hero. In this room, at least, he was Somebody."

Nothing, though, had explained away the anger that came through the telephone wire when Dennis had threatened me. I could not imagine that he could allow himself to die until he had exacted some devious form of revenge on the man who had invaded his house, his bedroom, and his wife's body if not her heart and her mind. And I admitted a sense of relief that he hadn't waited for us.

It wasn't that he was hurt by his wife's infidelities: he was hurt that she could have desired another man once she had been in the presence of

Dennis himself.

Wadsworth, who had been looking through the room carefully, found the note. It was actually inside a book that had been lying on a coffee table.

The note said, simply: "I loved them all, and I killed them all, just as I loved myself and killed myself."

"That does it," Wadsworth said. "The guy played it out as far as he could. He knew, after he left your house, that he could not keep it up. He had gone too far, and he knew that we could not miss identifying him. So he did what most of this type of person does: he killed himself rather than face humiliation in the public eye."

He extended his hand for me to shake. For a brief moment the contempt for me almost disappeared. I took the limp hand and gave it the perfunctory shake. Rick did the same.

"This one is wrapped up," Wadsworth said. "Thank God," he added as a footnote. "I had him in my mind's eye from the start of this orgy of death, but I couldn't find the link between him and the deaths. Not until he went over the edge and killed his own wife. This will keep the batting average at the top of the league. A real Hall of Famer."

"It's a great one," Rick said. "It'll keep you in the lineup, if this is a game. But I don't think Dennis killed the women. I don't even think he killed his wife. Why would a man trail his wife to her lover's house and then kill and rape her? And I am willing to bet the farm that he did not kill himself."

Wadsworth was referring to the fact that he had investigated a zillion or so murders and had solved all of them and had obtained convictions on the entire batch. He didn't want Lurch to cause him to miss out on this one.

I was the one he missed. He had officially charged me with the murders of my wife and Edney Parkins, and he was convinced that I was guilty beyond any shadow of any doubt. When I walked, he took it personally. I remain convinced that he'd have been much happier if I had gone to prison or to the gas chamber, even though I was innocent, than for him to have his perfect string broken. I wondered how many of his other convictions had been no more just than mine would have been.

The truth about his perfect record was, like so many of the statistical garbage journeys, subject to much question. The vast majority of his convictions had been the domestic type, where the wife calls the police and tells them that she has just killed her husband, who had been beating her with an axe handle. Or the ones when the poolroom fight leaves a dead body and nineteen people can identify the killer.

I think that, if chilling truth could be told, Dallas Wadsworth harbored until the very end the suspicion that I had somehow managed to kill the women, or have them killed, and if he could find a way to pin it on me, then his record could still be considered intact. Like the guy who gives up a base hit early in the game and, when he allows no more hits, the official scorer goes back and changes the hit to an error, and the no-hitter becomes official.

It was, after all, to Wadsworth a game, nothing more. It was his own private ego trip from which he would never return. He was another Dennis in this respect.

"Of course Dennis killed them all," Wadsworth protested. "I had him in my sights all along. I'd have had him within thirty-six hours at the outside. I was closing the net all along."

He strode about the room in agitation. Someone was trying to rain on his parade and he wasn't having any of it.

"He killed them all," he repeated. "It's all as clear as night and day. Anyone could have seen from the outset that he was guilty."

"If you say he did, then he did," Rick said. "It's your own party. But he didn't."

"Well," Wadsworth said with bluff good cheer, "You can have facts and you can have theories. I prefer to depend upon facts. I suppose one of us ought to call this in. And maybe let the press know. Sheriff Ivy, do you want to do the honors, or shall I?"

I didn't hesitate. "You call it in, Special Investigator Wadsworth. Get the medical examiner and all the others over here, and, if you don't mind, what about giving Gallager a call at the newspaper office. Tell him how you solved the crimes. It'll be good for a front-page spread."

He was grinning from ear to ear when he picked up the phone and punched in the numbers. Rick and I stayed with him until the press and the death teams arrived. Then he pulled me outside the house.

"He didn't do it," he said. "Jeff Dennis did not kill those women."

I didn't realize until then how elated I had become at the thought that the killings had ended. A weight like that of Atlas had rolled off my shoulders and for the first time in what seemed like years I was able to breathe easily, to relax. The tightening in my chest had disappeared; the constriction was gone. There was, of course, the lingering pain connected to the dead women and their loved ones, and I felt the evisceration in my own gut area about Laura Dennis.

But the crimes had been solved, and we could all begin to put lives back in order. If such a thing were possible.

And then Lurch dropped his bomb, and I was back at the starting gate and wearing concrete shoes.

"Why?" I asked helplessly. "Why would you say that he didn't kill the women? What earthly reason....?"

Lurch's face should have been carved onto Mount Rushmore. It would have been totally in place there. He turned to face me. We were standing in the back yard of the Dennis house, almost at the spot where Laura planned to have her asparagus bed. She had even hauled in mulch and had mounded it, ready to be worked into the soil as soon as weather permitted. She had bought the crowns and they were in a cool corner in the back of her pantry. I felt more than a twinge of pain as I looked at the heaps of snow, which now were graves rather than plots for new life.

"You stood in the Shrine," Lurch said. "You saw what I saw. The man set up a temple in which to worship himself. There is a color portrait of himself dominating the room. His face is in every photo in the room. Now ask yourself: would this man, this Adonis, devotedly in love with himself, do what he did? Would a man in love with his own face blow his head off with a shotgun? He'd take sleeping pills. He'd never under any circumstances do anything that would destroy his looks."

He turned his face up to the light snowfall. When he looked at me again his features were granite. "This man shoved the barrel of a shotgun under his chin and pulled the trigger with his toes. We have the shotgun and the bare foot as proof," he said.

At times like these I am reminded viciously of how little reason I have to be in law enforcement. I had not noticed the bare foot.

"The shotgun fell across his foot," Lurch went on. "That's the first thing wrong with the picture. When the gun went off, there was a terrific recoil. The gun would have been thrust halfway across the room. It would never have gently fallen across his foot. A shotgun is not a bazooka, but it has its points of comparison: for every action there is an opposite and equal reaction. For all the force going out the muzzle, there is an opposite and equal force moving backward. The gun would have been a mini-missile."

I nodded in silent agreement. We talked for another fifteen or twenty minutes, long enough to permit Ed Gallager to arrive and get his story and photos of Dallas Wadsworth, long enough to let the crime teams take their photos and prints and all the rest that they are obligated to do.

When the body was finally hauled away and the house was deserted, Rick and I returned to the inside of the house. The special investigator was gone; apparently Wadsworth had ridden with Gallager to be sure the editor had all the facts in his possession. The house, except for us, was empty.

The phone rang, startling me so that I jerked spasmodically and whirled toward the noise. My heart was thumping wildly as I looked for the phone, which rang a second time before I reached it. Before my hand could lift the mouthpiece, the recorded message began to play.

"You have reached the residence of Jeff and Laura Dennis," I heard the electronically immortal voice of Laura Dennis say.

The caller hung up. I looked at Lurch.

"Two rings," he said. "Most people allow four rings. But if there is already a recorded message, the next call gets only two rings before the machine is activated."

"I left a message," I said.

"Maybe someone else did, too."

There was no answering machine in the den.

"Laura's bedroom," I said. "She kept it there so Jeff would not be likely to see the message light and play her messages."

I hurried to the bedroom and saw the phone on the table beside the bed. There was no answering machine. Then I remembered that the last time I was inside the house Laura had shoved the machine under the bed. I dropped to my hands and knees and peered under the huge spread that nearly touched the carpet. A light blinked rapidly at me from the semi-darkness. I pulled the machine from under the bed and set it upon the table. Lurch stood over me as I punched the message retrieval button.

The first voice I heard was that of me, urging Laura to protect herself. The third message drained me of all the subdued elation I had felt earlier.

"I have had your wife," the voice said. "I left her in the bed of our idiot sheriff. You can find her there, if you hurry."

I looked helplessly at Lurch. "It's snowing harder," he said.

TWENTY

L urch said, "He's changing. The call did not go through the editor or the editor's office. I wonder why. Is it because he's having to work faster than he originally planned?"

"One even came to me," I said. I had forgotten that he had not been told of the call while Gallager and Rockwell were in my office.

I had pocketed the tape, after first placing it in one of the bags we carry with us everywhere now. I know they serve a fantastic purpose in big-city crime, but to us their best use was as litter bags in our cars. Still, I felt better having the tape in the bag, in case Wadsworth or Rowena or some of the others should ask later.

I wondered about Rance. I had neither seen nor heard from or about him since our run-in earlier, and I admit to having spent an inordinate amount of mental time to wondering which tree he was behind or when he planned to strike without warning.

What befuddled me most was that he was a martial arts expert and a massively strong human being. How did I happen to defeat him? Did I get in the first punch, which took the wind out of his sails? Did he take a dive? If so, why? Was it possible that I had more strength through anger than I thought possible? Or was he just a huge smoke screen?

"I'll call the editor," Lurch said before we left the house. We had been standing on the porch when he went back inside and then returned only seconds later.

"No one answers," he said. "The guys must be oiperating the presses by now. I can see Wadsworth setting type, except that they don't set it now that offset and computers have made the scene. Maybe he'll be selling autographed papers on the street corner. This is what the man lives for: taking bows and accepting plaudits after he has solved a monster case."

Lurch obviously did not like Wadsworth any more than I did. Wadsworth and Jeff Dennis could have made a lovely couple.

"Except that he didn't solve this one," I said. "Where do we go from here? Back to the office? Back to my house? Do we wait for him to call again? What the hell are we supposed to do?"

There was no need for me to clarify who "him" was. I was confident we'd be hearing from him soon, and my insides churned at the thought. But not as bad as before. I wondered why. Maybe I was becoming so inured to the grossness and vileness of the entire scene that I had become immune to horror. I dreaded the acceptance of that idea almost as much as I abhorred murder.

"I wish I had something to tell you," Lurch said. "You and I have seen too many bad movies where the hotshot detective is always on the cutting edge of everything. The truth of the matter is that we're not hotshot detectives. We're both defective detectives. Me more than you."

"How could that be?" I asked. We were driving back toward Sherman again. Between the trees I could see the lake almost at every turn. The waters, almost invisible in the swirling snow, were as smooth as the top of a table. One of the weather quirks we had long ago learned to accept was that even the coldest weather warms when the snow starts, just as fog guaranteed calm waters. We had the warming effect of the snow already, and the heavy mist above the water hinted at fog when the snow ended.

"I'm trained," he said. "You're not. I'm supposed to know what to do in crime waves and emergencies. I can open my personal file and show you credentials that are pretty impressive, on the surface. I've been to all kinds of police training schools, and I have finished at the top in many of them. Most of them, even, and on paper I'm the go-to guy in the crunch. You want to know a hell of a secret? I'm just as helpless in this as you are. So are Rance and Rowena Cullen and Wadsworth and Wooley, despite their posturing and officious and industrious attitudes when they are on the crime scene. Watch them. You'll see what I mean."

I already know what he meant. From the time they appeared on the scene, they bustled around the body like blowflies. They buzzed and hovered and flitted and pushed and shoved. They all came equipped with notebooks into which they wrote incessantly. They could look at a doorknob or a cat's butt and immediately jot down five minutes worth of notes. I resolved at some time in the immediate future to steal a quick look at one of their notebooks. My wager was that they were making a grocery list.

"Where's Rance?" I had to ask, and not because of inquiring minds.

"Healing his wounds. He went off like Robert Cohn."

"Daunted," I said. "Like a cat."

"With his mouth full of irony and pity. He wakes up in the morning with it."

"Say something ironical," I said.

"Wadsworth sucks."

"I wouldn't be surprised," I said. "But terrible irony. Say something pitiful."

I expected him to say Robert Cohn. When I first met him, he was a student in my American literature class, and one of the works we read was Hemingway's *The Sun Also Rises*, which is still head and shoulders above ninety-nine point ninety-nine per cent of all the books written in the twentieth century. Lurch had latched onto Hemingway's dialogue at once, and in our free time we tossed bits and pieces back and forth to each other, like a huge inflated ball that never quite touched down.

"Jhon Rance," he said. "He's pitiful. Did you know that he is Robert Cohn?"

"Am I the steer? Who is Romero? And does that make Derry the Lady Brett Ashley?" We were casting a movie of Papa's first great book and filling the parts with members of our own cast. For those who have been away too long, Romero was the bullfighter beaten nearly to death by Cohn, the Jewish boxer and pseudo-intellectual who had been rutting with Lady Brett Ashley, the girl friend of castrated Jake Barnes, the steer. I was not certain that I enjoyed all of the parallels.

"You were Mike Campbell," he said. Campbell was the chap who was to marry Lady Brett, although she was whoring around with the bullfighter and the boxer and would have done so with Jake Barnes if Jake were not, like me with regards to law enforcement and the solving of crimes, impotent.

"Past tense?" I asked.

"Yes. You had been Jake, but you graduated from that. Derry had no control over what she did. She was unfaithful to you in the same sense that a rape victim is unfaithful to her husband or lover. She hated all those bastards who kept her drugged out of her head night and day. She was Frances Farmer with a lousy script writer and a perverted cell keeper."

Farmer was arguably the most beautiful woman Hollywood ever produced, but when her Invisible Gardol Shield evaporated, she was victim to the things that happened to Derry and she, too, had no control over what happened to her body while her mind was on a three-day pass. Or AWOL.

"She never betrayed you," he said. "Not while she was in her right mind. Those who used her were lower than whale crap. Rance was a hyena devouring the spoils left by the lions. He was a lover when the partner was helpless; he is a fighter under the same conditions. You fought back, and he folded."

"But where is he?"

"The message is that he is out investigating some angle of the killings. Loosely translated, this means that he is waiting for his wounds to heal slightly before he makes an appearance. And he is setting up his appointment as sheriff to replace you. I'll drive through Sherman," he said, changing gears rapidly. "I want to look at the streets."

He did. The streets that had been snow-plowed were now again white, but traffic still moved easily. At Lurch's suggestion we tried the two major highways entering Sherman. Both were clear enough that traffic could move into and out of town without real problems.

"Let's ride this way," Lurch said. I sat silently as he eased the truck through the Sherman streets and to the outskirts of town. He drove for several miles, then turned off on a road that must have been unpaved, judging from the bouncing of the truck, but there was no way to tell. The road wandered along the side of a mountain and along a small creek. At the end of the road stood a small house, barely a cottage. It was the sort of house a sharecropper might rent.

"Who lives here?" I asked.

"Possibly a killer," Lurch said. "Perhaps a man we're supposed to think is a killer."

He opened his door silently and I followed him to the front door of the cottage. He tapped at the door and waited. Then he knocked louder. Still no response.

He turned the knob and the door opened easily. I held my breath, waiting for the rose-colored muzzle flash and the blast of the shotgun. The house was silent. I heard Lurch's fingers rake the wall as he searched for the light switch.

"No switch," he said. "Stay here." I heard him move away, and seconds later the light came on. The house must have been built during the Not-So-Great Depression: the walls were thin enough that we could hear the wind whistling through. On a small table near a window there was actually a skiff of snow that the wind had forced under the window sash. It felt as cold indoors as it did outdoors.

"Who lives here?" I asked again, whispering, although I did not know why I demanded secrecy. We had knocked on the door and turned on a light. I didn't see how we could have made our presence much better known.

"Ed Gallager," he said. "I've watched the house now and then, when I had a moment to spare. Not a palace, is it?"

I looked around the room again. A single bulb glared in the center of the ceiling, and an old-fashioned string hung down to eye-level for me. The floors were bare, and the furniture was Early Goodwill. One chair in the room was upholstered, and the frayed fabric allowed the cotton to bulge through. A book case stood in one corner: a three-shelved structure five feet long. Inside it were some cheap novels, a thesaurus, a stack of high school yearbooks, and selections from the Pulp-of-the-Month Club. A wood heater stood near an outside wall. A pipe rose from the back of the stove and exited through a hole in the wall. A suggestion of heat exuded from the stove.

"You've been here before?" I asked.

"Never inside before. Let's see who else is here. You may be in for a

239

shock."

The house was a square, with two rooms on the front and two on the back. Lurch stepped into the other front-side room and turned on the light.

The floors of this room, too, were bare; rough-cut boards permitted gusts of air from under the house to enter the room. The paper drapes shook, like the house, when the wind blew. The walls were covered ineffectually with sheets from the Sherman *Guardian*. The newspapers were obviously intended to substitute for insulation.

There was a hospital bed in the center of the room, and in the bed lay a frail-looking woman who could not have weighed more than eighty pounds. Her face was drawn so that her nose looked too large and her eyes bulged like a bug's. Her body barely made a mound under the covers. Above her, thirty inches from her face, was a large sheet of glass suspended by a crude wooden framework that was somehow fastened to the floor. Six or eight books lay upside-down around the outside border of the sheet of glass, and the center space was filled by a late issue of the *Guardian*, also upside-down.

The woman's eyes darted from me to Lurch and back again, like the eyes of a terrified animal.

"We mean you no harm," Lurch said softly. "We are police officers. Are you Mrs. Gallager?"

She did not respond except to close her eyes for a moment, and then she opened them again. She repeated the process.

"When you blink, does that mean yes?" Lurch asked.

She blinked again.

"Does your husband live here with you?"

A blink.

"Does no one stay with you while he is gone?"

The eyes remained wide open.

"Were you injured in an accident?"

No response.

"Did you have a stroke?"

Blink. Blink.

"Can you read?"

Blink.

240

"You can hear all right. Can you move at all?"
Nothing.
"Does Ed feed you and care for you?"
Blink.
"How long ago did you have the stroke? One year? Two years? Three years? Four? Five?"
Two exaggerated blinks on the final question.
"During your husband's trial?"
Blink.
"Your husband was charged with theft and misappropriation of funds?"
Blink.
"Was he guilty?"
Her eyes seemed to bulge even more. She glared at us fiercely.
"Was he innocent?"
Blink. Blink. Blink. Tight blinks, emphatic blinks.
"Was someone else guilty?"
Blink. Blink.
"Do you know who?"
Blink.
"Was Lawton Calvin guilty?"
Blinkblinkblinkblink.
"Is he still alive?"
Blink. A world of hate was in that blink.
"Does he live in Sherman?"
Blink.
"Under his own name?"
No response.
"Under an assumed name?"
Blink.
"Is he killing the women?"
No response.
"Do you think he is guilty?"
Blink.
"Is your husband afraid of Lawton Calvin?"
A fierce glare. Then an apologetic blink.
"Does Calvin have some power over him?"

Blink.

"He is blackmailing him?"

Blink.

"Was your husband accused of something other than theft? Was he accused but not charged?"

Blink.

"Sex charges?"

She blinked fiercely.

"Was he guilty?"

No response.

"Was Lawton Calvin guilty?"

She blinked in an exaggerated fashion.

"Will your husband be home soon to look after you?"

She blinked confidently.

"Has anyone else been here?"

Blink.

"Someone to look after you?"

She blinked again slowly.

"Someone else? A woman?"

Blink. Blink. Blink.

"A huge woman? A tall, very fat woman?"

Blinkblinkblink.

"Are you afraid of her?"

Blink.

"Do you hate her?"

She closed her eyes and did not open them. It was a sign to us that the interview was over.

"Is there anything we can do for you?"

The pale blue eyes opened. Blink.

"Would you like for us to put a new newspaper down for you? And turn the pages in your books?"

Blink.

We prepared her reading matter and left the room. On the top shelf of the bookcase there was a photo of Ed and a beautiful young woman. "Mrs. Gallager," Lurch said. "When she still had a life."

"The yearbooks," I said. "Let's check."

We pulled them out and found the usual, except that page after page had rectangles cut from them. I returned to the bedroom.

"The yearbooks," I said. "Pictures have been cut from them."

Blink.

"Photos of Lawton Calvin?"

Blink.

"Was he here?"

No response.

"The giant woman was here?"

Blink.

"Does Ed know?"

Blink.

"Did she threaten to kill Ed?"

No response.

"Did she threaten to kill you?"

Blink.

"Was the killer the one who answered the phone the day I called?"

She closed her eyes again. They were still closed when I turned away from her and walked toward Rick.

We left the house shortly afterward. Neither of us spoke of the visit for a long time.

"The woman," I said finally, telling Lurch about the brief incident in the bedroom. "She was going to kill her."

Lurch nodded. "Or a huge man dressed as a woman."

"Lawton Calvin?"

"Perhaps. Let's go to the office and call the police in Wilmington and get them to ship us a copy of the yearbook and to fax us copies of pages eleven, sixteen, and twenty-nine."

I had not thought to note the pages where the photos had been cut from the pages.

It was three in the morning when we returned to the office. Bum, who seems to have slept there, was on the telephone. Zane, who apparently never slept, was on another line. Both were talking earnestly and taking notes.

Bum's tablet was almost out of reach and his eyes never seemed to rest on the page. His thick, stubby fingers moved with the least effort possible, and the resulting notes were little more than wavy lines that only he could decipher.

Zane was the exact opposite. Her tablet was close to her body, and her long, slender fingers moved with grace and speed, and the letters were tall, flowing, and beautiful to see. Her handwriting was, for a southpaw, as legible as I have ever seen.

She looked up when we entered, smiled quickly, and returned to her writing. She hung up seconds later and looked up at me.

"Everyone is calling either to thank us for solving the crimes or to tell us that the killer is knocking at the door and threatening to huff and puff. I've made a list of those who called for one reason or another."

She turned the tablet so that I could see it. At least two dozen people had called to thank us for catching the killer. I looked at her and she opened a desk drawer and pulled out the latest edition of the *Guardian*.

Wadsworth had wasted no time. In the hour or so that Lurch and I had spent at the house and on the road, he had dashed to the office of Ed Gallager and had given him the entire story: as he recalled it, or as he wanted it to be, starting with his initial suspicions of Jeff Dennis as the killer and how he followed up the most minute clue until the trail led him, only seconds too late, to the house on the north of town where he had discovered the body of Dennis.

Nothing that could have enhanced Wadsworth's character and talent and work had been omitted. Nothing that included the work of others on the force had been included. Gallager, in the true form of the astute news-paperman, had apparently laid out an entire dummy newspaper, leaving space only for the sensational story that he knew would come when the killer was finally caught.

"Fantastic," was all Lurch said when he saw the story. "Just fantas-tic." He had disappeared into the inner office as soon as we arrived, and now, the telephoning done, he joined us. He added, "You remember when the guy pitched the no-hit baseball game, and when the reporters asked him about it he said that it couldn't have happened to a nicer guy? I think that line was the only one Wadsworth left out."

"I'm expecting an important fax," I told Zane. "We'll be here until it comes, unless an emergency occurs first."

As soon as I spoke the phone rang. Zane answered, listened for a few seconds, and then spoke tersely to me.

"Edna Hamilton," she said. "Her husband is on the line. He says she's missing."

Seconds later Lurch and I were skidding along snow-packed streets and into the rural area on the east side of the county.

"This is a first," he said. "All the others have been on the west side. Along the lake where the rich people live."

"I live there, too," I said.

"I stand corrected: the rich and the lucky live there."

When we arrived the Hamilton house was dark. Three cars were parked in the drive. Lurch played the spotlight across the front and then the sides of the house, then leaped from the car and hurried to the front door. He pounded until lights came on all over the house and the front door opened.

A man holding a double-barrel shotgun peered through the opening.

"Sherman Sheriff's Department," Lurch said. "Are you Jerry Hamilton?"

"Yes," the man said, his voice filled with worry. The head and shoulders of a woman appeared in the space behind him.

"We just had a report that your wife had been kidnapped," I said. "When did you see her last?"

"Just five seconds ago," he said, turning to the woman behind him. "This is Edna. Now what's this all about?"

"A cruel joke," I said, explaining the call.

We climbed back into the truck and started back to the office. I thought about the yearbooks I had glanced at in the shack where Ed Gallager lived. Change the name on the title page and the same books could have been used in almost any other school in the nation. The students obviously fell into three essential categories, as do most high school students universally.

There were the hopefuls, the hopeless, and the confident. The hopeless were the ones on the periphery: they sat in the backs of classes, never joined clubs, seldom if ever starred on an athletic team, never held elected positions, and invariably wore the dullest clothing and concealed their lack of personality by affecting a clothes-store manikin's expression.

These were the future mill workers, the sanitation workers, the street sweepers, and the carpenters, plumbers, maintenance workers, and supermarket bag boys who never become adults; they simply became old. They would marry someone as unattractive as they and product children like them, and their role in the endless cycle would be perpetuated.

The hopefuls were the hangers-on who stood just outside the real vitality of the classroom and the social world. They would become in career worlds as innocuous as the dust motes floating in the air over the desks where they moiled. These future straw bosses, electricians, clerks, secretaries, and insurance agents built scenery for the senior class dramas, sat in the cheering sections at the footballs games, and excelled in one thing: they served as buffers to keep the confident and their hopes in their own distinct caste system.

The prettier girls would marry slightly above their social standing and the uglier boys would marry below theirs, and the great leveling tradition would continue. Those who attended college at all would sit through classes at a two-year business school, take computer applications programs, and commute from their houses to their classes. They would never see a college drama or musical program, and they would never join a club or appear in a superlative photo in any school they attended.

The confident ones had their lived mapped out with all the particulars delineated. They would attend the universities their parents attended; there they would star on the athletic teams, excel in the classrooms, drink the most expensive whiskey and use the coolest drugs and fornicate only with the most acceptable of the world's other sex. And then they would return to their home town, accept the top position in Dad's business (after first serving a decently brief period of time in a subordinate position) and take their places in the country clubs, on the golf courses, at the banquet tables, on town councils, in civic seats, and professorial surroundings. They would write their books, have their own swimming pools, have their flings with what passed for the sophisticates of their cultures, and groom their children to take their places when the propitious times came.

Of this group, the rarity would be the one who earned or deserved a tiny fraction of what he received.

The confident ones made the best grades for three obvious reasons: they were born of educated parents who surrounded them with the best

246

of music, books, travel, and social acquaintances; they met, talked with, drank with, and cohabited with those of similar fortunes who could open any doors that their parents did not hold the keys to; and their teachers and later their coaches and professors knew who donated to the football team or to the college endowment funds, and no one would dare give a failing grade to anyone who made a pretense of trying to learn.

I didn't bother with the hopefuls or the hopeless. Phyllis Tyler and Katherine Thennis and Laura Dennis did not hobnob with these necessary evils whose purpose was ill-defined but clearly understood by all concerned. Edwin Arlington Robinson said it best, perhaps, when he informed the confident ones that some of them could not be so far ahead if the rest of us were not so far behind. The function, then, of the hopefuls and the hopeless was to become cushions and door mats for the confident ones.

The group I wanted to know about would not be door mats; they would wipe their feet on the mats. I thought of the candid shots and the May Court and the Homecoming Dance and the rest of the accolade sections where the confident ones praised themselves and preened their feathers.

And then came the group of six or eight girls who seemed to be the tentacles of a social octopus. They were cheerleaders, drama club standouts, honor students, queen's court attendants, and presidents of all the appropriate clubs. They smiled, side by side in their formal dresses. They posted prettily in all the special occasion functions.

The confident ones were also the prettiest, in addition to being the smartest. While the hopeless ones grew up in homes where no one read books, even if there had been books to read, they also grew up in homes where attractive clothes could never be afforded, where dental work would never straighten teeth or repair them, and where skin-care specialists did not ever work to remove or cover blemishes.

The confident girls were trained to talk properly, walk gracefully, and conduct themselves appropriately in public. They did not have to work after school so they could devote their time to studying and being pretty and popular.

I thought of the Sherman yearbooks. Lurch, if he had come from a better family, would probably have been valedictorian without ever having to crack a book. Zane would have been the May Queen and the Homecoming Queen and all the rest, if the fates had put her into the backgrounds of the wealthier girls.

In each photo where she had appeared with the others, her face was the freshest, the prettiest, and the most personable. Only her clothes seemed slightly out of place: her gown was from the previously owned rack; her sweaters and skirts appeared again and again in photos, while her classmates sported a different outfit for each picture. She clearly was one of the school's leaders, and yet she was unquestionably the outsider.

Teachers appeared in virtually every group photograph, with the apparent favorites making repeat appearances with astonishing regularity.

Rockwell, the principal, had appeared in more than one-third of the group photos, often with other teachers. In the cheerleaders photo the girls stood in a semicircle with Rockwell in the exact center. The girls looked adoringly at him, while he looked casually at the camera. He also appeared in the Student Government Club, again with the adoring looks from the girls and, or was it my imagination, a resentful look from at least one of the SGA officers. I checked the caption and learned that the one with the grouchy face was none other than Jeff Dennis.

The same scenario was repeated in the Dramatics Club, except that in this case it was Tubby Tyler whose demeanor seemed to reflect an attitude toward the principal. I asked Lurch if there was a quick reference method and he told me that in the student directory at the end of the book there was in parentheses the page number where each student appeared in a photo.

Three more photo checks revealed similar conditions. In one it was Thennis whose apparent resentment registered like a red-hot brand. In another it was Webley.

In the photo of the Student Aides it was Zane who gazed with apparent admiration and even love at Rockwell, while a young man whose name didn't ring any bells glared at the principal. When I checked the photo caption I saw that the kid was named Harvey Andrews. When I referenced his name in the student directory I learned that he appeared in only that one photo.

It didn't take much imagination to arrive at the theory that the principal was a hunk to the girls and their boy friends were eaten alive with jealousy. Lurch, when I asked him, admitted the point.

"He was and still is, I suppose, a good-looking guy who got along well with all the students, men and women alike. He always dressed well and drove a status symbol car. He was married. Had been married to the same woman for fifteen or so years."

I didn't doubt it. Marlin Rockwell could keep a woman in love with him without trouble, I was confident.

"Whatever happened to Harvey?" I asked Lurch, remembering the one photo in which he had appeared in the Sherman High School yearbook.

"Harvey gave his farewell address to the entire senior class," he said. "He was in a student government association meeting one day when he rose from his seat and began to curse and rant and rave. He attacked the principal and two or three students before he was subdued. He was expelled from school the same day. He never came back. He went back after the principal two or three times before he was finally arrested. Then he got married all at once and he and his wife moved to a little house near the river. One day he went swimming while his wife was at work and apparently drowned."

I didn't miss the inflection on the one word. "Apparently?" I asked, repeating the word. "There is some doubt?"

Lurch shrugged. "He was a good swimmer. A good athlete all-around, and a fairly good student. He had college scholarships offered to him, but he turned them all down. No one knew why. To get married, we all supposed."

"You ever meet his wife?"

He nodded. "She was a student at the school."

"Still in town?"

"Yes," he said reluctantly. He seemed painfully embarrassed, or at least uncomfortable.

"Any word on the real fate of the husband?" I persisted.

"Killed in a car wreck."

"Don't tell me," I said. "Let me guess. He was killed in Jackman, Maine."

Lurch stared at me.

"And the widow works at the sheriff's office," I suggested.

"At the sheriff's office," he repeated. "Zane asked me not to tell you the entire story. She said that it ought to come from her to you, face to face. I agree with her."

I said, "I wouldn't have it any other way. But in the meantime I'm going to call to see if the fax has arrived."

Bum answered and told me what I dreaded to hear.

"She's not here," he said in surprise. "She got the fax you wanted and she's taking it to your place. She said to tell you to meet here there, that you needed her. She said something about photos in your office."

He was right. I *did* need her. But not at my house. I needed her as far away from my house as she could get. I needed her out of the clutches of the madman who was killing all the left-handed girls in Sherman County.

TWENTY-ONE

The soft new snow was a blanket of cold love, of death. The night was jet black except for the eddies of snowflakes, huge and downy and deceptively cruel, that swirled in our headlights as we made our excruciatingly slow way to my house.

Rick drove, which was wise. If I had been behind the wheel I'd have either gotten us there in record time, or I'd have had the car wrapped about us in the bottom of a roadside ravine. In the shotgun seat I writhed, twisted, and mentally urged Rick to give the engine more gas.

The thunderbolt hit me ten minutes into the drive. We lurched along, jerking, sliding, and careening from one side of the road to another, and it struck me suddenly just how much I had started thinking about Zane. Not just occasionally, but in all of my waking moments she was there, somehow, smiling, asking questions, offering help.

Losing, or nearly losing, someone or something you have admitted in a major sense into your life can do that to a man. Or a woman, I suppose. I don't know when Zane invaded my mind, but I knew at once that she meant far more to me than I had admitted.

I don't know that I loved her. Don't know whether I am even capable of loving. But when I thought of her I didn't think of the broken promises, shattered dreams, and the failure to commit that had been a part of every relationship I had known since I lost Derry.

Was that love? Or was it the reaction of a man incapable of doing anything with his life, with his mind, his opportunities, and his spirit?

Was it possible that there existed someone who could rescue me from the coldness of heart that not even the weather could have paralleled?

I had nearly lost everything, once, and I knew the value of all of it, starting with freedom. Before I went to prison I had a vague notion of what it must be like to have the steel doors clang shut behind you, but vagueness does not equal reality.

It was only when I saw the compound with its dull gray cement block buildings and razor-wire topped steel mesh fence that I had my first reality laboring pains. Months later, I still dream of the huge mesh square with the guard towers at each corner and the huge rows of powerful lights that could illuminate the darkest night until it was brighter than a sunny day.

In broad daylight I can close my eyes and see the huge snarling dogs that prowled around the fence, glaring balefully at the misery in human form that inhabited the interior of the square. I see those teeth, too, in my mind's eye, and I cannot pass near a growling dog without recalling in terrifyingly real detail the sight of a mob fight inside the compound and the dogs hurtling themselves like vicious and hyper-animated robots into the tangle of men. Teeth clicked, throats emitted guttural sounds that cannot be recalled except as the ecstasy of teeth sinking into hot, moist flesh, the pungent and sickening aroma of hot blood, and the indescribable odor of fear, all mixed into one teeming mass of terror. The cruellest men, the strongest and the most malevolent, abandoned their anger and their pain and ran like terror-stricken sheep pursued by a wolfpack.

But most of all reality hits with the weight and mass of a sledge hammer to the gut when you enter the cell block and smell the evil, the hopelessness, and the fears that exude from every pore of every person there. Even the bedclothes, the toilets, and the water reek of the smell that penetrates sinuses and brains and refuses to leave, even when you leave the prison.

You know that you can never, ever leave the caged world behind; it will always be a part of your most horrible memory.

Having nearly lost, and then recovered my freedom, at least temporarily, I now lived with the terror that I might again lose it. I had also nearly lost my cabin, my forest on the shore of the lake, and the beauty that became a part of me so that in prison I could again smell the sweetness of the pine needles and the delicate and rose-laden aroma of the sweet shrubs that grew throughout the forest. I knew I could never live in a city; could not wake and hear the traffic and the frightened and frustrated voices of the people, or smell the exhaust and layers of body scents intended to cover the discontent that was drowning the neatly dressed and quietly desperate members of the rat race.

I lost Derry forever, but I could deal with the loss because I had lost her long before she died. The drugs, the booze, and the men had stripped her of her dignity, her beauty, had removed all that had ever been the woman I loved. She had been slowly leaving me even before I was hauled away to prison, and each day there increased the pain of being without her. But even open wounds heal, if imperfectly, and I knew that I could live without her because the world continued, even though I was lost sensually and spiritually.

And I had nearly lost my life as well. This did not frighten me until much later, when it was all over but the slow recovery. I knew that I could face death and even die without a conscious sense of loss. It would merely be oblivion. I had seen rats die with courage if not dignity, and I knew I was equal to a rat if not to a good man.

But I could not face the loss of Zane, even though I had never owned her even in the most spurious sense of the word. I had never made love to her, never kissed her or held her in my arms except briefly, never spoke a loving word to her.

But I knew, but not until now, that I loved her deeply and painfully as I am capable of loving, that I desperately needed to share my life with her.

And I knew, wrenchingly and infuriatingly, that I was losing her, too. I closed my eyes tightly and succeeded only in blotting out the swirling snowflakes and enclosing the smell of death and the sight of black and cracking coagulated blood.

I turned toward Rick, sending him a mental urgency.

"I know," he said evenly. I had never seen him mad and hoped that I never would. I was confident he could be as devastating as a buffalo herd. "I can't go any faster and still get us there."

I wanted to tell him that if we arrived too late it would do no good, either, but I knew what his response would be. And he would be totally correct. I had no right to consider Zane's life to be more important than the lives of the other women.

He leaned forward, his face now only inches from the windshield. He strained to see past the white barrier that filled the night. Even when I closed my eyes briefly, I could still see them: still see the chaotic white stars in a disintegrating universe.

Then, incredibly, we were turning off the state road and into my drive. My drive!

I had long ago, it seemed, stopped thinking of it as my drive or my house or my woods. The killer had taken over my car, my forest, my basement, my bed. My life.

A single set of tire treads could be seen through the light covering of snow. Rick saw it before I did.

"One vehicle went in," he said. "It did not come out. She's possibly there, waiting for us."

"Or he was there. Waiting for her."

I recalled too well the absence of tracks of any sort into the area before, and I knew that if the killer traveled by snowshoe or skis he could carefully brush away his tracks.

The damnable weather had been his greatest ally. I could not believe that it had all been accidental, that each time he killed the snow obligingly covered all traces of him. No, he obviously waited for the snow. He, I was confident, would have killed during the summer only in desperation. His motivations had been recent, and he used the coming snow as his camouflage. Nearly every winter brings the five-day snows that cover the visible world of tracks and scents on the trails.

He knew that bloodhounds were worthless, that the keenest eye could not see a footprint under five inches of snow. That had to be it. He could not travel by vehicle, even with four-wheel drive, without leaving tread marks. He had to have the snow for his bloody work!

Rick eased onto the driveway bed, and I felt the lurching and dipping of each irregularity in the road. I had traveled it so often that even blindfolded I could have told you exactly where on the road I was. And because I knew the drive so well, I also knew which trees, which dead stumps, which carpets of creeping cedar, which crocuses, and what growths of poison oak or ivy were nearby. In my sleep I could have picked wild flowers without brushing against the noxious plants.

I had learned long ago from painful experience that the poisonous growths are as potent in winter as they are in summer, and the only benevolence was that the absence of leaves meant that the stems had to be crushed. I knew, too, that the saw-briars cut as deeply and the nettle, dried and sere, left its own marks.

Just as I knew that killers lurked under the cover of beauty and pristine purity.

The headlights illuminated tracks of deer that had crossed the road only minutes ahead of us. They had crossed from the left side of the road and disappeared into the darkness on the right, and I could tell from the distance between them that the deer had been frightened. They were not walking but leaping.

They could have been frightened by a falling heap of snow when wind dislodged it from the tree branches above. A dead limb crashing through the vital limbs could have spooked them. Or a pack of wild dogs.

Or a killer.

If the killer had indeed come through the woods, he'd have likely made his way down the right side of the creek, to the edge of the lake, and through the woods to the cabin. I mentioned this to Rick.

"I saw the deer tracks," he said. "But if someone came through the woods, how did he get this far without some means of transportation? Where did he leave his car? The man's visible, no matter how clever he is."

I shook my head. "He dumped a body into the trunk of my car while it was parked in the lot outside the office," I said.

"Not necessarily," he said, verbalizing what I had dreaded to think about.

"Say it," I said. I had to hear it. I had heard it in my mind often enough. He repeated what he had said earlier.

"The body was put in your car while you were in bed with Laura Dennis. You hauled it around all day. Face it, Chess."

It was nauseating to think that while I slept, some pervert had slain a woman, carried her body through the woods, and silently placed the still-warm, and possibly still living, body in the trunk of my car.

It could have happened easily. I never locked the car while I was at home because I never knew when I might have to leave hurriedly in the middle of the night.

During this time Rick had inched the truck slowly down the forest road. He was scanning the snow by the road carefully and analyzing every shadow created by the headlights. I knew that he was thinking what I had thought: how easily one or both of us could be killed by someone standing behind one of the trees that grew within inches of the drive.

"Your lights are on," he said at the exact moment I saw the yellow gleam through the snow and trees. "Did you leave them on?"

"I wasn't the last one here," I said. "We left the house filled with people."

"They're gone now." Seconds later he pulled into the yard and nosed the vehicle into the edge of the bushes and then backed up so that we were again facing the road. I knew what he was thinking: that we may need to leave quickly. For whatever reason. I lifted the sawed-off-but-legal shotgun from the back seat as we left the vehicle. Lurch, I noticed, withdrew his own handgun and gripped it tightly as we closed doors softly behind us and crept through the snow that was as fluffy as pillow feathers and eased our way up to the porch. A yellow slit of light showed through the crack where the door had been left slightly ajar.

"He's been here," I said, my heart thumping frantically inside me. I fought the insane impulse to crash through the door and open fire on whatever alien presences might have been inside my house.

Rick nodded and held one hand, palm down, out in front of him, the signal to proceed cautiously. He held his pistol in the old western style, using the grips as they were manufactured to be used. He had never bothered to imitate the television conception of police work. He, like all real shooters, knew too well that one hand was far more maneuverable than two hands.

My own palms were sweating profusely despite the cold. I had removed my gloves as soon as we turned into my drive. I preferred cold fingers to clumsy ones inside leather. Weeks ago I had discarded the double-barrel shotgun in favor of more firepower at the touch of a finger. Automation has much going for it.

Rick used one toe to push the door open, again contrary to the television cop version of the house search. You use one hand to push the door open and the man inside grabs your hand and pulls you off balance while he shoves a muzzle into your gut and you learn a valuable if belated lesson. When the door swung wide, he reached inside and pushed the door all the way back until it touched the wall to be certain that no one was behind it.

All the while I stood with my right shoulder turned to him so that I could see behind us and at the same time be ready to turn to the interior of the house if necessary.

The inside of the house was warm, and I could feel the heated air rushing out toward us. I knew what that meant: the uninvited presence in my house had turned up the heat by opening the damper on the wood stove in the basement. I had never bothered to have central heating installed and had never regretted the decision. I was particularly grateful for it now.

Zane could not have done it. In the brief time that she had been there the wood stove would not have heated the house so that hot air would have reached the front door. Someone had beaten her here. There was no doubt about that. Someone had apparently spent several hours in my house while we were at the Dennis house.

There had been no cars in the parking area when we arrived, and my heart dropped like a millstone when I realized that if Zane had come here to meet me, she had left already. Or at least her car had.

I didn't like either implication. If she left, it was against her will; if her car left without her, it was because she had no control over matters.

We stepped all the way inside the room and closed the door behind us. I did not like the idea of being silhouetted against the light so that we were a perfect target for anyone outside.

The house was silent except for the fan on the wood stove that I had installed to help circulate hot air. The fan did not run unless the stove was hot. The electrically controlled fan thermostat turned off when the heat inside the pipe dropped below one hundred degrees, and the pipes stayed that hot only when the wood supply was adequate and the ventilation was good enough to feed the flames.

I wished I knew when the investigating team left, but I didn't. I told myself that while they might have left a door open, they would not have fed the stove.

No, there was no doubt. The killer had been here again. And possibly was still here.

We searched one room at a time, the two of us taking turns opening doors while the other covered him. We did the upstairs first, because anyone shooting from above us would have a tremendous advantage. The cathedral ceiling structure of the cabin had left the entire kitchen and den areas wide open, and a gunman could have picked us off easily.

I followed Lurch up the steps, keeping my back to him as much as possible while we climbed so that I could cover us from behind.

Upstairs I had built a sitting room that overlooked the downstairs area and two small guest bedrooms. We searched the rooms and found damp patches of melted snow. Someone had been in both bedrooms.

We descended the stairs, and I stayed in the den while Lurch searched the downstairs. He did not need to tell me that we did not want someone slipping from one room and climbing the stairs while we were in another room. I still didn't know enough about police work to justify my carrying a badge, but I learned every minute I was with Rick. He returned within three minutes. He nodded toward the basement and started down.

Only hours ago we had learned that the killer had been in my darkroom, workshop, and office, in addition to leaving a body in my basement den. As we crept down the stairs I wondered for the ten thousandth time if I would ever again be able to enjoy my house.

There was another crack of light appearing through the office door. Lurch motioned for me to go around and enter the office through the second door. I would need to pass through the workshop, or darkroom.

Opening the first door, I reached inside and flipped the light switch. In a split second I realized that the killer had been here only minutes earlier. There was unmelted snow on the floor. Deja vu all over again. Again.

Inside the darkroom earlier my paper safe had been opened so that when I turned on the light all the photo paper inside the safe would be ruined. Now two hundred-foot rolls of film had been pulled from the canister and lay curled and worthless on the floor. I didn't care about the paper or film: I cared about Zane.

Finally I opened the office door and saw the face of Zane, blood nearly concealing her features. I backed away, weakly, and leaned against the wall while Rick Blanton pushed past me and into the room where my hopes and dreams had just died.

TWENTY-TWO

O nly the face of Zane stared sightlessly at me. Where the eyes had been there were only jagged holes that appeared to have been made by a large knife. The crimson seeping down her cheeks from the eye area was obviously catsup, and the photo propped in the chair in front of the office computer had apparently been taken from Zane's apartment. It was one I had never seen before.

The computer screen was dark, but the lights on the monitor and computer told me again that the system had been turned on. I turned the brightness buttons and saw the message that had been left for me.

"I have a new toy," the brief paragraph told me. "She'll no doubt start to bore me soon. You know how it is, Sheriff Dumbo. Anything you do too long becomes a bore. Your hero Hemingway told you that. What he didn't tell you is what happens to toys when they start to bore people. But you don't need to be told, do you? Look for your friend Zane in the place closest to your heart."

The message was signed, "Zimri."

I felt as if I were paralyzed. He had Zane, and she was still alive. For now, at least. I felt certain that she was. She had been here only minutes ago, and he wouldn't kill her until he had enjoyed satiating his perverse lusts at her expense.

Where had he taken her? I turned to Rick, whose face was still like granite or an ice sculpture. In times of crisis, I learned long ago, it was a

259

waste of time to try to read anything from his face. He'd have been a helluva poker player. I had seen him punch a man's head so hard that you could hear bones and gristle crunching like popcorn, and the expression on his face was one of total disinterest. Sometimes I wondered if the man ever felt anything, and yet I knew that he not only felt but felt deeply. He loved music, poetry, art, and nature, and he hated whatever was the enemy of the things he loved.

He looked at the message quickly and turned to me.

"What does he mean?" I asked. "What's closest to my heart? He's already corrupted my car, my property, my house, and even my bed. What the hell is left?"

"Whatever is closest to your heart," he said. "That's one you must answer for yourself. I don't think anyone else can do it for you."

"My house!" I nearly screamed. "I love this place. I thought I'd die in prison if I didn't get to see this house soon."

"She's not here," he said.

"It's the lake," I shouted. "He's drowned her!"

Lurch shook his head. "He uses his victims before he kills them," he said. "He's too perverted just to kill her. In the lake he couldn't watch her suffer and die. And you don't love the lake. You never saw it until you came out of jail."

"Derry!" I said. "I loved Derry. He's taken Zane to the graveyard."

"You stopped loving Derry long ago," he said. "She has nothing to do with this. All you are doing now is missing her. And wallowing in self-pity."

The words stung like shotgun pellets, and I fought the urge to smash my fist into his emotionless face.

And I knew he was right. I no longer loved Derry: I loved what she had symbolized for me. She was beauty that faded, virtue that was demolished, goodness dragged through the dirt, morality that had lost all direction, and kindness turned into stone.

I nodded numbly. He had said what someone should have told me a long time ago. Maybe someone did, and I was deafened by my own selfishness.

But now I was becoming frantic. "Zane!" I cried. "She means more to me than anyone on earth."

Rick shook his head. "It's possible," he said, "but not likely. He could have taken her to her own place, but it's not the place closest to your heart. Have you ever been there?"

"Once," I admitted. "On office business. I don't know why I never went back. God knows I wanted to. For the first and only time in my life I knew that I desperately wanted to go back, but I was terrified of becoming vulnerable again."

I added lamely, "It's what Donne meant when he said that one little room can be an everywhere."

Rick grabbed my arm with such force that I almost crashed to the floor. "Let's go," Lurch said. "I know where they are."

The drive to Sherman University took fifteen minutes. We slid, swerved, skidded, and careened from one side of the highway to the other. We seemed to spend more time in the ditches than in the road, but somehow he managed to keep us in the road.

"If we get stuck we can run the rest of the way," he said. He was speaking for himself. There was no way I was able to keep up with him. His idea of a morning jog was ten miles. He was the most superbly conditioned man I have ever known, in addition to being the most intelligent.

We skidded into the parking lot at the back of the college where we were surrounded by a world of white. Classes had been cancelled for four days now, and even the dorm students wisely stayed indoors. Commuters had no chance of getting to classes, and not half the professors could have dug their way out of their drives.

Lurch killed the lights when we turned onto the campus and we drove in darkness across the huge, sprawling campus where the old and new buildings melted into one another and the lake and the campus lawns were one in their glistening white surfaces. The lake had long ago frozen over, and the snow lay a foot or more thick on the ice.

The only lights visible were the security bulbs that glowed at the entrances to the locked buildings. Lights burned in dorm rooms, but the classroom and administrative buildings were dark and deserted.

Nearly deserted, Lurch apparently thought. He seemed confident that at least two people were inside the enormous buildings that looked more like warehouses than educational centers. We leaped from the vehicle and I followed him across the parking lot.

I thought we were going to enter the building, but instead Lurch skirted the front of it and went to the back. There, he crossed a small masonry fence and followed a breezeway to yet another building, made his way around it, and continued his erratic way around this and the next three buildings until we emerged through huge clumps of shrubbery and stood at the back of the Languages and Literature Building.

The front door was locked, but Lurch climbed to the railing and stepped to the top of the low roof where the coal for the ancient furnace was chuted into the basement furnace room. He made his way across the steep and narrow roof to the final window and crouched beside it. Something metallic glistened in the dim light, and there was a soft grating sound as the window slid upward and he disappeared into the darkness of the classroom.

I followed him at a much slower pace across the roof, which was no more than six feet wide and was connected to the side of the building in a fragile and threatening way. I could feel the roof give slightly under my weight, and I envisioned myself falling through the shingles and fragile and decaying two-by-six rafters and tumbling down to the concrete steps.

As I finally reached the open window a thick, not totally unpleasant smell hit my nostrils. I recognized it instantly and mentally cursed that I did not think of it before. It was the smell of oil-treated floors, the aroma that is part of every ancient schoolhouse in the nation. The custodial staff every Friday afternoon at the end of classes dutifully pushed their oil-saturated mops, three feet wide, up and down the halls and over the floors of classrooms. Another faint smell mixed with the oil: the acrid but faint odor of coal smoke.

It was the same smell that I recognized at the high school, but I had the right idea and the wrong location.

That was the smell on the bodies of the dead women. They had been criminally assaulted in one of the classrooms or offices and dragged along the walls where the ancient paint flecked away and clung to their clothing or hair. They were later killed in the boiler room of the school, where there would be no one who would hear their screams or witness their struggles.

I knew now what triggered the sudden understanding on Lurch's part:

the closest thing to my heart, he knew, just as I knew, was the classroom, my office where I stayed, surrounded by my books and the authors I loved, and the few good people who shared my interests.

But one of them did not share my feelings on humanity; one of them was a killer who tortured and murdered women after raping and humiliating them horribly before murdering them brutally.

But which one?

As we crept as silently as possible down the tomb-like hallway where every board seemed to me to creak with astonishing clarity and decibel levels, I tried to think which one of the professors, janitors, or even students could have been reduced in their levels of humanity to perform such atrocities, and I came up with nothing.

I knew administrators who would cheerfully cut the throats of a dozen professors in order to save a few dollars on their budgets or to increase their Full-Time Enrollment Allotment statistics and get extra funding from the state department. I knew coaches who would do whatever they deemed necessary to get a seven and a half foot center for their basketball team or a coed for their private recreation. There were students, not just the jocks who now and then located the classrooms where they ostensibly met their classes if they could find their way back, who, I know, would not have been above rape, but they wanted only to palliate the lusts created by raging hormones. They would have settled, as some of them were fond of saying, for anything hot and holler, a stove pipe or a horse's collar. But the literature I taught was my true love.

Professors chronically dispensed high grades as if they were supermarket coupons to any coeds willing to drop their standards and underwear for thirty seconds. But would they kill for the opportunity?

I could not believe they would take such drastic steps. There were too many nubile students willing to do whatever was requested in order to improve their scores while the profs did their own scoring.

Who was left? On a college campus there are thousands of people, composing a mid-sized city, all crammed and jammed into a society unlike any other on earth, a society in which there were no laws, no rules, no standards except those of the subculture. In no other part of our culture are so many people in such close proximity for so long without any restrictions except those which are self-imposed. They eat together, study together, cheat their way through exams together, sleep together, do drugs as a body, and plot, plan, and scheme means of making their lives better or at least easier and more desirable.

They go for days on end and never see a law officer; their parents hear from them when money is scarce; even their closest friends see only what the other wishes to be seen.

Any of them could be the killer, and that includes the women. A twenty-year old woman in the pink of physical condition and with the muscular development to rival that of many men could easily approach and over-power an older and unsuspecting woman.

The hallway was at least three hundred feet long, and as we moved silently yet as rapidly as conditions would permit and yet allow us to remain undetected, I envisioned a scenario: a woman not yet in middle age but out of the social whirl and essentially sedentary answers the doorbell and sees a neat, attractive young woman there, perhaps holding a package, a present. The woman opens the door and the younger one slugs her with a stick of wood, a length of pipe, a sock filled with sand or quarters, or even a fist. The housewife goes down in a heap, and the younger woman batters her into unconsciousness or into abject defeat and then drags her to the waiting car and hauls her away.

It was admittedly farfetched but possible.

A male student, particularly an athlete, could overpower the woman easily. So could a janitor, a maintenance man, or a campus custodian. These people work physically every day of their lives except Sundays and some holidays, and they are stronger than they ever intended to be.

Even more logically, many of the maintenance men moonlight as elec-tricians, plumbers, carpenters, welders, and other repair people. It was highly possible that one of them posted a note on the bulletin board and housewives learned to call these part-time experts and save half of the repair bills. The calls could easily get them into the house, and many of them drove vans, which would make it easy to transport an unconscious or trussed woman.

I wondered how many, if any, of the women took night classes at the college, and I cursed myself again that I had not taken the time to check.

Lurch was barely visible as he moved ahead of me. I could make out only a huge bulk that occasionally blotted out the faint light from the windows at the doors at the end of the hallway.

Then I bumped into him. I had not realized that he had stopped. His cable-like fingers tightened on my arm and pulled me closer to him. I could feel his body warmth, and yet I could not see him at all.

"No one's on this floor," he said. We were standing outside the classroom where I lectured on American literature and now and then British literature an eternity ago. "I thought he'd be in this room. Did you teach anywhere else?"

"No."

"Any special meeting places where you advised students?"

"There is a student-faculty conference room in the basement. At times I met with poetry groups there. It's a slight possibility. Then there's my office."

"I'll try the conference room," he said. "You want to check your old office?"

"How will I get in? It'll be locked."

"You don't still have your key?"

"Right. I have it." I had forgotten the Kwikset key on my chain. When I was arrested that night in the basement of the administrative building, I was hauled off to jail, and from there to court, and then to prison. My belongings were taken from me when I went into the jail and returned to me when I came out of the prison. I fumbled in my pocket for my keys. In the dark, and after all the time away from the college, my fingers found and closed upon the key without hesitation. It was as familiar as my own hand. Worse, no one had used the office since I left.

I left Lurch and found the stairway. The huge fire doors were closed but not locked, and I climbed the wide, oily, and creaking stairs slowly, putting my weight down on a tread a little at a time. I stopped every two or three steps and waited, listening for any indication that anyone had heard me.

At the top of the stairs I paused again, waited for any reaction to my presence, and, hearing nothing, turned left, passed the couches where students sat while they waited for classes to start, and made my way past the male students' rest-room and to the corner where I paused, desperately trying to force my eyes to focus on something other than darkness, and listened again.

265

A tiny sound reached me. It could have been a warped board in the floor creaking, a rat squeaking, or a muffled cry of pain.

My office was in the first alcove. The hallway was in the exact center of the floor, with small cubicles of offices on each side. Each alcove typically contained three offices and a work room that was also a supply room. My office was the final one on the left.

I crept forward, one microstep at a time, stopping to listen at each pause. The sound came again, and this time I was positive it came from my office.

Gripping the shotgun tightly in one hand and feeling in the darkness with my other, I made my way to the office door.

It occurred to me that I had no plan whatever. Now that I was at the office; now that I was within ten feet of the killer I had wanted to destroy since the first morning of horror, I did not know what to do. I realized that I was sweating profusely.

I pondered my options. If I waited for Lurch, it might be too late. If I tried the doorknob and it was locked, the sound would surely announce my presence. If I tried to use a key, the killer would have ample time to kill Zane.

Or me. Or both of us. He would know at all times where I was, while I had no idea of his location. I did not know how he was armed, whether with a baseball bat, martial arts skills, or his own version of the sawed-off shotgun.

Two grotesque and horrifying visions filled my mind: in one I crashed into the office I had occupied for so many months and the orange-red muzzle flash and explosion of the .357 Magnum would register shortly before the slugs ripped through my flesh; in the other, I stood outside and debated while the razor-sharp knife slashed silently through Zane's throat.

The latter vision won, and I stepped backward three soft steps and threw my weight forward with all my energy and felt the panel door break loose at its latch and swing inward. My momentum carried me through the doorway and I crashed into the desk I had called my own when I first came to the college.

A sharp pain flashed from my knee to my brain and back again, and something sharp crashed into my shoulder, or vice versa. Then what felt like a briar scraping my skin raked over my face and neck rapidly several times. It took a full three or four seconds before the pain registered completely and I felt the warmth of my own blood trickling like a wet-weather spring down my chest.

I twisted to land on my back and folded my arms over my face and neck and kicked upward with all my strength and connected with nothing. I writhed in a quarter-circle and kicked again, and this time I heard a deep grunt and felt a jarring pain in my knees and ankles. I kicked repeatedly until I again connected with nothing and felt something rake across my shoulder and then I felt the cool air as the fabric split open.

From somewhere in the darkness I heard screaming that I recognized as Zane's voice, and I twisted again and kicked upward and felt the jarring pain again as my boots connected with flesh. Then something landed atop me and the razor-sharp knife flashed repeatedly toward me. It was too dark to see, but I know the knife flashed: in my mind's eye I could see it coming at me rapidly and furiously, like a blind and starving bird frantically pecking at unseen seeds. My arms were covered with the thick leather of my jacket, but the point of the knife penetrated the sleeves and I could feel the flash points of pain in a dozen places as I flailed and threshed and tried desperately to dislodge my attacker.

Something hard dug into my hips, and I suddenly remembered the sawed-off shotgun. Defending myself with one arm I managed to pull the shotgun from under me and grasp it by the stock so that my thumb flicked off the safety and my finger reached inside the trigger guard while my fingers curled around the grip portion of the stock.

I shoved the gun upward and pulled the trigger. The orange explosion filled the room with enormous impact and concussion. For a brief moment I could hear nothing but the ringing inside my head, and then I could make out the sounds of two voices raised in screams. Then there was a crashing of broken glass and the room was again silent except for the suddenly subdued sobbing of Zane and a deep voice at my shoulder. The shotgun was gone.

A rush of cold wind struck me in the face, and from somewhere outside and below us I could hear another voice, this one filled with pain and fury as it moved farther and farther from us. Footsteps raced from the room and into the alcove. I could still hear them as they reached the hallway and turned toward the stairs.

I struggled to my feet and searched for the light switch. When I flipped it, I saw blood everywhere, much of it mine and the some of it Zane's. A trail of red spots led to the broken window, and I knew that some of the pellets connected. Zane was now crumpled in a chair in the corner beside a bookcase, her hands over her face. Blood seeped through her fingers and dripped onto her naked body.

I could see cuts on her breasts, her stomach, and across her abdomen. Her thighs bled in a dozen places. I looked quickly and saw that the cuts were shallow, designed to inflict pain and terror rather than to cause shock and death, although both would have followed in time.

My own wounds were deeper but not life-threatening. Not while the killer was dragging himself across the snow and toward whatever shelter or hiding place he had. I picked up the phone and heard nothing. The line had not been cut or pulled loose, so I assumed that the lines were down all over the college campus.

Sherman University had once been a high school, and for close to a hundred years it stood on the side of a mountain that seemed to rise on and on until it reached the low-hanging clouds. When the school board voted to close the school when the state built a consolidated school, the buildings stood vacant, a haven for vandals and drug-heads, until Andrew Bannister bought the buildings and started a business school that kept growing, thanks to G. I. Bill of Rights money and returning vets who wanted either an education or an excuse not to go to work. Little by little the school grew in numbers, if not in standards, and the Board of Trustees decided that it was time to change the name from a college to a university. So they hired a sign painter. As far as anyone could tell, that was the only change.

Most of the buildings were two-story, long, and barely usable. A spark or carelessly dropped cigarette would level the entire campus in a matter of minutes. The campus also covered several acres, and there were dozens of places a man might hide. But only one stood out in my mind.

Quickly I removed my jacket and waited for her to pull on slashed and tattered clothing and then draped the coat over Zane's blood-striped body. I urged her to her feet, which mercifully still had shoes on them.

"Lurch may need us," I whispered urgently. "We can't leave him. Can you walk?"

268

She nodded, and I pulled her to her feet. When she slipped her arms into my coat I could see that the pervert had cut her face and neck. Something dropped softly to the floor, and I stared at it for only a moment before I averted my eyes.

I hurried her from the room.

Outside we stumbled across the campus. I had located my flashlight, and as I directed its beam onto the snow I could see patches of bright red. I had no idea where the shotgun blast caught him, but he was losing blood. We followed the red trail between buildings and toward the grove of trees that lined the campus lake.

We followed rapidly, but soon the blood trail stopped. I assumed that the sudden cold had helped the blood to coagulate. All we had were footprints in the snow.

The prints entered the laurel slick that surrounded the lake, and we plunged ahead. Just outside the thicket another set of footprints, these much larger and farther apart, trampled the first ones, and I knew that Lurch was not far behind him.

The lake surface was frozen solid, except at the north end where the creek flowed over the rock cliff and crashed into the frothing water. The footprints moved in the direction of the waterfall, and we made our way toward the towering hill when Zane seemed to slip and fall. She dropped to one knee, and when I helped her to her feet she looked at me and shook her head.

"I can't keep up," she said. "My ankle is damaged. You go on. I'll stay here."

"No," I said "You're not staying alone. I'll carry you."

I lifted her and stumbled toward the waterfall. I noticed that the snow had stopped and the clouds had parted. A full moon glowed brightly over the frozen lake and the waterfall.

The scene would have been one of unspeakable grandeur and beauty had it not been for the ghastly necessities facing all of us. The two-hundred foot waterfall poured over the sheer rock cliff and fell straight uninterruptedly to the plunge pool where it crashed into the dark waters. The automobile-sized boulders on three sides of the plunge pool were glistening white with the snow and ice that had formed where the spray clung and hardened. It was a postcard scene, except for the occasional droplets of blood in the snow..

I had carried Zane for a hundred yards when we reached the plunge pool. There the footprints in the snow disappeared into the laurel, and I knew that the killer had headed for the top of the rock cliff. From there he could reach the highway.

At the base of the cliff I stopped, helped Zane to a nearby boulder, and gently seated her upon it.

"Rick is up there," I told her. "With the pervert. He may need help." Fear darkened her eyes, but she nodded and whispered for me to go. Her bleeding had nearly stopped, and her color, even in the reflected moonlight on the snow, seemed better. I dreaded the thought of leaving her alone, particularly if the killer knew she was unguarded. Or even if she thought it.

That way there would be more pain and terror, which were the foods of the pervert. I kissed her bloody lips quickly and turned to climb the rocky cliff and follow Lurch and a killer.

And I knew who he was, now and without a doubt. I remembered who Charles Lutwidge was. He was a classical scholar and a true genius in mathematics who wrote only a handful of books in his life, but those pages will live forever. Charles Lutwidge Dodgson is better known to the world as Lewis Carroll, author of *Alice's Adventures in Wonderland*.

He was also known in smaller circles for his peculiar sense of humor that endeared him to adults and children alike. Some of his characters had a way of stating truths in the most absurd manner. They linked well with the vicious satire of Alexander Pope.

And that link took me to the identity of Zimri and Ehud.

TWENTY-THREE

If there had ever been a trail up the cliffside, and I was certain the college kids had worn one, it was obliterated by the snow. I had to follow the tracks of the two who had gone ahead of me, and I had the advantage of being able to see where the two of them had slipped and slid over ice-covered rocks. I carefully avoided the obvious pitfalls, but I nevertheless experienced more difficulty than I would have thought possible in the short climb.

I was climbing with my feet and one wounded hand; the other hand held the flashlight. Ahead of me, although I could see little, I could hear an occasional grunt, a yelp of pain, or a curse.

Then I heard the shotgun blast.

Silence followed the blast, and I could not determine whether Rick had shot the killer or whether he had been the victim. Or if the shot had gone wild, although with a shotgun it's hard to miss by much if the gun is aimed in the general direction of the target.

After the fight in my onetime office, I had lost the shotgun. I had no way of knowing whether it had been kicked under a desk or whether Rick or the killer had it.

I now knew. I reached the top of the climb and started to push my way through the final fringe of laurel when a shotgun blast shredded the leaves all around me and I felt the sting of the pellets ripping my flesh. My right arm and shoulder were hardest hit, and my neck and cheek burned as if a thousand bees had stung me.

Flattening myself in the snow, I crawled forward. My knee scraped painfully over a small rock, the size of an orange, and I closed my fingers over it quickly. Even with the covering of snow, the rocks were apparent, and within seconds I had gathered a dozen of them and piled them within easy reach.

There was a long silence, during which time I assessed my damages. The thick year-round foliage and the close-growing branches of the laurel slick had deflected most of the pellets, and I had not been seriously wounded. My own bleeding had slowed to an ooze, and I flexed my left arm back and forth to determine whether I could actually heave a rock.

I decided that I could.

I had used one shell in the office, and I had heard another shot as I climbed. Then the third was fired as I started out of the laurel slick. He had three more shots.

Waiting, barely breathing, I could see the dark figure moving slowly toward me. I could not wait until he was within certain range; to do so would mean that he would be close enough that the shotgun blast would shred my body. Even a sawed-off shotgun packs a wallop at twenty yards.

He knew too much about me not to know that I did not carry a hand gun, and he moved with agonizing slowness toward me. I could not afford to wait any longer. I picked up a baseball-sized stone and lobbed it like a hand grenade toward the dark figure.

The rock arced slowly and landed harmlessly in the snow beside him. But it distracted him long enough for me to rise and fire the second like a fastball. It caught him in the side of the face just as he started to pull the trigger.

Diving into the snow, I could hear the pellets ripping through the foliage like the first one, then one more blast rocked the night and more pellets shredded foliage.

He had one more shell. I rose slightly and fired another rock, this one catching him in the gut. The one that followed hit him squarely in the forehead, and as he staggered, I rushed from the laurel thicket and dived headlong at him. The two of us fell heavily into the snow, and I heard him grunt with pain as we went down. I thought I could smell the sour-sweet odor of blood on him.

Despite his wounds, he was powerful, and he was desperate. In his weakened state he lashed out at me with both fists and both knees, and he butted and bit at me like a wild animal. I was fighting for my life at that moment, but all I could think of when I felt his teeth sink into my cheek was AIDS.

I was never a fighter, and I had never managed to teach myself the necessary tricks of the literal hand-to-hand combat, but there are many actions that are born of instinct, not training, and I kneed, slugged, kicked, and elbowed.

Somehow we broke apart, and we scrambled to our feet. In the brilliant moonlight we looked like two abominable snowmen in mortal combat. The gun had been lost somewhere in the scuffle, and, unarmed, he lowered his head and charged me. The deep snow made it difficult to move my feet, and his head caught me in my gut and we were down again. As we fell I brought my knee up hard between his legs, and I felt most of the wind leave his lungs.

One thing I knew about fighting: if you do something, no matter what, that really hurts your opponent, do it again and again. And as we fell, I kneed him repeatedly. He tightened his legs in an effort to stop the punishment, but I kneed harder and harder. At the same time I threw one arm around his neck and pulled his head to my chest, in a deadly embrace. Holding him as tightly as I could with my wounded arm and shoulder, I lashed out at his face with my left fist, hitting him until his face felt like mush. I was certain that his testicles were oatmeal by this time.

He suddenly collapsed. Whether from the wounds, the pain, or the exhaustion, I could not determine. I rolled him off me and stood over him. He lay there, inert, in the snow. He lay on his back, with one arm thrown backward over his face.

I stepped back to look for the shotgun, and when I did he was on his feet in a blur of motion and charging me again. This time the snow was his enemy, and his feet slipped and he went down on his knees.

I kicked him in the side of the head with all the strength I could muster. To hell with fair fighting and with law and order, I thought. He fell, and I kicked him again and again. Then I dragged him to the edge of the creek that flowed across the north end of the campus. There I broke the laws governing police actions one after the other.

I read him no rights, used no cuffs, showed him none of the basic consideration people seem to think criminals ought to have. I showed him the same mercy he had shown his victims.

It took only a slight shove to roll his body into the swift current that slithered across the surface of the solid rock that was the foundation of the mountain. His weight caused him to cling to the rock for a moment, and then he looked up at me just as the current caught him and pulled him away from me. The light of the moon caught the look on his face and imprinted it in my mind for, I knew, the length of my life.

It started as a look of bewilderment, surprise that I would do to him what he had done to others. The shocked look evolved into a sudden expression of realization and fear, and the fear in his eye was transposed to yet another look. This one, final.

It was a glare of pure hatred. It was unadulterated and total abhorrence, loathing, and malignity.

Then he disappeared over the ledge and fell two hundred feet to the frigid plunge pool below.

I could have taken him to jail where he'd hire a hotshot lawyer and the trial would be delayed for months, even years, and then when he finally faced a jury and judge the killer would either be declared insane and sent to an institution or he'd go to prison for a few months. I had seen too much wrist-slapping: enough to last me for a lifetime.

After a few months he'd be released, and he'd start all over. If he was indeed criminally insane, that is. If he was just killing from a personal motive, he could return to freedom and live out the rest of his life in whatever environment he chose. But his victims would spend eternity in their graves.

I didn't like either of the possibilities, which is why I gave him the shove. When the report was filed, I'd state that in the fight he lost his balance and fell over the falls. And Lurch, if he was still alive, would have memory troubles.

Was I immoral, wrong? So was the killer.

I made my way to the edge of the cliff and peered into the darkness of the plunge pool for some sight of his body. There was none.

Then I searched for Rick Blanton. Strange, he was Lurch to me when all was well; in a crisis, he became Rick or Blanton.

Whoever he was, I had to find him.

I searched the plateau quickly and found nothing. Then I began to move in a half-circle around the fringes of the laurel slick. On my first try I found the blood. By moonlight I followed the trail into the laurel, and there between two rocks I found him.

He was alive. But I knew that I had to get him to medical aid quickly. It would take half an hour to climb back down the cliff, haul him to the vehicle, and then drive him to the hospital. If I left him alone and went for help, it would take almost as long, plus the time needed to get the stretchers up the cliff and the time to work out the logistics of getting him back down. A helicopter was out of the question. There was, as far as I was concerned, only one way.

"Rick," I said in a low but firm voice, "can you hear me?"

He nodded slightly.

"I've got to get you down to the bottom of the hill," I said. "It's going to be rugged. Can you take it?"

He didn't answer; instead he squeezed my hand.

I knelt beside him and pulled as gently as I could until he was out from between the rocks where he had crawled to escape the deadly fire from the shotgun. I knew from the dead weight that nearly exhausted me that I could never carry him down the cliff.

"Rick," I said again, "I can't carry you. I've got to find another way. Can you hang on while I work it out?"

He squeezed my hand again, then released me. I stepped onto the open area of the plateau again and looked around frantically. I saw nothing that I could use. I had hoped that the killer had dropped his knife in the snow. If he did, I could not find it.

Then I saw the eight-foot spruce tree leaning across the snow. The weight of the snow and ice had pushed it over, and when I approached it I could see that the roots had been nearly pulled from he ground. I grasped the top and pulled with all my energy and strength, and I felt the tiny roots breaking. It took less than three minutes to pull the tree the rest of the way loose.

I dragged it to the edge of the laurel slick and then returned to Rick. I turned his body so that his head was toward the open plateau and then reached under his arms and pulled as hard as I could. He moved perhaps four inches. I tried again and again, and finally I had him moved to the flat snow field.

Then I rolled him onto the tree. I recalled that years ago when we had to move something heavy across the floor, we'd pry up one side and then slip the business end of a broom under the weight. Then we'd pull the broom handle and, miraculously, the object would slide obligingly across the floor.

I hoped the same principle would work with Lurch.

When I had him loaded onto the tree, I grasped the root end of the tree and pulled. Despite the agonizing pain in my arms and legs, it worked.

I found that I could slide the huge form of Lurch across the snow with little difficulty. At the laurel slick on the other side of the open area I knew it would be different. I'd have to pull him and the tree through the dense growth and then somehow get him down the cliff.

It turned out to be much easier than I dreamed. Once I had his head and shoulders into the thicket, I'd back down the cliff three or four feet and then pull. The weight of the wounded deputy, aided by gravity, moved forward, and the thick limbs of the laurel held him back sufficiently that he didn't bobsled down the trail.

I could hold the root end of the small sapling at waist level and thus keep his head from banging into rocks. At the steepest points I'd wedge my back against a tree and pull, and the tree I leaned against served to anchor Lurch and keep him and his spruce from getting out of control.

In far less time that I would have believed I had him at the bottom of the cliff. The spruce sapling had served as a travois and also as a cushion against the shock of the rocks I had to pull him over. As I pulled him into the open area at the base of the falls, I paused to check him.

He had made the trip safely. I asked if he could hold out a few more minutes, and he replied in a whisper, "You've not killed me yet." I thought I saw a hint of a smile flicker.

Then I heard the scream.

I whirled, and in the moonlight I could see Zane. She was running out onto the ice-covered lake, and a lumbering figure moved relentlessly toward her. She kept backing away from him, and he pursued, flopping and floundering, like a manatee or crippled moose, toward her. I could see the glint of the knife as the moon beams struck it.

"I've got to go," I told Lurch. "Zane's in trouble."

I lumbered as fast as I could along the lake shore thirty yards to the point where I could see evidence of a struggle. A wet trail led from the plunge pool to where I had left Zane. Every few feet there was an area of depression in the snow, suggesting that the killer, who had somehow survived the fall into the pool, had collapsed and somehow had clambered to his feet and continued his quest to kill Zane. His wide path through the snow suggested that he was forced to drag one foot.

Apparently he had broken his leg in the fall.

Zane was twenty yards from the shoreline, and the killer was closing in on her. Her feet had slipped from under her and she fell heavily on the snow-covered ice. Even above the roar of the waterfall I could hear the sharp cracking sound as the ice began to fracture. It popped, then squealed like an animal in pain.

Then the killer had her by the foot and was edging closer to her body. She kicked at him with her free foot and jerked free, and she began to edge backward faster and faster, toward the plunge pool where the ice was thinner.

A sheet of ice ten feet wide broke and the dark figure lay inert for a moment, then rose and began to crawl again toward Zane. I limped forward and reached the huge ice floe just as the figure turned to face me. He lunged forward, the knife glinting in the moonlight.

I stepped heavily on the floating ice sheet and heard it crack. I stepped again, harder, and the sheet cracked ominously, like tree limbs snapping in an ice storm, and the man disappeared into the water.

"Don't move!" I yelled at Zane. "Lie perfectly still. I'm coming to get you."

I hobbled the short distance back to where Lurch lay and rolled him not-too-gently from the spruce tree and dragged it behind me as I staggered back to the edge of the lake.

I lay flat on the ice and pulled with my hands and pushed with my feet three feet forward and then pulled the tree even with me. When I was within ten feet of Zane I slowly and very carefully maneuvered the sapling until the tip of it was within her reach.

"Stay flat," I urged her. "The ice is too thin. Distribute your body weight as much as you can. Hold on to the tree. I'm going to start backing away."

Like a disabled crab I wriggled backward. Snow had worked its way up inside my shirt and I felt its frigid presence embalming me. My hands and feet were numb, and I had to command my limbs to obey what my brain told them.

The ice under her cracked ominously, and I could see that her feet were in the water now and the ice sheet was sinking with terrifying speed.

I squirmed backward as fast as I could move, pulling her with all my strength, but suddenly she refused to move. I tugged with all my strength, and she did not budge. Her knees were in the water now and she was having trouble holding on to the top of the sapling. She was kicking again, rapidly, and suddenly the face of Marlin Rockwell, filled with hatred and determination, glowered at her, then at me. Somehow, he still held the knife, and his hand lifted it high above his head.

Then he seemed to pause in mid-stabbing motion. The physics of his upward movement had the opposite and equal effect of sending him under the frigid water again, but he rose to the surface almost instantly and his hand rose again and seemed to remain motionless in the air as I abandoned the tree and rolled across the ice until I was at the edge of the water. The knife arced downward and I swung my foot forward and let my boot take the force of the blow.

At the same moment I kicked at the contorted face and felt my booted heel crunch into his mouth and nose. There was a gurgling sound and he disappeared again. He bobbed to the surface almost immediately, and for a brief instant the knife rose, poised, and then fell from his fingers and disappeared into the lake. For a moment the hate-filled face hung suspended, then slowly sank from view and did not reappear.

Zane was pulling herself forward now. Her entire body was out of the water, and together we snow-swam back to the shore where we could see red and blue lights blinking in the early morning darkness. When we reached the shore of the lake Bum helped me to my feet while Wadsworth pulled Zane from the snow and helped her to the ambulance.

Lurch was already inside. I looked at Bum. His face was wreathed with both worry and happiness.

"Zane called in," he said. "She told me that you were on the cliff and that Lurch had been hurt. She hobbled to the truck to call and then ran back down to see if she could help. Sorry it took so long to get here."

"You got here," I said. "That's what matters."

The ride to the Sherman hospital was sheer torture from the moment we started until we were deposited in the emergency room where the bright lights and toasty warmth had the double effect of waking us from our pain-induced state of near-shock and at the same time the painkillers left me in a dreamy state.

I could vaguely remember the events that had occurred only minutes earlier. My brain was a cluster of random flashes of light and actions that included snow, ice, water, glistened knives, blood, pain, fear, arctic wind, horror, and a grim satisfaction as the face of Marlin Rockwell sank for the final time into the waters beneath the ice.

Doctors and nurses swarmed all over us in a no-nonsense manner, except for one man with a cocky moustache who grinned at me and said we were going to have to stop meeting this way. I remembered him from the night he treated me for a broken leg. I had no idea who he was.

They took Lurch first, wheeling him quickly into the inner recesses of the emergency room. Grim-faced nurses and doctors hovered over him like mother hens protecting one chick. Zane was next to go. That left me and Bum in the huge room where they had taken us all.

"Thanks," I told him. He hadn't told me, but I knew that while he was helping at the lake he was also finding time to get the hospital alerted to the serious extent of our injuries. He spent the night in the hospital, going from room to room to secure the information he knew the rest of us would need to hear. He disappeared at dawn when it was obvious that we'd not lose anybody.

The three of us spent the night, what was left of it, in the Sherman County Hospital. At noon the next day Zane and I were released, but the doctors told us that Lurch would be a guest there for perhaps a month. They were going to have to go inside to stop the bleeding.

I told him earlier that they'd be lucky if Lurch stayed two days.

I left the hospital and accepted a ride back to the office. Wooley, Wadsworth, and Rowena were waiting at the outside door and escorted me back to the cubicle that I had begun to associate with freedom. They wanted two things: answers and the right to leave the snow fields of

Sherman.

"Rockwell killed the women," I said, telling them of the fight on the plateau and the clear view I had of his face in the water. "Divers can find his body in a day or so. Let him stay there as long as you like. I want to be damn certain he's dead this time."

"He's already dead," Bum said. "We checked, after you suggested the similarity between the deaths and those in eastern Tennessee. Marlin Rockwell was killed in a car wreck shortly after he left Johnson City. For the past week we've all been chasing a dead man."

TWENTY-FOUR

The pain killers had begun to desert me, and I wanted to make this session as fast and easy as possible. I told them I had called the Tennessee Department of Public Instruction and learned that Rockwell had died in a flaming car wreck. Except that his name was not Rockwell then. It was Redding Willis, a high school principal and then district superintendent who had, they told me, a shady career. They did not elaborate.

"His name was Willis then," I said. "He had designated a woman named Bea Gross as his beneficiary. She collected a check that was equivalent to one full year's salary. That was in the area of sixty thousand dollars. She did not get to enjoy it for very long. She drowned not long afterwards."

Wadsworth nodded. "At least he didn't kidnap her and torture her. You know, of course, why he faked his death." It was not a question.

"Yes," I told them. "It was the only way he could stay out of trouble. He apparently found a convenient body, or persuaded a living person to die, and then planted the body, along with personal items that would identify Redding Willis as the victim. At least a dozen irate fathers and about that many husbands and boyfriends were interested in having a long talk with him."

"I was told that he had actually raped a young housewife, a former student of his," Wadsworth said. "The police there say we could multiply the case by several. He was killed, or so they thought, and all cases were closed."

"How did he manage it?" Rowena asked. She was dressed all in black today: black cap, a leather beret type that sat jauntily on the back of her head; black pants, black shirt, and black jacket that reached to her hips. Her boots were, of course, black. I wondered if her underwear was also black and silently prayed that I'd never find out. "I mean," she added, "he wasn't that good looking."

I saw Wadsworth and Wooley glance quickly at each other and I could read their thoughts: For Rowena to think a man handsome, he would have to be a woman.

"Who can predict what will appeal to a woman," I said, then added quickly, "or to a man. We've all seen beautiful people who were married to and madly in love with unattractive mates. What he had, I suspect, was the combination of sensitivity, quiet air of authority, understanding, and sympathy. He worked on their heads and hearts and needs. And it worked for him."

"You think he actually killed someone to fake his own death?" Wadsworth asked. He, too, seemed restive and nervous. For the first time he appeared frightened and uncertain.

"I don't know what happened," I said. "My guess is that he either saw a roadside wreck and switched identification with the dead man inside, or he killed someone or found a body and stole the car and pushed it over the cliff. My gut feeling is that he killed someone that he had personally selected to die. Someone whose death could serve a real purpose for him. My best guess would be that the person was Herman Brittain, Ralph Brett, or Benjamin Collins. There are other possibilities."

Wadsworth's face was a huge question mark.

I told them about the post office boxes and the vacant trailers on the lonely roads.

"It's only a guess," I said, "but my take on this is that when he knew he had to leave Tennessee he looked around for a victim who could serve two purposes. He found or knew someone with tons of teaching experience. A retired person."

"How did that help? Something isn't quite—"

"I'm fuzzy on it, too. And it's only a guess. But say he chose to kill an acquaintance who had taught thirty or so years. The man would have to be little more than fifty years old and he would ideally be a loner, either a bachelor or a widower. And the man we knew as Rockwell could kill the man, burn his body beyond recognition in the faked car wreck, and then locate the man's state teaching credentials, including his retirement number and social security number. Then in the first wreck it would be Rockwell's body. The man we know as Rockwell, I mean."

"So he collected the insurance, or the woman did. He killed the woman and then he moved on."

"To other victims. Think how many teachers you know who are unattached socially. Mates die or leave. The teacher lives alone, or he decides to move. His checks are forwarded to a post office box in Monbo. Or Cato. Or Arden."

"And the man we called Rockwell collected the checks? Is it worth it? To risk all he did for such a small amount of money?"

"Not so small," I told them. "Assume the teacher collected only $2,000 each month, plus $1,400 in social security. That is a total of more than $40,000 in a year. Or $400,000 in ten years. Now multiply that number by the total number of teachers whose checks he might have stolen over the years."

"Still," Wadsworth began, "he'd have to wait a long time to collect that much money, and it still isn't a very high amount."

"If he had ten such amounts coming in, from ten teachers who died and no one knew it, it would amount to $400,000 in a single year and several millions in ten years. Are you familiar with the old Rule of Eighty? I don't recall all the details, but if a military retiree became a teacher, if his age and years of total service to state and country added up to eighty, he could retire on three different paychecks. That doesn't include the other people, such as retired servicemen or cops or just plain mill workers. It might take us years to nail down all of them."

"So the amount would be at least $30,000 more for each of the retirees. As the man said, a million here, five million there, it adds up."

"To a rather shocking total. Marlin Rockwell made lots of trips out of town. He made speeches, attended seminars and other professional meetings. Maybe senior citizen gatherings. At these functions he could have met his future victims: retirees who were at loose ends. He could persuade them to move to Sherman. Or at least to tell people that's where they were going."

"And then he'd eliminate them and keep the checks coming. So how many of these did he have?"

I admitted I did not know. "We can check post offices in all the nearby towns. He might have a mailbox in all of them."

"So why have the women check the mail?"

"To keep from being seen himself. He was a man known by people all over the area. Someone would start to wonder why he had mail coming in all these places. But one of the women could have easily picked up mail in two or three cities."

"Why would the women have agreed to do this for him?"

I shrugged. "We'll ask the ones who are left. My best guess is that he selected the DOLLS women for a purpose. They found that they were in trouble in high school and dropped out to have a baby. In a mountain community like this one the social stigma would be much greater than it would in a large city. Protestant Work Ethics are still strong here. The girls would have been alone and worried. And then their old high school principal shows up to befriend them. One by one, I am assuming, he seduced them. Or he let them seduce him. They had married for money and had a life with a slob. There was no love in the marriage, and even if there had been, the morganatic marriage would have killed it. I don't know how the women felt, but I'd be mad as hell if I had to start a marriage on such mistrust."

"Still, the women might not want to help him."

"Chances are they did not have any idea what they were doing," I said. "To them it was helping out the man they loved. Or perhaps he paid them. I rather think he did. They knew that if they ended their marriages, they were essentially penniless. We can check to see how many of them made regular deposits into a private savings account."

The room was cozy and warm, but the pain from my wounds kept me from getting drowsy. Wadsworth kept probing for answers, no doubt for his personal use when he wrote up his account on how he solved the crimes.

"What about Lawton Calvin?" he asked.

"One of the several names Rockwell used. That's another guess."

"What about Gallager?"

"He apparently taught for enough years to collect at least a partial retirement check. I'd guess twenty years. Legal problems hounded him out of education, so he bought a small newspaper. We can ask him. His wife suffered a debilitating stroke several years ago and her health is fragile."

"She's dead," Wadsworth said. "Her house burned to the ground last night, with her in it."

I nodded. I could feel no grief for the loss. She had no life as it was, not even the power to end her existence.

"The wood stove?" I asked.

He nodded. "Chimney fire, apparently."

I wondered. The timing was too perfect.

"And Gallager?"

"Hospitalized. He collapsed when he learned that his wife was dead. Was he guilty of the crimes he was charged with?"

"I doubt it. Like the girls, he was a pawn for Rockwell. My reading of the whole thing is that he was set up all the way. And he not only lost his job and his career but his wife suffered a paralyzing stroke as the stress and anxiety mounted. All so that a man could continue to satisfy his appetites."

"But didn't Rockwell—or Lawton Calvin, as he was known at the time—speak out in defense of Gallager? Why would he do that? Why not let the man rot in prison? He'd be out of the way there."

"Rockwell seemed to have a sort of perverse integrity about some matters," I said. "He was willing to let Gallager take the rap for crimes he did not commit, but he wanted the sentence to be as light as possible. He may even have wanted Gallager free, in case he needed another fall guy. I mean, a man with a record would not be hard to sell as the guilty person in a different setting."

"The left-handedness? That had no role in this?"

"Only to the extent that the girls had the silly club in high school and continued it in their married lives. Remember: these were not school leaders. They were fringe students who would never be popular in the classic sense. They were smart enough to make good but not great grades; they were pretty enough to attract slobs like Tyler and Dennis and Webley, and they were expected to be grateful enough to remain docile and servile."

Rowena laid her hand on my arm. Her flesh was clammy and cool, like that of a reptile. "I misjudged you badly," she said. "I was confident that I knew people well. You did a great job. But I am still concerned about the giant woman."

"Nobody knows all people well," I said. "Some of us fall outside the norms and conventional channels. As for the woman, I doubt that we'll see her any more."

"She's dead?"

"She never lived," I said. "She was the other persona of Marlin Rockwell. It made a wonderful disguise. I'd have never recognized him in that atrocious getup."

"The man was a satyr," Rowena said. She had been sitting and fidgeting during the entire time. "He deserved to die horribly. But why kill the women here? Didn't he have a wonderful game going on? For him, I mean."

I shrugged and wished I hadn't. It took several long seconds before the pain subsided and I could speak again. "My guess is that Rockwell either boasted about how much money he was taking in, or one of the women saw the checks and told the others. Or he thought she told the others. Maybe it was blackmail and he couldn't take the chance that he'd be fingered. So he decided to eliminate them, all during one massive snowstorm. He damn near succeeded."

"Why Zane?" she asked. "She wasn't involved."

I shook my head. "No, but she had been to the meetings on a couple of occasions. She was close to us daily, and Rockwell had assumed that sooner or later he'd be implicated."

"What now?" Wadsworth asked.

"I'm going to call around," I said. "We'll see what develops."

Wooley shifted uncomfortably in his chair. He, too, longed to be on the road, and for a fleeting moment I tried to imagine him as a loving father and husband, a member of the PTA, or a volunteer at the Bloodmobile give-in. Maybe he played the violin in the community concert series.

"What about the rose beryl?" he asked.

"The girls married slobs, but the girls themselves were sort of damaged goods to the rich brats. They married them. But the blobs knew—or suspected strongly—that they were not the father of the girl's earlier child. That resulted in the prenuptial marriage agreement part of the deal, and the girls added the rose beryl bit as a constant reminder that they were simply married whores."

Wadsworth seemed disappointed. "That's all?" he asked.

"No. That's not all. The left-handedness translated into the morganatic marriage. The custom started when the groom gave his left hand to the wife. The morganatic marriage was one in which the husband's gift to his wife on the first morning after their marriage was a token, often rose beryl, that she accepted in lieu of inheritance. The women in the club became drawn together more and more by the realization that they had all been treated like medieval serfs. That's when they became angry."

"But at whom?" Rowena wanted to know. "What had anyone done to them, other than the things men do to women generally." She'd never be able to let it go.

"They were mad at life, obviously. Their life had brought them close to the better things in our existence, and they knew that the best they could hope for would be to rent the status symbols for a while. The idea was not appealing."

Wadsworth rose. The others followed suit. "We're off," he said. "Tons of records to deal with. You might want to get out of here, too. I suspect you'd like to have a chance to eat a meal, take a shower, and maybe even catch a nap."

"Nice," I said thickly. I had been enervated by the cold and the struggles, but the warmth of the hospital room and the office had negated the couple of hours of sleep I had snatched after the doctors had stopped probing and picking and pronounced me reasonably healthy. "I hope you folks aren't leaving Sherman with a bad impression of the folks here."

"No problem," Rowena said. "Maybe we can come back for a visit."

"Where's Zane?"

"Released an hour ago. She left with Bum."

We didn't talk any more until we stood on the landing at the top of the stairs outside the building. I vaguely remember that they helped me with the elevator and the doors. When we stepped outside, to my shock the sun was shining and the air was suddenly warm.

"It's not spring yet," Wadsworth said, "but it's on the way. Radio weather reports said that it would be in the sixties for the next eight or ten days. Enough to melt the snow. Give us a chance to check the terrain around your cabin for signs that Rockwell was in fact there. Although it really doesn't matter now, does it?"

I had the feeling that he was ready to wash his hands of Sherman.

"No," I said. "It doesn't matter. Anyhow, I know how he did it." They looked at me strangely.

"It occurred to me while I was lying on the ice on the lake. The ice was thick enough to hold me and Zane and him, all at one time. And it was thinner near the waterfall than it would be on the calm part of the lake. It's only a short walk from the edge of the lake to my cabin. He used the lake. That's why we never saw tire tracks, except from victims' cars."

"But how did he carry the victims?" Rowena asked. "That's a tough job even for a strong man."

"Sled," I said. "A child's sled. Big enough to hold a tied-up woman and easy for a man to pull. The runners make tiny marks in the snow and he brushed these away. None of us checked out on the ice. We assumed that he was moving by car. Keep in mind that the lake comes up to the back yard of nearly all the houses in this part of the county. It would be a short trek."

"But surely someone saw him—"

I cut him off. "No," I said. "Remember that he was coming to the women's houses as a lover, not a killer. The wife picked a time when he could arrive and leave unseen. It worked. Too well."

"Why didn't the girls come to you, when the killing started?" Wooley asked. He had taken off his heavy coat and had it draped across his arm. "You'd think that when their friends began to die, they'd get scared as well."

I shrugged. "Who can explain why a criminal terrorizes a complete neighborhood and not one person will report him or agree to testify against him? Why do the vast majority of rapes and domestic violence go unreported? Why do we refuse to prosecute criminals from petty shoplifters

288

to major crime czars? I have no answers. Except that Rockwell was such a con man that he capably argued to each of the women that he was not the killer, and they apparently believed him. Remember that sometimes multiple killers are not even suspected by their wives."

"His voice," Wadsworth said. "On the phone. The voice was described as a soft, intimate voice. Rockwell's voice is crisp and masculine. And he was with us when some of the calls came."

"I've got that covered," I said. "I'll mail you each a complete report."

It didn't convince me, and I doubt that it convinced them. We shook hands without feeling and I watched them drive away. I had encountered them twice and hoped that I would never see them again. I know they are the best we have, and my response to that is: God help us. And them.

It wasn't that they were inept; it was more that they were so set in their ways that anyone who didn't conform to their preconceived notions of how a criminal should behave was wrong. I supposed I'd never understand or accept how the women could have remained loyal to Rockwell, but I had seen the same scene played over and over in my own sphere of experience, and I found nothing that surprised me greatly.

When they left I went back inside, called the room and learned that Lurch was still making progress and was not in any real danger. Time was his greatest ally.

I went outside to look at the sunshine again, and a car pulled up to the curb. Zane was driving. She rolled the window down and smiled painfully at me. She had been patched up at the hospital and from what I had been told she was bandaged virtually from head to toe.

"Need a ride?" she said weakly.

"Thanks, I do," I said. "If you don't mind going a bit out of the way."

"Fine with me," she said. "Where to?"

"Rockwell's house," I said. "Someone has to check out the place for evidence."

"You have a key?"

"I'll get in," I said.

"What about Mrs. Rockwell?"

I looked up at the crystal blue sky and thought of the days and nights I had spent chasing Rockwell across the county.

"Figment of his imagination," I said. "I talked with people who knew

289

him. And with a couple of teachers. They all tell me that Rockwell's wife never made it to Sherman with him."

She bit her lip and was silent for several long seconds. "I never heard of her. Certainly never saw her during the whole time I was in high school. No one else did. You think she actually died, or did she have help?"

A bluebird perched high above us emitted a cascade of notes that echoed off the nearby trees and buildings. "If she had an insurance policy of ten dollars or more, he'd have done her for it. Maybe she knew what he was doing and ran out on him."

"Hop in," she said. "I'll drive you there, but I'm not going in. It's a half-day job for me to get in and out of the car."

I grimaced. "I'll get in," I said. "But I won't be doing any hopping for a while to come."

With difficulty I managed to climb inside the vehicle, and she eased gently away from the curb. Even so I felt every tiny bump the wheels hit: the pain reverberated in every part of my body. I could have sworn it hurt even when we crossed shadows of the huge trees that lined the street.

Snow was piled high on both sides of the road, and we eased our way along the deserted streets until we reached the lakeside home of Marlin Rockwell. Zane parked in the drive, shut off the engine, and tilted her seat back. She closed her eyes.

"Be back in five minutes," I said.

She didn't answer. I thought she had fallen asleep even before the engine ceased its groaning.

I rang the front doorbell as a courtesy, but there was no response. I rapped with my knuckles with the same results. I looked both ways, then stepped off the porch and rounded the house. There were two doors on the back side: one on a deck that rested on a series of metal supports, and one beside the double-garage doors.

Choosing the basement door, I tried the knob. Locked tight.

Tentatively, I tugged gently at the garage door. To my shock it rose easily to a height of three feet. Painfully, I crouched low enough to slip under the door and found myself in a dark and spacious basement. I pulled back a curtain and instantly I saw the sled hanging on the wall. Patches of moisture under it suggested that it had been used recently. I

290

knew how he had transported the women across the ice on the lake. And I wondered if it was the same sled the huge woman had been pulling.

A desk stood against an inside wall, and I limped to it and opened a drawer. Amid the clutter inside, I found a ledger. I opened it quickly and saw a series of neat rows of figures, ranging in amounts from a thousand dollars to more than twice that amount. I counted mentally, rounding off to the nearest thousand, and realized that, according to the entry dates beside the figures, that Rockwell had taken in more money in one month than I earned in two years. Five years, perhaps.

A mouse scurried across the ceiling, presumably between the floors. I flipped page after page. The entries continued as if they would never stop. I checked dates and saw that some of them had been made ten years earlier, while the most recent ones had been entered less than a month earlier. The house groaned as the cooling caused the timbers to shudder. I wondered if there was a dog on the premises.

A dog that might starve if I didn't call the humane society to come get it. Perhaps a cat, although I could not imagine Marlin Rockwell permitting a cat near him.

Steeling myself, I gripped the stairway rail and pulled myself upward with agonizing slowness. I wanted to see what else Rockwell had in the house that might incriminate him. Careful not to touch anything except with my gloved hands, I climbed the rest of the steps and entered a wide hallway. To my right I could see a spacious living room with immense fireplace. To the left were the bedrooms.

Betting that he wouldn't keep anything unusual in the living room, I made my way down the hall to the first bedroom and opened the door. It was apparently a guest bedroom, neat, tidy, and more than adequate for the king-sized bed, chest of drawers, and dresser. I opened several drawers and found them either empty or containing only the things people always leave in drawers.

I opened the huge closet and found towels, linen, hangars devoid of clothing, and little else. I flipped a light switch and nothing happened. Either the power lines were still down in this part of the county or there was a problem inside the house. I went to a window to open the blinds when a foul odor penetrated the air. I struggled to place the distinctively unpleasant smell that defied description.

Nothing of interest could be found in the room, and I went back to the hall and opened another door. This was clearly the bedroom of Rockwell: it reeked of masculinity, from the huge and ponderous furniture to the dark oak panels of wood and the wide oak flooring. I flipped another switch.

No power. I approached the chest or drawers and began to search. I found nothing of value. In the walk-in closet I found rows of suits, jackets, and shorts, all ranging from dressy to outdoors wear. Rockwell apparently envisioned himself as a rugged outdoorsman, the lumberjack type.

In this room there was the scent of a piney fragrance that filled the air, but under all the aroma of pine needles and the perfume of the outdoors world there was only a hint of another smell: the same one I detected in the guest bedroom.

Ten minutes later I gave up on the room and tried the third and last bedroom. The door was locked, and it took me several long seconds to slip the blade of my pocketknife inside the latch and slip the door open.

When I opened the door I nearly lost it all. The stink was beyond belief. I clutched my handkerchief and clapped it over my mouth and nose as I tried the light switch.

Nothing.

I hurried to a dresser and began to search frantically, as if I would suffocate if I didn't finish soon. I found hair brush, combs, and little else.

There was another large desk against the outside wall and I opened the middle drawer. Under an array of clutter I found the clipboard and legal pad. Flipping through it rapidly, I saw the same names scrawled repeatedly, hundreds of times.

Ralph Brett. Herman Brittain. Benjamin Collins. There were more than two dozen of them, the same names I had encountered in the post office: the box renters. The ones to whom the retirement checks had been mailed. The repeated signatures were obviously an effort to forge a signature perfectly.

A locked box was under the clipboard. I snapped the puny lock and opened the lid. Inside were a small stack of envelopes from the state and other addresses from which retirement checks and social security checks would be mailed.

A sudden wave of the foul odor struck me like a blow, and I knew at once the source of the odor: the giant woman I had once encountered at the courthouse. The same one I had seen on the street in Sherman and the one who had been at the post office. At the same time I heard the floor boards creak. I turned just in time to see the immense woman rushing toward me. In her upraised hand she held a baseball bat.

She swung viciously at my head, and I rolled away, catching the majority of the blow on my shoulder. She raised it again and I rolled desperately. The blow struck the edge of the desk and splintered the bat. She advanced relentlessly as I dodged, rolled, and twisted.

Now she was using the broken end of the bat as a spear. She stabbed at me with it, and half a dozen times I felt the jagged wood rake my flesh.

Stumbling to my feet I lifted the heavy oak chair with my least-damaged hand and used it as a shield. She dropped the end of the bat and hurled herself at me like a filthy avalanche, and the two of us collapsed into a heap in one corner of the room.

I found myself buried under her weight and strength. I could not seem to get my breath, even if I had wanted to breathe. From somewhere a knife appeared in her hand and she slashed at me again and again.

The door slammed open and I heard a distant scream. I opened my eyes and over the shoulder of the obese woman I saw the face of Zane. She was swinging the large end of the baseball bat with one hand, the blows raining on the head and shoulders of the giant woman. Zane kept swinging until the huge form slowly sagged and rolled to the floor.

With Zane's help I extricated myself and staggered to the window and tried to unlock it. The latch was stuck, and I used my elbow to smash the glass pane. Fresh air flooded into the room, and for several moments I stood there, gasping and drinking in the cold and wonderful air.

When I turned back into the room, the woman was sitting up and Zane had her weapon aimed at the massive chest.

The woman's gray face crinkled into what was intended to be a smile.

"You're looking for my husband," she said, her wheezing filling the room. "He's not here, and he's not coming back." The voice was softly masculine, a Peter Lorre voice without the trace of an accent. She struggled to her feet.

She stood well over six feet tall, and she had to weigh in the vicinity of four hundred pounds.

"You are Mrs. Rockwell," I said. I hoped my voice did not betray my fear of her, even while she was at gunpoint.

She laughed unpleasantly. "I'm not what you'd have expected his wife to be, am I?" She wheezed horribly, and the stench was unbearable.

"Tell us," I said. I didn't offer her a deal or make any sort of promise. It was a simple request, and she granted it.

"I'm the mole woman," she said. "The owl woman. I live underground and go out at night. Or in snow storms. But I wasn't always like this. You see, I was once a beauty contest winner. I even competed in the Miss America contest. But I was never enough woman for my husband, whose real name, incidentally, is Roy Church. He had to be looking, sniffing, poking somewhere else all the time. And he made those men angry enough that they made their girl friends tell them the truth, that it was not Ed Gallager but my husband who stole the money and seduced the girls. The men beat us, especially me. Roy deserted me and left me at their mercy. They raped me all night and all the next day and the next night and day, and when they finally let me go, my face was hideous and my body was totally defiled. I was determined that I'd never again be attractive to any man. So I went on an eating binge that has lasted to this day. See the results?"

She turned in a mock pirouette for us.

"Roy eventually came back," she said. "Even he had a sort of conscience. Or he was scared to death that I would rat on him. He supported me well, and he let me eat and grow into a monster. He took me out of town to eat out, at first, and then he started bringing in the food. He bought it by the ton, it seemed, and he gave much of it away, so that no one really thought anything about it. When I was fat enough, corpulent enough, he banished me to the basement and this room. I stayed down there or in here and listened to him and his girl friends in his bedroom. But what would I do? I couldn't drive. I can't even get inside a car now, except without great difficulty. So I couldn't leave him. And I couldn't lose weight. I wasn't going to go through that again."

There was more, but it amounted to the same story. I asked about the fake identities and the checks. She waddled to a desk and pulled out a sheaf of checks I had seen, still in the envelopes.

"He had it all figured out," she said. "Do you realize that he had over three million dollars in overseas accounts? That's not counting the hundreds of thousands he had in banks around the state. He was going to retire at the end of this school year, and the two of us would buy a houseboat and we'd float around the lake, down the Mississippi, wherever we wanted to go. We were going to become the happiest couple in the world. You see, once you knew him, it was impossible not to love him. No matter what he did, he could also make you feel like the most special person in the entire world. That's how I felt. And still feel."

"It was you who called the editor and the others, and me," I said.

"Yes. He couldn't run the risk that someone would reeognize his voice. And he had to be present for some of the calls, so he would never be suspected. He wanted to be close to you, so that left me to do the calling."

"But why me?" I asked. "Why leave the bodies around me?"

"Simple," she said. "You had already been charged with two murders. Everyone would think you were doing it again. There was a good chance that you'd actually be charged. At any rate, you'd lose your job and go back to prison. And we'd be free to enjoy the rest of our lives."

"Who were the people at the store: the hippies?"

"You don't know? The little slut is Roy's daughter. The punk is Gallager's son. I don't know what names they are using now. The two of them followed us around, wherever we went, and they tried to bleed Roy dry. Finally he hired them to kill you and make it look like either suicide or an accident. By that time Roy would have finished with the stupid sluts in that ridiculous club, and the killing would have stopped. With you."

"Did you kill Mrs. Gallager?"

"I got careless with matches," she said. "So sue me. She lost her life, now maybe he can find his. What'll happen to me?"

"I don't know," I said. "But if I were you, I wouldn't plan any long Mississippi River trips. Not for a long time. And don't try to run away. You won't make it."

She laughed. "Fat chance," she said. Zane turned the gun over to me and went to the car to call the office. Within minutes Bum was there to take charge.

We left then, and Zane drove us to my place. When we arrived melting snow was dripping from the eaves of the cabin and Dr. Pangloss, my world-mouth cat, was lying in a patch of sunlight.

"Can I come in?" she asked. I nodded, and we climbed out and held on to each other as we mounted the steps.

"Will you be all right?" she said as we entered the den.

I shrugged. "Who knows?" I said. "I'm feeling better."

She was silent for a long time. She had wandered to the window where she stared at the still-frozen lake.

"He was in good shape," I said. "A sled offers very little resistance."

"But wasn't he taking a terrible chance? I mean, there is no cover whatever on the lake. Anyone could have seen him."

I moved to the window and stood near her. "Seeing wouldn't have been proof of guilt," I said. "He worked mostly at night or in the early morning. Most people near the lake would have been inside with windows and doors locked. Remember how some of the mass killers operated within a few feet of neighbors and no one ever saw anything."

She turned to me, and in the light from the window I could see discolored skin. Her bandages looked like death in the now bright light.

"Chess," she said tentatively, "this is a hell of a time to bring this up, but you know how I feel about you, don't you?"

"I think so."

"I'd be asking a lot to expect you to forgive and forget. I can't ask it."

"You don't need to," I said.

She smiled faintly and I saw tears in her eyes.

"May I stay longer?" she asked.

I touched her lips lightly with my fingertips. "No," I said. "Let me ask you." She waited.

"Zane," I asked, "I have been an idiot, an ass, a dolt, and a buffoon. Can you put all that aside and let me start with a reasonably clean slate?"

"Done," she said.

"Will you stay? Not just for now. For as long as we both want it. For me, that will be a long time."

She nodded. "I'll stay, for as long as you want me. For the next few days I'll be worthless in bed."

"That's two of us," I said. "This could be the most clinically pure honeymoon of all time."

"It'll be more than I could have ever hoped for," she said. "When the snow melts, we'll fish. We'll walk in the woods. Make love. What about your job?"

"I don't care what we do," I said. "Or don't do. Do you know what I want most? To be with you. That's all. I don't need the bells and whistles or sirens. Right now, I think I'd like nothing better than to sit and rest."

"For six months, at least," she said.

"And eat. And take hour-long showers."

"Alone?"

"Only when necessary," I said.

She was silent for a long time, her face suddenly sad and worried. When I asked what was wrong, she shook her head and turned away from me. She rose and walked across the deck and stood looking at the lake. When she turned back to me, her face was wet.

"This is a wonderful place," she said. "You are a wonderful man. We could be happy here for the next two hundred years, if the world would leave us alone."

"Maybe it will."

She shook her head. "No. It never does."

She walked back to me, took my good hand in her good one, and she leaned against me.

"What are we going to do, Chess?" she asked almost plaintively.

"I don't know. We'll see. If worst comes to worst, I'll open an office, put you in charge, and I'll work for you. Does your legal-eagle mind find a flaw in that?"

"Sounds great," she said. "I've always wanted to be in charge."

She tugged at me and led me to the deck. The sun was full on the porch now, and we removed, with difficulty, our coats. Dr. Pangloss came over and leaped up on her lap. She winced slightly but did not complain. Instantly he purred loudly. Then he slept.

And I knew everything would be all right. Dr. Pangloss is a terrible mouser, an awful glutton, as damaging as a cyclone in the house, and under foot at all times. But he is never wrong about the character of people. Unlike me, he knows a champion the moment he sees one.

I could learn a lot from that cat.

In the incredible hours following the death of Marlin Rockwell and the arrest of his wife, who somehow managed to end her miserable existence in the county jail the first night she was incarcerated there, Jhon Rance, who resigned his position with the state offices to become the temporary sheriff of Sherman County, informed Zane that her services were no longer desired or required.

That's all that was necessary. Law does not require a sheriff, appointed or elected, to give reasons. There is no such thing as tenure in a position like Zane's.

Rick Blanton resigned within minutes of Zane's dismissal, and Bum Harley submitted his resignation five minutes ahead of Rick's.

The other state people left the hills of Sherman County and went back to their routine daily chores. No one missed them.

I had been unfair to them, I know. They were, after all is said and done, good law officers. They were also unappreciated and were in every sense professionals who knew their work but somehow managed to let training get in the way of judgment at times.

I received a call to the effect that conditions of my parole were that I must be employed at all times, no exceptions. The letter that followed stated that in view of my injuries, I would be allowed a reasonable time for recuperation. If I did not comply in full with all of the conditions of my release from prison, I would be returned to jail immediately.

With my good hand, I spent hours dialing the telephone and listening to potential employers tell me lies about why they would not be able to use my services. The arm of Sherman University and its administrators was much greater in length than the long arm of the law.

I called prison officials and explained that I was filthy rich and therefore not in need of money. They listened politely and told me that the terms of my parole were not subject to negotiation.

"Then," Zane said as cheerfully as she could manage, "let's use the next few days to the best advantage. Something will turn up. I know it. There's no way you're going back to prison. We'll find a way. I know we will.

I'd have given lots of my money to have only a tiny part of her confidence. Except that she didn't have it. She knew as well as I did that there was no hope. My only consolation was that I'd be the richest convict in the state prison.

TWENTY-FIVE

Bum Phillips came by daily to keep us informed of news in the town hall and county offices. And from around the county.

All of the victims of the killings had been buried, and Bum said that the cemeteries looked like a winter spring, with countless flowers of all descriptions springing from the snow. He told us that Blanton was making steady progress and that he would be released from the doctor's care within a few days.

Zane asked me if I'd be willing to relocate to another part of the state, if the prison heads would allow me to do so. I told her that I did not want to start our life together as fugitives and that I was fully determined to learn again to love my cabin and enjoy the lake.

"Then I'll make the most of what we have," she said, "and, if necessary, I'll use my savings to hire the best lawyers available. We can spend the money on a legal defense and we'll eat hickory nuts and bark, if that's the best we can do."

I assured her that hickory nuts are indeed delicious. I also told her that I'd drive to Asheville to talk to a lawyer as soon as I could manage the highways. The weather had turned incredibly warm, as it always does in the latter stages of winter. Crocuses and daffodils had somehow managed to force their way through the snow and the banks of the lake looked like gold waving in the breeze. I could feel my heart crunch a little more each time I looked at Zane, at the lake, and at the woods springing to life and thought that I might have to leave them again. We spent most of our time outdoors, away from television, the newspapers, and the telephone.

Bum Harley arrived close to dark on our tenth day at home. He began to unload a huge bag of charcoal, grill, and sacks of food. He did not park close to the house, and he set up his grill at the edge of the lake. One huge stack of something in the back seat was not taken out of the vehicle.

"Stay there," he called to us. "Rest all you can. You're going to need it in a few minutes. These are the toughest steaks this side of an old boot. Besides, I have news for you, but you get none of it until the food is ready."

Within a few seconds, it seemed, the charcoal was blazing like a forest fire, and within minutes the food was sizzling. From the back of his station wagon Bum unloaded a small folding picnic table and chairs, and between chores he fussed over the food and made a weak pretense of casting spinning lures into the lake.

It was too dark to see by the time the food was ready, so he hung a lantern on a broken snag on a huge pine tree. Then he called for us to come eat. When we reached the table, the lump in the back seat moved, and Zane screamed in joy and rushed to Lurch and flung her good arm around him. She cried like a baby, which was good, because that way no one paid a great deal of attention to me wiping my own eyes.

Rick looked pale, weak in the yellow glow of the lantern. Bum had to help him out of the vehicle and guided him to a chair. As Lurch looked at us sheepishly, Bum loaded a plate for him and even cut up his steak. Dr. Pangloss scrambled down from a nearby tree and found a spot on Lurch's lap, where he remained while we ate.

"Be as good as new in three more weeks," Lurch said. "Chess, I don't think I ever got around to thanking you for saving my life up there. So here."

He passed two manuscript envelopes to me. Nobody said a word as I opened the first envelope and saw the corporation papers. I looked at Rick in astonishment.

"You want to explain this?" I asked.

"Eyes going to the bad?" he asked. "It's a simple partnership agreement. You and I now own a school of our own."

I shook my head in bewilderment. "No," I said. "I'm through with teaching. You know that."

"You are through teaching for other people," he said. "Do you know how many people in and around this county want to become published writers? In case you don't know, I can enroll enough this week for us to start our own classes. The four of us, if you like."

I didn't know what to say, so I said nothing. Rick continued.

"You have published more books than most people have read," he said, "and you know the tricks of the trade. Enough of them, as least. I've had an attorney in my room at the hospital for hours on end, and he assures me that the school fulfills every requirement of the prison department and the state. Zane and I can work with students in a one-on-one fashion, and Bum will be the general administrator. I've made a few calls and have tentatively enrolled more than forty students. All of whom, incidentally, have written me a check to hold until we know which way you want to go with this."

"Lurch," I said, fighting for self-control, "this is the dumbest thing I have ever heard in my life. Where will we meet, for starters?"

"In the basement of your house. There's enough room for all of us to work. In good weather we can meet along the lakeshore or on the deck. You can count part of the house as a business expense, and you can deduct any money you spend for supplies and equipment. And the three of us will be paid out of the tuition costs. What do you say, chief?"

Zane reached over and took my hand in hers. "Chess?" she said, her eyes pleading. "This is perfect. Please say you'll do it."

"Wait," Lurch said. "There's another envelope. Just in case you don't like the first one. Read it now."

The smoke from the grill seemed to slide across the surface of the lake, and a sudden breeze reminded us that there was much more of winter to come. There was a huge splash near the bank and we saw the head of a huge bass surface to hit a large insect that had landed on the water. My fingers trembled as I wrestled with the envelope while six anxious eyes and two curious ones watched me.

The contents of the envelope looked almost identical to the first one. The agreement in the second envelope was for another business deal. This time it was a private investigator's corporation.

"I'm the boss of this one," Lurch said. "Bum is my second in command. Then Zane. Chess, you are the administrator. And the chief cook and bottle washer."

I looked at him curiously. His face betrayed no insincerity.

"This is legal?" I said. "Will the state permit a convicted felon to work as a private detective?"

"No problem. Largely because of the third envelope."

"What third envelope? I see only two."

"That's because I haven't reached into my shirt pocket yet." From his pocket he pulled a third envelope. It contained a brief letter.

301

It was from a law firm in Asheville, and in it the attorney stated in an uncomplicated manner his views on my original conviction, and he assured Lurch, and me, that my original trial was riddled with procedural errors and biases and that it should be a simple matter to have the conviction overturned. He added that he was ready to start to work the moment we gave him the word.

It was too much for me! I laid my head on the table and let out all that had been building for the past months. I felt Zane's hand on my shoulder, followed by the huge mitts of Lurch and Bum. Dr. Pangloss sensed that he was being left out of something, and I felt him crawl from Lurch's lap into my own. He began kneading my leg with his toes, and the claws dug into my flesh like small medieval torture devices.

It felt wonderful. And I knew that everything would be coming up roses within a short time.

The cold air forced us into the house, where we opened a bottle or two of wine that I had been saving for a celebratory occasion. We talked, made plans, and reveled in the happiness of freedom-to-come until the wee hours of the morning. Lurch and Bum spent the night in the guest rooms, and the following morning I woke to the incredible aromas of strong coffee, steaks, eggs, hot biscuits, and steamed apples from the basement.

"Consider the house reclaimed and purified," Zane said. I told her there was no question about it. And when Lurch and Bum left, she told me that she had prepared the entire meal by herself, lame arm and all. When I congratulated her on her work, she blushed suddenly and delightfully.

"If you think I'm good with one arm," she said, the crimson rising again in her face, "you wait until I have both in use."

"I can't wait," I said.

"You won't have to," she said, pulling me toward the bedroom.

And we didn't.

ABOUT THE AUTHOR

Robert L. Williams is author of 36 other books. He has written magazine articles and stories for some of the leading publications in the nation, including *Money Magazine, House Beautiful, Southern Living, Modern Maturity*, and a number of others. He has for years written special assignment articles for the Charlotte *Observer* and, before that, the old Charlotte *News*.

A well-known public speaker, Williams has appeared before audiences ranging from church congregations to university and college audiences to civic clubs and special interest groups.

He and his family have appeared on such television programs as NBC's Today Show, local and national segments of the old PM Magazine show, and dozens of other mainstream offerings. He has also written a number of television scripts.

Together, Williams and his wife Elizabeth and their son Robert have written a popular travel book now in its seventh printing, and Elizabeth Williams, who has collaborated with Williams on several of his books, has also been a successful photographer, magazine writer, and newspaper editor. She currently teaches at Cleveland Community College in Shelby, NC. Robert L. Williams III, the son of Robert and Elizabeth, distinguished himself when he was only three years old by becoming the youngest person in history to sign a photography contract with a major firm and to sell his photographs to a wide range of magazines, newspapers, and book companies. He appeared on dozens of television shows as well as making special appearances at the World's Fair in Knoxville, and when he was five years old his photos were on exhibit at the Las Vegas Convention Center.

The Williamses live, along with four cats and two dogs, on their 40-acre farm in Belwood, NC, a short drive from the mountains they love.

Want to read more Chess Ivy mystery/suspense novels? Order the following titles, which are either in print or will be shortly:

* *Eye of the Cockatrice.* The story of a giant precious stone that is found miraculously and then disappears mysteriously, leaving a trail of violence and death as Ivy, Zane, and Rick Blanton try to unravel the mystery of the emerald and its relationship to the legendary creature, the Cockatrice, as depicted in the Bible.

Mad Dog's Tooth. The first in the Chess Ivy series, this story relates the murder of Chess's wife and best friend. Ivy, charged with the murders, must act as his own attorney in the murder trial that he cannot win and can't afford to lose. And live!

The Gallows Birth. A helpless, illiterate young woman becomes the last person hanged in North Carolina, and she gives birth to her son as she hangs from the gallows. Her body is stolen from the grave the first night after burial, and Ivy, Zane, and Rick set out to prove the woman's innocence, more than a century after her execution.

Fingers of the Rain. When Ivy attends the funeral for a man he had never met, he discovers the man was Ivy's brother, whom he had not seen in decades. The man had lived the second half of his life under an assumed identify, and Ivy looks for the reasons and discovers murder, CIA drug trafficking, and more danger in the North Carolina mountains than he had seen in his military time in Vietnam.

Arrow for the Heart. Ivy, Zane, and Rick investigate a series of murders written about in a sensational new book, only to learn that the narration is not about murders that occurred a century ago but instead is about murders that will be committed in the near future.

Children of an Idle Brain. Ivy returns to Sherman University to teach *at the request of the man who hated him enough to have him fired, sent to prison, and ruin his entire life.* On the college campus Ivy learns of a multimillion dollar corruption scheme. And of murder!

To order, call (toll-free) 1-877-922-5263, write to Southeastern Publishing Corporation, 3613 Dallas-Cherryville Highway, Dallas, NC 28034, or check out your local newsstand or book store.